CW00832028

ONE LITTLE SECRET

AVERY MAXWELL

That's What She Said Publishing, Inc.

This book is for every reader who has worried about Ashton. Some of you started asking for him before I even knew he was broken. Trust me when I say breaking him broke me too.

But fixing him was the best kind of salve.
I know you've waited ten books for him, and I hope I did him justice.
Ashton is for you.

AUTHOR NOTE

ONE LITTLE SECRET

Dear Reader,

We've known for many books now that Ashton is broken. We first met him in *Cross My Heart*, my debut novel, when he was just a young, naïve nerd.

Or so we thought.

Over the course of ten books, we've seen him grow. We've seen him harden. We've seen him scar. We've seen him break.

His road is dark. His road is heartbreaking.

His redemption is everything.

Themes of self-loathing, bullying, difficulty conceiving, self-harm, extreme gaslighting, betrayal, and self-worth are all explored via various characters.

As a mom to four beautiful children who fought for each of my pregnancies, and lost several others, I know that not everyone's HEA includes children. But I write what I know. Most of my stories, including this one, have an HEA with babies or children however they come to my characters: pregnancy, IVF, adoption, surprise, and of course, found family.

You, my reader, are always my top priority. If you have any

questions or concerns about any of my books, I encourage you to reach out.

Info@AveryMaxwellBooks.com

Luv & Kindness,

Avery

PLAYLIST

ONE LITTLE SECRET

There were so many songs, stories, and emotions that went into
this book.
It was hard to break it down for a playlist.
But I did my best.
https://geni.us/AverysOneLittleSecret
xoxo,
Avery

The WESTBROOK FAMILY

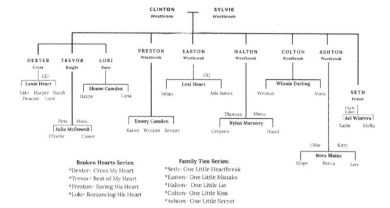

Broken Hearts Series:
*Dexter- Cross My Heart
*Trevor- Beat of My Heart
*Preston- Saving His Heart
*Loki- Romancing His Heart

Family Ties Series:
*Seth- One Little Heartbreak
*Easton- One Little Mistake
*Halton- One Little Lie
*Colton- One Little Kiss
*Ashton- One Little Secret

The Westbrooks: Family Ties is a spin-off series of The Westbrooks: Broken Hearts series. If you're looking for Dexter, Trevor, Preston, or Loki's stories, you'll find them in The Westbrooks: Broken Hearts.

Seth's story, One Little Heartbreak, is a bridge novella that connects the two series.

You can read The Broken Hearts series for free in Kindle Unlimited.

Happy Reading!

CHAPTER 1

ASHTON

"*How* ow are you today, Ashton?" Dr. Benson asks in a monotone voice.

"Same as Monday and Tuesday and Wednesday," I respond dryly. Dr. Benson is used to my snark by now. At least I'm not yelling at him as much.

"Still not sleeping?"

A heavy sigh escapes as I lean back on the sofa. I really don't want to fucking be here, but I've promised my family. There are so many of us these days. We just keep expanding, and I can't even keep track. But my mom and Sadie are the most important, and they're worried, so here I am.

"Not really."

"And you won't take the prescription I gave you?"

And risk being caught unawares? I'm as safe as I can be in my secluded mountain house, but I've made a lot of enemies in the past few years. Enemies that would love to catch me with my pants down.

"No."

"Ashton, as I've said before, needing medicine is not a sign of weakness."

1

AVERY MAXWELL

"I never said it was," I bark.

"Okay. Have you been journaling?"

I glance down at the notebook in my lap, knowing exactly what the new entry says. Instead of answering, I nod and hand it to him. He reads it out loud.

He always fucking reads it out loud.

Dear Dad,

Reason #732 why I hate you: Because of you, I've lost my best friends.

Reason # (unknown) why I love you: Because you meant to make the world a better place.

"Hate is a powerful thing, isn't it?"

Barely resisting the urge to roll my eyes, I keep them focused on the ceiling.

If I always look up, he can't see straight through me when our eyes meet.

"You're the doctor," I say. There are seven points on the popcorn ceiling I can count without moving my focus.

"I am. Some would say that hate is the easy way out. Forgiveness is harder."

"They're probably right."

"Why do you think so?"

Oh my God. It's like going around in a circle with this guy. Growing up, I didn't care that I was on the outside of social norms. I've always been more concerned with technology than people, but I've been like an ogre since my attack. I can't even be nice if I try—the exception to that being my family. And even they have become a daily exercise in niceties.

The door bursts open, jerking me to high alert. A symptom of PTSD, according to the good doctor. But my spine tingles with an awareness that something's wrong. When the receptionist enters holding a phone out to me, I'm on her in two long strides.

"What's wrong?" I growl into the phone, knowing it'll be one of my brothers or their wives.

2

"Ash, something's up. We need you. Can you meet us at your house in ten?" my brother Colton says. I hear others in the background, not that it matters. I've let them down enough that when they call, I go running.

"I'll be there in five." I hand the phone back to the stunned receptionist, not caring what the hell they had to tell her to get her to interrupt the session. "Sorry, Doc. I'll see you next week."

Fear pushes me out of the room at a sprint. But whether it stems from worry over what's wrong with Colton or avoiding what's wrong with me, I'm not sure.

True to my word, I pull into my driveway five minutes later to find Colton, Preston, and Colton's friend, Lochlan, on my porch. By the way Loch is pacing, I assume he's the one in trouble.

Despite how fucking cold it is outside, they've opted to wait for me out here. My skin prickles with unease.

"Why aren't you inside?" I ask when I'm close enough for them to hear me without yelling. My voice is much stronger than it used to be, but still raspy and deeper than before some asshole crushed one of my vocal cords.

"Ah, we were just talking," Preston explains, but he looks shifty.

Hurrying past them, I press my palm to the scanner, then narrow my eyes because someone has already disarmed my system.

"Bloody hell," Lochlan mutters with his almost British lilt.

Once the door opens, we all hurry in out of the bitter mountain air.

~

"How long has this been going on?"

"We aren't sure. A couple of weeks, at least. He was her assistant. I vetted him myself. He'd been working for her

3

for three years." I can feel Lochlan's guilt eating away at him as he speaks.

"It wasn't your fault," Colton placates.

Those words. *It wasn't your fault.* They never help, and yet people continue to say them.

"Any idea what made him snap?" I ask, fumbling to insert the flash drive he gave me into my computer. USB drives always cause flashbacks for me, and it's a fight to keep my hands steady. It doesn't help that we're not in my actual office. That's private. The façade we're standing in is the only one I allow others to enter.

The small screen on my back wall lights up, and we all turn toward it.

"What is this?" I ask, fighting to keep the memories at bay.

"We found cameras planted all over her apartment," Lochlan grumbles. "Who knows how long he's been watching her."

The camera zooms in on a sleeping woman—Lochlan's sister, Nova—as a dark shadow moves around the bedroom. She stirs, and another person comes into view in the bed next to her. Like it's a B-movie, we see the dark shadow lift a lamp overhead and smash it down onto the person next to Nova.

She screams. The other body doesn't move. There's yelling, but I can't make out what they're saying without filtering it down. She runs around the room, trying to escape, and the shadow follows her.

My breathing is harsh, chest ready to explode, when we get another view from a different camera. In this one, Nova's face is clear. The fear in her eyes. The confusion. It's clear to me that she knows the intruder, but she's terrified. She starts throwing things at the wall, probably to draw attention to her apartment.

Smart girl.

There's a knock at the door, and she takes her eyes off the shadow for half a second. He uses it to his advantage. We can't hear what he says to her, but his lips move next to her ear. She screams, and what looks like security runs into the room. But they're too late. The shadow is already heading down the fire escape.

The frame freezes on Nova's tear-stained face, and I know in my heart I'm going to help her. She has a magnetic pull that draws me closer to the screen.

"Is this a hotel?" I croak.

"Yes," Lochlan says. "One of mine in New York. I live in the unit next to her."

"What happened to the boyfriend?" The question tastes like acid on my tongue.

"Not a boyfriend. One of her one-night stands, I guess. He was knocked unconscious, but he hightailed it out of there when he came to. I'm sure I'll get a lawsuit at some point, but she'll never see him again. The fucking wanker."

"Where is she now?"

Their eyes shift from one another but never quite meet mine.

"Where. Is. She. Now?"

My brothers pinch the backs of their necks, and I know exactly where this is leading when Colton steps forward. "She's in your guest room, Ash."

CHAPTER 2

NOVA

$\mathcal{M}$y brother has been friends with the Westbrooks most of his life, so I thought I was well-versed in their chaos. Turns out, I was wholly unprepared for the giant parade of blended, blood, and chosen family members that met us at the small airfield in Burke Hollow, Vermont.

"I'm sorry. We can be super overwhelming," Rylan says. She clasps her hands in front of her with an apologetic half-smile.

She's a beautiful woman with bright green eyes, and the only one in this room I know. After she filled in last-minute a couple of years ago to photograph my fashion show, she became my go-to photographer, and eventually, my friend.

"Overwhelming but honest," a blond woman says. She towers over my five-foot-four frame, and she's stunning.

She must read my blank expression because she introduces herself to me. Again. "I'm Lexi. I'm married to Easton, the second oldest Westbrook."

"Gah!" someone else says. "I can't imagine how overwhelming this is for you. I'm Ari. I'm married to one of the Westbrook adoptees."

Right. Because the Westbrooks have a habit of collecting family members. Like the mob, once you're in, there's no getting out. That thought has a choked giggle escaping from deep within my throat.

The ladies all flash me a worried expression.

"Okay. Maybe we should draw her a map?" Rylan whispers.

"Probably. She looks a little freaked out, and not just because some pinprick tried to kill her lover."

I'm unable to hide my flinch, but I recover quickly and offer them all a small smile. It's better to focus on the mafia family dynamics. My shoulders bounce a little as I suppress the weird emotions filtering through me.

Glancing around, I decide I'll call them the Westbrook mafioso. Like an inside joke that will keep my mind occupied until I can be alone again.

"Lexi!" Ari hisses. "Tone it down."

"Oh, right. Sorry, chica. I forgot you don't know me. I don't hold my tongue often. I'm blunt but fair." She shakes her head at my blank expression. "Okay, I'll break it down for you. We're on GG's mountain. She's my grandmother and she's batshit crazy. She reads cards, tells fortunes, and is a scary matchmaker. All the men are either Westbrooks by blood, by choice, or because the matriarch, Sylvie, said so. We all married into the crazy. You still with me?"

No. My brain is mush. But I nod anyway. Her words go in one ear and out the other.

"Great. There are five Westbrooks, four adoptees, and eight daughters-in-law floating around Vermont or Waverley-Cay where they grew up, and far too many kids to name. I'm sure you'll meet everyone eventually, except Dillon, because he's in New York now, running that branch of Envision, Ashton's security firm. Actually, you may have already met him. Anyway, that's the gist of us."

I look at these women and shake my head. They don't seriously expect me to remember any of that. Do they?

"Ashton is the youngest Westbrook. You're in his house." Lexi stands back, obviously proud she got that all out in only a few breaths.

She stares at me with her hands on her hips, and I nibble on my lip like I'm about to be sent to the principal's office.

"You didn't follow any of that, did you?" Rylan asks gently.

Not a word of it. I thought my family was insane, but we have nothing on these ladies.

"No worries." Lexi sits beside me on the bed. "We're overwhelming, but we all care." Her words are gentler than I'd have thought possible just moments before. "We've all had shit in our lives that left a scar, but we love hard and protect those in our circle. Since you're here, you're ours now. We won't let anything happen to you, okay?"

My own mafia-esque protectors. I almost grin at the nickname.

God, I must be exhausted. My emotions are all over the place.

"The truth is, I'm not really sure why I'm here." The words are a whispered breath full of fear, regret, and anger at myself for missing all the clues. My fingers ache, and I look down to find my hands twisted together in my lap. Carefully, I flex them flat on my thighs and don my carefully constructed mask of indifference. It takes more effort than it should, but the weight of exhaustion threatens to take me under.

All the women in the room share a look over my head.

"Well," Ari says. "My guess is that you're here because it's quite possibly the safest place in the northeast. My husband has worked with Ashton for a long time. They've seen more than their share of trouble, so Ash has made his home a fortress that's nearly impenetrable unless he allows you in."

I glance up at Ari as she speaks. Her kind eyes tell me there's a story here I'm not privy to.

"Ashton has his own demons, but Ari's right," Lexi says.

She stands then flits around the room. The woman never seems to stop.

"He'll protect you with everything in his arsenal. Well, after he gets over the initial shock of having someone in his home." She snorts, and dread sits heavy on my chest.

"He doesn't like strangers?" Anxiety, meet my throat.

"Geez, Lex. Put a lid on it already." Rylan groans but pats my hand. "I've known Ashton nearly his entire life. He's quiet. He's always been shy. And he has the biggest heart I've ever known. He has scars that he hasn't allowed to heal, and I'm not talking about the ones on his body."

I gulp. "Scars?"

Rylan squeezes my trembling hands. "How much do you know about Ashton?"

I shake my head as my mind goes blank. I'm so damn tired, but even the thought of sleeping, of being unaware of my surroundings, has the room tunneling and words echoing in my ears.

"Nova?"

Shit. Who's talking to me? A full-body tremor courses through me, and another bout of nausea hits like a tsunami.

"Fuck." Lexi puts her face so close to mine I can't focus on anything but her eyes. "Nova? Can you nod for me?"

My head obliges even as I'm still processing her words.

"Good. That's good. Can you stand? If I help you, do you think you can make it to the bathroom right over there?" She points to the right, but my gaze doesn't follow. I nod again. "That's great, sweetie. Let's get in there and put a cool cloth on your neck, okay? And while we're moving, can you try to count out loud for me?"

"One. Two." My voice sounds hollow and nearly unrecognizable.

"That's good. Keep going," she murmurs.

When we reach the attached en suite, she leaves me at the sink while she turns to grab a small towel.

"Remember when I told you we all have our demons?" she asks.

With a forceful gulp, I answer. "Yeah." It comes out weak and small. I hate it. I've spent years building myself up. It's that thought that has me coming out of my daze.

"Well, someone I trusted once took me against my will. Caused a pain that will never heal. He took away my choices, and I almost lost myself because of it. What I'm trying to say is that it's human nature to trust people. Especially when they've been in our lives, learned our secrets, and built a bond. I need you to know that trusting this guy isn't your fault. Evil comes in many forms, and they're usually quite adept at masking the devil."

As I stare up into her light blue eyes, she allows her own mask to fall, and there's a world of emotion shining in her irises. She's a fighter, and I am too. I always have been. I won't let Sam change that.

"Thank you, Lexi. I think I needed that."

And just like that, she's back to the no-nonsense woman I initially met.

"I decided long ago that my circumstances may have been victimized, but I will never be a victim—even if that's how everyone else describes me. I took control of the situation by acknowledging it wasn't my fault. None of it was my fault. By releasing the blame I was putting on myself, I could direct it exactly where it belonged. It's amazing how free you'll feel when you place the blame where it deserves to be, Nova, and it isn't with you."

Without thought, I launch myself at this giant of a woman. Lexi chuckles but embraces me like family.

"You'll fit in well here. They're all a bunch of freaking huggers." Her tone is sassy but filled with fondness.

When I pull away, I feel stronger than I have in days.

"Sometimes wearing a mask protects us, and sometimes it keeps us from healing. Remember that over the coming days. You don't have to hide from Ash. At first, he may seem grumpy and off-putting, but no one knows pain like him. Let him in. And we're all here for you too. He can show you the paths through the woods that lead to our homes."

I think about what she said as we walk back into the bedroom together. Rylan smiles hesitantly, and I return it. I realize with a jolt that I'm not pretending. This motley crew of found family has some sort of voodoo magic in them.

"So—" Rylan starts, but the bedroom door crashes open.

Standing in the doorway is a dark knight. That's the only way I can describe him. His rich brown hair is disheveled. Not in the *I used a lot of product to get this look* kind of way, but the *I rolled out of bed and couldn't give a shit* kind of way. His piercing blue eyes and the way they see straight into my soul have my heart beating steadily for the first time since this all started.

His hands grasp the door's wooden frame like an anchor as we stare at each other. So many stories pass between us while the seconds tick by.

My shoulders relax as I watch him. His nostrils flare with heavy breaths, but his eyes are pools of kindness. Beneath the scars that mar his cheek is a very handsome man. He's beautiful and beastly, yet I'm drawn to him. I take a tentative step closer. My movements are cautious, like I'm cornering a wounded animal, but he doesn't flinch. Doesn't even blink.

I have the uncanny sensation of my heart being drawn to his on a string that binds us. It's like my body knows this man, even if my mind doesn't. My sense of trust might be bruised, but watching this man's features, I know I'm not broken.

I could trust him with every secret I've ever held. That thought makes me shudder just before I reach him.

I've read about the lightning-strike feeling some people get when they meet, and for better or worse, that bolt of awareness has traveled all the way down to my toes.

Tilting my head to my side, I flash him a shaky grin. "I suppose you're my babysitter then?"

CHAPTER 3

ASHTON

*M*y skin prickles with a painful awareness and I rub at a phantom ache in my chest. It's like a rush of adrenaline is coursing through my veins at an uneven tempo I can't control.

"You left her by herself?" The words are a graveled demand that barely sounds human, and I immediately tamp back my desire to hide.

My voice is like something created by the devil himself and I'll never escape it. Not even my brothers have gotten used to the painfully harsh tone.

Lochlan steps forward, his face a menacing mask. "Is this going to be a problem?"

"Is what going to be a problem? The fact that you left a frightened girl in an unfamiliar bedroom after she was just attacked in her own?"

"Bloody fucket," he curses.

Colton places a hand on his shoulder, but he doesn't relax.

I can't blame him. Seeing Nova's face frozen on my screen causes a riot of angry emotions to well in my chest.

"The girls are with her," Preston says, watching us all closely.

My eyes don't shift from the fear I see in Nova's gaze. Even through a cheap-ass camera feed, her fear is palpable. Pinching the bridge of my nose, I let out a heavy sigh.

"Ashton?" Lochlan's voice is low, and I recognize how he's struggling to keep himself under control. He tugs on his vest and focuses on me. "Can you keep her safe? And find this asshole?"

I glare at him, but finally force my face to remain calm. It isn't his fault he has no idea that all I've done for the last eighteen years is keep people safe.

His question doesn't require a reply. They wouldn't be here if he thought he had any other options. Besides, my body is already moving toward the girl.

And yes, I need to refer to her as a girl. A girl is untouchable. A girl won't produce the uncomfortable ache trying to make a resurrection in my chest.

Nice try, moron. You may lie to everyone in your life, but you can't lie to yourself.

It's time to meet the girl they've maneuvered into my house.

With each step, my internal body temperature rises. By the time I cross the family room my skin is on fire, like the raging inferno in my chest is shooting sparks from my pores.

When I finally reach Sadie's room, any semblance of finesse I may have once possessed flies out the window and I burst through the door.

It's like I'm no longer in control of my own body, and all the air is sucked straight from my lungs like a siphon is snatching it away.

Nova is no girl. She's a woman in every sense of the word, from her silky brown hair that glints under the soft glow of the lights above to her amber eyes that shine with worry even as she offers a shaky smile.

It's her smile that disarms me. While my brothers and I grew up looking like spitting images of each other, my features have changed over time. Hardened. Scarred. I'm the living, fire-breathing dragon from Sadie's fairy tales.

And yet she smiles at me.

I flare my nostrils as if I'm truly breathing fire. Nova tilts her head to the left, and her unsteady grin widens, but I don't miss her shaking hands or how her eyes dart to the exit every thirty seconds. And I definitely don't miss her short, shallow breaths.

"I suppose you're my babysitter then?" There's humor in her trembling words that reassures me she isn't stuck in a spiral of panic from the attack. She takes tentative steps toward me, like she's trying to walk on water, and I'm not even sure she's aware she's moving.

I can't reply. Even if I could form words, my mouth is so dry my tongue sticks to the roof of my mouth.

Blinking, I glance around the room—Sadie's room—and shake my head.

"You can't stay in here," I bark.

Nova flinches but nods and slides away from me.

"Ashton Westbrook."

I simultaneously close and roll my eyes at Lexi's tone. I clench my teeth as I respond. "Sadie will be here soon. It's Friday Funday, and this is her room."

Nova's eyes go round with interest, and she moves in my direction again, but my grasp on the doorframe keeps her from stepping past me.

With as gentle a tone as I can muster, I explain. "Sadie is my niece. This is her room. We have a standing date every Friday. Give me ten minutes, and I'll prepare the other room for you."

Her hand presses to the center of my chest like a branding iron. Apparently, she has no use for personal space, and I nearly pass out. The pads of her fingertips press an uneven pattern, and I can't tell if she's trying to put distance between us or hold me close.

Dropping my gaze to hers, I see all the confusion I'm feeling in her eyes.

When was the last fucking time someone touched me? I jump back like a bullet propelled me and crash into Colton.

The ringing in my ears keeps me from understanding Colton's words, but he sees me. He's always seen me. Holding his hands out in a gesture to continue, he ushers me down the hall without saying a word.

It's an effort not to run. Not to scream. For the first time in years, my eyes feel too hot. Too damp.

I'm too fucking broken for this life.

I burst into Sadie's old room and finally take a breath, Nova's imprint still burning my skin.

Sadie hasn't slept in this room in nearly four years, but it still brings me comfort. When she turned ten, she told me she might be too old for the room decorated in sunflowers and sunshine. I hadn't hesitated. The very next day we went to Home Depot and started collecting what we needed for her "tween" room, whatever the hell that meant.

Technically, this room is supposed to be an office. Or a nursery. That thought sends a shiver down my spine. Perhaps if I were anyone else, this could have been a nursery. Now it will stand empty. It connects to the master bedroom through a small private corridor, and when Sadie Sunshine first started insisting on our Friday night sleepovers, I couldn't have her anywhere else. This was the safest room in the house—right next to mine. I could hear her if anything happened. I would always protect her.

Now that she's a teenager, it's inappropriate on every level to have her in here. I knew it would happen eventually, but I haven't slept a single Friday night in the four years since we switched her room.

Ari painted the room for us—the large smiling sun on the wall hovering just above the window, the sunflowers that seem to grow straight out of the carpet framing the entire room. I don't know if I'll ever have the heart to change it.

It's just another room that sits empty in this shell of a home.

Like me.

Giving myself a mental shake, I get to work removing the lamps from the end tables. I won't take any chances. They could incite flashbacks from her attack if she wakes in the middle of the night. I'm checking the window locks beside the bed when I feel his presence. Loki may be a retired spy, but he still has the uncanny ability to appear out of thin air.

My mother has a habit of drawing people into our family, and Loki was one of her first adoptees when we were kids. He moved in with us after his parents were killed. He knows me better than almost anyone else in my life. Shared trauma will do that to people.

"I'm fine," I say, interrupting whatever protest he may have come up with.

"I know." Loki isn't one for talking. Like me, he'll always have residual baggage from his father, who guided his life choices for so many years. Unlike me, he found Sloane. Or she found him, I suppose, and she's lightened his soul every day since.

I fight to suppress a chuckle, remembering how Sloane went toe-to-toe with him when they first met.

Loki enters the room holding the clean sheets and drops them onto the nightstand. Without a word, he strips away the sheets and starts to replace them before I snap out of it and help.

"She's pretty."

I grunt and lower my face to shield my eyes.

A wave of nausea rolls through me.

"It's been a long time since you've been in close quarters with a stranger."

"She's not exactly a danger to me."

My neck heats and prickles when he doesn't respond.

Squaring my shoulders, I cross my arms over my chest like armor, then swallow a lump when I see his expression.

"Not physically, no."

I narrow my eyes just as Colton bounds into the room like Tigger from Winnie the Pooh. He's always pushed the boundaries when he thinks it's for the greater good, and I get a sick feeling in the pit of my stomach.

He belly flops onto the bed, ripping the sheet out of Loki's hand.

"For fuck's sake, Colty," Loki growls, but Colton is like a baby bunny. It's nearly impossible to look at him and be angry.

He rolls over on the bed with a devilish grin and crosses his arms behind his head. "So," he drawls. "Nova?"

"She's terrified and putting on a front for everyone else." I surprise myself with those words, but the fuckers before me nearly split their faces in two as their grins grow so wide I swear I can see all their teeth.

"She's smiling and talking with everyone." Colton goads.

"Her hands were shaking, she was checking out any possible exit every thirty seconds, and she didn't take a full breath the entire time I was with her."

Colton shoots up into a sitting position like he knows a secret. "That's a lot to extract from a person in less than a minute."

Loki claps him on the shoulder, and Colton's face falters for a second. "You learn to read people when you do what we do."

My brother pinches the back of his neck and shakes his head. "Shit. Sorry. Yeah, that makes sense." He stands then, and in the process, his easy smile returns.

The words of a lost friend ring in my head. *"It's not his fault he has no idea why you're the way you are. Keeping these secrets will always put a barrier between you and your family."*

"Why didn't you bring her to Dillon? He's running the New

York office of Envision now. Wouldn't it have made more sense to let him handle this?" I ask.

Dillon is another Westbrook by proxy. A friend of my brother Easton who keeps himself apart from the chaos these days.

"Would you bring Sadie to a stranger to protect, or would you bring her to someone you know and trust?" Colton asks.

Asshole. Everyone knows our niece will always be my Achilles' heel.

"Lochlan doesn't really know me," I bite out.

"No, but I'm one of the only people he trusts," Colton explains. "He trusts me to know how best to keep his sister safe. Plus, he really felt like she needed to get out of New York. She hasn't been sleeping."

My chest clenches at his words, but I only nod.

"I wouldn't trust anyone else with Sloane," Loki adds. "This place is locked down better than Fort Knox, and when you're invested, you protect with every piece of knowledge you have in that oversized brain of yours. You're the best, Ashton, but..."

His pause incites a little swirl of anxiety.

"Can you handle the social aspect of having her in your space twenty-four seven?"

I picture the fear in Nova's eyes in that video. A blessing and a curse of having a photographic memory, but my body heats with the same protective instincts as the first time.

"She's scared. I'll do my best not to be an asshole."

Colton's eyes mist as he shakes his head. "Someday, Ash. Someday you'll remember that you're the best man I've ever known."

Loki, always knowing me better than I know myself, says, "I'm going to clear everyone out. In situations like these, it's best to get the victim comfortable and safe in their new space. I doubt she can do that with the ladies interrogating her every move."

I nod, and he exits as quietly as he came.

"Thank you, Ash," Colton says. "Thank you for helping them. I know you like your privacy, but she's a good girl. She needs you."

"I'll keep her safe, and we'll start tracking down this asshole."

She needs you.

She needs you.

She needs you.

Fuck me. Why do those three little words send my world rioting into chaos?

CHAPTER 4

NOVA

"*M*aybe this wasn't such a good idea." Lochlan curses.

"It's the safest place for her," Colton says with conviction. "And a change of scenery will be good."

I roll my eyes so hard I feel a headache coming on.

Exasperated, I wave my hands in their faces. "I'm right here. Don't talk about me as if I'm a child."

Lochlan's gaze shutters. "Sorry, Nono." After a long pause, he adds, "I'm scared. He got past all our defenses, and I'm worried about you."

My jaw hangs open until I remember to close my mouth. Lochlan isn't one to emote his feelings. My chest warms, knowing his wife, Tilly, has softened him. He opens his arms, and I happily slip into his embrace. We're not siblings by blood, but he's my brother in every way that matters. He's been my rock, my friend, my biggest cheerleader, since I was three years old.

With my cheek resting on his chest, he hugs me so tightly his fingers dig into my shoulder blades. He's not just scared, he's terrified, and guilt nearly takes me out at the knees.

"She'll be safe here," a low, raspy voice promises from behind me.

Holy shit, that voice. His gravelly tone causes a high I could easily become addicted to.

What on earth is happening to me?

"You should head home, Loch." This time it's Colton's voice, and Lochlan's arms go rigid around me. Taking a step back, I look up into his eyes and give a subtle nod.

I turn just as Ashton speaks again. "The longer you're here, the harder it will be to conceal where Nova is." His gaze drops to mine, and I forget to breathe. "I will keep you safe."

God help me, but I believe him. I also hate that I'm in the position of needing protection. Anger replaces the fog around my brain caused by fear.

"Thank you, Ashton. Lochness, he's probably right. It's not like you're exactly incognito with your private plane taking up an entire airport."

I'm surrounded by big, powerful men, but my gaze keeps snagging on Ashton. On the scar that covers the right side of his face. A dizzying number of theories about it tumble through my mind. When he catches me staring, he furrows his brow and angles his body so his right side is hidden from me.

He's hurting. It's so painfully obvious. Doesn't anyone else notice it? His external scars have clearly healed but his wounded heart, and maybe his pride, is hanging on by a thread.

I'll need more than a crowbar to crack Ashton Westbrook's code. Of that, I'm sure.

There's a whirlwind of activity as everyone packs up to head home and…oh, shit. I'm about to be left alone with Ashton Westbrook. My stomach drops, but not with fear. Apprehension, check. Intrigue, check. We'll leave all those other messy emotions buried deep though.

"Fair warning," Lexi says. "I have no idea how long we can

hold my grandmother off, but prepare yourself for the circus of chaos that surrounds her like happy hour."

"And don't let her read your cards," Ari adds.

"And whatever you do," Rylan laughs, and the sound sets me at ease, "do not, I repeat, do not drink her truth wine. Or anything she hands you in an unmarked bottle. Halton made that mistake and woke up the next morning with a newfound fear of GG."

I've never been able to keep many friends. At least, not close friends. I can't allow friendships like you read about in novels. Not when one little mistake I made as a teenager follows me like a dark cloud, but Rylan is as close to a real friend as I've had in years. She and Lochlan's assistant, Penny, are the friends I hold at arm's length just so I can keep them in my life.

They're not like Kate, who wields friendship as a bargaining chip. But I decided a long time ago that sometimes it's better to just accept companionship, than to feel so alone all the time.

Acquaintances are a way of life for me now. Thankfully my brother married someone great. Tilly rounds out my circle, even if I seem to be on the outside of it looking in most of the time.

Their warnings of the infamous GG help me relax. The love these people all have for each other is obvious, and that more than anything else puts me at ease.

They're the epitome of chosen family, and chosen family is all I've ever known. After my mom married Lochlan's dad, Ollie, he adopted me. My biological father is a narcissistic asshole, and I've only ever met him once. Lochlan's mother also stepped in after my mom passed away and has been a surrogate mom ever since.

Chosen family. Too bad I've spent the last ten years living in fear that a mistake I made as a teenager might eventually take them from me.

"Nova?" Ashton's voice tears me from my dark thoughts like a bucket of ice water dumped on my head. His tone tells me it isn't the first time he's attempted to get my attention.

"I'm sorry. What did you say?"

His scowl deepens as he stares at me. And he's again turned so I can't see his right side.

Does he do that with everyone? Or am I making him self-conscious?

I hate the idea of making him uncomfortable in his own home, so I promise myself I'll make a valiant effort not to stare at his scars again. I know better than anyone that we all carry scars. His just happen to be on the outside.

Before Ashton repeats himself, Lochlan wraps me in a hug. "Listen to Ashton, please. You wouldn't be here if I didn't trust him with my life. No one is better suited or more capable of finding this bloody fucket asshat than him. And, for the love of God, please do not give him shit like you do with me."

I grin against his chest before pulling away. I can't stop my gaze from drifting over to Ashton. His expression darkens when I openly stare straight into his eyes, and it feels like a challenge. I'm strangely satisfied when he doesn't turn away from me. He may be the one protecting me, but I think I might be able to help him too.

"I'll be on my best behavior," I promise.

"That's what I'm worried about," Lochlan grumbles before walking forward and offering Ashton a hand.

"Thank you, Ashton." Emotion clogs my brother's voice, shocking me right back into the seriousness of my situation.

Luckily our parents are stuck in London, or Ashton would be saddled with a whole new kind of crazy I'm not sure he could handle.

"You have my word," he whispers. "She'll be safe with me, and that trashy excuse for a man can't hide forever. Not with everything I have at my disposal."

Lochlan claps him on the shoulder, and I watch as every muscle in his body tightens. He doesn't relax again until Lochlan moves toward the front door with Colton at his side.

"Thanks, Ash," Colton calls. "I'll check in with you tomorrow after Seth picks up Sadie Sunshine."

Ashton nods but never takes his gaze away from mine.

The front door shuts with a click and an odd sound like a mechanical wheel turning.

"Automatic locks," Ashton answers my unasked question. "The doors lock automatically, but the alarm system only activates or deactivates with a biometric code. We'll get your fingerprints and a retina scan so you can move about the house and grounds without getting locked out, but most of the time you'll only need your fingerprint."

His voice is unlike anything I've ever heard before. Hoarse, like he spent all day yelling at a football game, but rough too. Whispers filtered by tree bark. If he didn't speak with such a neutral expression, I'd guess every word was painful, but he doesn't give any indication that it's true. He seems so quiet, so controlled, I wonder what he sounds like when he yells.

Does his control ever slip?

"Do you want me to give you a tour and show you where your room is before Sadie gets here?" His voice holds a sandpaper quality that smooths over my ragged edges. He breaks into a smile that transforms his face. "Sadie is…" He pulls on the back of his neck. It's a gesture I've seen Colton and Halton make. "Well, Sadie is pure sunshine, but she's also a tornado no one can escape from. If she becomes too much, we won't fault you for retreating to your room."

I flinch and look away to hide it. My being here uninvited is probably an aggravating disruption to someone who appreciates solitude.

"I don't want to interrupt your plans." I glance down at the floor but gasp when I feel his touch under my chin, lifting my gaze to his. I hadn't even heard him approach.

By the look in his eyes, I'd say he's just as shocked by the contact as I am, and he releases me quickly and tucks an unsteady hand into his jeans pocket.

"Sadie is a the more the merrier kind of kid. She has been her entire life. If she knows you're here, she'll want you involved in every conversation, every game, every moment."

I gulp, much louder than I anticipated, and heat rushes to my cheeks.

"She sounds like my kind of girl." I don't know what comes over me, but I wink at the man. Watching his face, I can see the dark clouds that engulf him, and it makes me ache with sadness. "But I don't want to impose. If you have a routine, I'm happy to hide out in my room."

His chuckle is low and if I were anyone else, it would be so very dangerous to my heart. "When I say Sadie is a tornado wrapped in sunshine, I mean it. She has never once stuck to a routine. She's like the wind, floating around, waiting to knock you off-kilter and then wrap you up in her warmth. You'll see."

"She sounds very special."

He nods thoughtfully. "She proved that sunshine can crack through even the darkest of souls." He doesn't give me a chance to respond before he turns on his heel to continue our tour, and honestly, I'm not sure I could even if I wanted to.

What happened to him?

"This is the family room, obviously. It's all run on voice commands. We'll set that up for you too, so you can turn the TV on, adjust lights, get online, et cetera. But you must be very careful about what you put out into the world. Do not tell anyone where you are. If you post pictures online, check the background for anything that may give away your location."

His intensity calls back the fear I've been trying to avoid all afternoon. When I don't say anything, he lets out a heavy breath.

"You will be safe here, but it's going to feel a little over-whelming until we set the ground rules to make that happen."

Once I nod, he takes me through the first floor, bypassing

only one door so expertly hidden in the wall that I almost missed it. Maybe it's because I'm so used to aligning the seams of my dresses to make sure they're perfect that I notice the lines of the wall don't quite match. We pass it again on our way upstairs, and curiosity gets the best of me.

"What's in there?" I ask, pointing at the space with my thumb.

Ashton freezes, and I walk right into his muscular back. My palm lands on his shoulder blade to steady myself, and his back expands with a sharp intake of air. He's strong, but not bulky like his brother Halton. Ashton is leaner. His muscles are powerful in a way a swimmer's might be.

Slowly I remove my hand and watch as his shoulders rise and fall with each steadying breath he takes before he turns around. I haven't moved back, and neither has he, so when he completes the semi-circle, our faces are mere inches apart.

A tremble runs through my hands, but it has nothing to do with fear. My mouth goes unbearably dry, and I wet my lips. Ashton's gaze follows the motion. We're frozen in time. Entranced, I shouldn't feel this need, yet I don't want it to stop.

Ashton breaks the spell first with a small step back. "How—" He clears his throat before trying again. "How did you know it was there?"

"I spend my life putting pieces together so they look like they were always whole. I guess I just got good at looking between the seams."

His eyes bounce back and forth between mine like he's trying to divine some epic truth from them. I don't hide my expressions from him as I do with everyone else. Something tells me it wouldn't work anyway. So instead, I do something I haven't done since I was a teen. I let him in. I give him a front-row seat to my insecurities, my failures, and the pain I've so expertly hidden behind plastic smiles. I let him see my jagged edges and pray my trust in him doesn't tear me apart for good.

A car door slams, breaking the spell that ties us together.

"It's my office," he announces abruptly. "No one has access to it but me."

I open my mouth, but before I can speak, a lock clicks at the front door. My brain is still trying to process all of this when a bubbly, curly-haired teenager bounds into the family room. I know immediately why they call her Sadie Sunshine, and when her happy gaze lands on me, she breaks into a smile that surely means trouble.

She immediately wraps her arms around me. I thought I hugged a lot, but I've got nothing on the Westbrooks.

CHAPTER 5

ASHTON

I see it the minute it happens. Sadie has hearts in her eyes as she shines her light on Nova like a goddamn cheerleader. Ever since she turned thirteen and found boys...

The girls both glance at me, and I realize a growl escaped. It happens whenever I think about teenage assholes getting close to little Sadie.

Teenage boys are no good. End of story.

I hate that Sadie's even old enough to think about boys. It was just yesterday that she was a squishy little six-year-old kissing my boo-boos better. My only saving grace in this situation is that she's still convinced she'll marry Tate, one of my many "adopted" nephews.

Those two have been glued together since the moment they met. And if they do actually get married, they'll bind two of our chosen families together legally. Not that any of us give a damn. We know what makes a family. It isn't blood or a piece of paper notarized by a judge.

With a defeated sigh, I watch them, knowing Sadie already thinks Nova will be "the one" for me.

"Hi. I'm Sadie. My mom told me all about you. She also said Auntie Lexi thoroughly confused you, so I won't tell you that my mom is actually my bonus mom. I have a mom in heaven and a mom here with me. I'm very lucky that way."

Sadie shrugs with that sunshiny smile of hers. "Oops. Well, I'm not very good at keeping things inside. But don't worry about getting us all straight. We're just a big ball of found family chaos. That's what GG calls it anyway. Oh, geez! Have you met GG yet? She's a trip. How long are you here for? Can you show me how you make a wedding dress? Holy wow. Did you bring designs with you? Will you be making your next runway pieces here in Uncle Ash's house?"

Nova is blinking at her like a deer in headlights, so I run interference. "Sadie, I think we should let Nova settle in before we play twenty questions."

Though Nova's mouth is opening and closing like she can't decide which question to answer first, her lips still draw me in. Sadie elbows me in the side, breaking my fascination.

"Oh, okay. I guess that was a lot of questions." Sadie smiles and sweat dots my hairline.

Turning, I force my gaze to stay on my niece, not the temptress standing next to us. "I was just about to show Nova to the sunshine room."

For a brief moment, I see a glimpse of the little girl she used to be. Then she waggles her eyebrows like Colton would, and I duck my head to break the eye contact. This has already been a long fucking day. My throat hurts. I've spoken more words in the last two hours than I have in the last two weeks.

"Sadie." I infuse as much warning as possible, but her face brightens even more. "I need to get my throat spray. Why don't you show Nova upstairs?"

"Gladly. It'll give us a chance for girl talk." My niece lets out an excited squeal, and I groan.

"Nova has been through a lot in the last few days. Don't harass her."

My houseguest finally smiles. "I can handle a teenage girl," she says sweetly.

My lips twitch at the corners and I break into a grin, and it isn't until she's backing up that I realize I'm facing her full-on. *My scars.* I begin to shift, but Sadie stops me.

"Don't you dare, Uncle Ash."

I know she's talking about hiding my scars away, but Nova glances between the two of us, seemingly at a loss. But she's not paying my scars any attention. At all. When her focus lands on me, it's my eyes she won't release from her gaze.

Like the coward I am, I look at the hardwood floors. "Sadie isn't your average teenage girl," I say with fondness.

Though I'm not looking at her, Sadie's eye roll is dramatic enough to be obvious. Nova laughs, a musical sound that freezes me in place as it fills every corner of my consciousness. It envelops me, and I memorize it like a photograph.

I can't be anything but her protector. Fuck karma and hell for giving me glimpses of what I'm missing out on. In another life-time, she could have been my dream girl.

When their footsteps land on the stairs, I finally let out a deep breath and go in search of my throat spray. It's more of a habit now than truly beneficial. But I hold on to routine any way I can. Especially now.

~

"No. No, you didn't." Nova's gentle laughter spreads through the dining room like a shooting star, sprinkling Sadie and me in her happiness.

"Oh, he did. But he made the store owner close the shop for everyone else."

I try to hold in an exasperated sigh and set down my fork.

Nova's expression tells a thousand stories, and I glance away before she catches me staring again. When I feel her gaze land on me though? I'm drawn to her like a moth to a flame.

"You're a great uncle," she says, full of sincerity. Does she ever do anything that isn't heartfelt?

"It wasn't an altruistic move, Nova. I don't like crowds. Sadie needed a tutu or tap shoes..." I run a hand roughly through my hair. "I've never been able to say no to her sunshine, so I did what I had to do."

"Why don't you like crowds?"

Sadie's big blue eyes go wide. Her blond curls bounce as her focus volleys between Nova and me, ready to jump into the conversation, but I give her the slightest shake of my head. If Nova is going to be in my space, she deserves to know a little about why she's living in a home even the CIA couldn't gain access to.

"I worked for a special military organization for a long time..."

"He started when he was really young," Sadie interjects, probably excited to hear me talking about this with someone.

A shiver runs through my entire body. I was only a year older than Sadie is now when my world fell apart. It hits me harder now, just how ill-prepared I was to do what I did. Fuck, Sadie's practically still a baby.

Was I this innocent before it all went to hell?

"Sadie," I say in warning. I may be giving a glimpse behind the curtain, but that doesn't mean I'm going to spill my secrets.

"What?" Nova gasps. "How young?"

"It's not important. Anyway, I wasn't always this—this monster." I gesture to my face, then down my chest, and Nova's gaze follows my hand with a furrowed brow. "I made a mistake that hurt a lot of people. These scars are a physical reminder to never let my guard down again."

My heart thunders in my chest. I should feel shocked that I shared even this tiny bit so easily with a virtual stranger, but the only thing coursing through me is unease that I like talking to her as much as I do.

I don't share.

I don't chat.

Ever.

Especially with a stranger.

What makes her so different?

"You did that to punish yourself?" Nova's words are barely a whisper and full of...of what?

Reluctantly, I face her, and the sadness in her amber eyes blows me away. Remembering she asked a question, I blink rapidly and force myself to focus. "No, Nova. I didn't hurt myself on purpose. Someone else used the blade, but it was my mistake that caused the scars."

Sadie stands abruptly, holding her plate. "That's not true," she says to Nova. "Mistakes are just that. They don't force someone to hold a knife. They don't force people to make crappy choices. The bad guys did that all on their own, and someday my uncle will realize he isn't responsible for the safety and well-being of everyone that ever meets a Westbrook."

"Sadie..."

She turns, pointing her fork in my direction. "I said what I said."

I shouldn't feel proud of her, but I am. This little girl who once kissed my boo-boos with the slobbery precision of a kindergartner is growing into a woman to be reckoned with. I hope I've had some small part in that.

"And just for that," she continues, "we're going to watch *Hello, Goodbye and Everything in Between* tonight. Again."

Pinching the bridge of my nose, I attempt to push a migraine back into the recesses of my brain. She makes me watch this teeny-bopper movie anytime she wants to punish me.

"Have you seen it, Nova?" Sadie asks.

Nova sits in the chair to my right, her knee bouncing wildly under the table and brushing up against my thigh. Scanning up the length of her body, I find she's also chewing on the inside of her cheek.

Fuck.

A phantom pain in my chest causes me to rub the hollow space absentmindedly with the heel of my palm. Scaring her is the last thing I want to do.

Reaching across the table, I place a tentative hand on her balled-up fist, but I don't retreat when she flinches. It's an effort to keep the contact, but I can sense it's important for her to feel safe with me. And fuck me if I don't want that for her. "You are safe here, Nova."

"I know." Her words are full of conviction, and it confuses me.

"Geez, Uncle Ash. She isn't worried about herself. She's upset for you." Sadie rolls her eyes and stalks off to the kitchen as only a teenager can.

My eyes are glued to where our skin touches. The searing pain I usually feel at human touch doesn't come, and it makes it hard to breathe.

Nova slowly raises her other hand and places it on top of mine. More contact. I wait for the pain to come.

Sweat trickles down my spine when it doesn't.

"Are you okay, Ashton? Is it too much? Me being here? If my brother knew you needed your privacy, I'm sure he would have found another solution."

Me? Am I okay? She was the one recently assaulted. This woman confuses me every time she opens her mouth.

It takes great effort, but I carefully slip my hand from hers without looking like a complete asshole. "I'm fine, Nova." Clearing my throat, I will myself to maintain eye contact. "You're here because this is the safest place for you. I will find this guy so you can go back to your regular life, and the Westbrook Beast will just be a fun story you tell people."

Nova's eyes narrow, and if I knew her better, I'd think I've made her angry somehow. Then she squares her shoulders, and I try not to notice how the position presses her cleavage forward.

"You know, in the fairytale, the Beast was just a prince who had a lot to learn before he got his happily ever after."

I scoff. The raspy bark is rough like the edges of a scab that fades into some semblance of a chuckle. "Trust me, princess. There's no happily ever after in my story."

I track her movements as she slowly stands, then places her palms flat on the table and leans closer to me. So close I can smell the tannins on her breath from the red wine she's drinking. The bitter scent is at odds with the sweet creature before me, wearing a gentle smile.

"Oh, *peto*. There's always a happily ever after if you look hard enough."

I feel my brows raise in surprise. Languages have always come easily to me, and I speak many fluently, but Finnish was one of the more difficult to learn. "Peto, huh?" Does she know she's calling me beast in Finnish?

She shrugs with a knowing grin. "My mother was from Finland. She read the Beast to me in Finnish. You may not believe in the fairy tale, but you are a prince, a protector, a hero in every sense of the word, even as you view the world as a dark and scary place." She pauses, and the last trace of humor leaves her beautiful face. "There's a princely code of honor in you, peto. I'm sure of it. And if I'm the princess here, you sure as hell will be the prince." She winks and picks up her plate. "Did Lochlan tell you that I'm kind of a handful?"

I can't help but smile back at her. "He did not. Are you a handful?"

Nova's eyes sparkle in the dim lighting as she smirks, then walks toward the kitchen. "Guess you're about to find out."

Yeah, she's a handful, all right. And now I know I need to find this fool who broke into her apartment, and quick, because I can hardly handle a passing brush of fingertips. What would I do with an entire handful of Nova Blaine?

CHAPTER 6

ASHTON

*W*e sit on the sofa in my great room. The opposite wall has floor-to-ceiling windows with bullet-proof glass that overlooks the valley of Burke Hollow below. On the large pull-down screen, Sadie streams her movie from the overhead projector, but she's the only one paying attention.

Nova hasn't said a word since she left the dinner table. When we entered the family room, Sadie had already plopped down in the center of the sofa. She held out her arms, tugging us down until we bracketed her on either side. Then she covered us all with the blanket she uses for movie nights. It's oddly intimate and not all that uncomfortable.

She won't admit it now, but Sadie has had this blanket since the first time she waltzed in here with a Hello Kitty suitcase and made herself at home.

With their eyes on the screen, I find myself angling my body to watch their reactions. Sadie's emotions flit across her face as words I barely register come from her movie. But Nova? Nova chews on the inside of her cheek again, eyes staring straight ahead rather than following the movement on-screen. Her legs are tucked under her, and she holds onto her elbows like a lifeline.

What's on your mind, Super Nova?

As if sensing my eyes on her, she fidgets with the frayed edge of the fluffy gray blanket in her lap before tucking a piece of silky-looking hair behind her ear. I've never seen hair color quite like hers before. A sun-kissed brown with threads of gold. It glitters in the light that dances across her features.

The urge to reach across and tap her cheek is strong. She's going to chew a hole right through it soon, but she doesn't seem to notice.

While I watch her, I process all the information Lochlan gave me on her former assistant, Samuel Jacobs. Lochlan did a thorough background check on Sam, I'll give him that. But you don't just snap overnight, and Sam's record is too neat. Too tidy. I've been doing this long enough that when my instincts kick in, I trust them. He's hiding something, but what?

I'll need to ask Nova questions, but the thought of hurting her sends an uncomfortable pang through me. It's a protective feeling normally reserved for my family, and if I let myself, I'm going to dwell too long on why she brings that out in me.

I don't know how long I sit there studying my sleeping house guest, but when Sadie rises from the sofa with a mischievous smirk, I know she's caught me staring. Has the freaking movie ended already? It's the kind of film meant to make raging teenage hormones weep, but I'd do anything for the little golden girl who kept me from total darkness for the last eight years.

Sadie shakes her head and leans in to hug me. She and my mother are the only two that I can fully embrace without fighting an anxiety attack. "I think it'll be good for you to spend some time with Nova," she whispers in my ear, then kisses my cheek. She never misses the chance to kiss the most brutal scar on my face. A subtle reminder that she's only ever seen the goodness in me that I was sure had been extinguished the night I was attacked.

"I'm just here to protect her, Sadie Sunshine."

She pulls back, her eyes wild as she stares me in one eye, then the other and back again.

"Even protectors can wish on a shooting star for a chance to feel alive."

My gaze darts to Nova who drifted off to sleep at least thirty minutes ago. Returning my attention to Sadie, I offer a small smile. "Good night, kiddo."

"Good night, Uncle Ash. I like her, you know."

I nod because Sadie likes everyone.

"No one has slept in the sunflower room in a long time."

Damn this kid. Pure sunshine with the ability to burn if you're not careful.

"I just thought she'd feel more comfortable having me close by."

"Mm-hmm," she whispers while retreating toward the hall. She blows me a kiss, and then she's gone, leaving me in the silent blue glow of the blank movie screen. The light reflects on Nova's face, and I take a moment to stare now that no one's watching.

It's been a long time since I've had any reaction to a woman. Granted, the only women I'm around on a regular basis are family members, but still. What is Nova bringing to life in me?

I settle deeper into the sofa. She seems so peaceful right now. *When was the last time you had a restful sleep, princess?* She's tried to hide the dark circles under her eyes with makeup, and she's quite adept at it, but after years of watching Pacen attempt the same thing, I'm in tune with all the signs of duress.

Silence often stirs memories of my childhood friend Pacen. She was the one person I let down more than myself. Her wedding was last month, but no matter how hard I dig, I haven't found out who she married. Not being there for her was like a dagger through the heart, but I understand. I represent every

39

nightmare she's ever experienced. I wouldn't want me around either.

Nova shifts in her sleep, and I lean over to tuck Sadie's blanket around her. Up close, I get a whiff of strawberries that reminds me of innocence. The strange urge to touch her has me shooting back to my own side. Shaking my head, I allow my thoughts to drift back into the darkness where I belong.

~

The jarring sound of a camera shutter jerks me awake. Alert and on edge, I scan for threats until I spy Sadie behind the sofa with her phone pointed at me. When I lower my defenses, other sensations flow in. The warm, supple body plastered to mine. Strawberries. The painfully hard erection pressing against the zipper of my jeans.

Well, there you are, you little fucker. I thought you'd died years ago.

Dropping my chin, I find Nova's head resting on my chest, and my hands begin to shake. I lick my suddenly dry lips as I force my surroundings to stay in focus.

Sadie's small hand lands on my forearm, and I take much more comfort from her than I should. But it's always been that way between Sadie and me, hasn't it? I'm a broken man with nothing to offer, and she's the little ray of sunshine who refuses to let me drown in my darkness.

I rest one hand over the tattoo on the left side of my chest. A reminder that she's saved me before.

Then I force a smile for her benefit.

"Tate is landing soon. Colty is taking me to the airfield," she whispers just as my front door crashes open.

I swear, Colton is worse than the Tasmanian Devil sometimes.

"Ash?" he shouts. He rounds the corner and stops mid-step when he finds me on the sofa, Nova sprawled on top of me.

His unannounced visit has the blessed reaction of causing my inconvenient boner to subside, but he startles Nova, and the fear in her eyes as she stares at me is palpable. I hold a hand up to stop Colton in his tracks and speak softly, directly to Nova.

"We fell asleep, princess. You're okay."

Forcing my gaze away from Nova, I watch Colton's eyes go as wide as his smile, and I curse myself for letting that stupid nickname slip past my lips again.

Nova's heart beats rapidly against my chest, so I consciously take a deep breath. An obscene level of satisfaction fills me when she mimics the action. Colton takes a cautious step forward, and I hold my hand up again, silently commanding him to stay still. But Nova notices the shift and lifts her head to look around.

She spots Colton, and her entire body stiffens against mine, making my cock jerk in my jeans. Once again, my body is confused by everything Nova.

"It's okay. You're okay," I repeat, hating how the tone of my voice has me forever sounding like a villain in a children's movie.

She looks down at my shirt and gasps. When I follow her line of sight, an unexpected bout of laughter fills my chest. "You're a drooler."

"Ugh! I am not. Not normally. I can't help it if you had my head in a submission hold. I probably couldn't breathe through my nose because you had it pressed into the pine-scented rock wall you call a chest. You don't make a very good pillow."

I sit up with her still attached to me. "You seem to have slept just fine."

A jolt passes through me as I realize I also slept through the night. For the first time in years, I slept through the night with Sadie in the house. It doesn't take my Mensa rating to attribute that to Nova's presence.

"So did you, Uncle Ash," Sadie unhelpfully butts in, but I don't have time to ask her how she knows I don't normally sleep because Nova is scrambling to disentangle herself from my limbs.

"Yeah, he doesn't make a great pillow, but at least he didn't piss the bed. The last time we had a sleepover, he peed all over me." Colton's light laughter fills the room.

"I was five years old, and we were in the woods after drinking a case of Gatorade. And that wasn't our last sleepover, you dickhead."

Nova's face flushes a delicious shade of crimson as she gets to her feet. "Ah, I don't even remember falling asleep."

"You passed out about an hour into the movie," Sadie says. "When I went to bed, Uncle Ash was watching over you. Not in a pervy way." She giggles. "Like he wanted you to rest, and he was going to stand guard so you could. I've never seen him fall asleep too though."

"Sadie," I groan. But she smiles with her brows raised.

"Tell me you don't sit out here every Friday night to ensure I'm safe. All night long."

"I work, Sadie. I…"

"Don't lie to me, Uncle Ash. I've seen you out here at all hours of the night. And you used to do the same thing in the sunflower room. It's okay—I know it makes you feel better, but I like that you felt comfortable enough to keep Nova safe while also taking care of you."

I open my mouth to protest, but her curls start bouncing as she turns to my brother. "Come on, Colty. I don't want to be late picking up Tate! We have so much to do before he has to head home."

Colton holds out his arm, and she slips in beneath it. "Let's go, kiddo. Can't keep your destiny waiting."

"Okay, boomer. Bye, Uncle Ash. See ya, Nova."

Colton's face pales. "Did you just call me boomer? As in outdated? Old?" His horrified expression is amplified by the crackle in his voice.

42

"Geez, Colty. You're low-key rocking the dad vibes, okay?"

That has him smiling again. "Can't help it, Sunny. Winnie's law practice is *booming,* and little Wes makes me a better man every day."

It's all true. Colton's wife, Winnie, is a miracle worker for the underprivileged, and adopting her baby brother changed something in Colton. He's a great father and a better man, even if he is annoying.

When he pauses at the door and flashes a smirk our way, I push off the sofa but not fast enough to keep the words from leaving his mouth.

"Don't worry, Ash. I won't tell Loch you're playing house with Nono. At least not yet."

"Leave," I grit out. My teeth are clenched so tightly that pain radiates to my cheekbones.

"Do it," Nova challenges. "And if he says a damn thing, I'll tell his wife to replace all his suits with sweatpants the next time he goes on a trip."

"Brutal." Colton laughs, shaking his head. "I bet Lochlan would wear a three-piece suit to a nude beach."

My head swivels between him and Nova. Her stance is relaxed like she enjoys this banter. Nova may be a victim now, but she's stronger than I've given her credit for.

I wave them out the door. "Go, Colton. If you're late, Sadie might never forgive you."

His laughter follows him out the door. And then it's just Nova and me. The silence I usually crave feels suffocating as she turns to me in slow motion.

CHAPTER 7

NOVA

I take a deep breath through my nose and slowly exhale. Then I do it again, placing my hands on my hips, and slowly turn toward Ashton.

"Your family is very…"

"Invasive? Intrusive? Giant pains in the ass?" he says while scratching the scruff along his jaw and shifting his weight from foot to foot.

I search his face, but he can't hide the love in his eyes. I shake my head. "Caring. A little unconventional, but whose isn't these days? Do they always pop in unannounced, or is that because I'm here?"

I seem to make him nervous, so while I wait for an answer, I walk toward the only photo in the room. A giant framed piece on the back wall filled with close to fifty people. Some of them I recognize as Westbrooks, while others are familiar but I can't place them.

"I think they're on a rotating schedule," Ashton grumbles low enough that he may not have meant for me to hear it.

"Why?"

"Why what?"

"Why are they on a rotating schedule?"

He places a hand low on his hip, and I half expect his foot to start tapping at any moment. His body language screams exasperation. Oh, peto. If I'm annoying you already, you're in for a lot of trouble. The thought makes me smile. I'm going to like ruffling his feathers even more than I do my brother's.

"I don't know if you've noticed, Nova, but I'm not exactly Mr. Social. They take turns checking on me to make sure—to make sure I don't do something stupid."

He doesn't say hurt himself, but I have no doubt that the dark shadow that follows him around has whispered those words in his ear more than once.

"Have you always been this way? Or just since..." I wave my hand up and down his body when I can't find the right words.

"Since I became the Westbrook monster hidden away in his tower?"

This guy is really starting to piss me off with this crap. With my hands planted firmly on my hips, I stomp over to him until we're toe to toe. "Listen to me, peto. You're only beastly if you want to be. Is that your family?" I point to the photo behind me.

"Yes."

I figured it must have been, but it still shocks me. With the exception of the two older women, they all seem to be about the same age. "All of them? Are they cousins or something? Was that taken at a family reunion?"

"I'm sure you've heard by now that my mother has a habit of adopting people regardless of their age."

I furrow my brow as I search my memory bank for anything Loch would have told me. I know Lexi was trying to explain it when I arrived last night, but it's all foggy in my brain.

Maybe I'm quiet too long because Ashton rolls his eyes, skirts around me without touching me, and stalks over to the photo.

"These are my biological brothers in birth order." He points to a different face with each name. "Preston, Easton, Halton,

Colton, and me. Preston is married to Emory. Easton has Lexi, Halton is married to Rylan. Colton has Winnie."

He circles a cluster of kids with his index finger. "These are all my nieces and nephews. These guys, Dexter, Trevor, Loki, and Dillon, grew up with us. They started as my brothers' friends, but Loki and I are closer in age and, well, we were put on the same path. Seth worked for Loki, and my mother likes to make sure everyone has a home for the holidays. Lanie, Julia, Sloane, and Ari are their wives." His chest heaves, but I can't tell if he's annoyed or overwhelmed as he takes a giant step back.

"And they have way too many freaking kids to name, but they're all family by choice. Blood doesn't make a family, princess. Love, circumstance, and trust do."

"I agree. Lochlan is my stepbrother. I don't have a relationship with my biological dad, but when my mom married Lochlan's dad, Ollie, he adopted me. Before my mom passed away, Lochlan's mother, Kitty, promised her that she'd always be there for me, and she has. They're the best parents I could ask for. And given my situation, I'll never question anyone's family dynamic. I wasn't judging, Ashton. Just asking. And you're changing the subject."

He raises his brow in challenge. "How am I changing the subject?"

"Your family, all of them?" I point over my shoulder with my thumb. "They love you."

"Of course."

"And they check on you daily?"

"Unfortunately."

"Do you think they feel obligated to do that?"

I can tell he senses a trap, but he begrudgingly answers anyway. "No, that's not how family works."

"Exactly. But if one of your brothers hurt Sadie, would you stand by them?"

"They would never do that." He paces three steps to the wall, then turns back to me.

"But if they did, would you stand by them?"

"No." His words are barely audible, but anger radiates from every tightly corded muscle in his body.

"And if you were truly a monster, this beast you keep calling yourself, would they stand by you?"

"If they knew the truth, no. They wouldn't."

It's like he sucked all the air out of the room.

"Wh—What do you mean?"

His eyes have turned dark, the blue colors swirling like a storm cloud as he watches me. In the silence, the mechanical sound of the lock has us both turning just as the front door opens.

"Jesus, GG," Ashton grumbles, but he crosses the room with long strides and takes a pan from the old woman's shaky hands.

Didn't Lexi tell me to stay away from GG?

"Well? Where is she, warden? I gots to see her for myself, ya know?"

I watch with a smile as she pauses to stare into Ashton's eyes with the all-knowing expression that comes with age.

"That's it, ain't it? You're the warden."

Ashton's eyes dart to me, then back to GG.

He gulps, making his Adam's apple bob. "It's as close as all the other nicknames you've tried, GG. What are you doing here?"

Her unwavering gaze hasn't left his. "Nah, this is it. It's sticking. You're everyone's keeper." She glances around the room, then back at Ashton. "Hattie made those for your girl. He's been in my kitchen for hours pacing like a zoo animal, and I had a feelin'. I knew she'd come, just took her long enough."

"GG…"

"No, don't ya go GG'ing me." The old woman spins on her heel, and Ashton instinctively reaches out a hand to steady her.

Her face is wrinkled with time, and her gait is unsteady, but the sparkle in her eyes tells decades' worth of stories.

"Nova?" I tear my eyes away from the old woman to find a flummoxed Ashton watching me closely. "This is Lexi's grandmother, GG. She's a…"

"Menace," GG interrupts with a wave of her hand. "You listen to me, warden. Have I been wrong yet?" When Ashton doesn't answer, she elbows him in the gut. "Well, have I?"

I can't help myself. I laugh. GG might be my hero, and I want to know everything. "Been wrong about what?"

Her wise and aging eyes finally land on mine, and she shifts forward. I can't tell if she's dragging Ashton with her or if he's trying to guide her, but they move as one.

She ignores my question for a long moment. "Mm-hmm. Been waitin' on you, all right." She narrows her eyes and scans my face with such determination that unease settles in my gut. "Ya know, some secrets are like spoiled milk. When it starts to stink, it's just time to let them go."

My throat goes dry, and my skin suddenly feels itchy, but I mentally shake my head. There's no way she knows my secrets.

Over her shoulder, I catch sight of Rylan, and relief hits me. I like this old lady, but the way she stares makes me twitchy.

"Don't worry, starlight, you're in the right place."

Ashton pales. Rylan gasps. GG smirks, then leans in to kiss my cheek. When she does, she whispers, "They've been waitin' a long time for me to pick his match."

"Let's get you a seat," Ashton barks and leads her to the kitchen island.

There's no mistaking that I've missed something big here, and judging by Rylan's expression, everyone but Ashton is happy about it.

Rylan holds up a bag and nods to the stairs just as her husband walks in with a large box. The picture on the side shows an industrial sewing machine and table just like the one I use at home. My knees go weak at the sight.

"You brought me a sewing machine?"

"I know you're still working on a piece for CFDA. I spoke to Lochlan—he's going to have Tilly and Penny gather up all your material, and it'll be here this afternoon."

"What is the CFDA?" Ashton interrupts. "They can't just ship shit here. No one is supposed to know where she is."

Turning my attention to him, I see the agitation in every muscle of his face.

"The CFDA is like the Oscars of fashion. Lochlan wouldn't keep anything from Tilly, and Penny is his assistant and my friend. They're both one hundred percent trustworthy."

"What part of 'not a soul' didn't he understand?" Ashton says more to himself than anyone. "How the fuck do they expect me to do my job if they can't follow a simple command?"

"Take a breath, peto. Your beast is showing." An uncomfortable silence fills the room as everyone stares at us, but I'm fuming. "Tilly is family. You can trust her. And I don't have friends. Not many anyway, but I would trust Penny with my life."

"Like you trusted Sam?" he spits.

Direct hit. I have never trusted the right people, but I know Penny. Don't I? Instead of answering him, I deflect. "She's with Lochlan every day. She would have been worried."

"Yup. You're good for him, glowy."

I turn a confused expression on GG. "Glowy? Wait. Starlight? Are you talking to me?"

"Nova means new. New star. New light. New start. Your heart glows like the light of stars, child. It ain't yer fault people are trying to make that fade away. But mark my words, you're the one who will blaze a path in his darkness."

A loud snap makes me flinch. Turning my head, I realize Ashton punched the wall before storming out of the room. My mouth drops open, but I don't know what to say.

"I'll talk to him," Halton mumbles after setting the sewing machine box against the wall.

"I—I don't understand what just happened."

Rylan takes my hand and leads me into the kitchen. "Remember how Lexi told you GG reads cards and plays matchmaker?"

I feel my brows pinch together, but I nod and sit at the island next to GG as Rylan pulls out a teapot.

"Well, she uses those fortune-telling cards to make love matches. She never tells the couple though."

"I'm still missing something," I admit, more confused than ever.

GG cackles, startling me, and I nearly fall off my stool. I've never heard a sound like her laugh before. I can only picture the old woman who gave Snow White the apple, but GG looks nothing like the evil queen. Her eyes are shrewd but kind, and love wars with mischief behind them.

"She doesn't tell any of her matches. She simply gives them nicknames."

I drop my chin into my palm, waiting for more information. When Rylan remains silent, I turn to GG, who cackles again.

"She's eight for eight with her matches," Rylan explains.

"O-kay?"

"We were all given nicknames."

I peer over my shoulder, searching for anyone who can give me answers, and GG pats my forearm. "Enjoy the cookies, glowy. They're the warden's favorite kind—coconut chip."

I gasp as her frail bones attempt to slip off the high stool. Rylan is right there to catch her while flashing me a look that says, "See? I told you."

I round the island to the sink as they walk to the front door. While they head outside, I splash cold water on my face. I take back everything I have ever said about my family. We have nothing on this shit show.

CHAPTER 8

ASHTON

Thump. Thump. Thump.

My fists connect with the punching bag I've set up in the center of the ring. Left, left, right. Right, right, left. The comforting thwack, thwack, thwack regulates my thoughts.

Fucking GG.

"Are you just going to stand there, or are you going to come hold the bag for me?" I hiss through clenched teeth.

My brother Halton has been leaning against the wall for the last ten minutes, not saying a word. But talking has never really been his thing. Not like Colton, thank God.

I feel his sigh from here, but he pushes off the wall and walks into the boxing ring I have set up in my basement. If only he knew what these mats are really used for.

He grabs the bag that's extended from the ceiling and holds it still as I continue to pummel into it with unprotected hands.

"It's not the end of the world, you know."

"What isn't?" My breathing is heavy and erratic, much like my thoughts.

"Letting someone in. Falling in love," he says quietly.

"Get the fuck out."

"No."

"Halton, I fucking mean it. That woman has been in my life for less than twenty-four hours. I don't give a flying fuck what GG says or does. I don't care if her meddling has magically worked out for the rest of you. I'm not you. I'm not any of you. I don't believe in her bullshit. I don't need a woman to save me. I don't need a light to guide me."

I throw another punch with so much force my shoulder aches from the effort. My form is off. My stance is unbalanced, but I keep going. For years, my life has been spiraling toward an explosion, but I'll be damned if I let it take down everyone else too.

"Don't you?"

I spin and kick the bag so hard that Halton falls backward, but he doesn't back down. He charges me. Halton isn't the brother I expect a physical reaction from, so he catches me unawares as he grabs me by my shirt and pins me against the ropes.

"No," I yell. The anger I've carried for almost eighteen years is dangerously close to the surface.

His eyes jump between mine, and when I expect him to punch me, he pulls back just enough so his hands aren't pressed against my chest. The move is so small most people wouldn't have noticed, but Halton has struggled with anxiety his entire life. He knows unconventional pain, and I realize for the first time that he recognizes it in me.

He doesn't release me. He just takes extra care not to touch anything but my shirt.

"Colton said you fell asleep on the sofa."

Motherfucking cocksucker.

"So. What."

"With Nova on your chest." He intentionally stares at the scar stretching across my face.

He's making a point, but I can't be rational right now. The pity in his eyes sickens me, so I slip my hands between his arms to break his hold on me, then shove him back.

"When is the last time you let anyone get that close, Ashton? Anyone other than Mom or Sadie?"

I stomp back to the punching bag, but when I clench my fists, my knuckles pull painfully. They're swollen and bloodied. I normally keep the bruises hidden, but I won't be able to hide these.

"Don't you get tired, Ash?"

I spin and stare but keep my lips sealed shut.

My brother shakes his head as if he's disappointed in me.

Yeah, well, fuck you, Halton. I'm disappointed in myself too, but the asshole keeps talking in my silence.

"Carrying around the hatred? The secrets? The pain? We all see it. We just don't have a goddamn idea how to help you." His heavy sigh hits like a brick to my heart.

"It isn't your burden to carry. Let it go." A shudder racks my body as exhaustion rolls in. I don't know how much longer I can keep fighting.

"We can't do that, Ash. That would mean letting go of you, and you know we'll never do that. Whatever demons you're fighting, it's time to lay down your sword. Let us in."

For the briefest of seconds, my guard drops. "And if I'm the demon?"

He tilts his head and registers my question, but before he can answer, my walls rebuild like the final stages of Tetris. Fast and unyielding, I shutter my expression.

Halton shakes his head and bends to slip through the ropes. "Even a peace lily can grow in the dark, but it won't flower without the sun."

"What does that even mean?" I ask his retreating form.

"It means you can keep living in the dark alone, or you can let the light in and see what it's like to finally breathe."

His footfalls echo on the stairs. So I leave the ring and head to the freezer in the corner for an ice pack.

Fucking metaphors.

~

I step out of the shower and pause, swamped with a dread I can't place. Something sounds eerily like a fisher cat screaming to the beat of Coldplay. After another second, I relax marginally. It seems my houseguest likes to sing. Badly.

As I dry off, I can't help the chuckle that bubbles up in my chest despite the clusterfuck with Halton. I tug on my jeans, not bothering to do much with my hair, and cross the small hallway that connects my room to Nova's.

It's odd that she opened this door, but I'm not complaining. I lean against the doorframe and observe her.

She bounces merrily. There's no other way to explain it as she dances around the pile of wood and metal in the center of her room. In the corner, I see the discarded box of her new sewing machine.

How the hell is she carrying that thing around? It must weigh close to a hundred pounds.

Her hair is piled on top of her head in a way that should look messy, but on Nova, it looks…innocent. And real.

"And the light…" she sings, and I swear to all that's holy, my ears try to bleed, but when her eyes land on mine, that blood attacks every nerve ending in my body. She reaches up, removes the headphones that kept her brain happily distracted, and gives me a sheepish shrug.

"Is that what you do? Do you fix people?" I ask, not sure why my voice has gone several octaves lower.

She eyes me for a moment, before peering down at the headphones in her hands. "'Fix You' sounds a lot better when Coldplay sings it," she answers evasively.

"I agree," I deadpan, but lose the battle and laugh outright when her face goes slack. "So, do you?"

"Do I what?" The sultry, hypnotic tone of her voice goes straight to my balls.

God, I love her voice.

Wait. What? I'm worse than a horny teenager with a hot teacher.

Focus, Ashton. "Ah, do you fix people?"

"People don't need to be fixed, peto. They need to be loved."

"Love fixes everything?"

A gentle smile shows off her perfectly straight teeth and reaches all the way up to hug her eyes. "There you go thinking people are things to be fixed. Furniture breaks. Dishes break. When a person feels broken, it's because someone let them down. Or…"

My right hand clenches as she traces the scars on my chest with her eyes. In my rush to find the offending sounds, I forgot to put on a shirt.

"Or what?" My voice is lower than normal, my ability to breathe hinging on what she says next.

"Or a person feels broken because they let themselves down."

This princess with eyes that glow like the souls of stars sees too much.

Her gaze locks on the tattoo on the left side of my chest. Icarus lies below one of my most brutal wounds, and on the upper side of the scar, an avenging angel floats, blocking me from the sun.

Nova just stares but doesn't ask any questions. It's like she already knows that the mistakes I've made will eventually burn me to the ground.

"It's been an—" I swallow to buy time and feel myself frown at the pile of crap sitting at her feet. "It's been an intense twenty-four hours. Let me finish getting dressed, then we can go make dinner."

"Make? You cook?"

I like the skepticism in her voice.

"Princess? I can do anything I set my mind to."

"Hmm. Promise?"

It's a challenge that makes me feel alive, but I also sense a trap.

"I promise." If I fall victim to her challenge, I have a feeling it'll be worth it.

"Remember that, peto. Remember that promise. I will be collecting before I leave here."

A challenge and a threat. Two things I've built my life on.

~

*N*ova makes her way around the kitchen with her bottom lip between her teeth, a slight hesitancy in the way she moves.

"Have you always lived in a hotel?" I ask. That would explain why she's uncomfortable in the kitchen. The princess has been waited on her entire life.

I skirt around her to place the pork and potatoes in the oven, but never take my eyes off her.

"For the most part." She stalks toward me at the end of the island, dragging her finger along the leathered granite like she's admiring the hard stone.

I lean back against the counter so I can watch her approach and give myself space. There's an elegance that surrounds her. She's cultured and sophisticated, yet standing here in my kitchen in ripped jeans and a Nirvana sweatshirt that slips off her shoulder like an '80s pop star with messy hair and bright eyes, she feels almost…sad.

"You must miss out on a lot living your life in a hotel."

"Or you learn a lot," she snips.

Fuck. I've offended her. I have the social skills of a pigeon. Unsure of what to say, I push off the island and walk to the fridge. I pull out everything we'll need for a salad and set it next to her.

"Can you handle chopping a salad while I make a glaze for the pork?"

I can't see her expression with her back to me, but she shrugs and nods. I watch her for a few stolen moments as she removes a cucumber and red pepper from their plastic confines.

Silence hangs heavy, making my shoulders tense. Nova has been talking since the first moment I met her. I don't know what to do with this muted version of her. As my frustration comes to a boil, I walk to the pantry to gather what I'll need to start the glaze and leave her to her task.

When I come out of the pantry, I nearly drop the bottles in my hands as I rush to Nova's side.

"Are you messing with me?" I give her the side-eye as she holds the knife in her hand like a three-inch golf pencil. When she crosses her left arm over the knife to hold the end of the cucumber at an odd angle, I swear my heart stops. "You're going to cut your goddamn hand off," I grumble, moving in behind her.

She picks up the cucumber with a smirk, and I freeze. My arms nearly cage her in as I reach around her for the knife.

Strawberries and innocence fill my nostrils, but this woman is no innocent. A temptress, maybe, and the gleam in her eyes as she turns her head is full of seduction. Her lips are dangerously close to my skin. She can wield her beauty as a weapon or a defense. Does she realize it?

I take a step back and let my arms fall to my sides. "You know how to cook."

"I know how to cook."

"I'm sorry. I just assumed because you live in a hotel..."

"You know what they say about people who assume?"

A dark chuckle pulls a smile from me. "Yeah, they make an ass out of you and me."

Her eyes twinkle, but she cuts out the sass.

"I can cook, Ashton. I'm not some great chef, but I can get

around a kitchen. I just wanted to see how far your conde-scending instructions would go."

She sets down the offending vegetable and grins at me like she's the definition of trouble, then continues speaking.

"Growing up, our parents made Lochlan and I try every job at the hotel. From the front desk to housekeeping, we did it all. My favorite was working in the kitchen, even when I was relegated to doing dishes. The energy and the mayhem that happens in an industrial kitchen is unlike anything else I've ever seen."

Nova's body heat seeps into my soul and I put a little more distance between us.

"Eventually," she laughs, "chef Pat took pity on me and started giving me lessons. I loved it, but culinary life is not for the faint of heart so, in the end, fashion was more my speed." She picks up the cucumber again. "Did you have to learn to put a condom on one of these in high school?"

Hello, whiplash. Meet my neck.

"No."

Nova's eyes go wide. How does anyone ever say no to those eyes?

"What did you use? A banana?" She makes a crude motion with the vegetable, and my heart vibrates in my chest.

"I didn't have a normal high school experience, princess."

"How come?" she asks nonchalantly and begins chopping the cucumber so fast I turn to watch her. She slices the vegetable with the precision and determination of Gordon Ramsay, and I'm left shaking my head. "How come?" she asks again.

Because at fifteen, I was learning how to save children from monsters. It almost slips out before I catch myself.

Dangerous. This sassy little princess is dangerous.

"Ah, I was graduating college when other kids my age were getting their driver's license."

"Ooh, brainy. I like that in a man."

Nova doesn't lift her head as she says it, but the flirtation in her tone sounds easy. Does she even realize it? Is she just a natural-born flirt?

Something Lochlan said pops into my head. *"Not a boyfriend. Another one-night stand, I guess."* Does she have one-night stands often?

When she tosses the cucumbers into the bowl sitting between us on the island, her body brushes against mine. Her heat seeps into my thigh. Turning my head to the left, I don't mean to make eye contact, but it's like she reached through the air and trapped my gaze in hers.

My skin feels too tight, like a sunburn that can find no relief. Flexing my hand, I attempt to relieve the tingling sensation that's taken over my body. My eyes drift down her face to her lips, then dip lower, to the pulse point in her slender neck. The rapid thump, thump, thump betrays her calm exterior.

"Peto?" The way she says it sends a shiver down my spine.

Why does her calling me peto have such a profound effect on me?

It's like she controls the pleasure center in my body, and with a single word, she can ignite me. I'm feeling strange things. Things I've only been able to feel from my fist for a very long time, and it's deeply distressing.

I need to get my shit together.

"Tell me about your boyfriend," I command in a tone so harsh it surprises me. I try again. "The one who was injured. Who is he? Where is he? How long were you together?"

"Not much to tell." Nova tucks a piece of hair behind her ear and squares her body to me. Her right hand falls to her hip like she's about to scold me. And hell, I probably even deserve it, but I mimic her position, and it angles our bodies close enough to touch.

I lower my chin but raise my eyebrows, waiting for her to continue. She huffs out a long breath, fluttering the hair around her face. For the briefest moment, I imagine her hair splayed across my pillow.

Clearing my throat, I take one step back, then another, and pull the bowl closer to the edge of the counter to keep my hands busy.

"Tell me what you can then."

"What was your voice like before you were hurt?"

My entire body tenses like prey who just noticed they're being hunted. "I don't remember," I answer honestly.

She steps closer and pushes the scent of strawberry fields my way.

"You're very short," I blurt. I don't mean to, but it's like every step she takes into my space eviscerates another layer of control.

She snorts in response. Her laughter causes her cheekbones to become more prominent as her eyes tilt up at the edges. It's as if the happiness escaping her lips pushes her entire face to the heavens. But it's her eyes that light me up like a million tiny shooting stars.

"I bet your voice was always soft, Ashton. Deliberate but gentle when you spoke. It may have a rough edge now, but it's no less powerful. You are no less powerful unless you let your fears win."

My skin feels itchy. And my throat closes like I've swallowed a mouthful of sand, but I force the words out anyway. "You have no idea the kind of power I've been forced to control. Tell me about the asshole in your bed, Nova."

CHAPTER 9

NOVA

I glower up at the insufferable man assigned to be my protector, but I don't back down. He may have gotten the short end of the stick having to babysit me, but he needs someone too. He's hurting even if he won't admit it. I see it in his eyes. In the way he holds himself apart, on the periphery of his life.

Focusing on other people's problems keeps me from shining a light on my own, but something tells me it will be tit for tat with my sexy, broken peto.

Because, let's be honest here, Ashton is freaking sexy as hell, but he needs a giant shove into life.

The asshole in my bed.

My chest flares with anger. "Which one, *Ashton*? Which asshole would you like to know about?"

Why am I antagonizing this man? He's gone out of his way to open his home to me, yet I can't help picking. Pushing. Just a little. His resounding growl causes a wave of pure pleasure to ripple through my entire body.

We definitely have chemistry, even if he denies it, but I won't go there with him. I can't. He's too close to my family, even if by proxy. I can't risk him finding out what I am. I can't risk my family finding out. So I'll flirt. I'll push. I'll help him out of his shell. But I will not, in any way, cross the line with Ashton Westbrook.

"Start with the one who had his face bashed in."

I wince and can't stop my shoulders from hitching around my ears.

Another direct hit. He's skilled at those.

When he leans forward, his manly scent of pine mixed with fresh linen and hints of leather make my throat go dry.

It's so much easier to focus on my bodily reaction to this man than my embarrassment and fear over my one-night stand, Jason, being so publicly exposed. No one has ever drawn purely sexual, raw tension from me as Ashton does. It's confusing. And terrifying. But oh so intriguing.

"Princess?" He grunts the warning through clenched teeth. I blink rapidly, causing my eyelashes to flutter up until I'm trapped by his baby blue irises.

My breathing is shallow, my body is flushed like I've just had the most epic orgasm, and we're not even touching.

"God. You're like a super-sized vacuum."

Ashton frowns, and it does nothing to tone down his growly sex appeal. Neither does his gruff response or the brute strength lurking beneath his unassuming clothing. A strength and power I can sense but have yet to experience.

Maybe I am a sex addict. Maybe Kate was right and it isn't my fear of one stupid mistake keeping me from a relationship…it's because I'm attracted to everyone who gives me the tiniest amount of attention.

"Whatever you're thinking, stop. Why am I a vacuum?"

"You have no idea what I'm thinking," I huff.

Somehow, he inches impossibly closer, sending a whiff of pine my way. I'll never be able to go near a Christmas tree again without thinking dirty thoughts about this near stranger.

Ashton leans down so we're nose to nose. "I have a pretty good idea what causes that type of flush, princess." He pulls away so quickly it makes me dizzy. "Now, answer my questions. Vacuum? And who was in your bed?"

Thankfully, he turns to grab a mixing bowl and gives me a reprieve from his all-knowing gaze. He slides a glass of water in front of me, and I realize in my flushed state that I spaced out for a minute. I turn to thank him, but the jerk winks at me and returns to his pork glaze.

Puffing out my cheeks, I slowly exhale. "You're like a vacuum because you suck all the thoughts from my head without saying a word. And you take up a lot of air. Like all the air and space. Just, sucking it all right into your vortex and taking everyone with it." My hands gesture wildly with each word, and I can't stop them.

"Everyone? Or you?" He chokes and shakes his head. "Never mind. I mean. Jesus, princess. Who was in your bed?"

"Are you jealous, peto?" I keep my tone light and teasing but damn it, I really want to know!

He gives me a dead stare, but his right eye twitches ever so slightly. Interesting. I cross my arms over my chest and wait for him to say something, but he doesn't. He just stares right back with an intensity that could melt glaciers.

My eyes burn with the need to blink, but I will not back down.

"Do you often engage in staring contests?" I taunt.

"Only when I need to prove a point."

"And what point are you making right now?" A tear slips out of the corner of my eye.

His breaths are even but heavy. So heavy that when he exhales, the faint scent of mint washes over my face. "Right now, I'm proving that you're playing by my rules, sweetheart. Mine, and mine alone."

That's all it takes. I blink. Rapidly. Then glance anywhere but directly at him. It's like trying to stare at the sun. You can't do it

63

without protection. And in Ashton's case, I can't begin to decipher who needs protecting—myself from him? Or him from me?

"I win," he whispers. "Lochlan said the man was a one-night stand. Do you have a boyfriend?"

"I wouldn't be having a one-night stand if I had a boyfriend," I hiss.

"Sorry, I didn't mean it like that. I just need all the details I can get."

"I haven't had a boyfriend in years."

"Bullshit."

His outburst shocks us both into silence.

He wipes his mouth with his thumb and fingers, then pinches it closed for a second too long before releasing it with jerky movements. "Ah, I just mean that's hard to believe."

He's flustered. It's cute. Very cute.

"You can wrap up ugly in the prettiest packaging, but it's still ugly underneath, Ash. Sometimes it's better to keep the paper on."

Jesus, Nova. Mayday. Mayday. Too close to the truth. I take a surreptitious glance at the water he gave me earlier. Could he have drugged me? Would he? I almost laugh at my absurdity. I'm just a loudmouth that feels some kind of connection to him, like a kindred soul. That's the only reason I'm blabbering on like an idiot.

"I choose not to have relationships right now. That's all you need to know."

"Do you have one-night stands often?" He sounds...angry?

Placing my hands on my hips, I step forward, forcing him to either move out of my way or let me run into him. He steps back. "This is not the 1950s. Women can have a healthy sex life. Gasp! They can even enjoy sex. A lot of sex. We can have sex with whoever we want, whenever we want, and not be made to feel like a slut. Men do it all the time, Ashton. If I want to fuck someone I just met, that's my prerogative. And yes, one-night stands are *all* I do."

I'm not sure who moves first, but he's crowding me against the wall a second later. I'm pinned in place by Ashton's large body, even though the only part of him touching me is his palm splayed flat across my collarbone.

"You talk. Too much. For the love of God, stop saying sex, and for fuck's sake, don't say fuck like that."

That's when I notice the heavy rise and fall of his chest. The flex of his fingers against my skin. How his gaze seems to devour me from a foot away.

As quickly as he came, he steps back. It's all I can do to hold myself upright and not stumble forward in his wake.

"Holy intense," I mutter.

Ashton spins on me quickly like he's about to say something, then reconsiders and stalks to the other side of the island. He's putting a physical barrier between us.

"What was his name?"

"Jason." I remain plastered to the wall like I'm wearing a Velcro suit.

"Where did you meet him?"

"O'Malley's."

"Were you by yourself?"

"I rarely go out alone," I mutter. "Kate's usually with me. She's gone everywhere with me since the tenth grade."

"Does she know where you are now?"

For the first time since high school, I haven't had a constant barrage of text messages from her. I glance around the room at the same time as I pat my empty pockets.

Ashton has kept me so preoccupied I didn't even realize my phone was missing until this very minute. Who gets so wrapped up in a stranger they don't notice a missing phone? It's like an extra appendage to most people. What is going on with me?

"What's wrong?" The worry in Ashton's voice has me focusing on him again, and for a moment, the dread I carry subsides.

"I don't have my phone," I groan. Kate is going to be pissed.

"I know."

"What do you mean, you know?"

"I sent it back to New York with Lochlan," he says, shrugging his left shoulder like he had every right to make that decision.

"All my contacts are in that phone, Ashton. I need it for work."

"In all likelihood, that phone is being tracked by your attacker. Having it here would lead him straight to you—if it didn't already."

Do you know when people say they feel all the color draining from their face? I never thought that was a real feeling.

I was wrong.

Before I can open my mouth, Ashton stands in front of me with a firm grip on each of my biceps. "I didn't say that to scare you, princess. But it is the truth. You cannot use that phone and you must keep contact to a minimum with everyone until they're cleared by me. So far, that list only includes your immediate family and Lochlan's assistant."

"Penny." I nod.

"Yeah, Penny."

"She's kind of like a big sister." I don't know why I'm babbling.

"Are you okay?" His voice is barely a whisper when he's gentle, and I wonder if it's intentional or from his injuries, but now is not the time to ask him.

Pulling myself together, I stand taller. "Yeah, sorry. You just caught me off guard. Do you think he'll know where I am?" The words sound strong but are full of false bravado, and somehow, I know Ashton sees through it.

"No, I don't. As soon as I got here, I wiped the pings from every tower it could have hit here in Vermont. But you have to be careful. Until I have more information, I have no idea how dangerous this guy is."

"Okay," I answer quietly. "Can I call Kate though? She'll probably file a police report if I don't check in."

He scans my face. "Is she a good friend?"

I force my shoulders to remain relaxed. "She's my only friend. Well, besides Penny, but Penny has three kids and is in her forties. Not quite the same vibe."

He doesn't release my arms as he continues to study me. "Sometimes we're better off having no friends than the wrong friends." He steps back and runs his hand through his hair. "I'll be right back. I have a burner phone you can call her from. But keep it short. And you can't give her any details."

"All right. Thank you," I say, but he's already gone. I finally take in a deep breath. Ashton Westbrook is more than intense. I'm not sure how long I'll be here, but I do know I'll need a better game face with him around.

CHAPTER 10

ASHTON

*F*ucking Nova.

It's a thought that has run through my brain on a loop since she arrived twenty-four hours ago. Has it really only been a day?

I drop heavily into the chair at my desk and rest my palm on the scanner. When the light turns green, I open the bottom drawer and remove a phone and a battery, but my gaze lingers on the other phone. The one I've checked every day for a year. The one connecting me to my childhood friend, my biggest regret, Pacen, and I'm immediately drawn into a memory.

"So she wanted more from the relationship than you could give," Dr. Benson comments without emotion.

"It just didn't make sense."

"You were intimate with her."

If this fucker isn't careful, he'll end up with a fist in his face.

"We slept together to save her from the virginity auction her father signed her up for," I hiss.

"You only lose your virginity once, Ashton. What about the next time?"

My throat closes up as it always does when I think about this.

68

"You slept together a few times over the years, correct?"

I nod, unable to form words.

"Ashton?"

The constant ticking of the clock is the only sound in the room. The good doctor has always been willing to sit in the silence until I respond. But the pleading tone of his voice this time makes me cave and look him in the eye.

"You were young. Hormones are a messy thing sometimes. For men and women. It can be hard for people to differentiate between love and lust, especially as teenagers or young adults. I need you to stop and think about the conversations the two of you had. Were you honest with her? Did you discuss what was happening?"

Did I? "I'd always told her she was my best friend. I never wanted to lose that. I told her to date. I... Fuck. I don't know. We hadn't even slept together in years when she left that night."

The night I almost lost everything.

"You're struggling for closure because you care. But you can't get closure if she isn't willing, so you have to find a way to forgive the innocence of your youth to have the benefit of age."

My phone vibrates in my pocket, startling me to the present. Before I even reach for it, a song begins to play.

God damn it, Colton.

The Dixie Cups' "Chapel of Love" plays through my iPhone speaker. The fucker has set it to his text tone.

(Brothers Group Chat)

Colton: Goooo-in' anywhere today?

Ashton: Are you fucking twelve years old?

Preston: What did he do now?

Ashton: He changed the tone in my phone to "Chapel of Love."

Loki: Well, I heard you had a sleepover.

Easton: Y'all are assholes.

Easton: Lexi likes her, though so (shrugging emoji)

Halton: Just because GG gave them nicknames does not mean anything will happen.

Halton: Nova has been there a day. One day. Give him time. Two days…at least. (laughing emoji)

Loki: You got a nickname?

Colton: He did. A real one.

Loki: And Nova got a nickname?

(Ashton left the chat at 6:45 p.m.)

(Colton added Ashton to the group chat at 6:46 p.m.)

Colton: We're your brothers, dude. There's no escaping us.

Ashton: What do you want?

Colton: Just checking in. The girls are bringing over some more stuff for Nova tomorrow. Consider this your warning.

Fuck me.

Ashton: I have to go.

My phone continues to vibrate, ding, and sing, so I shove it into the desk drawer with the others and lock it. I don't need any distractions while dealing with Nova anyway.

I slide the battery into the burner phone and head back to the kitchen, where I find Nova singing to herself at the stove.

Jesus. How long was I gone?

Whatever she's making smells delicious, and my stomach growls, announcing my arrival.

She jumps in place but settles quickly.

Why do you wear so many masks, Super Nova?

"I'm sorry I scared you earlier. Even if he knew you were here, you would be safe. *I* would keep you safe."

"I know." She smiles brightly, but her cheeks don't scrunch up, and her eyes may carry the souls of stars, but right now, they aren't pointed to the sky.

That's my new measurement for her masks. Her eyes.

She's hiding at the moment.

You learn a lot about people, doing what I've done for nearly twenty years. Their fears, their hopes, their tells. And the thing they all have in common is their inability to completely shutter their eyes all the time. There's always a spark if you're willing to wait for it.

"You can call your friend on this," I say, handing her the phone. "But it has to be a quick call, and I can't stress this enough, you cannot give any indication of where you are."

"Okay." She grabs the phone, but I hold on to it for half a second. When she gives it a tug, I smile. Finally, her eyes dance with questions, and I feel like I've done my job. Her face was made to shine, but her eyes? Her eyes were made for laughter.

"I'll finish up dinner. Anything I should know about…" I peer into the pot on the stove and freeze. "Is this…is this rice pudding?" I immediately pick up the spoon and start to stir as it begins to boil. I remember making this as a kid with Loki's mom before she passed away. The number one rule was to never stop stirring.

"Sorry?" She says like a question. "I should have asked you, but I needed some comfort food. My dad told me my mom used to make this. It's a little different than most recipes because I use a lot of cinnamon, but it's, well, it's good, okay? Just trust me."

My grin tugs at the scar on the corner of my mouth, but I smile through the discomfort. "Okay, princess. I'll trust you. Five minutes." I nod to the phone in her hand, and she does a funny little hop before spinning and settling into my sofa.

Images of waking up with her on top of me flood my brain, and I lower my face to the steam coming off the custard. The heat trying to melt my skin causes just enough pain to push back the unsettling feeling of contentment.

At least until I hear Nova's friend answer the phone. Then I push all my messy emotions to the side as my bullshit radar goes into overdrive.

"Kate? It's me." Nova isn't quite whispering, but it's clear that she's searching for privacy without being downright rude and walking out of the room.

I can't make out her friend's response, but I hear the intensity of it in her volume, and instinct makes me want to be closer. Checking on the rice pudding, I decide to chance it and turn off the heat, then slowly make my way into the family room.

"Wait, how did you know that?" Nova asks.

I sit down next to her and motion with my hands until she turns the phone over. I immediately press the speaker button and hand it back to her.

Her eyes shoot flames my way, but rather than deterring me, I'm mesmerized by how expressive they are. She doesn't have long to be mad though, because the clock is ticking and so is her friend's mouth.

"Sam called me looking for you, of course. He's out of his mind worried about you. Frankly, I'm disappointed in you, Nono. You've always been a little selfish, but to be so blatantly careless isn't becoming. You know he worships you. The least you could have done before traipsing off with some booty call was let your PA know you're okay. Where are you anyway? We missed the opening of Chez Piaze last night. You promised we could go. Now that I think about it, you're letting everyone down lately. Not cool, lady."

"You can't—"

Nova's loudmouthed, narcissistic twuntytit of a friend forges on. "Where. Are. You. Nova? Where are you? I need to borrow that pink dress for tonight, and you had better not tell me you're running late because I've already told everyone we'll be there with a VIP table."

Nova rolls her eyes to mask the hurt lingering there. Her and her damn eyes. I wonder if she has any idea that she's an open book when she gives me a look beneath those long lashes.

I tap my watch and make the wrap-it-up signal with my finger.

"Kate…"

"Seriously, Nono. You're backsliding. You were doing so well, but if you can't follow through—"

"Kate?"

"On a single promise, I might have to reconsider things. I can't be your emotional support person if all I do is give, give—"

"Kate," Nova finally yells, and silence ensues.

"Jesus, Nono. What the hell has gotten into you?"

"Kate, please listen to me. You can't answer Sam's calls anymore, okay?"

"What? Why not?"

I place a hand on Nova's knee and shake my head.

"Ah, some things were brought to our attention, and Lochlan had to let him go. He isn't happy about it, so just steer clear of him. Okay?"

"Ugh. Fine. He loved you though. You know that, right? Anyway, whatever. He's just the help. Listen. What time will you get to your place? I'll meet you there for the dress."

"I'm not going to make it back tonight, Kate. I'm sorry."

More silence. I can imagine the steam coming off her friend's ears.

"I hope you're joking. You know how long I've been waiting for tonight."

"You can still go, Kate. Just take someone else."

"No, I can't, and you know it," the other woman screeches. "I can't believe you're being so selfish. Again. They never let me in without you. And I can't get a VIP table on my own. This is a new low, even for you, Nono. After everything I've done for you? After all the secrets I've kept…"

Nova picks at imaginary lint on her pants and shakes her foot so wildly the sofa cushions rock with the motion. Her anxiety radiates through her, and I've had enough of this bitch. I yank the phone from Nova's hand, but it slips out easily.

"Kate," I growl, "Nova is on an extended vacation. She'll be with me for the foreseeable future. If you or anyone else has a problem with it, you can suck a dick. Keep her name out of your mouth. Stay away from Sam. And while you're at it, get a fucking—"

Kate gasps, but it's Nova's fevered head shaking and clawing at my arms that makes me pause.

"Please," she hisses. "Please don't make it any worse." She scrambles over my lap and takes back the phone.

"Sorry, Kate."

"Who the hell was that, and who does he think he is talking to me like that?"

"Sorry. It's just—" She glances at me then faces the floor-to-ceiling windows. "It's just a friend Lochlan set me up with. I'm going to a wedding with him in—in Bali, so I won't be home for a couple of weeks. I'll have Penny let you in to my apartment so you can get the dress, and I'll call my publicist. She'll get you on all the lists while I'm gone."

I don't wait for her to finish. I take the phone back, end the call, remove the battery, and chuck the entire thing into the trash can on my way back to the kitchen.

I don't speak, and neither does she, but the words fly around my head like fists in a UFC fight.

The timer goes off, and I turn to the oven to remove the pork and potatoes. Nova stays put on the sofa, looking out the window, but I doubt she's seeing anything.

Peering into the pot on the stove, I try not to make a face at the gelatinous glob of rice pudding I've probably ruined by not stirring long enough. I place the cover on it and put it aside to deal with later, then plate two portions of dinner and set them on the table. When she hears the cork of a wine bottle pop, she turns her head, a fake smile firmly in place.

"It smells great," she says, standing slowly and taking a seat to my right.

It should say something about her that I'm not trying to turn my body away from her anymore. She's never once stared at my scars since our first introduction, and honestly, right now, I could give a fuck about them. For once in eight years, I'm more worried about someone else's scars than I am about my own.

"Just tell me one thing," I say.

She takes a giant gulp of wine. "Okay."

"Is your friend blackmailing you over something?"

Her laugh is unexpected.

"B-blackmailing me? Are you serious?"

"Why else would you put up with a friend like that?"

Nova's expression goes hard. "Kate has been by my side every day since we were fifteen. When others turned away from me, she stayed. She's the only friend I have who knows everything about me and still shows up, Ashton. Can she act like an entitled bitch sometimes? Yes. But so can I. Sometimes you take what you can get, and sometimes you get what you deserve."

The muscles in her jaw twitch, but she's not done with me yet, so I remain silent.

"She's also the one who shows up with chocolate and wine when I'm lonely, or when a relationship ends, or when I don't close a deal, or when a client is unhappy. She's the one who holds my hand when everyone else treats me like the pariah of high society. That's why I put up with her. Anything else you'd like to judge me on tonight?"

"Nope. That was it."

And it is, for now. I'll find out everything I need to know about twuntytit Kate on my own.

CHAPTER 11

ASHTON

$\mathcal{T}$he thing about Nova and her many masks is they just keep fucking coming.

Dinner went by...perfectly pleasantly.

I hated it.

Her years of etiquette training kept her appearing engaged, but she wasn't really there. I know because I do the same damn thing.

Why do ya care so much? I narrow my eyes at the thoughts in my head and silently curse them for sounding just like GG.

After dinner, she sat on the sofa and watched a movie while I sat on the other end with my laptop, digging into everything I could find on Samuel Jacobs. In a darker web dive, I also had a search going for Kate Green. And on another screen, I had a list of questions.

1. Why does Kate feel like you owe her something?
2. Why did she say Sam loved you?
3. Why can't she go out without you?
4. Why does she feel entitled to your clothing? She's a fucking adult. She needs to get her own clothes!

5. Did Sam ever make you uncomfortable?
6. Has anything strange happened that you couldn't explain since he started working for you?

Eventually, she quietly went to her room while I stewed in my thoughts. I waited until the silence became too much, then headed upstairs also.

It's easier to keep her safe when she's close by. And that's what I'll keep telling myself until it becomes my reality.

I'm still staring at the list in my bedroom long after Nova said good night, but I haven't added to it because I'm too busy watching the light shift under her door.

Back and forth. Pause. Back and forth. Pause.

Waking up my computer screen, I check the time. Why is she pacing her room at three in the morning?

Her bedroom door that leads to the hallway creaks open, and I watch through my open door as light filters out into the space, followed by the pitter-patter of bare feet on the hardwood floor.

Where the hell is she going?

I open the security app on my laptop and watch her move through the house from my screen. I can almost feel her exhaustion when I zoom in on her face. It's there in the circles under weary eyes. In the way that she carries herself when no one's watching. Like she has the weight of the world on her shoulders.

I know that feeling well.

She walks from room to room, touching random points like she's memorizing the space with her fingertips. Nova is a tactile person. This seems habitual for her—feeling, touching, and experiencing.

My body reacts as if it's me she's touching, not objects in my house. It's disconcerting to feel pressure from a phantom caress, but then she stops outside my office, and I switch cameras to get a good look at her face.

She's frowning but doesn't look guilty. I almost laugh when

she runs her nails along the seam of the door like she can find a secret lever.

Hands on her hips, she steps back, still staring at the space. Then she presses her face against the wall and closes one eye as she slides up and down it.

"What are you looking for?" I whisper, then shake my head because I can just ask her.

Slipping out of bed, I avoid all the spots on the floor that creak and silently make my way down the stairs. Watching her in the darkness for a few seconds, I appreciate her tiny sleep shorts before the self-loathing for doing so has a chance to kick in. I swear those things were made by the devil himself.

I shouldn't even be noticing such things after an eight-year drought.

I know why I am though.

Eight fucking years is a long time to be alone.

But it's necessary.

It's a requirement of the life I lead.

I open my mouth to say something, but the little minx has found the secret panel in the wall, and I watch with interest to see what she'll do with it.

The only light in the room comes from the reflection of the moon, which gives her an angelic glow, but the lip caught between her teeth speaks to my depraved side.

I want to bite that lip myself.

Nova delicately places her hand on the concealed scanner and lets out a silent huff when nothing happens. Nothing that she can see or hear anyway. My phone and computer will lock down at the unauthorized attempt.

"I hope you give me more credit than that?" I keep my voice gentle and soft, but she still screams and panics, flailing her arms like she's searching for a weapon.

"Nova. It's me. Take a breath."

"What the hell, Ashton? Why are you sneaking up on me in the dark?"

That's a good question. After what she just went through, it wasn't very sensitive of me.

"I wasn't thinking. I'm sorry."

That stops whatever diatribe she was about to send my way.

"I was curious," I say with a shrug. "I hadn't expected breaking and entering from you. Elpis, turn the lights on low."

At my command, the lights slowly brighten the room around us.

"I wasn't breaking and entering. I'm already entered. I mean, here. I—wait. Elpis? Did you name your house computer Elpis? The Greek goddess of hope?"

"She was more of a spirit, I think, and some say she encompassed both hope and misery."

"Like you," she says without any humor.

Yeah, princess. Like me.

"What are you doing out here, princess? Can't sleep?"

Her shoulders sag, and she shakes her head. "What goes on in there?" She points to my office with her thumb.

"Work."

"What kind of work?"

"My kind. Why can't you sleep?"

"Why do you always answer a question with a question?"

"Same reason as you, I'd guess."

"I thought you ran security for the Westbrook Group."

"I do." I don't know what possesses me, but I cross the room and place my hand on the scanner, gently applying pressure with the pads of my fingers in a pattern that will ensure every screen in my office is black. After a brief pause, the Murphy door opens with a silent woosh.

She watches me closely but doesn't move. "Then why all the secrecy?"

"Ex-military." I shrug. "No one can get in here without me."

"Like a safe room."

"Yes."

"And you're the only one who can access it?"

"And Sadie. Just…just as a precaution. She's the only one who stays here regularly."

Nova nods and enters the room when I gesture her inside.

"You have a lot of secrets, peto."

"I do." Following her, I try to take it in with new eyes. What does she see when she enters the only place I ever truly feel safe?

The room itself is utilitarian. Clean. Nothing out of place. Nothing personal, except for the huge wooden desk that belonged to my father that sits in the center of the room. The walls are black with chrome highlighting various panels. The warm tones of the desk do nothing to make the room feel comfortable, but it stands as a reminder that my life is not my own.

"Do you spend a lot of time in here?" she asks, walking the space, learning it with her fingers as she did everywhere else.

"Most of my time."

She turns to study me, then glances around the room again. "So, these walls turn into screens, right? What would show up if you turned them on?"

I'm surprised that she picked up on that, and it must show in my expression because she smiles.

"Lochlan has something similar in his office. So, peto. What are you hiding here?" She motions around the room, and a piece of hair falls into her face.

Innocence.

Shaking my head, I hide a smile. "My life," I answer.

And the reality of those two words crushes the smile.

"Huh."

"What?"

"You're going to be a tougher nut to crack than I thought. Your secrets go deep."

"Is there a reason you're trying to crack me, princess?"

Princess. A reminder that she can never be mine.

"Yup." She pops the p with a wide grin. "You're helping me. I'm going to help you."

Oh, sweetheart. If only you knew. I'm beyond redemption.

"I don't need help here," I say, gesturing around my safe space. "You're the one wandering around in the dark at three in the morning."

She crosses the room until we're just inches apart. We're so close she has to lift her head to look at me. From this angle, I can see her long dark lashes flutter across her cheeks.

"And yet you found me only moments later. So you were awake too. Don't try to deny it. I could hear you rage typing. Do *you* ever sleep, Ashton?"

Swallowing is difficult.

"You have boundary issues, princess," I say instead of answering her.

Nova inhales deeply and I swear her breasts reach for me. "There you go answering a question with a question again," she whispers.

"That wasn't a question."

This room is a goddamned inferno. She lifts a tentative hand like she's about to touch me, and I force myself to hold still even as sweat trickles down my spine, but at the last second, she frowns, and pulls her arm away. With a question flickering in her eyes, she studies my face.

Can she read me so easily?

She runs her trembling hand along her collarbone, and I track her movements with a need I've never quite experienced before.

The darkness that lives in my chest aches with urges I can't act on, no matter how much my entire body begs, pleads, and weeps for a physical connection with this woman. I don't deserve it. I don't deserve her. That reminder has ice filling my veins.

My muscles ache with pent-up frustration, and when she

reaches up on her tiptoes, it takes a Herculean effort to keep my arms tethered to my sides.

She's careful not to touch me anywhere but my forearm, which she uses to steady herself, as she leans close. Her lips graze my jawline because she can't quite reach my ears.

"Some boundaries are meant to be broken, peto."

CHAPTER 12

NOVA

*M*aybe Kate's right. I'm so desperate to be loved that I search for attention wherever I can. So broken that I seek affection as solace in the bed of any man willing to give it to me. But for the first time I can remember, I feel a connection. Maybe I want more than just the orgasm or warm body. I fear I might want Ashton Westbrook even knowing I can never have him.

Tit for tat with this man.

Lowering my chin, I stare at the weave of his shirt. "I have trouble sleeping."

Hmm. Admitting that wasn't as hard as I'd expected it to be.

Ashton's finger lands under my chin, and the contact sends a bolt of longing through me. Like watching lightning hit the tip of a tree and work its way down, the zing flies through my body until my toes tingle. He electrifies me everywhere.

"For how long?" His low, rumbly baritone with rough edges is a balm to my battered soul.

I'm losing my freaking mind. Two days, Nova! Get a grip! You cannot feel so comfortable. You cannot feel *things* after two days.

It's your desperation talking.

"How long?"

"I don't know." I sigh dramatically. "High school?"

I try to force a laugh, but it won't come. Not when he sees things too clearly. Too deeply. His intensity has a weight, a texture, that I've never encountered before.

"Tenth grade, maybe?" he asks with narrowed eyes. A dark expression lurks in his baby blues, sinking dread into my chest.

Does he know? He can't. But what if he does? I fight to keep my body relaxed, even knowing I'm going to lose the battle.

"It's been a while," I finally admit. Turning my face, I break our connection and step back. "Why don't you sleep?"

"It's hard to sleep when the faces of those you failed are embedded in your brain."

"What do you mean?"

"I have a photographic memory. Every mistake I've ever made is branded in my head like a torture device." His jaw tenses for a moment, the thick vein in the side of his neck bulging as he clenches his teeth.

Ashton Westbrook is not a man who allows words to slip.

The realization nearly floors me. "You're comfortable with me."

He says nothing, and my grin nearly splits my chest open as relief consumes me.

"You might even like me."

"Of course I like you," he growls. "You wouldn't be here if you weren't important to my family."

"Mm-hmm. Okay. I'll tell you a little secret. I like you too."

He's inched closer to me, our breaths mingling, his eyes questioning. We're a stolen kiss apart.

"Sadie bought me some Sleepytime tea," he whispers, staring down at me with heat and anguish swirling in his eyes. "Why don't you go pick a movie while I make it, and we'll try to drug our secrets with ancient herbs."

"But…"

"I think that's enough show and tell for one night, Nova. Movie. Tea. Now."

I want the intimate moment to continue. Here, in the darkness of night, when no one knows where I am and my secrets can't hurt me or anyone I love, it's a special kind of freeing. But Ashton's tone irks me, and his troubled expression pulls at the worry I keep just below the surface.

My emotions are all muddled, so I focus on the one thing I can do without effort—irritate the living hell out of him until he forgets the vulnerable pieces of me that he's unraveled too quickly.

"Keep bossing me around like that, you Neanderthal, and you're likely to end up with a foot up your ass."

His laugh is rich and husky—and unexpected. The sound is like a heavy blanket on a cold night, and I could easily snuggle into it and never ask for another thing.

He takes a sudden step forward, and his nearness consumes me. His knee presses between mine, but our thighs are the only place we touch because he's angled his upper body away from me. My breathing quickens, and I hope he doesn't ask me a question because my tongue is stuck to the roof of my mouth.

"The pulse in your neck."

"W—What?" I stammer.

"Your breath. The dazed look in those pretty amber eyes of yours." He leans in just a fraction more, and I nearly catapult myself onto him. "Your mouth says one thing, princess, but your body tells the truth."

"What truth?"

"You like to be bossed around." His eyes narrow as he searches mine so intently I'm unable to blink. "Sometimes."

Oh, if he only knew! Take back control, Nova. Dammit. Don't let him see all your secrets.

Tilting my head so we're almost cheek to cheek, I let my breath ghost along his skin. He rounds his shoulders, creating a small bubble between us. "So, peto. What you're saying is, you think I'm pretty."

"This house has over six thousand square feet," he says, side-stepping me and taking all the heat in the room with him.

I'm so confused I feel my nose scrunch up as I try to make sense of what he's saying.

"Six thousand square feet, and we keep sharing breath. You have boundary issues."

"And you love it," I singsong. "Face it, peto. You like me and my boundary-pushing ways."

He stares so long I don't think he'll say anything at all, then the smallest of smirks pulls at the scar above his lip. It makes him seem so much younger. "The things I like never have been good for me." With a shake of his head, he points behind me. "Movie. I'll be out in a minute."

I don't move for a second, and he tugs at the back of his neck before stomping past me. It would be more effective if he weren't barefoot, wearing low-slung pajama pants and a Westbrook Group Security T-shirt that hugs every lean muscle of his giant frame.

"You're sexy when you're irritated," I call after him.

There's a hitch in his step, but he plows forward to the kitchen, and I silently laugh to myself. It's like he's all but forgotten there's a sexy man under the scars and pain.

And suddenly, I have a new mission that just might burn me to the ground.

Show Ashton Westbrook how loveably sexy he is, then go back to my lonely existence and one-night stands.

The thought guts me, but I made my bed, and I'll lie in it until the day I die.

～

"*N*o."

"Have you seen it?"

Ashton blows out a harsh breath and shakes his head.

"Then you don't know what you're missing."

"Why the fuck would I want to watch a live-action version of *Beauty and the Beast* when I…" He sets the serving tray down on the coffee table with a loud thunk.

"When you what?" I press.

"Do you want sugar in your tea?"

Avoidance. I know that tactic well. He may be the super spy, but I'm pushy as hell.

"Why would you want to watch a live-action version when you're living it? Is that what you were going to say?"

"Sugar it is." I watch from the sofa as he drops a sugar cube into the delicate teacup.

"Wait. You have an actual tea set and sugar cubes? You just keep surprising me, peto."

"Every nice thing in this house was done for Sadie. Every girly touch, every comfort. It would be utilitarian in every way if it were just me." He hands me a baby blue teacup decorated with a paisley design that's dwarfed by the size of his fingers.

"Can I ask you something?"

He gives me the side-eye as he sits on the end of the sofa. As far away from me as he can get, I notice, then lifts his own mug to his lips. His is stainless steel. Utilitarian. "Now you're asking permission?"

If I could see his lips, I'd be willing to bet there was a smirk on them.

"I have my moments," I say with a shrug. Unlike Ashton, I don't hide my smile. "You have a lot of nieces and nephews." My gaze darts to the only photo in the room, the giant family portrait on the wall.

"Not a question, princess." He's back to grumbling like he

knows where I'm going with this. But his grumpy disposition won't turn me off. I grew up with Lochlan. He was the grumpiest bastard I've ever met until he found Tilly.

Turning sideways, I sit crisscross with my feet tucked under my body and stare straight at him. "How come you're so close to Sadie?"

"Aren't you tired?"

"Sadie."

He crosses one long leg over the other, so his ankle rests against his knee. It's a relaxed position, but I can tell he's just stalling for time because there is nothing else relaxed about him.

"Jesus Christ," he grumbles behind the safety of his stainless-steel mug.

I shimmy a little in my seat, catching his attention. He turns a humor-filled glare my way. "Are you getting comfortable?"

"Yup. I'm settling in to wait you out, mister, so spill. You and Sadie."

"Sadie Sunshine." He sighs and places his mug on the end table next to him. "What do you want to know?"

"Exactly what I asked. Why are you so close with her in particular?"

"Because when she was six years old, she showed me that the sun can break through the darkest clouds."

"How?" The array of emotions playing across his face makes my voice crack.

He shifts uncomfortably, uncrossing his legs, only to cross them in the other direction a moment later. "You don't give up, do you?"

"No."

"If I answer, you have to answer a question of mine."

Tit for freaking tat. My fingertips run along my bottom lip, and I'm not surprised to feel the smile there. I'm always smiling around this guy.

There's a seriousness to his gaze though that causes goosebumps to rise on my forearms. It's not like he could already know about my past. So, what would he want to know so badly he's willing to play this game? Not that it matters. I know I'm going to risk it before I even have time to think about the consequences.

"Deal." Reaching over, I hold out my hand.

Ashton takes it in slow-motion, but the formality of a handshake breaks down the second our skin touches. The inferno engulfs us. He drops his hand into his lap, with my smaller one trapped in his. His thumb's slow, gentle caress smooths the skin between my thumb and forefinger, and I force a steady breath.

"Right after my injury, she kissed my boo-boos. They were still gnarly, ugly, raised, gruesome cuts, and she loved them."

Tears burn hot in the backs of my eyes.

"This little ray of sunshine, with golden blond curls that bounced with every syllable she spoke, loved the wounds of my mistakes because she could see them. She could kiss them better every day, and she did. My heart felt like it was being torn into tiny, jagged pieces every time she did it because to her, it was a blessing."

Without glancing at me, he reaches over, grabs a handful of tissues, and hands them to me before continuing. "Ari isn't her biological mom." He chuckles, and the sound lances my chest. "You must know by now biology has nothing to do with family when you're a Westbrook."

"That's exactly how a family should be," I manage to choke out. He still won't look at me, but maybe he can't. He can't tell me these stories while looking at me because he still doesn't fully believe the love in them. I do the only thing I can. I squeeze his hand that still holds mine.

He jerks in his seat and drops his head to stare at our joined hands in his lap. With gentle movements, he places my hand back in my lap, and the rejection makes my stomach lurch.

"Anyway, Sadie's mom, Rebecca, died when Sadie was a baby.

She had cancer, and Sadie always told me that her mom's boo-boos were on the inside, so she couldn't kiss them better."

Jesus. That poor baby. "And yours are on the outside."

He nods. "She's been kissing boo-boos better ever since. Even the ones she doesn't know exist."

"She's a special girl." I can barely get the words out. They seem so inadequate for a little angel so full of love and light that she kept a full-grown man from drowning in darkness.

"She is. She's why I'm still here."

Oh, you broken, handsome, man.

"I'll have to thank her then."

He tilts his head and studies me, but I go into self-preservation mode before he can make good on our deal. Distraction is the name of this game.

"You ready for our movie?"

He nods, and I press play. Fully aware that he's watching me and not the giant screen that rolls down from the ceiling.

CHAPTER 13

ASHTON

It takes twenty minutes of me not watching the film for my fucking heart rate to calm down enough that I can ask her the question plaguing me.

I turn to Nova and freeze.

She's curled into a ball in the center of the sofa. Fast asleep. Her back is to me, so I can't see her face, but I can tell she's sleeping by the slow, rhythmic rise and fall of her ribcage. Goosebumps sweep down her exposed skin, followed by the slightest shudder.

I get up quickly, grab a blanket from the ottoman under the window, and cross back to her, unfolding it as I go. Standing before her with my arms spread wide, I'm struck by her beauty. But there's something different about her in sleep. I noticed it last night too. There's a peacefulness about her that's missing when she's awake. You'd have to watch every reaction to notice, but now that I have, I doubt I'll see anything else until I have answers.

Carefully, I tuck the blanket in around her small frame. The urge to carry her to bed, my bed, hits me like a sucker punch, but I don't pick her up. I can't. She doesn't belong to me. She never will. Straightening up, I intend to leave her there, but a small whimper escapes her lips, and her eyelashes flutter with a dream.

The breath stalls in my lungs as her face contorts as if in pain, and I place a hand on her shoulder.

She stills instantly, her face relaxing again.

Well, fuck.

Maybe I can just sit with her for a little bit? She needs her sleep. I check the clock on the wall to see it's now four fifteen. It's almost time for me to be up anyway, so as gently as I can, I sit down beside her. I'm careful not to touch her again, but close enough that her body knows she's safe.

I'll just sit and watch her for an hour. She'll get some sleep, and then I'll go to work finding the asshole who brought her to me.

~

*C*lick. Click. Whir.

I awaken immediately but keep my eyes closed. Training that kicks in no matter how long it's been sitting dormant has me alert and waiting for the next sound.

I don't have time to process what woke me though, because by the time I've registered the noise, the front door is opening and voices echo off my bare walls. My sisters-in-law.

A low, disgruntled moan much closer than the front door has all my training taking a fucking nosedive, and my eyes fly open to find Nova's head pressed into my chest. Asleep. Again.

She inhales deeply, and her pelvis rocks against my thigh. The damp heat from her pussy scorches my skin through my sleep pants.

"More," she whispers, and my cock reacts like it will do whatever she commands.

"Not everyone reads smut." Lexi's voice does little to alleviate the semi in my pants.

"Stop calling it that," Rylan scolds from the foyer.

Fuck. They're going to round the corner any second. If I yell at them to stop, they'll think something's going on. If I don't, they'll get an eyeful, and this will stop anyway.

What the hell am I thinking? This has to stop, regardless.

"Princess," I whisper, shaking her shoulders gently. Her body stills, and mine is rock hard because I know she's waking in the middle of a sex dream. "The girls are here…"

My warning is interrupted by Lexi rounding the corner like a runway model. Her arms fly out at her sides when she spots us, effectively corralling the other girls behind her.

"So," she begins, turning her back to me and ushering the girls back into the foyer. "We'll come back. Just put the bags down here."

"What?" Ari asks. "Seriously, Lexi. She probably needs some girl time."

"Not right now, she doesn't." Lexi's tone is determined, and I feel Nova trying to shrink away from me. I'm not sure why, but I hold her tighter.

Tighter to my chest because the shards of glass that normally protrude at human touch aren't cutting me open. They feel more like small needles. Like she's tattooing herself to my skin instead of slicing me open just to watch me bleed out.

"What's going on?" Rylan asks. Of any of them, Rylan will be the one to push past Lexi.

"They're, ah, they're in Ashton's office," Lexi lies.

Silence.

"Nova's in Ashton's office?" Ari whispers, and my shoulders shake with silent laughter. "The hidden one or the fake one?"

I really have turned into a monster.

"Hidden," Lexi hisses. "Out. We'll call before we come back." She says it more loudly than before, obviously for our benefit.

When the front door locks engage, Nova groans. "They must think I'm the most messed up person ever."

I tense beneath her. That her brain automatically goes there triggers something protective, but anger is the predominant emotion that comes out.

"Why would you say that?" My voice is gruff with...with sleep, I realize.

Disoriented, I check my watch to see that it's almost noon. That means I slept for nearly seven hours. Seven peaceful hours. Hours not filled with faces of children I couldn't save. Not filled with regrets that claw from the afterlife, trying to bury me alive.

Nova sits up, and the action has her straddling my legs. My erection presses between us like a beacon calling her home.

She notices it and smirks because she's a fucking ballbuster. Her eyebrows raise when it twitches in my pants.

"Like I can fucking control it." I grunt. I refuse to allow my gaze to follow hers. Instead, I focus on her eyes. Her amber, glowing eyes that seem a little less haunted this morning. The dark circles under her eyes are a little less pronounced today, her skin a little less sallow.

"You look good," I say without thinking, the double meaning not intended to be audible.

She shimmies against my legs, and I fist my hands at my sides to keep myself in check.

"Stop moving. I meant you look rested. You look..." I'm not sure how much to push this early in the morning. For all I know, she could be one of those women who get stabby before their coffee. But you know what? Fuck it. She's sitting on me. She's making fun of my cock that's so fucking hard I don't know how I'm even forming a coherent thought. If she can push, so can I.

"You look less haunted."

"You still make a crappy pillow," she deflects. Swinging a leg over the top of mine, she hops to the floor.

"But you slept."

She pauses at the end of the sofa and gives me a once-over. "So did you. I look good on you, peto."

She spins and strides toward the stairs.

"You still owe me a question."

She waves a hand in acknowledgment but ducks her head and takes the steps two at a time.

I fold the blanket, about to put it back in the ottoman, then stop. Maybe she sleeps better out here? If so, she'll want this later. Right? Instead of second-guessing myself, I toss it over the back of the sofa and frown.

How can a blanket tossed so carelessly make a room look alive? An uncomfortable energy buzzes in my ears. But it's not the blanket. It's the girl. A war within me rages as I battle not to rip the blanket off and tuck it away.

This isn't a home. It's a house. One blanket. One temporary houseguest will not make my reality any less harsh. A home is where you settle. A home is where your heart is safe. A house is shelter against the storms of life, nothing more. And even that's better than I deserve.

I chuckle darkly. Soon Nova Blaine will be out of my house and back to the life she was meant for.

Crossing the room with angry steps, I stumble to a stop. I left the door to my office open after I caught Nova snooping. I've never left that door open. Not even when I had Covid and was hallucinating with fever.

What does that say about Nova, or me, that she can twist me up so completely?

My skin is on fire as I step inside and kick the door shut behind me. Once the third lock engages, I can breathe again. My phone buzzes in my desk drawer while the thoughts I don't deserve run through my brain, setting my skin ablaze. Stab after stab of pain traces the scars that mar my body. Phantom pains that feel so real they bring me to my knees. One cut for every ounce of happiness Nova gave and I was too weak to push away.

I sink to the floor, covered in sweat as I wait for the episode to pass. My body twists and shakes with the memory of unimaginable pain that I'm helpless to control.

Tears slip down my face, reminding me I'm still alive.

This happened weekly when Sadie first insisted on her sleepovers with me. She was the only one I could accept slivers of happiness from. No one else—until Nova—has even come close.

Focusing on Dr. Benson's words only prolongs the agony, but I breathe through the pain. The memories.

"Your brain is forcing you to relive that pain because you don't believe you deserve happiness. Every time Sadie breaks through that wall of self-loathing, your brain punishes you for feeling happy. But you forget that you are a victim in all this. You forget that you deserve happiness, not the pain. And you're the only one who can fight it, Ashton, so fight it. Fight for happiness. Every single day. Fight for your happiness."

"Me," I scream in agony, rolling around the floor like a wild animal. "I fight it. Me. It's my fight."

My fight.

Happiness and pain.

Right and wrong.

Hope and fear.

The fear of hope.

I'm going to need Killian.

By the time the episode subsides, my body trembles with aftershocks, but I drag myself across the floor to my desk. It takes all my strength to pull myself into the chair, and my head hits the desk with a thud.

I blindly reach for the drawer with my phone. The incessant buzzing makes it easy to do. I pull it out and without looking at the screen, I press the side key for voice command.

"Call Killian."

"Calling Killian," a robotic voice responds.

It rings once, twice, and he finally picks up on the third ring.

"Been a while. I was hoping you'd sorted your shit out."

"How soon can you get here?"

I can feel his sigh cross the Atlantic.

"You know I'm in Ireland, yeah?"

I stay silent.

"Next week. It's the best I can do. Don't do anything stupid in the meantime."

My grunt is painful.

"I fecking mean it, Ashton. Stay away from the club. We're done if I find out you were there before I get back. I won't help you anymore, and then you can explain this shit to your family."

"Just fucking hurry up."

Ending the call, a text message comes in.

Seth: Ari was home pretty quickly.

Seth: Everything okay?

Easton: I heard they had another sleepover.

Halton: Give him a break.

Seth: Ash?

I turn it off and throw it back into the drawer. Leaning into my chair, I hit the switch that illuminates the walls. The faces of those I've failed fill the darkness.

Abby Miller, 17 years old.

Jordan Bath, 14 years old.

Michael O'Connor, 19 years old.

On and on and on. My failures stare at me with dead eyes, and once again, the darkness drowns out the ray of light.

CHAPTER 14

NOVA

I haven't seen Ashton in a few hours, and it's just as well. I know he'll ask the hard questions, and I'm happy to avoid it for as long as possible.

Using my leg to hold one piece of wood, I precariously try to screw another into it. The instructions for this sewing machine might as well be in German for all I can read them. If I could use the machine without having to build the table around it, that would be one thing. But this particular one has a foot pedal that connects to the wooden frame.

A frame that is much larger than it looked in the box. Once it's together, I think it will take up most of the sunshine room.

With a frustrated sigh, I stand. I'm covered in a light sheen of perspiration, but I'm determined to get this thing together. Plus, I have to work.

Designing something beautiful helps me push away the ugliness in the world, if only for a little while.

My stomach growls, and I start to check the time on my watch, except I don't have that either. An Apple Watch would probably be too easy to trace.

Grabbing the instruction manual, I head downstairs in search of food. I'll just make a quick sandwich or something and then figure out how to put this together.

The bags Ashton's sisters-in-law brought earlier still sit at the bottom of the staircase, and embarrassment heats my skin.

Was I really dry humping him like a horny teenager?

Peering into the first bag, I find workout clothes, sneakers, and some books. The half-naked man on one cover has my interest piqued, especially when I catch sight of the author's name. Sloane Camden.

I don't know her personally, but I know of her. Her book covers routinely occupy billboards all over New York City.

That's when it clicks. Sloane Camden is Ashton's sister-in-law. One of them, anyway.

Picking up the bag, I carry it with me to the kitchen, only pausing briefly outside Ashton's office. I'm not at all surprised that I don't hear anything inside his iron fortress, but I am surprised by the slight pang of disappointment that fills my chest.

"Needy, needy," Kate's voice whispers.

Shaking my head, I move through Ashton's home and place the bag on the counter, next to a bowl of fruit that wasn't there yesterday. I glance around but see no other evidence of his presence. When did he go to the store? Is he even here?

Reaching for a plate, I set it on the counter, then search the kitchen until I find some peanut butter. As I cut up an apple, my mind keeps wandering to Ashton.

He was awake for most of the time I was pacing last night, but how had he known I'd gone to his office? Looking up at the ceiling, I scan from one side to the next.

I bet he has cameras everywhere. That's what ex-spies would do, right? With the amount of security he has in this place, cameras would make sense.

Just the thought of the cameras in my apartment still makes me shiver. Why doesn't Ashton's setup bother me the same way?

Leaving the apples on the plate, I grab the tub of peanut

butter in one hand and a spoon in the other, then dig into the creamy goodness. With Ashton and security cameras on my mind, I walk into the family room, scanning the ceiling and walls there too, but find nothing. I'm staring at the chandelier above the kitchen island with a mouth full of peanut butter and the spoon hanging from my lips when Ashton's voice comes through the sound system.

"The cameras have facial recognition. Now that you're entered in the system, it doesn't record you unless you're in a restricted area."

There's a click, and I think he's hung up, but then he's back. It makes me smile, even with peanut butter clinging to my throat like cement.

"There are no cameras in your bedroom or bathroom."

"Where are you?" I ask the empty room.

"Working."

My eyes dart to the hidden door.

"Are you telling me you're behind that wall and talking to me through a speaker instead of coming out here to face me?"

Silence.

"Ashton?"

"I'm in a meeting. Eat your snack, and I'll come out to make dinner in a little while."

"I'm capable of making something myself."

There's the slightest sound of static, so I know he's on the line, but he pauses before answering. "I'd like to have dinner with you, Nova."

His irritation comes through loud and clear, and I laugh.

"Okay, peto. See you soon."

He doesn't answer, so I take my peanut butter, sit at the island, and rifle through the goodies the girls brought me. I pull out the well-read paperback and skim the description.

Pages are dog-eared, and because I'm nosy, I open to the first one. Within a few sentences, I'm engrossed in a sex scene hotter than any porn I've ever watched.

Holy shit, this girl can write.

~

"What's wrong with your apple?" Ashton's deep rumble startles me from the pages of Sloane's book, and I almost fall off the stool.

"Huh?"

"Your apple. Why didn't you eat it?"

I blink rapidly, pushing back the dirty images and staring at the sexy man before me.

"Princess? Are you okay?" He's on me instantly, swinging my chair around, staring into my eyes, then checking me over. His hands roam over my body, searching for an injury.

"Yeah. Yeah, I'm fine." I swat him away.

He scowls and looks around me. When he spots the romance novel on the counter, he closes his eyes, pinches the bridge of his nose, and I would bet money he's silently counting to ten.

When he steps back, he ignores the book completely. "What do you want for dinner?"

"I'm not picky. Just no mushrooms. What do you want me to do?"

He shakes his head. "Nothing right now, but I will have some questions for you tonight, Nova. And it's important that you tell me the truth."

"Am I going to need some wine for this?"

"I'm on your side, remember?"

"Yeah, yeah. I remember. Have you read this book?" I ask, holding up the cover for him to see.

"No," he grunts. "The last thing I want to do is picture Loki and Sloane…practicing."

"Hmm."

I can't help it. I want to see how he'll react, so I flip back to the second dog-eared section and begin to read aloud.

I hear the moan again, and panic rips through me. Is someone in there with her? Did someone find us?

Pressing my ear to the door, I listen for half a second before...

"What are you doing?" Ashton looks genuinely concerned, and all my nervous energy flutters low in my belly.

"Reading. You cook. I'll read."

"That's not a good idea."

"It's a very good idea, peto."

He opens his mouth to say something, but I continue narrating.

It takes a moment to process what I'm seeing, but when I do? Holy fuck, I nearly come in my pants.

Rose leans against the shower wall with a hot pink vibrator between her pussy lips.

"Nova," Ashton grinds out with his back to me. Every muscle in his body is tense as he adjusts himself, but he doesn't turn around, so I skip ahead in the book.

"You like to play with toys, Rose? How much can you take?"

"More," she moans against my neck. "More, please, more."

Ashton is frozen in front of me.

"Tell me what you want, baby." I read in my most masculine tone, but the words are also beginning to affect me, and my voice wobbles.

"Fill me," she commands.

"You think you can handle me in your ass while I fuck you with this vibrator? I don't think you can. I think you'll explode around me the second I enter you, and then where will we be?"

"Yes," she mumbles, and I smirk down at her. My masterpiece. Bound to the bed, completely at my mercy, she's fucking edible.

"Princess," Ashton warns more gruffly, but I ignore him.

Smearing lube over her puckered hole, I enter her from behind while turning the vibrator on in her pussy. I freeze, pressed into her as far as I can go as she spasms around me. Loud, violent cries explode from her lips as I press her deeper into the bed.

Ashton slams his hands down on the counter before spinning on me with a dark look in his eyes. I want nothing more than to see that expression when he's on top of me, and my breath hitches when he takes a step forward.

The air is thick, like trying to breathe through a morning fog. Ashton's restraint is the only thing keeping us apart. Placing the book on the island between us, I lick my lips in anticipation because I know I'll detonate like a nuclear bomb when he kisses me.

Keeping the island between us, he leans in close. So close I can feel the war inside him.

"Why do you only have one-night stands?" I feel his scratchy staccato all the way down to my toes.

Then his words register, and the fire burning in my core runs face-first into an iceberg.

CHAPTER 15

ASHTON

*O*y heart attempts to escape my chest, and my cock uses the zipper of my jeans like a punching bag in his fight to be set free.

Lust has never consumed me this completely before.

Nova's eyelashes flutter as I lean in close. How easy would it be to tempt fate and my fucked-up mind and for once, for one fucking time in my life, take what I want?

Too easy. Too dangerous. I'm too close to losing the thread of control that keeps me from her.

But then, where would I be? I could barely handle waking up with her next to me, and that was completely innocent. What would happen to me if I gave in?

What would happen to her?

"I can't figure out if you use sex as a weapon or a defense."

"Isn't that the same thing, just taken from different points of view?" Her admission is husky.

"Why do you only have one-night stands, Nova?"

"You know, you've only known me a few days, right? You're making an awful lot of assumptions based on what?"

She hops off the stool, and a dark satisfaction fills me when her legs tremble.

"Why?" I step around the island even though I know I'm entering dangerous territory.

When we're toe to toe, she looks up into my eyes with a million words playing across hers.

"One night is fun. There's no risk of getting hurt…"

"There's a fuckton of risk, Nova."

"But only to me. The only risk in a one-night stand is to me."

My stomach turns because I know the truth. "Someone hurt you."

She shrugs and turns to walk away, but I grasp her bicep and don't let go.

"Who was it?"

"You don't know me well enough to demand these kinds of answers," she whispers.

"If I'm going to help you, I need to know." That's not strictly the truth, but if today is any indication, I won't be able to think straight until I know what motivates her. When she stares back at me defiantly, I change tactics.

"Do you know what made Samuel snap? What was different about the guy he attacked? Had anything changed leading up to that night?"

She immediately looks away, and my heart feels for the guilt in her expression.

"Tell me so I can help," I demand. "What happened?"

"He stayed," she hisses.

I blink down at her, but I don't understand.

"He stayed," she repeats and slips past me. With jerky movements, she takes her uneaten apple slices, sticks them in a plastic bag, and tosses them into the fridge.

When I don't say anything, she walks out of the kitchen. "I never let anyone stay the night. It never ends well."

"For who?" I call after her. Anger fills me, and I don't even know who to be angry with. I'm not a man who runs on emotion, they're too messy, but she has me ready to chase down her ghosts.

"Me," she says simply. "I'm not really hungry after all. I—I have a headache. I'll see you tomorrow. Good night."

Nova heads up the stairs, and I go straight to my office. Once the door locks behind me, I turn on the screen that monitors the upstairs hallway. I want to be ready for her if she comes back out. Then I get to work diving into everything I can find about Nova Blaine.

~

"*A*sh?" Dillon's voice cracks with sleep, and I realize it's the middle of the night. "What's wrong?"

"You know I have a houseguest?"

He clears his throat. "Lochlan's little sister."

Dillon is an oddity in the Westbrook family. As a kid, he and Easton were inseparable, but then our lives got fucked twelve ways to Sunday, and they've never fully recovered. He's part of our family, but it always feels like he's trying to find his way out.

When he wanted to settle in New York, having him run a branch of my security company, Envision, seemed like the best choice.

He also might be the only one still connected to Pacen. He was like her big brother, and I doubt she cut him out completely. Not like she did me.

"Ash?"

"Yeah." Shaking my head, I run a hand through my hair. "Her attacker is in the Bronx. I need you to get there before the police."

"What are we looking for?" The sleep in his voice is replaced by anger. I know he's spent a lot of time working with Lochlan in the last few months, but only recently in his hotel, so it's likely he's feeling the brunt of Lochlan's guilt. But I gave up trying to placate feelings a long time ago.

Words are just words until you're ready to hear them.

"I'm not sure. He's been receiving money from her friend, but I don't know what for. Yet."

"Kate," he seethes.

His tone makes me sit straighter in my chair. "You know her?"

"She's a bitch, but I wouldn't have thought her dangerous. Loch and Penny never really understood why Nova stays friends with her."

"You know Penny?"

He clears his throat again, and I wish I could see his face. "I've spoken to her a few times while I waited for Lochlan. Nova can trust her."

"You're sure?"

"Yes."

I wait for him to expand, but he doesn't, and I smirk even though he can't see it. Dillon sounds smitten.

"Fine," I say. "My gut says there's something going on with Kate. Something that's been dragged out for years, but I can't find it. I'm sending you the address Sam is hiding out at, and I want you to tear it apart until you find something. Then let the police take him."

"Done. I'll send Mica. He's the most qualified."

Sometimes I forget that even though Dillon got caught up in our mess, he isn't trained like Loki and me. He's just a good guy who gave up everything to keep someone safe.

We have so much in common.

"Are you happy, Dil?" There's a long pause, but I can hear him breathing. "Envision isn't exactly what you thought you'd be doing with your life."

"We all make our choices."

"And if you decide to choose something else at any point, you know we would all support you, right? You don't owe us anything."

Where is this coming from? He's been working with us for years now. Why am I suddenly concerned that he's living his life trying to repay a debt that doesn't belong to him?

His laughter surprises me. "This might be a record."

"What's that?" I ask.

"I can't believe Nova's getting under your skin after only a few days."

"What are you talking about?"

"Nothing, *warden*. Nothing at all. Tell *starlight* she'll be home soon."

Fuck. I forgot he's on the group chat with my idiotic brothers.

I end the call without saying anything else.

I've spent the last few hours following the money that's been deposited into Samuel's account. The most logical explanation is he's keeping an eye on Nova for Kate. But why?

Knowing it will be a few hours before I get any answers, I shut everything down. Sleep is pulling at me, but first, I want to check on Nova.

When I exit my office, there's a faint glow coming from the family room that I follow to find Nova curled up on the sofa.

Oh, princess. How did I get so caught up that I missed her on the security feed?

I don't even pretend I'm only going to watch her this time. I may not be good for her long term, but I can help her now. Slipping out of my shoes, I cross the room and slide in next to her. As soon as I'm settled, her body twists toward mine, and I lie back, dragging her with me.

She won't be here much longer. She can't stay. But while she's here, I'll allow her to chase away my nightmares as I do the same for her.

As my eyes drift shut, I think about how I'll pay for this reprieve in pain all too soon.

"*W*hat do you mean?" Nova asks. Her face is free of makeup and rumpled with sleep. There are lines from my T-shirt spread out across her cheek. The simple markings trigger a primal urge to possess her and beat on my chest like a caveman.

She slept so peacefully. I did not. I held her in the silence, feeling a sense of peace I'm not sure I've ever known. Right up until Dillon sent me a text message.

Holding her hand in mine, I deliver a blow I know will hurt. "Kate has been sending Samuel money every month for the last two years."

"How much money?" Her chin quivers until she bites down hard to stop it.

"Double the salary that you pay him."

Nova's eyes dart around the room like a cornered animal, and I squeeze her hand.

How quickly times can change. If I wasn't so fucking angry at her twuntytit of a friend, I might be freaked out that I can touch her so easily.

"B—But it doesn't make any sense."

"Nova?" I say gently. When she doesn't look at me, I tug on her hand until we're thigh to thigh.

She gasps but meets my gaze.

"You know your relationship with Kate is not a healthy friendship. I need you to trust me. I need you to tell me what you've been running from and why she's the only one you let in."

"No."

"Nova."

"No. There's no way it's all connected." Even as she speaks, realization is dawning behind her amber eyes. "She wouldn't— she wouldn't do that to me."

The despair in her words hurts more than the knife that sliced my skin.

"Do what, sweetheart? Please, trust me. I have eyes on Samuel. Kate has no idea what's coming her way, but I promise you, I will fix it. I just need all the pieces. What am I missing?"

"I need a computer."

There's a tightness to her voice. Like an empty, hollow shell of the woman I'm beginning to understand. She's withdrawing.

Without a word, I stand and drag her with me. Together we cross the room and enter my office. I set her in front of the screen and place my hand on the scanner to unlock it.

Nova types slowly and speaks so softly I have to sink to my knees beside her to hear.

"I had a boyfriend in high school. His name was Max. We went to a party and—and neither of us remembers much after about an hour. But there's a video."

My stomach lurches, and rage I've only ever channeled at real-life monsters threatens my control.

"Max and I broke up shortly after the party." Nova doesn't sound like herself. She's detached. "My senior year, I started dating Theo. After two weeks, the video was emailed to him, and he shared it with the football team. In college, I started seeing Ben. Ben was really sweet. And kind." Her heartbreak has me seeing red. "He didn't believe the video at first. I did my best to explain, but I don't remember it. Any of it. We lasted a few more weeks, but then he met Lochlan and said he couldn't handle it. After that, I stopped trying to have relationships."

One-night stands. Fuck me.

She presses a button on the keyboard and stands. "I love my brother, Ashton. But not like this. Never like this. I'm going to pack. I'm assuming it'll be safe to go home soon? Just, I know you won't see me the same after this, but please don't tell Lochlan. He and his parents are the only family I have. I don't know what I'll do if I lose them." Eyes swimming with tears she refuses to allow to fall, she leaves the room.

I lift myself into the chair as the party scene on the screen zooms in on a young Nova and a teenage boy to her left.

I'm drowning in her pain as the video cuts in and out with a shitty editing job. The party fades, and Nova comes into view wearing only a bra and panties. Another fade, and you see her with the shirtless teenage boy behind her. Their bodies are moving strangely, like she's being pulled back and forth. The editing makes it look like something I'm reasonably certain it's not.

The scene fades again, and she's lying on top of the boy, whimpering for Lochlan.

This video was edited to make it look like a sex tape of her lusting after her brother.

My chest heaves because I can see what she can't. This isn't real. Someone has been fucking with her since she was a child, and I'd bet my life it's that bitch, Kate.

Adrenaline courses through my body, causing my hands to twitch against the keyboard. It takes three tries to shut the damn video off. And another few minutes before I can get online and hack into Kate's computer.

I hadn't even thought to fucking check her photos or videos. I followed the money trail, which led to her, but this kind of betrayal never even crossed my mind.

Within five minutes, I find what I need.

Then it hits me that Nova would have been fifteen in this video. The same age I was when my life crashed and burned. A tiny piece of the burden I carry falls away when I vow to give her a piece of her childhood back.

I'm going to chase away her monsters.

And then I'm going to let her go.

CHAPTER 16

NOVA

*S*tumbling into the sunshine room, I trip over the sewing machine pieces that have yet to be put together.

What have I been doing for the last few days?

Has it really only been three or four days?

I guess it doesn't matter now, anyway. Once Ashton watches that video, he'll know all my secrets.

Shame has me bolting to the toilet on shaky legs. The dry heaving is loud and painful and never-ending.

I have to get out of here.

Facing Ashton after he watches it will be the worst kind of punishment.

Will he tell Lochlan?

I haven't cried for myself in a long time. Pitying myself, my situation, is a luxury I never allowed because I brought this on myself. Kate always said...

A new wave of nausea hits, and this time my stomach empties until all that's left escaping my throat is bile.

She's not a great person. I've always known that. But this? To do this? For so many years?

No. Not even Kate Green could be this evil.

But the longer I hurl my feelings into the toilet, the more memories assault me, and I know it's the truth.

Ashton has no reason to lie to me.

And now, no reason to want me.

My body shakes. It's shock, I think, causing me to spasm on the tile floor.

I've been here before. Two days after the party when I first saw the video.

"Nova?" Ashton's scratchy voice is soft. "Fucking Christ, princess."

He lifts me easily and cradles me to his chest. I should pull back, but his steady heartbeat against my ear brings tears so hard and fast that I'm too weak to do anything but let him carry me.

Ashton sits down and holds me in his lap. Brushing the hair from my face, he holds my cheeks in both of his large, calloused palms. He gently coaxes my eyes to his.

I blink back tears. Steeling myself for disgust. For pity. For anything except what I actually find in his eyes.

Understanding.

"This is going to hurt, sweetheart. But trust me."

Fog has encased my brain, and it takes far too long to understand that he's placed a laptop on my thighs. He presses play, and my fight or flight instinct kicks in, but he holds me to him like a vice.

"Please, Ashton. I've seen this. I don't want to…"

"You haven't seen this," he growls. "The full video. The unedited, unmanipulated version. You haven't seen the truth."

His body vibrates, literally vibrates beneath me, and I force myself to see him. To understand him. To really hear what he's saying. I shake my head at him before I find the courage to glance at the screen.

Sounds rush through my ears, causing a pressure that makes my head feel like it's going to explode. Clips I've seen and ones I haven't play on the computer before me.

Images freeze in my brain.

Me passed out next to Max.

Kate removing my shirt and pushing me on top of Max.

Me crying.

Me begging.

Me asking Kate to call Lochlan to take me home.

Kate taunting me.

Me whimpering for Lochlan to save me.

Even with Ashton holding me steady, I shake like a person in a movie suffering from hypothermia.

"It wasn't real, princess. None of it was real. But I will slay your demons. You're safe. You are safe. I promise."

I'm paralyzed. This is too much.

Ashton wraps me in a blanket, and the next thing I know, I'm lying in a bed that smells like him with his arms wrapped around me like a protective shield.

He's pushing past all his own wounds to comfort me, and that knowledge makes me tremble even more.

"W—Why are you doing this?"

His face nuzzles into my hair. He inhales deeply before replying in a voice so low that I'm almost convinced I made it up. "Because you broke through my darkness, princess. I'll hold you through yours. Even if it kills me."

⁓

I wake to raised voices and know I'm alone. In Ashton's bed. The pounding in my head is worse than any hangover I've experienced. My throat tastes bloody from the abuse it took emptying my guts into the toilet, and my heart races so fast I'm afraid I might be at risk of a heart attack.

But beneath those immediate physical responses, there's something I never thought I'd feel again.

I feel free.

Hysterical laughter bursts out of me, breaking through my defenses. Not just crazed laughter but full-on hysterics.

Anyone looking on would commit me for having a mental breakdown. I pull Ashton's pillow over my face and scream.

I scream for the years I spent in fear. And for the rage pounding through my veins. I'm going to fucking ruin Kate. Ruin her.

The door bursts open, and Ashton slides into bed behind me before I can remove the pillow, spooning me so tightly that I can barely breathe.

His rough hands press across my chest and around my belly, molding me to his form.

"Shh, princess. It's okay. I'm here."

The truth of that cracks something inside me. He said he would be, and he is. For everyone, I fear.

"I'm okay," I choke out. "I'm angry, peto. Really fucking angry."

Ashton freezes and slowly loosens his grip as I feel the bed dip at my feet.

"There's my girl," Kitty coos. My stepmother leans against the foot of the bed, and Ollie, my dad, paces behind her. I've never been so grateful to see his purple hammer pants as I am right now.

His always insanely outdated wardrobe makes a warm sensation bubble in my chest.

"Your family's here," Ashton whispers. Lowering his voice, he says, "They're even weirder than my family." His arms slowly slip from my body, and I sit up.

He stands, angling his body away from Kitty to prevent her from staring at his face as he rubs at his nape.

Lochlan is in the doorway behind him, scowling more fiercely than I've ever seen. His three-piece suit is pressed to perfection, but the storm behind his eyes is ready to touch down.

"I'm going to let you all talk. I'll bring back lunch," Ashton mumbles. As he passes Loch, they exchange a look I can't read. "You know my thoughts. You brought her here because you trusted my expertise. She needs—"

"I brought Nova here so you could protect her, not fuck around with my baby sister."

"I'm right here, you giant turd. Ashton never even kissed me."

Lochlan glares at the two of us, but he'll never understand. Everyone has pain, but not everyone can understand it quite the same way Ashton does.

Ashton nods. "I'll be back." Without a pause, he ducks out of his own bedroom and crashes down the stairs.

CHAPTER 17

ASHTON

I can't get out of my house fast enough. My family's strange, but apparently you can't appreciate their kind of crazy until you're faced with the crazy of someone else's family.

Not even bothering with a car, I just walk through the woods on the path leading to GG's lodge. Not that I want to deal with her particular brand of crazy either, but she'll have food there, and if I'm lucky, I'll avoid my brothers too.

I'm rounding the corner when Halton comes into view carrying two large baskets. He pauses when he sees me, then flashes a sheepish grin.

"You don't want to head that way." He nods toward the house. "The Westbrooks are descending like someone sent up a bat signal."

"Fuck."

He stops in front of me and hands me a basket. "Heard you had some company this morning."

The fact that we've kept Nova's whereabouts a secret at all shocks me.

I lift the basket lid to find an array of sandwiches and snacks.

When I cast him a confused look, he shrugs. "You haven't exactly hosted many people, Ash. I thought you could use some help."

He's right. I don't know that I've ever had anyone in my house who wasn't considered family. "I'm not very social, I guess. Thank you."

He bumps my shoulder with his and watches me closely. I hate that he has to tip toe around me to see what my reaction will be to something so simple, but it is what it is. When I don't flinch, I see the tension release from his clenched jaw.

"Neither am I, dude. If you hadn't noticed, I had this all prepped to drop and run." His sly grin tells me he isn't joking.

"What's in that one?"

Halton's eyes twinkle. "Cookies and alcohol, in case you forgot how to turn on the charm."

"Charm?" I scoff. "Why would I need to charm anyone?"

I see Halton staring at me out of the corner of my eye, but I don't respond to it.

"I don't know. I just thought you might want to make a good impression on Nova's family. That's all."

My scars tingle like a warning. Don't chase it, Ashton. That happiness isn't meant for you.

Even if I wanted to make a good impression, what would it all be for?

Instead of fighting him on it, I simply say, "Thank you."

We walk in silence for a few beats. When he breaks it, I stare at the ground.

"You know, I spent a long time fighting battles I had no business taking on."

Halton thought he was the reason our father died at one point. It still makes my throat ache to think about it.

"I hated him too. Dad? For so long, I hated him."

"You thought he tried to keep you and Rylan apart," I say. "Anyone in your position would have felt the same way."

He nods and kicks a rock in the path to the side. "As much as I hated him though, I loved him. That was the confusing part. How could I simultaneously love and hate someone for the same exact reason?"

"What did you come up with?" I keep my gaze averted. I swear fireworks are being lit in my stomach, and I try not to cringe.

"I realized I could love and hate him because he taught me the difference between them."

"What's the difference?" It sounds like frogs are dancing in my throat, and my shoulders tense as I wait for him to answer.

He stops walking in the path and turns to me. I do the same. He scans my face like he's trying to determine if I'm ready for whatever wisdom he wants to impart. But then his eyes mist, and my lip trembles under the effort of holding it all together.

"The difference between love and hate is forgiveness, Ashton. And he taught us that too."

"I don't know if I can forgive him." It's a hoarse confession full of fear and regret.

Halton wraps his free arm around my shoulder, then pulls my head to his. Forehead to forehead, he grips my neck tight. My skin prickles at his touch, but the raging fire it usually causes merely simmers at a dull roar. "Dad isn't the one you need to forgive, little brother." Another forceful squeeze, and he lets me go. "He isn't the one you have to forgive," he repeats.

Handing me the other basket, he beats his chest, then points to mine. "Forgiveness isn't for other people, Ash. It's for you." He slams his chest again, right above his heart. The sound echoes through the trees that surround us. "For this. Forgiveness is so this can beat again."

He turns and heads back toward the lodge, leaving me with two baskets of food and a lifetime's worth of baggage.

I stand there, watching the clouds above float by like the questions swirling around my head. When the weight of the baskets gets to be too much, I push forward and head home.

Fuck. Me.

I'm heading home.

Hope flutters in my chest just as the scar on my face burns. Like a battle between good and evil, right and wrong, who will win? And will I be able to survive either way?

~

"*I* just don't understand why you didn't tell us, Nono." The British accent belongs to Ollie Blaine, Nova's father.

"Stop badgering her, Ollie." Kitty Bryer-Blaine is no-nonsense, but the love she has for her family is evident in her tone.

I set the baskets down quietly in the entryway hall, unsure where to go in my own home.

"What's done is done. It's our job as her parents to make sure we never make that mistake again. Whatever we did to make you think you couldn't come to us will never happen again. We are your family, Nova. For better or worse, we will always stand by you. Always," Ollie says. There's a gentleness to his voice that happens only between a father and daughter.

"The Greens are your best friends, Papa—"

"And she was a child. She must have been terrified, and I didn't protect her," Lochlan curses.

"Lochness. I swear to fucking God, if you don't stop talking about me like I'm a child, or like I'm not here, I will give you a titty twister to end all titty twisters."

Nova's father snickers and I have to suppress a chuckle myself.

There's a heavy sigh I imagine coming from Lochlan before he speaks again. "I'm sorry, Nono. For everything. I'm so sorry we weren't there for you."

Lifting the baskets, I enter the family room and head to the kitchen. I half expect them to stop talking, but they carry on like I'm already part of the conversation.

"Kate is a great manipulator," Nova mutters. "I played right into her hands."

"Nono?" Ollie's calm demeanor puts me at ease, and I instantly like the man. Nova lifts her face to his. "I don't care if the Greens were my own flesh and blood. Had I known what was happening, I would have cut their heads off like a snake in the grass."

"Not would have," Lochlan interrupts. "Going to. I'm going to bloody fucket ruin them."

"Time out, Lochness. Kate's parents didn't have anything to do with this." She freezes, then turns to me. "Did they?"

Silently, I shake my head.

"I'm going to fucking kill that twat," Lochlan murmurs darkly.

"It's already done," I say without thinking, and I'm met with a chorus of gasps. Fighting a flinch, I face Nova. "Not literally. I didn't kill the twuntytit. But I did ruin her. She's facing so many counts of dissemination of child pornography, conspiracy to commit murder, blackmail, and a litany of other charges, she'll be in prison for the rest of her natural life. And if, by chance, she does get out, the consequences of her actions will follow her to the depths of hell."

"What?" Lochlan barks. He seems to have two tones. Pissed off and more pissed off.

"She blackmailed Sam into spying so she could keep Nova dependent on her. That's why she kept sending everyone that video. My guess is she got off on swooping in as the hero best friend each time."

I try to catch Nova's gaze, but she's staring at the floor, so I walk around the island to be closer to her. Lochlan glares at me with disapproval, but I continue.

"The pressure she put on Sam and the lies she told him finally made him snap. But regardless, Nova was fifteen in that video.

Twuntytit was an adult when she sent it to Nova's college boyfriend. I have, ah, contacts with the FBI who don't fuck around with kiddie porn."

"Oh, dear." Kitty fans her face and slips onto the sofa.

"I didn't exactly tell them what was on the video, peto," Nova hisses.

Fuck.

"I mean, it's not porn. It's just. It's…" My face heats, and I don't know how to proceed for the first time in a very long time.

Ollie breaks into a full-blown belly laugh, and I'm convinced he's gone mental. "You should see your face, my boy. Oh, Lordy. Yup. You're going to be so much fun to rile up."

Turning my head, I frantically search for a way out of this shit show, but find they're all laughing at me. Laughing. At a time like this. Maybe they're fucking nuts.

Nova walks closer and places a hand on my bicep. "I told them about the video. We're just messing with you."

"This is not something you mess around with!" I bellow. "This is…this is… What the hell is happening?"

"Lexi welcomed me to the chaos of your family. I'm welcoming you to our circus, and Ollie is the ringmaster."

"Right. Right, then. Okay," Ollie says, patting the sofa like I'm going to cuddle in next to him.

Lochlan's chuckle is short-lived. "It wasn't really your place to dole out punishments."

Feeling a fight coming on, I cross my arms over my chest. "Wasn't it, though? The second you dropped her off on my doorstep, serving justice became my only priority."

"And now?" he growls.

"And now, it's going to be a media circus. I told you, the best place for her to ride it out is right here. What you all decide to do is up to you."

Nova moves so fast I don't have time to react, but Lochlan is obviously well versed in her grabby hands because he dodges her, and she reaches for my ear instead. Then she twists. It's just hard enough to get my attention, but every scar on my body flares to life as I attempt to swat her hand away. But what scares me is that the pain—the sensation I usually seek to feel anything at all—just twisted into pleasure and diverted straight to my cock.

What the fuck is happening to me?

"Do not talk about me as if I'm not here. I may have a bruised ego, but I'm perfectly capable of making decisions."

"Samuel is in custody as well." I finally pull away from my little she-devil. I'm torn between rubbing my sore ear and not rubbing my sore ear because it seems to be directly connected to my dick.

My signals are crossed. My brain is misfiring. And all I can do is stare slack-jawed at the tiny shooting star before me. Nova shines more brightly than any sunny day, and I just might be too tired to fight it anymore.

CHAPTER 18

NOVA

"*I*t's all settled then," my dad announces, reaching for another peanut butter cookie. "Nono will stay here until the media frenzy dies down."

"That could be months, Dad. Months. The Greens are going to fight this, you know they are, and where do you think Kate got her love of the spotlight? Mrs. Green will eat this up and drag it out as long as she possibly can while trying to turn it around on us." Lochlan's exasperation is evident when he tugs hard on the bottom of his vest. Too bad Tilly couldn't have come with him. She's the only one who can keep him calm.

Lochlan becomes more agitated as he moves about the room, but my mind keeps snagging on one word in my head. Months. Months here. With Ashton.

Heat pools in my belly as I chance a peek at him. Like every other time I've glanced in his direction, his gaze is singularly focused. On me.

"It'll be fine," Ashton mutters. "However long it takes will be fine. You can stay with Rylan or in GG's lodge. There are plenty of safe spaces here."

It's like he threw me into the deep end of the pool, and I don't know how to swim. "W—With Rylan?"

He nods, and Lochlan curses, but I can't drag my blurry gaze away from Ashton.

"I'll handle that bitch Green," Kitty says, shocking everyone.

We all stare at her.

"What?" she asks. "No one will mess with my little girl like that for years and get away with it. Lochlan may be the grumpy one, but where do you think he learned it from?"

I can't help it. I leap at the woman. My mind is a mess, and I need her comfort. She wraps me in a hug and murmurs into my hair. "Sweet, sweet girl. We all make mistakes. Sex tapes are not—"

"Holy mother of Christ, if you're about to tell us you have a sex tape, Mother, I'm going to burst my own eardrums. Just. Stop. Talking," Lochlan commands.

I pull back in time to see Kitty roll her eyes, and for just a second, I forget all about Ashton pushing me away. "He gets the dramatic side from his father. I was going to say sex tapes are not the end all, be all of life," she says.

"No," my dad chimes in. "Just look what it did for that Kardashian girl. Someone took advantage of her once, and now she claps back twice as hard."

Noticing the confusion on both Ashton and Lochlan's faces, I laugh. They have no idea who or what a Kardashian is.

"We're getting sidetracked," Lochlan announces at the same time Ashton says, "It wasn't a sex tape."

Lochlan and Ash glower at each other, but at least they realize they're on the same team.

"Oh, dear heaven. Is this a signed copy?" my dad asks. Turning to face him, he smiles and holds up my copy of Sloane's book. "Oh my God. It is. Kitty. It's a signed copy. Do you remember that outdoor shower scene? Up against the wall when he pulled her—"

"Stop," Lochlan bellows.

"What the hell?" Ashton's raspy voice slices through the air right behind Lochlan's.

"Yes. Yes, and remember when he used the plug to—"

"Oh my God. Kitty! Stop." Heat rushes to my face, and all hell breaks loose as Lochlan reaches over to try and rip the novel from our dad's hand.

Ashton spins in a circle as my dad tosses the book to Kitty, who opens it to a dog-eared page and whistles. "Woo-ee, Ollie. And this one. When he was chopping wood, then pounded her—"

"Stop," Lochlan, Ashton, and I all scream to joyous, teasing laughter from my parents.

"Yup, I think she'll be all right here, Kitty. We can go."

Kitty snaps the book shut with a wink, and Lochlan's muttered curses follow him down the hallway. Halfway to the door, he spins and returns to wrap me in a warm embrace.

"I'm sorry I wasn't there for you, Nono." He tilts his head in Ashton's direction. "Do you like him?"

"He's a good man, Loch. And before he did any of this, he made me feel safe for the first time in a very long time."

Lochlan recoils like I struck him, but it's the truth. His chin nods on the top of my head. "Okay," he says gruffly. Then lets me go and stalks to Ashton. Puffing up his chest, he makes himself as menacing as a man in a three-piece suit can be and holds out a hand. "Thank you, Ashton. For…" He pulls down on his vest, then smooths his free hand over the top of it. "For taking care of her."

"Again, right here," I say, flinging my hands in the air.

Ashton shakes his hand with a curt nod. Ollie attacks him next, but Ashton is ready for him. My heart pinches painfully as he adjusts his hips to put space between himself and my father as they hug awkwardly.

How long has he been like this that he can so readily make accommodations for the well-meaning strangers in his life?

Kitty, always a little better with personal space, pats him

gently on the shoulder, then leans in and whispers something that makes him swallow hard. When he nods, he can't hide the emotion welling in his eyes.

"Well," Kitty announces. "We should get that bird in the air before everyone and their mother knows our girl is here."

"Burke Hollow takes care of their own," Ashton says with a gruffness that's beginning to feel like an embrace. "The residents don't let strangers go snooping around. Nova will always be safe here."

"With you?" Kitty asks with a knowing smirk.

"Y—Yes, ma'am," Ashton stutters.

Interesting.

$\approx$

"*B*ut how did you do it so quickly?" I ask, following Ashton around the island as he collects dishes.

"It's what I do, Nova." He says my name with emphasis, and I don't miss that he hasn't called me princess since my parents left.

"But, I mean, Halton brought a sewing machine. I thought that meant I'd be here for a while."

He pauses with a sponge on the counter, such a mundane movement, but it causes the corded muscles of his forearms to bulge.

I was wrong before. He isn't built like a swimmer. No, his muscles are from something much more militant. I can see it in his intentional movements now.

"My family doesn't do anything half-assed. They were trying to make you as comfortable as possible. I can get it packed up, and we'll put it together wherever you decide you want to stay. There are plenty of options." He lowers his head and aggressively scrubs at the counter. "They would all be happy to have you, so you don't have to worry about that."

"What if I want to stay here?" I sound like a petulant child, but I'm kind of pissed off that he's shipping me out of here so quickly, even if I have no right to that anger.

His body stills. I can't even tell if he's breathing. Other than the twitch in his jaw, he's motionless, and the air becomes heavy around us. Like right before a thunderstorm, I can smell it coming.

Ashton lifts his head slowly, that storm brewing behind calculating eyes. "Why would you stay here? You're safe now. There is no threat. Your dragon's been slayed. You can be with anyone you want." The words roll over his lips like the roughest sand.

Holy shit. He did it. My peto slayed my nightmare. I am free. I'm free to be with anyone in any way that I want.

"No more one-night stands," I murmur, almost to myself.

A scratching sound makes me lift my head, and I find him scrubbing the counter with so much force I think he might actually burrow a hole in the granite.

"You're free," he agrees without looking at me.

"Are you?" I'm not sure where the question comes from, but the answer is in his haunted eyes before he even opens his mouth.

"It's not an option for me."

"Isn't it?"

He tosses the sponge into the sink and crosses his arms over his chest. "Rylan's or the lodge? I meant what I said. Burke Hollow takes care of its people. No one will bother you, so you'll have much more freedom to explore the town and hang out with the girls now if that's what you want."

"Are those my only two options?"

He narrows his eyes.

"I want to stay here, Ashton," I finally sigh. "Just because he's in custody doesn't mean everything just magically goes away. I feel safe here."

"You'll be just as safe with Rylan or at the lodge." I've never heard him so cold.

"You don't want me here?" The rejection stings.

He traces a scar I know runs along his chest and I don't think he knows he's doing it. Does it hurt him? After all this time, do his scars still cause him pain?

"I'm not a prince, Nova. I have the social skills of a gnat and the temper of a raging bull. I have work that keeps me occupied all hours of the day. I cannot babysit you forever."

Even as he says it, I see the regret in his expression, but he doesn't take it back. No, Ashton Westbrook doubles down.

"It's a small town. I don't suggest any one-night stands here unless you want to talk about it over coffee with the town crier the next day, but hey, you do you."

A direct hit to my heart. I nod past the lump in my throat as he slides something across the island. I recognize my phone and watch.

"I entered everyone's numbers. You'll be able to reach all the girls, and there are paths to all their houses that are clearly marked too if you want to explore."

The front door opens, and before I realize what's happening, Rylan and Halton are loading my stuff into their car to take me to the lodge.

"Are you sure you don't want to stay with us?" Rylan asks quietly while glaring at Ashton.

"Yeah, I'll be fine at the lodge. I don't want to put anyone out. Plus, I'll be able to spread out and work without worrying that I'm *bothering* anyone."

Rylan nods, and Halton grunts behind me, followed by angry whispers, but I don't turn to look. I know I should thank Ashton for all he's done, but I can't bring myself to look him in the eyes right now. I'm too afraid of what he'd see in mine.

CHAPTER 19

ASHTON

I sit in the corner of the family room, staring at the offending blanket draped haphazardly across the sofa. It's been there for four days now. Four days of my family waltzing through, dropping Nova-sized bombs every two seconds.

"She isn't sleeping," Colton said.

"You're being an asshole," Lexi helpfully supplied later.

"It's okay to feel things." This one was from Halton.

I haven't slept either, but that's nothing new. What is new are the dreams that happen anytime I close my eyes. Not nightmares, but daydreams that are followed by painful episodes of PTSD when I finally wake.

Leaning back in the chair, I stare at the ceiling, and my mind wanders to thoughts of her. Thoughts that bring a smile to my face and set fire to my scars.

How did I end up so fucked in the head?

My phone vibrates on the table next to me, and warning bells ring in my ears because it's the middle of the night. When I see her name, my heart clenches so painfully that I gasp for air.

"Princess?" I wheeze.

"Are you awake?" she whispers. Her voice is even sexier on the phone. Raspy with sleep, or more accurately, exhaustion if Colton's intel is correct.

"Always."

She sighs into the speaker. "You're an asshole, you know that?"

Not what I was expecting.

"Yeah, I know."

Her silence tells me she wasn't expecting my response either.

"You could have at least called to see how I was doing. That would have been the gentlemanly thing to do."

"I'm not a gentleman, Nova. I haven't been in a very long time, if I ever was."

"You were, and you are."

I nearly smile at her conviction. "How are you so sure?"

"You held me the other night. You held me against your own pain. I could feel you fighting yourself in every tense muscle. I could hear it in your breathing. You held me even when you wanted to run."

"Why aren't you sleeping?" I imagine her in her bed at the lodge and sink deeper into my chair. She's in the maple room, my favorite in the lodge.

Fucking GG.

"I guess I'm not much of a sleeper these days. Why aren't you sleeping?" Her voice is like a salve on a fresh burn.

"Work," I lie.

"Do you ever get so tired...so tired of secrets?"

Here in the darkness of night, I allow my guard to crack. Just a bit.

"Yeah, princess. I'm fucking exhausted."

"Tit for tat," she mutters.

"What's that?"

"A secret for a secret. I'll show you mine if you show me yours."

Now a full smile tugs at the scar on my lip. "Sweetheart, I have so many it would take years to break the surface of my secrets."

"Fair enough. Is that a yes?"

I feel lighter than I have since she left, and I know I'll pay for this later, but I can't stop myself. She's like the most addictive drug. A hit of her light, and I'm a junkie for more.

I put her on speakerphone and set it down on the arm of the chair. "That's a yes, princess. You first."

She doesn't hesitate. "I'm afraid of being alone."

I sit up instantly, hating myself a little more. "Do you want to go to Rylan's?"

"No, peto. You misunderstand. Not alone right now. In life. I think I always have been."

"Your mom died when you were very young, Nova. I think that's a rational fear."

"I think keeping everyone at a distance has broken me. I'm afraid to be alone, but the one-night stands? They were a temporary reprieve. Now I'm afraid to be alone and afraid to let anyone in. I'm going to end up living out my greatest fear."

"You won't," I promise. "You won't."

She sniffles, and self-loathing stabs me in the eye.

"Your turn," she says, then clears her throat. "What's your secret?"

My nostrils flare as a million things I've never told anyone dance on the tip of my tongue. A million stories of greed and death. Of the worst humanity has to offer, and yet the thing that comes out is the most honest truth I've ever told.

"I liked having you here."

Nova's laughter is sad, but the sadistic part of me loves it just as much. "You could have fooled me, peto. You couldn't get me out of your home fast enough."

"I'm not a good man, princess." Another whispered confession. "You're better off far away from me."

I swear I hear a grumbled "martyr" before her words become

clear. "One more?" she asks with a sultry tone that makes me feel alive.

"One more."

"You looked sexier than anyone I've ever seen when I read to you."

Wild images flash across my vision, and I can't speak.

"Did you like it? When I read to you?"

"Is this my second secret?" I grind out with a heaving breath.

"Sure," she whispers.

"I've dreamt of it." And paid the price of those dreams with a nightmare once I woke. But she doesn't need to know that.

There's a rustling sound, and I wait to hear what she'll say. A groan escapes long and low when she begins to read.

I stare, unblinking, at the raven-haired woman before me. But what scares me more than the gun she's pointed at my chest is that I think she sees straight to the soul of me. She sees more than the money. More than the sum of all my parts. She sees what I could be. Maybe what I was meant to be if given the chance. And for once, I actually contemplate walking away from this fight.

I stay silent as she reads page after page. When the sun begins to rise, I interrupt her.

"Princess?"

"Hmm?" Images of her lying naked in bed, touching herself like the heroine in this book, have me slipping a hand beneath the waistband of my boxers.

"You need to at least try to sleep," I say raggedly.

"Peto." It's not quite a moan, but dirty visions explode before my eyes.

"Sleep, Nova. I'll talk to you tomorrow. Sleep."

I don't wait for her to answer. I end the call and toss my phone to the floor. I haven't stripped myself naked this fast since before. Before, when I was just a weird kid watching porn on computers I built in my room.

Fifteen-year-old me could never have imagined someone like Nova though.

Fuck.

My hand wraps around my cock, and electric currents run from my base and shoot out, tearing open every scar, real and imagined. Pain and pleasure. Pleasure and pain. The pain of a pleasure so intense I see stars. I see fucking Nova Blaine and come shoots from my tip as a tortured cry rips from my lungs.

The pleasure morphs into pain and back again. My body shakes with violent aftershocks. Dark, vicious images attempt to kidnap my brain, but thoughts of Nova keep shoving them back. With both hands, she fights the darkness, and I weep.

Tears. Years and years' worth of tears spill over my face and onto my battered chest.

I'm so broken.

I'm so fucked up.

I'm so fucking broken.

A grown-ass man, sitting alone in a chair with come all over his chest, crying because he'll never know a love like hers.

I can't. And the pain of that knowledge causes my vision to tunnel, and finally, finally, sleep overtakes me.

∼

I wake with a start.

Staring down at my naked body, shame washes over me. I clutch the arms of the chair, waiting for the attack to come.

And wait.

And wait.

Air fills my lungs painfully when I realize it isn't happening.

What the fuck?

I don't bother showering. I throw my clothes back on and sprint to the basement.

I can't hit the bag hard enough as I fight my memories.

Nova.

The kids I couldn't save.

The ones I did.

Nova.

My father.

Secrets.

So many fucking secrets.

Screams and laughter sound in my head, getting louder and louder like the crescendo of a drum solo. They pound against every inch of my skull until I'm sure it's finally going to crack open and give me peace.

Sometimes I know death is my only out.

Someone grabs my arms and kicks at my legs. I fall to the mat, pinned, blinded by memories. I can't see my attacker. I can't hear over the sounds of my own screams in my head.

The metallic taste of blood snaps me to consciousness, and I release my lip from my teeth along with an animalistic scream that only comes from torture.

"Mate. Feck. Mate, it's Killian. It's me, Horseman!" A thick Irish brogue melds with the screams until I'm so hoarse no more sound comes. "Ghost. It's Horseman. Snap the feck out of it, Ghost."

Ghost. Horseman. Me. Killian.

He lifts my torso off the mat, shaking my shoulders almost violently.

I choke for breath as he releases me, and my face hits the mat hard. Shoving up to hands and knees, I continue to gasp and settle my breathing, knowing Kill is here.

I hear him muttering in Gaelic, but I don't make a sound as I push to my feet. Turning to him, I open my arms and wait for the blows to come.

He shakes his head with a string of curses. "You haven't punished yourself in years, mate. Why now?"

"The light is shining through," I say, but he can't understand me. My voice is raw and bloodied.

"I ain't going to hit you until you tell me why the feck now."

I shake my head, and he takes a step back.

"Why, Ghost?"

Ghost. For years that's all anyone knew me by. That's all most of my crew knows me by now. I've lived in shadows, sending men to do what I couldn't while sitting safely behind a computer screen. It wasn't until Killian met me in the ring that he learned my truth.

He gets in my face, spittle flying as he demands answers.

"A girl," I whisper, and shock registers just before the first punch lands on my right side.

Killian has a very specific set of skills. He inflicts the most amount of pain in strategic places that can be hidden by dress shirts and ties.

A punch to the ribs, and I feel it crack. He always hits just hard enough that I'll feel it for weeks but not hard enough to do lasting damage.

He's the only reason I'm still here.

The fight club he found me in would have killed me years ago.

For a while, he thought the needles of a tattoo machine would be enough of a distraction. He learned how wrong he was when he set the first needle to my skin.

When I stumble on my feet, Killian wraps me in a hold I don't have the energy to even attempt to escape from.

"It's time to let go, Ghost. Let it the feck go before you lose everything."

"I thought I already had." Blood trickles down my throat as I force the words to come.

He pulls back to glare into my eyes. "If the light is getting through 'cause of a girl, there's still something to live for."

He tosses my arm over his shoulder and guides me out of the ring.

"This thing between you and me is coming to an end, mate. You've paid the dues for whatever debt you've been trying to pay. Whatever wrong you feel obligated to make right. I've never seen someone so consumed by misplaced guilt. You've saved thousands of people, Ghost. It's time to hand over the reins. Let someone else fight the darkness now."

I shake my head, but he sets me gently on the edge of the sofa and leaves the room. I know he's gone to get the first aid kit, so I twist myself around and collapse onto my back.

The pain is a penance for my guilt. But even the pain can't block Nova's light. Without even knowing it, her memory alone battles the darkness of my mind, and sleep takes me once again.

CHAPTER 20

NOVA

"*He* wasn't always like this," Rylan says, holding her arms above her head while I pin a dress in place.

Without a dress form at GG's lodge, Rylan agreed to step in while I put the final touches on my new gown. It might be my most favorite yet. With delicate lace sleeves and a square neckline, it has a regal look to it. But the wide open back gives it a sexy update I adore.

"It's business in the front and a party in the back," Halton grumbles from the corner of the table.

"The mullet of wedding gowns. I like that, Hattie," Rylan winks, and I stare between the two of them.

"Did you just call him Hattie?"

"Yeah." He shrugs. His cheek shows the faintest blush beneath his scruff, but the love in his eyes when he looks at Rylan is what fairy tales are made of. "She's called me Hattie since she was six years old."

I remove the pin I was holding with my teeth and set it on the table. "You've known these guys *that* long?"

Rylan grins. "My entire life. Colton's my best friend, but

Hattie was my forever. So, trust me when I say Ash wasn't always like this."

"What was he like?" My voice wobbles. I've tried my hardest not to pepper his family with questions, but because they seem to be taking turns babysitting me now, I can't help it.

"He was the best part of all of us." Halton's voice is thick with emotion. "He still is. He just can't see it."

"His attack made him this way?"

I look at them and realize we're all missing pieces. No one but Ashton knows his full story.

Halton shakes his head. "No, I don't think it's just his attack. He's been keeping our father's secrets and won't let anyone else in. We don't know how to help him."

The front door bursts open with a gust of cold air, and a giant of a man stomps in. Halton stands immediately, but Rylan jumps off her dais and places a hand on his arm.

"Who is that?" I whisper as the dangerous-looking man heads through the lobby and up the stairs.

"Killian O'Connell," Halton growls.

"I take it we don't like Killian?" I ask Rylan because Halton is scary as fuck right now.

"He's a friend of Ash's," she says without looking at me. "But we don't know him. We just see the change in Ash when he's around."

"What kind of change?" My voice is three octaves too high.

"Like the pain he carries around is a little closer to the surface when Killian is here." Halton slams a fist down on the table and stands. "He hasn't been here in over a year. I'd hoped we'd seen the last of him, but Easton said he checked in last week."

"So, he's not really a friend?" I ask, confused.

"I think he might be the closest thing Ashton has to a friend that's not family."

I watch as Halton storms to the back of the lodge, where GG's private residence is, and Rylan gives an apologetic shrug. "Is it okay if we finish this later?" she asks, pointing to the dress.

"Oh, crap. Yes. Sorry. Let me undo the clips." I hold the gown up as she slips out of it. Rylan's athletic wear clings to her body as she steps into her sneakers.

"Regardless of what Ashton tells you about himself, he is a good man. All the Westbrooks are."

I nod and catch movement on the stairs behind her. She gives me a hug, but I keep my eyes on the hulking frame of Killian. Just before he reaches the bottom step, our eyes connect. He pauses, gives me a once-over, looks at Rylan's retreating form, and then turns his dark gaze back on me.

A frisson of unease skates over my skin.

He gives a shake of his head and smirks, nearly provoking me to march over there to slap it from his face, before he turns and walks outside.

The grandfather clock in the foyer chimes, and I jump into motion. If I don't have my stuff cleaned up before GG leaves the kitchen, I'll be stuck having dinner with her again. It's not that I don't like her, but too much GG is like too much vodka. That extra shot always pushes you over the edge.

Tossing the gown over my shoulder, I quickly pick up all my scraps and scramble to the stairs just as I hear the click-clack of her cane. I take the stairs two at a time, thankful for the cheese and crackers I stashed in my room's mini fridge earlier.

Every day here has become a silent countdown to my nightly calls with Ashton. It should terrify me how much I want this man. He has more secrets than the US military, and I'm sure he'll take them all to the grave. But there's something in his blue eyes that won't leave my heart. A connection I've always longed for.

I know it will hurt when I eventually have to go home, but until then, I'm basking in every conversation I can drag from him.

~

"*H*ow was your day, dear?" I ask when Ashton answers his phone.

"Like every other day of my life."

"How's that?"

He grunts, and the gasp that follows tells of pain. Physical pain.

"Moiling," he finally answers. He sounds weaker somehow. Gruffer.

Moiling?

"Are you okay?"

"Yeah, princess. I heard you dressed up Rylan today?"

My mind shifts to Killian, and it's on the tip of my tongue to ask, but he doesn't give me a chance to answer.

"This is the best part of my day," he admits like it pains him. "Of all my days," he adds, so quietly that if I hadn't been holding my breath, I would have missed it.

"Ashton?"

"Hmm?"

"Are you okay?" I ask quietly.

There's a sharp intake of breath, then a low exhale. "As good as I've ever been, princess."

I don't believe him. "Hold on. I'll call you right back."

"Wh…"

Ending the call, I press the video button and FaceTime him. It feels more intimate this way, and that's why I've never done it before, but I need to see his face. See that he's okay. I'm not sure why I've stayed away. He's literally a five-minute hike down a well-established trail, but he didn't come to me, so I stayed away.

Perhaps that was a mistake.

His handsome face is covered in shadows when he answers, and I realize he's sitting in his family room. In the dark.

"Why aren't you in your bed?" I scan every bit of his face that I can see in the four-inch screen.

He looks around the room with a frown, but when he twists, even the tiniest bit, I see the flash of pain in his eyes.

"Are you injured, Ashton?" I'm careful not to ask if he's hurt, because that's obvious to anyone who knows him. He's been hurting for so long that he doesn't know any different.

"I'm more comfortable here. What are you reading tonight, princess?"

"Peto?" I plead.

"Read, sweetheart. Read to me."

Emotion clogs my throat. "Well," I try. "We finished *Don't Let Go.*"

"They lived happily ever after." A whisper of a smile appears on his face.

I nod, watching him close his eyes and rest his head against the back of the sofa.

"Have you always read romance novels?" he asks with his face pointed at the ceiling.

I'm nodding, but with his eyes closed, he can't see that. He pries one eye open and searches my face through the screen.

When he quirks his brow, I answer. "For a long time, I thought the only way I'd find a happily ever after was in the pages of these books."

"And now?" He's gruff yet gentle, like he's making an effort. For me.

"And now you happened."

He nods, closing his eyes again as I memorize the lines of his face. "What's your favorite part about them?"

I'm not imagining it. His voice is weaker than normal. Scratchier too. Like every syllable is being raked across razor blades.

"Ash?"

"Please, princess."

I'm not sure what he's asking me for, but at this moment, I would give him everything.

I swallow. Once. Twice. Three times before the words will come. "The first kiss."

His eyes open, and he watches me with an intensity that overpowers his exhaustion.

"There's a magic when it's well-written. A power that builds with seduction and longing. When two characters dance around each other for so long that the chemistry between them threatens to set fire to the pages in my hand, that first kiss is like a ray of hope that all the angst, all the turmoil of their lives will just melt away when their lips finally meet."

A crack of lightning lights up the sky around us, followed by the loudest clap of thunder I've ever heard. The windows shake as an ocean of raindrops descends on the mountain.

"Do you think a kiss can be that powerful, princess?"

"I think if it's not, you're with the wrong person."

"Have you ever had a kiss like that?" His eyes burn a hole through me, and I shake my head.

"Have you?"

"I don't have a lot of experience in life. Love. Or... No. I haven't had a kiss like that."

"You're not a...wait. Are you a..."

"Virgin?" He smirks. "No, I'm not. But I haven't had..."

"A string of one-night stands either?"

"Don't do that," he says roughly. "What's your favorite first kiss?"

"What book?"

He nods.

"That's easy—Kathryn Nolan's *Bohemian*. Her hero is this nerdy—" Oops. Too many similarities between the hero in *Bohemian* and Ashton.

"Nerds are people too," he teases, and it shocks a laugh out of me.

"Yeah." I giggle. "Yeah, they are. And they're hot as fuck."

He growls his approval. "Read it to me."

"*Bohemian?*"

"Yes. Read me their first kiss."

Dropping my phone into my lap, I scroll through my Kindle. At this point, I probably have this scene memorized, but I want him to have the full Kathryn Nolan experience, so I tap the screen until I get to the part that lives rent-free in my brain and begin to read.

Every once in a while, I lift my eyes to find him studying me. I pause after the first kiss, wishing he wasn't covered in shadows. It's too hard to read him like this.

"Keep going?"

He grunts in response, and I continue. The rain pummels the roof above me as I read. I read and watch him watching me until my voice becomes hoarse, and he interrupts like he has every other night.

"Sleep, princess. You need to sleep."

The clock beside me ticks away the seconds. Two a.m. "It's early."

"Sleep," he repeats.

The weight of his pain sits heavy in my heart, but all I can do is nod.

"Good night, princess."

"Good night, peto."

He ends the call, and I stare at the blank screen, thinking about first kisses and broken hearts. They always seem to go hand in hand with me.

CHAPTER 21

ASHTON

*T*he wind picks up, and I cross to the wall of windows. The rain coming down in sheets makes it feel like we're underwater, but I can only think about Nova. And first fucking kisses.

I rub my side, feeling the bruise there from the beating Killian gave me last week. It healed much quicker than I was expecting.

I'm beginning to think he's pulling punches.

My phone vibrates with an incoming text, and my heart skips when I see an image from Nova. It's a screenshot that says #kindlequotes at the bottom. Reading through, I see she's sent me the moment she waits for in her books. The first kiss.

A dangerous kind of reckless energy rages in my veins, and I move before I can stop myself. The truth is, I'm weak. I always have been. But right now, I wouldn't be able to stop myself, even if I wanted to. I'm possessed, and there's only one thing that will keep me from burning the world to the ground.

Nova's lips.

Her kiss.

Her.

Walking outside is like jumping into a swimming pool. The

second I step into the rain, I'm drenched to my core, but I don't stop. The early fall rain is a frigid barrier keeping me from full beast mode.

It's raining so hard the sounds of the forest are drowned by plops of water. Despite the mud that squishes beneath my bare feet, I never consider turning back. I can't see more than five feet in front of my face, but I know these trails like the back of my hand.

So when I see a tiny light flickering back and forth halfway between my house and GG's lodge, I take off at a run.

No one should be out here at two in the morning in a storm like this. I'm preparing for a fight. For an intruder. For an unnamed enemy.

I'm not prepared to come face-to-face with Nova. A red-faced, shivering, covered-head-to-toe-in-mud, Nova.

Our bodies collide, and I scrub the muck from her face with my fingertips. She looks like she face-planted in the dirt. "Are you okay?" I yell over the storm raging around us.

She nods with a grin, and every sound, every touch, every sight around me blurs until it's just her, standing here in my arms, soaked to the bone and smiling up at me like I'm responsible for the sun and the stars and every good thing in between.

"I fell." She laughs.

My eyes search hers. When was the last time anyone saw me like this?

Has anyone?

"What are you doing out here?" She has to yell to be heard through the storm, but her smile is so wide I can see her teeth chattering.

"I…" I shake my head. What do I say? "What are you doing out here? You could have gotten lost. That little flashlight isn't doing shit."

"I was coming to…to you." Her body shivers in front of me.

A twenty-year-old knot loosens in my shoulders. A smile I

didn't know I had breaks through as I lower my mouth. I hover above hers. "You were coming to me? On a night like this? For what?"

As she shudders against me, her warm tears mix with the rain pounding down on our heads. They wash a clean streak down her face that I can't look away from.

Our eyes dance back and forth, blinking rapidly to clear the raindrops from our vision. Our breaths expel puffs of hot air into the chilly night. Our heartbeats are searching for the rhythm of the other.

I don't know who moves first, but like magnets, our bodies fuse to become one.

My hands wind tightly in her hair, angling her face to the left so I can devour every inch of her mouth. The second our lips touch, the sky lights up with a parade of lightning bolts that could rival any fireworks show, and it sends a frenetic energy darting between us.

Limbs entwine. Teeth smash. Tongues war.

It's the most heavenly fight of my life.

I sigh all my fears into her lips, and for a moment, I'm just a man kissing his girl. The weight of lives and secrets exists only on the periphery. I'm forced to stay in the moment. In the moment that smells like first rain kisses, of promises, and of Nova. My shiny little star that sparkles so brightly she eviscerates my darkness.

Her tongue darts into my mouth, teasing. Tasting. I savor every new exploration.

My teeth nip at her bottom lip, and it seems to spur her into motion. She jumps, and I catch her under her thighs without thinking. Her legs wrap around my waist, but we never break our kiss.

Thunder claps, and our eyes open at the same time.

This is what peace feels like.

Rain seems to fall in slow motion as I lick the taste of her from my lips. Nose to nose, mouth to mouth, we stare into each other's souls, knowing if we break the connection, real life will crash us back into reality.

Closing my eyes, I cup the back of her head and pull her into my chest so tightly I fear she'll snap in two.

"Peto?"

"Shh," I beg, already regretting my weakness. Regretting my weakness, but never her. I regret not being strong enough to stay away from her. I regret that I'll never be her knight in shining armor. And I regret that I won't survive our inevitable end.

Every rib and muscle in my body protests when I swing her sideways to carry her in a wedding hold. Without a word, I turn toward the lodge.

I don't dare look into her eyes. I know I'm an asshole. A bastard. A fucking prick who will bring her tears.

Instead, I trudge silently through the night storm. I walk us into the lodge, up the stairs, and into her room, where I head straight to the en suite and turn on the shower.

Unsure of my next move, I place her on her feet and take a step back.

Nova doesn't hesitate. She drops the ridiculous bright yellow raincoat she's wearing to the floor and then, with her eyes holding mine hostage, she lifts her sleep shirt over her head.

My princess stands naked before me except for a tiny g-string I could shred with one finger.

Every normal life experience I've never dared dream for races through my mind, and the scar on my cheekbone tingles with a numb sort of pain.

"You're perfect," I force through a swallow. "So fucking perfect."

I close my eyes when the first trickle of sweat slides down my spine.

"Fight the panic, Ashton. Fight for your happiness." Dr. Benson's words are like nails on a chalkboard.

My breathing becomes labored, and I rock back on my heels and force my eyes open. Concern shows on Nova's face as her lips move, but I can't hear her words.

"You're so perfect, princess," I croak. Lowering my head, I kiss her gently on the cheek, then take her arm and spin her toward the shower. With a gentle nudge, I urge her forward, and when the warm water spills over her skin, I turn away and walk out the door.

I'm pretty sure whatever was left of my battered heart is swirling down the drain with the mud that covered her feet.

CHAPTER 22

NOVA

*F*our sets of eyes stare at me with blank expressions. Lexi is the first to break away and glance over her shoulder at Ashton, who sits with his back to the wall a few tables over, watching the door of the pizza place like an armed intruder might bust through at any given second.

"But…" Lexi begins, and for once, I realize she's stunned into silence. "But then what happened?"

"He left," I say, trying to mask the hurt in my tone.

Her blond ponytail swings wildly when she spins back to me. "He just…left you there? Standing naked in the shower? After a kiss like that?"

A kiss that could make romance books blush. Yeah. He left me.

"I mean, I think we really need to give Sloane some notes. Imagine the story she would write around that kiss," Winnie gushes, fanning her cheeks. She's an adorably sweet woman, and I can see why Colton loves her so much.

Ari opens her mouth to speak, then takes a giant gulp of her beer instead. Shaking her head, she opens her mouth again. "But that kiss?"

I shrug, feeling the unease settling in my shoulders.

Rylan is the only one who hasn't spoken. After a month on this mountain, I'm getting to know them all pretty well, and I see the effect Halton's fight with anxiety has had on her. She sees more than most.

"I'm going to come back to him in a second. But first, I want to know how you're doing with everything?" she asks.

I know she's talking about the media shitstorm that hasn't subsided as my parents had hoped. I shrug. "It must be a slow month. I'm sure some celebrity will have a meltdown or affair soon, and they'll forget all about me."

The girls grimace, but I try to ignore it.

The truth is, my face has been plastered across every social media outlet for weeks. The hotel heiress as a promiscuous airhead has been the major headline, with one man after another coming forward with tales of my sordid love life. Some of the men I've never seen before. Some of them sting with betrayal.

"Is this going to affect your nomination for the CFDA award?" Rylan asks, and I sit back, stunned that she cared enough to remember. "What? You're my friend. Obviously, I follow this stuff. It's not every day someone I know could potentially win Emerging Designer of the Year. This is basically the Oscars of fashion."

Nervous laughter starts slow, then rolls into an uncontrollable fit while these women simply smile politely at me. Maybe they're used to this kind of crazy, but no one has ever cared about what I'm doing. No one but my family or Penny anyway. I laugh until my belly hurts and the hairs on the back of my neck rise.

My eyes are drawn to Ashton, and I find him staring at me even as he speaks to Sadie, who sits across from him. I'm guessing she's reading him the riot act about something by the way her hands fly through the air.

I really like that kid.

And I give him credit. Obviously, he wants to be anywhere

but sitting in a booth at the Marinated Mushroom, but it's Friday night, and he's here with his Sadie Sunshine because it's what she wanted to do.

"You haven't had many people care about what's important to you. Have you?" Winnie asks gently.

My smile falters when she reads me so clearly, but Rylan saves me from having to answer.

"Tell me I'm wrong?" Rylan huffs, and my attention falls to our black-and-white checkered table.

"No, sorry. You're not wrong. The Council of Fashion Designers of America awards are all about who you know and lobbying for votes though. With me here, it's not likely that I'll win, or even secure a nomination at this point. I'm being portrayed as the slut of Manhattan. That isn't exactly the look the CFDA goes for."

A collective gasp from the girls makes me smile. "It's fine. I'm not someone who can kiss the asses of board members to get ahead, and the truth is, I was a little promiscuous. I had sex. A lot of it. And the idea of trying to change myself into someone I'm not makes my stomach turn. It's why I would never be able to run the Bryer-Blaine empire with Lochlan. I kind of do my own thing."

"Good for you, chica." Lexi holds up a mug in cheers. "And for the record, there is nothing wrong with taking control of your body or your needs. As long as it's done in a consensual manner, it's no one's fucking business."

I smile at her tenacity.

"Now, on to Ashton. What in the ever-loving fuck is going on? Seriously. The guy just left you there?" Lexi gasps, then looks around the restaurant. "Wait. You don't think he's a virgin, do you?" She spins on Rylan. "Has he ever had a girlfriend? Ever?" She whispers with such urgency it's hard to take her seriously.

"He's not a virgin," I blurt much too loudly, drawing the attention of everyone in the restaurant.

Including Ashton.

His gaze narrows in on me, and my entire body flushes, causing me to fidget in my seat.

"Well, he's not," I whisper, then lean over the table. "He told me."

"I've never seen him with a girl except for Pacen," Rylan admits.

The beer in my hand freezes at my lips.

"Pacen?" I ask casually, but then I inhale beer foam that gets lodged in my throat, and I choke.

"She was his best friend for as long as I can remember. Her dad is the one who was trying to ruin the Westbrooks for all those years. He was arrested not that long ago. Maybe a couple of years ago? Anyway, I hadn't seen her in, geez, I don't even know, but she found Hattie and me on Block Island and basically gave us a message for him."

Rylan leans in conspiratorially, and we all follow suit. "She wanted him to stop looking for her and to spill his father's secrets before they buried him. She was, well, it was so sad seeing her. She was despondent. Cold. Like..." Her gaze drifts to Ashton, and sorrow fills her expression. "Like a more broken version of Ash."

"He isn't cold," I huff, crossing my arms and leaning back in my chair. The need to defend him makes my scalp prickle.

Rylan's expression softens. "No, Nova. He isn't. He's..."

"Hurting," I finish for her with downcast eyes.

"Yeah," they all nod in agreement.

Our server drops a gooey deep-dish pizza in front of us, and I smile as they all dig in. The girls I grew up with wouldn't be caught dead eating this carb-overloaded slice of heaven. As if reading my thoughts, Rylan refills my mug. She winks when she sets down the pitcher in the middle of the table.

"Have you heard anything about *her*?" she asks.

"Way to ruin the girl-gang vibe we had going on here," Lexi mutters.

Using the napkin to give myself time to process a response, I finally ask, "You mean Kate?"

Rylan nods.

"No. I mean, what could she say? Ashton handed my attorney everything on a silver platter."

"It's kind of a *Single White Female*-type situation," Lexi muses. "She's obsessed with you and fucked up enough to do something about it."

"Being here has been a good distraction," I admit.

"Are you still having trouble sleeping?" Ari asks patiently. She sneaks a peek at her daughter, and Sadie waves with a smile that lights up the entire restaurant. "Sorry," Ari shrugs. "Sadie has a big heart, but a bigger mouth, and she's been worried about you. She told me she overheard you having a nightmare at Ashton's house."

Embarrassment hits hard. Has Ashton talked to her about me? Before I can ask the question, Ari shakes her head. "Sadie has been worried since she found you on the sofa with Ash. Ash and Sadie have a special relationship, but he's kept you apart, even from her. Trust me, his brothers have each taken turns trying to get info from her this week."

"Oh," I say, unsure of how to proceed.

"He isn't keeping you a secret, if that's what you're worried about," Lexi says through a mouth full of pizza. "But he is trying to protect whatever it is that you have. He told Easton last week that you talk but refused to go into any details. I'm not surprised though. That's Ash."

That's Ash. Secrets built on secrets.

"He doesn't sleep much either," Rylan says.

"I know." I can't help but look at him again, and the intensity in his gaze warms me to my core. I have to turn back to the girls before my entire body goes up in flames. "I look forward to talking with him," I say honestly. "Even if we're not really talking about anything, it gives me a peace I hadn't known I needed, but by the time he makes me hang up the phone, I'm…"

"Horny and takes care of business, then falls fast asleep with visions of Ashton's balls dancing in her head." GG cackles at the table next to us, and mortification burns in my cheeks.

"Jesus, GG. How the hell did you hear what we were saying but couldn't hear Easton ask you to pass the salt last week at dinner when he was right beside you?"

The crazy old lady taps her ear with shimmering eyes. "Doc got me a new hearing aid. I can turn it down when it suits me and drown out background noise when I need to hear the gossip."

Lexi stands abruptly and marches around the table with her hand outstretched. "Hand it over, GG. Right now."

"You can't take my hearing aid, ya ninny."

"I can, and I will. Dr. Carter said you don't even really need one. Hand it over, you eavesdropping menace."

GG's lips purse to a straight line, but she drops it into Lexi's palm. When Lexi turns around, GG smiles at her blue-haired companion and pulls something from her purse. As Lexi returns to our table, I try not to laugh as GG inserts another hearing aid. "Back up," she mouths to me.

"You can have these back after dinner," Lexi grumbles, and GG's shoulders shake with unconcealed laughter. "She put another one in when I turned my back, didn't she?"

I nod, laughter escaping us all. I forgot how good it feels to laugh. It's liberating, and I realize I'm relaxed here. For the first time in my adult life, I feel like I belong, and not just because people want something from me.

My eyes snag on Ashton's again to find him watching me with an expression I can't read, but his eyes are soft and crinkle at the corners. When I smile, he gives me the smallest tip of his head.

There are so many layers to this man. The only question is,

can he shed the ones weighing him down so he can finally be free?

The conversation carries on around me, and even though the girls do their best to bring me into the fold, my heart just isn't in it anymore. I have too many questions about the man behind all the secrets, but I still spend every day counting down the hours until our call.

Because at some point over the last couple of weeks, it's become our routine to keep each other company in the dead of night, when nightmares try to steal hope and dreams search for a way into our realities.

Is he only placating me? Talking with me nightly out of a sense of duty? Or does he feel this connection too? This string that keeps me tethered to the hope of him.

I'm pathetic. Old insecurities of being too much, too needy, too messed up rattle around my brain. I'm still deep in self-loathing when Rylan's voice cuts through my thoughts.

"Nova?" she asks, and I can tell by her expression that it isn't the first time she's said my name. "You okay?"

The girls are all standing around our table wearing the same worried expression.

"Gah! Sorry. Yeah, I spaced out for a minute." Tossing my napkin on the table, I stand.

"We'll give you a ride back to the lodge," she says.

"I've got her," Ashton's voice rumbles behind me, and I shiver.

His hand lands on the small of my back, setting fire to my core. His fingers gently press into my skin, and I can tell he's fighting the urge to pull it back.

"You sure do. Maybe you won't let her go this time," Lexi mutters under her breath.

What is it with Lexi and her grandmother? Were they not born with a freaking filter?

"Ah," I splutter.

"Stepping right into GG's inappropriate shoes, I see," Ashton grumbles while ushering me forward.

"I..."

He cuts me off. "It's a Heart family thing. None of them have a goddamn filter. At least Lanie attempts to keep hers in check. Lexi is going to out-GG GG before she's forty." His words are a whispered growl at my ear that causes a tremor straight to my pleasure center.

Turning my head, I catch his satisfied smirk as he watches the goosebumps appear along my exposed skin. When he catches me eyeing him, he tugs on the back of his neck and looks away.

The heat from his hand seeps into my bones and claims a piece of me I didn't even know was for sale.

"Let's get you home, princess."

I swear my body trembles from the inside out. "What about Sadie?" I ask, searching the small restaurant to see her sitting in the corner with a group of kids.

"She's going to the movies with her friends, so it's just you and the *not a virgin*," he whispers.

CHAPTER 23

NOVA

"*A*h, funny thing about that." I nearly choke on the words as he helps me up into the cab of his truck.

"I bet," he says without looking at me.

Before I form a sentence, he's leaned in and is securing my seatbelt around me like a child. How does this man steal my breath with the stupidest things? The only movement I'm capable of is fluttering my eyelashes like I have dirt in my eye until his shoulder brushes the side of my breast. Then the air comes rushing back into my lungs.

My hand lands on his, halting his forward motion. "I'm perfectly capable of buckling myself in."

He shrugs me off, and the metal clicks as he inserts the latch. "You're capable of doing anything, Nova."

My brows pinch together in frustration. "Then what are you doing?"

He pulls back just a fraction but remains in my space, the spicy marinara from his pizza lingering on his breath between us.

"Because unlike some men, I'll never have what I want, so I get small snippets in time and force myself to be happy with it."

"Like what?" The words are too breathy. They give away my desire.

"Like feeling you strapped in under me."

I gasp, and he lowers his gaze to my lips.

"Like feeling your body next to mine and knowing you're safe." He pulls back and shuts the door, leaving me with the scent of him short-circuiting my senses.

I watch him as he rounds the hood of the truck, and I instantly know something's wrong. He's carrying himself like he could collapse at any moment. It's in the way his body shuffles. There are no fluid motions. Every part of him moves to control his next step.

I scan him head to toe as he opens the door and climbs in.

"Are you mad at me?" Angling my body so I'm leaning against the door, I search his face for the truth as he pulls out of the parking space.

His gaze darts to me. "Why would I be mad at you?" His tone holds genuine surprise, and I bite my lip as I think.

"I didn't tell them anything, not really."

Ashton's eyes dance with mirth, but he keeps his focus on the road. "Sweetheart, the girls thinking I'm a virgin isn't news." He grins, and my heart knocks against my ribs. "Hell, my brothers probably wonder the same thing. It comes with the territory in my family. Welcome to small-town life, where everyone knows your business, and if they don't, they make it up."

"So, you're not mad?"

His chuckle is deep and raspy. I swear it vibrates against my clit like the most powerful toy.

He reaches across the console with an open palm, jerks it back, then slowly, as if he's in pain, holds it out to me again.

Something about that movement tells me more about the man than any of our late-night share sessions.

"Secret for a secret?" I whisper into the darkness and place my hand in his.

His fingers twitch in mine, and I give them a gentle squeeze that he returns as he turns onto the long drive that will take me to the lodge.

"You first," he rumbles.

"I dream of you." I swallow and turn my head toward the side window. "At night, after we hang up. It's always the same dream, but I wake up before it ends."

He slips his hand from mine and puts the truck in park. The overhead light turns on as he opens his door then gets out. I sit as darkness engulfs me in slow motion. I think he's about to open mine, but when the light turns on next, I realize he's reaching into the back seat.

I try to look over my shoulder, but then he's there. At my side with the most intense expression on his face.

"Dreams are the only place my happiness lives, princess."

I close my eyes as sadness consumes me, and I force myself to hold it together when I stare up at him next. "Is that your secret?"

Leaning over me, he unbuckles my seatbelt and shakes his head. With my hand in his, we walk up the front steps of the lodge in silence. He stops at the front door and faces me, searching for answers to unasked questions just like I am. When he doesn't speak, I give him a nudge.

"What's your secret then, Ashton?"

"The consequences might kill me," he answers quietly, then holds up a small bag I hadn't noticed.

When I don't reach for it, he presses it into my chest and places a chaste kiss to my temple. The moment is so intimate and sweet that my throat clogs with emotion. Then he reaches around me to open the door and gently ushers me inside before I can open the gift.

He tenses behind me, and I lift my gaze to find Killian sitting at a small side table in the entryway.

"Killian," Ashton says in greeting. "Give me a couple hours."

Killian nods as I stare between the two men. Ashton is resigned, and Killian appears...tormented.

"What's going on?" I tug on Ashton's sleeve, but he won't hold eye contact. His eyes flicker everywhere but at me, and my stomach plummets to the floor. His jaw flexes and I take a step back.

I'm positive that whatever he says next will be a lie.

"Nothing, princess. We have a meeting that's being rescheduled. That's all."

My temper flares and I know my face is turning red. I normally respect most of his boundaries. I normally follow his lead. But I've never seen him lie to me either, so I step forward and poke him hard in the chest. Feeling the scar tissue beneath my fingertip has me stumbling over my words for a second.

"You know, peto, for all the secrets you keep, you're a fucking terrible liar. If you don't want to tell me the truth, don't tell me anything at all."

His mouth drops open, and Killian's muttered curse follows me to the stairs. It's the first time I've heard the man speak, and it draws my gaze to his. He stares at us, shaking his head. His expression is the epitome of sadness and loyalty.

It's confusing.

With quick steps, I take the stairs two at a time. "Have a good meeting," I say like a curse, not even trying to listen to the angry hushed words the two men share below me.

It isn't until I'm in my room with my back pressed to the door that I realize I still have the small gift bag in my hand.

Tossing it on the bed, I stare at it like it'll strike if I get too close. I need a nice long shower before I can handle anything else tonight.

CHAPTER 24

ASHTON

The phone rings again, and again it goes to voicemail. How many times can you call someone in an hour before it becomes inappropriate?

Three? Four? On the sixth time, she finally answers. "I'm mad at you," Nova states plainly, devoid of any emotion.

The sigh of relief still hits me when her face fills the screen, but it's like a kick to the nuts. I want her more than I've ever wanted anything for myself, and I don't know how to have her. Even if I could claim her as mine, I would never be able to keep her.

Could I?

"I know you are," I say as the war of want and need faces off in my head.

"I don't like Killian."

Her words surprise me, and I frown. "You don't even know him," I say lightly.

"I know enough."

Her stubborn tone coaxes a grin from me despite my best effort.

"What do you know, princess?"

"Don't you princess me, peto." Her shoulders bounce with anger, and I suppress a chuckle.

"Did you just stomp your foot?"

"My foot is going to get crammed up your ass in about two seconds," she hisses.

"Okay, I'm sorry. Why don't you like Kill?"

"First of all, because his name is Kill. *Kill*. That's not normal. And secondly, because—because you've been different with him in town."

"Different how?" That's concerning. I don't want this side of my life darkening her world. When she doesn't answer, I ask again with more urgency. "How am I different, Nova?"

"Like the torment that hounds you is closer to taking you away for good. Your pain is more visceral with him here. It's closer to the surface somehow. I don't like it, and I don't like him."

"You see things so clearly?"

"When it comes to you? Yes."

"It isn't his fault, sweetheart. He's only ever done what I've asked of him. He's a good friend, and he likes you."

"Well, he can fuck right off. I don't care what you say. Something is wrong with him."

"Not him, princess. Me. It's always been me." There's a clicking noise on her end of the line, and I can't place it. My ears strain to listen as fear swirls. "What's that sound?"

She turns the camera, and I see her fingernails drumming against the table right in front of her unopened gift.

I'm losing my mind.

"I owe you a secret," I mutter. Staring at her fingers, I swear I feel them dance across my chest. The camera turns back to her face, and I smile at her narrowed eyes.

"Okay," she drawls. "Let's hear it."

"You're my dream catcher."

"What?" Her voice is small as she eyes the bag.

"Even when you're not here, you fight the dreams that have plagued my nights. You've forced a little of the darkness out. I—I wanted to do the same for you."

"How?" I like that when she's with me, her voice is unguarded. She doesn't put up pretenses. She doesn't hide anything from me.

"Open your gift."

She reaches into the bag and pulls out the plush beast toy, and I instantly regret everything when her eyes go round, and her jaw drops.

"I didn't want you to be alone. I'm not made for the happily ever after, Nova. But you've given me pieces of one I'll cherish forever. I just didn't want you to forget me. I thought he could keep you company when you're feeling alone."

Tears stream down her face, and I tug on the ends of my hair.

This was so fucking dumb. That's what I get for listening to a teenager.

"Please don't cry," I plead. "I. Fuck. This is so dumb, but I have one more surprise for you."

"You do?" She sniffles.

"Thank Christ books are online now, and I didn't have to go into a fucking bookstore to find this." I hold up the iPad with the book loaded into the Kindle app.

"You bought me a book?"

I shake my head. Jesus, this is the worst idea I've ever had.

"I don't understand," she murmurs, reaching for a tissue.

"I'm going to read it to you. It's supposed to be a *Beauty and the Beast* dark retelling. Whatever that means. The reviews say the smut is good."

A very unsexy, gurgled giggle escapes her lips, and even with red-rimmed eyes, she's never looked prettier.

"I mean, I can just give you the damn book too. That's probably a better idea. I just…"

"Peto?"

I lift my gaze to find her sad eyes smiling in the screen. "Yeah?" I ask gruffly.

"Read to me."

I nearly swallow my tongue when she steps back from the table, and she's only wearing a tiny silk robe. Her hands play with the ties that hold it closed, like she's trying to decide on her next move. I almost come in my pants when she lets it slide off her shoulders.

"But be naked with me while you read."

"I'm not sure that's a good idea," I growl, unable to look away from her.

"Give me the memory, Ashton. Please."

I can't say no to her. I'll give her anything she asks for, even if it means the end of me. Pleasing this woman will be worth my inevitable end.

I nod and lift my shirt over my head. The self-conscious pang of guilt and fear I normally feel at my scars is washed away by the longing in Nova's eyes.

She sees a beast and wants the man anyway.

The weight of what she's doing nearly suffocates me. After everything Kate put her through, this has to be the ultimate act of trust for her.

I can't place the emotion building in my chest as I shuck my jeans and boxer briefs. It isn't until I'm standing, laying myself bare before the screen for her, that I realize it's gratitude and love. For her. It's a warm feeling that spreads through my body, slowly defrosting every crevice of my heart I thought had been killed off by self-loathing.

My dream catcher is also a unicorn because I never thought this feeling could exist for me. With her hungry gaze on me, I don't have to push back the pain or the worry about the aftermath. It will come, but for once, I don't have to chase it back. It's being tethered by this beautiful creature before me.

"You're beautiful," I croak.

"So are you," she whispers, walking backward until her bed comes into view behind her.

I scoff, but it dies on my tongue as she climbs onto the bed and situates herself on the pillows.

"I…" I gulp. Nova props the phone up on something next to her so I have a full-length view of her naked form. "I don't think I can read with you like that."

"I'm going to give you two choices, peto. One, read to me."

"Or two?"

"Or two, you come here right now, and we make our own story."

It's a struggle to stay in place when everything in my soul wants to sprint through the woods naked and bury myself deep inside her. But the memory of what one kiss did to me has me rooted to the floor.

With a heavy sigh, I pull the covers back on my bed and climb in. It's the first time I've even sat on my bed since Nova left. I've spent every night on the sofa with memories of her.

What will happen after tonight?

Swiping the iPad screen, I open the book to the first page and begin to read. Nova's eyes never waver from mine, and I feel her watching me intently as I read. I stumble over paragraph after paragraph when my focus shifts from the words on the page to Nova's naked body tempting me toward the light.

I get two chapters in before I lose the ability to multitask.

"Touch yourself," I command. A low, agonized growl escapes from the back of my throat when she doesn't hesitate.

Her hands slide up her sides to cup her full breasts, and I bite my tongue when she pinches her nipples and pulls roughly.

"How do you want me to touch myself?" She whimpers through the words.

"Like I'm the one touching you."

"Tell me what to do," she begs, and I toss the iPad to the side. I knew what I was doing when I started this, and I also told her I might not survive it. Just not for the reasons she might think.

"Fuck." I stare up at the ceiling to gain an ounce of control. "Suck on your finger."

She does as I ask.

"Bring it to your clit. Show me how you come."

Nova shakes her head. "Please, Ashton. Please touch me."

I lean into the screen, so close my nose nearly touches it. Her eyes catch mine, and eventually, she nods, snaking her hand down her smooth skin until it lands between her legs.

"Are you wet?"

"Yes." She moans. She's too far from the screen for me to see, but I find everything I need in her face as her hands move over her body.

"Do you dream of me touching you, sweetheart?"

"God, yes."

"How do we do it? Am I gentle and slow?"

Her head thrashes against the pillows.

"No? Do I suck on your clit until it almost hurts?"

Her breathing hitches, and I watch with desperation clawing at my chest as her hand speeds up.

"And when you're about to come, I'll pinch your clit as my cock enters you in one thrust. Tell me, baby, could you take all of me?"

Her eyes fly open and search the screen. "I—I can't see you," she whimpers.

The last thread of willpower snaps, and I grab my dick with a rough tug. Nova licks her lips when I put it in view of the camera. Her body convulses, and she comes with the sweetest sounds and my name on her lips.

Her belly quivers and her legs go stiff as the aftershocks continue. I've never seen a more beautiful sight.

"I want to see you come," she pleads, and I have to grip my base to the point of pain to keep from shooting off.

I lift the phone back to my face, she does the same with hers, and we stare at each other for a few seconds.

"You came so nicely for me, sweetheart. Sleep now." Knowing I won't be in any condition to see her tomorrow, I stumble over a lie. "I won't be able to call tomorrow. But I'll talk to you in a couple of days."

"Ashton," she warns.

"Sleep, baby. Sweet dreams."

I disconnect the call before I'm forced to tell another lie to her face.

Even knowing the pain that's coming has nothing on the pain that lances my chest every time I walk away from her, and it's growing more excruciating each time.

"Ghost?" Killian calls from downstairs. "Let's get this fecking thing over with."

And like a sad balloon, my cock deflates. Pulling on a pair of boxers and gym shorts, I head down the stairs to pay for my sins.

CHAPTER 25

NOVA

The blissed-out state that usually comes with an epic orgasm is short-lived because Ashton hangs up on me.

I tap an irritated beat on the floor with my feet, and stare at my knuckles as they turn white from gripping the edge of my mattress.

He barely said anything, and I came like a war missile hitting its target. Have I ever come that hard?

Who knew phone sex could be so satisfying?

But it wasn't really phone sex, was it? Ashton hardly touched himself.

And then he hung up on me.

Am I reading this wrong?

Who has he turned me into?

Maybe he doesn't want me.

I stomp to my feet and pace my room in an angry fit. Briefly, I consider heading down to the main floor of the lodge where GG set me up with a sewing room to get some work done, but then the image of Ashton's face right after I came gets stuck in my head, and I sink back onto my bed.

I'm not misreading that expression. He wants me. He doesn't want to want me, but he does.

Scanning the room that's beginning to feel like home, I land on the doll. The beast. Ashton. Picking it up, I run my hands over it tenderly. It might be the sweetest gift I've ever received.

He said I was his dream catcher. He has to know he's mine too, right?

I clutch the toy to my chest and feel my eyes grow hot as I replay the last few hours in my head.

I know he wants me. At least, I'm reasonably certain he does. I know I want him. But our most honest conversations only happen over the phone. Why? Why can't he tell me these things in person?

Anger flares hot, and I pace my room again. "Why?" I hiss into the empty room. "He kisses me, then walks away. He makes me come, then hangs up on me. Who does that?"

I'm forcing my foot into a pair of leggings before I realize I'm getting dressed. But once a plan forms, I know I won't back down. If Ashton wants to play games, we'll play games in person.

A nervous smile tugs at the corners of my lips. Ready or not, Ashton. Here I come.

∾

Standing on Ashton's porch, I half expect the door to open on its own. I mean, the guy has more security than the Pentagon, but the longer I stand here, the more a sense of dread pounds with every heartbeat.

Do I knock? I'm about to raise my fist when the scanner to my right lights up, and I hesitate. Does he still have me in his system? What's the worst thing that'll happen if I place my palm on the reader and he's booted me from the system?

He's going to know I'm here soon anyway, right?

With a breath so deep it hurts, I place my palm against the flat surface. It immediately turns green. The mechanical sounds of the lock whirring are followed by a click. Slowly, I open the door and poke my head inside.

Here goes nothing.

Removing my shoes, I leave them by the front door. It's dark as I make my way to the family room from memory. I'm tempted to ask his smart home to turn on the lights, and that's probably the intelligent thing to do, but I have a sinking feeling in my gut that has me holding the baton-sized flashlight a little closer to my chest.

When I don't find him in the family room or the kitchen, I place my ear to his secret office door. A stupid move on my part because I'm willing to bet it's soundproof, but I do it anyway as my heartbeat picks up.

The feeling of something being wrong beats like a ticking time bomb in my chest. Especially when I see a jacket too large to be his own tossed carelessly on the floor beside the sofa. The need to shout for him, call out to him, is so strong, but it gets lodged in my throat as I head toward the stairs.

My right foot lifts to the first step when I hear a whoosh and freeze, straining to hear it again. I can almost make out sounds.

Where are they coming from?

For the first time since I arrived in Vermont, Ashton's home has an ominous feeling to it. It's too still. Too quiet. He hasn't even spoken to me through the speakers yet. Where is he? It's like I'm walking through the haunted house of horrors all alone and blood rushes in my ears. The safety this house usually creates is nowhere to be found tonight.

Standing alone in the dark, true fear makes my head pound. I flatten my body to the wall and slide silently against it. The sounds slowly become more pronounced. Though I have no idea what they are, they beat in time to a soundtrack my mind wants to flee.

It feels like it takes an eternity to follow the sounds that come and go like the wind until I'm at a door that leads to the basement. Ashton's gym? Would he be working out this late?

I almost laugh when I realize that's probably exactly what he's doing. He didn't allow himself to come. He has to work off that energy somehow. Right?

As quietly as I can, I slide the door open and tiptoe down the stairs.

The lighting is muted and only illuminates a boxing ring in the center of the room.

My brain is playing tricks on me. It can't compute what it's seeing.

"This has to be enough, Ghost. Enough. You have to fix your shite, mate, before it kills you." Killian's thick Irish brogue breaks through my confusion, and I sprint toward them. "Say it's enough," he yells just before throwing a bone-crushing punch into Ashton's side.

I don't hear Ashton's reply. Just the sickening sound of another punch hitting skin as Ashton stands there with his arms spread wide.

"Stop it," I scream as I barrel into the ring.

Both men stumble, but I don't break my stride. I jump onto Killian's back and swing the heavy flashlight as hard as I can. It's the only weapon I have.

I know I can't take this man, but hopefully I can slow him down enough for Ashton to help me.

Nothing matters except keeping Ashton safe.

"What the feck?" Killian yells as the shaft of the flashlight connects with his forehead.

With one quick move, he has me flat on my back and is standing over me with blood trickling down his forehead.

"Oh, shit. I'm going to die," I mutter.

"Nova?" Ashton wheezes. "Kill, let her up," he demands, and I see the instant Killian's gaze clears. He didn't see me when he threw me to the mat. He saw an enemy.

"Feck. What the hell are you doing here?" Killian curses angrily, stepping back and hauling me to my feet with one hand fisting the front of my shirt.

"I…" I'm so confused. "I…" Without thought, I swing the flashlight again, but Killian catches my wrist easily and squeezes just enough that I drop my useless excuse for a weapon.

Ashton takes an uneasy step forward. Before he speaks, he spits blood onto the floor, and tears spill down my cheeks.

"You're hurt." I dive for my flashlight in case this monster decides to hit Ashton again.

But Killian is expecting me this time and pins me to the mat before I can reach it. "I'm not the enemy here, lass."

"Get the fuck off me!" I fight with everything I have. Scratching, kicking, biting blindly until he curses again. He lifts me to my feet, turns me around, then shoves me forward.

"Nova," Ashton's weak voice pleads, and I finally take in his face. I search him, turn to Killian and back again.

"I don't understand," I wail. I can't make sense of what I'm seeing. Why is Ashton a battered mess from his chest to his waist but not a bruise in sight on his face or hands? Why doesn't Killian at least have a single bruise or welt? Surely Ashton isn't this bad of a fighter.

Why isn't Killian trying to hurt me? Or Ashton? Why are we all just standing here staring at each other?

Ashton sinks to his knees, and I see unimaginable pain flashing in his eyes. But it isn't physical pain that causes it. It's something that runs much, much deeper than I could have ever imagined.

This is a pain he may truly never recover from.

"Oh, Ashton." My words are a sob as I shake my head. "You're…are you? Is this…?"

"He's punishing himself for not being able to save the fecking world," Killian spits, holding a towel up to the cut on his head.

Ashton sits on his knees in the center of the ring. His shoulders sag forward, his head dips, and he stays mute.

Every rational person in the world would tell me to run as fast as I can. Get away from whatever this is and never look back, but through teary eyes and hiccups, I still just see a man. A man I might love a little. A man so broken he needs superglue to be whole again.

What if I'm his glue?

My body makes the decision for me. Turning my head toward Killian, I glare at him, trying to decipher if I can trust this animal. When he makes no move to kill me, I nod.

"Where is the first aid kit?"

Killian glances between Ashton and me, and when Ash says nothing, Killian nods toward the stairs. "Probably in his office from last time."

I take a step forward, then turn on him. "The last time? You did this to him before?" I seethe.

"Nova," Ashton whispers.

"Listen, lass. If it weren't for me, he'd be dead. Think of that."

Tears clog my throat as I watch Ashton for a reaction. When one doesn't come, I know Killian is telling the truth.

"Do you want him dead?" I force out a shaky breath.

"Feck no," Killian growls. "I'm trying to help him."

"I think we're done with your help. If you touch him again, I'll cut your balls from your body and suffocate you with them. Are we clear?"

Killian smirks but nods with respect in his eyes.

"Can you help him to a chair without punching him again, asshole?"

"Nova," Ashton mutters.

"Don't. Don't you Nova me. This," I say, waving between Ashton and Killian, "is never happening again. I don't care if I have to handcuff myself to you for the rest of your life. This will not happen again."

Without waiting for a response, I turn and march up the stairs.

"It's time to let go, Ghost," I hear Killian's low words, and I pause. "It's time to walk away. It was never your fight to begin with. I think this girl proves it's time for you to live. Don't ruin it with a misguided sense of duty."

"Nova," Ashton says loudly enough that I know he's ushering me along. "My office."

Like a petulant teenager, I stomp up the stairs in search of the first aid kit.

CHAPTER 26

NOVA

I open the drawers of the desk for the second time like the stupid first aid kit will magically appear, but the drawer is empty. The entire room is empty.

Standing, I'm scanning the space when a thought hits me.

Did he mean his real office?

No one is allowed in there.

Right?

An unsettling feeling takes root in my stomach as I walk on wobbly legs to the Murphy door and place my hand above the hidden scanner. My skin tingles as guilt hits me hard. I glance over my shoulder like I'm doing something wrong. The wall lights up around my palm, and the door silently pops out a few centimeters. Just enough for me to tug it open.

He's letting me in.

When the door opens, it takes me three tries to get my voice to work. "Elpis, turn on the lights."

The room slowly comes into view, and my knees tremble. It's nothing like the first time I was in here. The dark wall at the back is lit with innocent faces of children and adults all overlapping each other, with notes attached to each one like something you'd see in a crime show.

A sick feeling has my gag reflex engaging, and I double over, dropping my hands onto my knees.

"He let you in," Killian's dark voice causes a riot of angry emotions to take over. But his words beat against my chest like a jackhammer.

He steps into the room and presses a button on Ashton's desk that illuminates another wall. Countless faces peer down at me, and I struggle for breath.

"These," Killian says, pointing to the wall, "are the ones he saved."

"Oh, God." I turn my head from side to side. "No—" My throat closes before I can get anything else out.

"Killian!" Ashton's volcanic tone causes my body to shake. He enters the room, grimacing with each step, and barks, "Elpis. Black out."

The walls go dark, but I'm unable to move. The low overhead lighting casts shadows all around the room, and I ball my fists so tightly at my sides my knuckles ache. The pulse point at my wrist stands out against my fair skin and I keep my focus on the unsteady thumping of it.

"Can you take care of him?" Killian asks, finally breaking the silence.

Slowly, I drag my gaze to his. "I hate you," I snarl, needing to release these emotions on someone. I want to throw something at him, anything, but there isn't a goddamn thing in this office either. No stapler, no cup of pens. Everything is too neat. Too forgettable.

"That's fair," he says with a shrug, even though it's anything but. "Nothing is broken, but he'll need ice and arnica cream—if he'll allow it—since he won't take anything else."

Killian turns to Ashton. "Mate?"

Ashton lifts his eyes to the monster.

"Let go. It's time. It has been for a long time. Learn who you can be without the weight of grief."

Ashton coughs and clutches his side.

"Get out," I yell. "Get out. Just get the fuck out, Killian." My rage might be misplaced right now, but I'll deal with that later when I can control my emotions.

"Nova," Ashton says grimly, crossing the room with measured steps.

"Don't." I hold up a hand to halt his forward motion. "Don't 'Nova' me. Not right now."

He nods and exchanges a look I can't read with Killian.

"You can hate me all ya want, mate. You were spiraling to burn out, and ya know it. Have been for years. It's time to let go."

My body trembles, and I wrap my arms around my middle when I hear Killian's heavy footsteps disappear. I become painfully aware that Killian is only seen when he wants you to see him.

Ashton and I stand in silence for what feels like an eternity. Each sitting with our own thoughts until I can't take it anymore.

"Why could I get in here?"

"You've had access since the first time I caught you trying to break in," he says quietly.

"Why?"

"Because it's the safest place I can offer. I did it right after you tried to get in. Before our nights on the sofa became our routine. Before our phone calls. I don't know why other than it felt like the right thing to do. I had to know I could keep you safe."

"Like Sadie."

"Similar, but the fatherly instincts I have with her have never been in my mind with you."

"Why, Ashton? Why were you hurting yourself?"

"Let's go into the family room."

I shake my head. "No. I have too many questions." I glance around at the dark walls again and feel a stab of sadness so visceral I clutch my chest. "And I need to know what the fuck this is."

As I wave my hand around at the walls, it's like all the fight leaves his body, and he sinks into the chair behind the desk.

"Sometimes—" His voice cracks, and he clears it before beginning again. "Sometimes, I need the pain to know I'm alive. To feel...to feel something."

"But you were feeling something, with me. Weren't you?"

He nods. "I'm fucked up, Nova. Really and truly."

"You were punishing yourself for feeling happy."

"I haven't needed this kind of outlet since Sadie was little. It's been years since anyone's light has shone through on me. I learned to accept Sadie's. It took time, but I did. You, this, it's unexpected, and I don't know how to process it when I still have so much guilt on my hands."

I scan the walls again. "Show me." My insides quiver, and I slowly lower myself to a chair in the corner of the room.

Ashton searches my expression, and with a sad nod, he gives the order. "Elpis, all bright."

The walls flicker like a neon sign coming to life. Face after face is illuminated with a note or a date attached to it.

"Killian was right. These are the people we've saved. For the most part, anyway. I'm not sure you can ever truly be whole after their lived experiences."

I stand and cross to the shorter wall.

"Those are my failures." His words are pained, his shoulders bowed, his hands clasped tightly in his lap.

"You have a photographic memory," I say, suddenly remembering something he'd said earlier about the faces of his mistakes haunting him.

He nods.

The wall has hundreds of photos that all seem to fan out from two in the center. A red-haired girl with fair skin and scared eyes. The one next to her is a dark-haired boy who can't be more than five or six, yet seems vaguely familiar.

"Why do all the photos connect here? Who are these two?"

Ashton answers without lifting his head. "Loki Kane and Pacen McComb. The beginning of my end."

CHAPTER 27

ASHTON

*E*xhaustion like I've never known toils through every muscle in my body with that confession. It also comes with an overwhelming sense of relief that nearly knocks me unconscious.

If I go down this road with her, there's no turning back. The world is going to crash and burn. I scan the walls around me.

What will happen to them if I walk away?

My stomach lurches with guilt that sits painfully in the back of my throat.

"I don't understand," Nova whispers.

"Why aren't you running from here kicking and screaming?" I ask instead of explaining. I know she'll have questions, and if I give in to temptation, I fear the floodgates will open and I'll never get them closed again.

Can I give this all up? Can I throw my responsibilities at her feet?

What will she say when she finds out?

My brain is firing in every direction, making it hard to focus, but every time she speaks, she draws me in like magic. My breathing evens out, and my thoughts converge.

"Because you're here," she answers simply.

Air whistles through my teeth at her admission. Fuck me.

"I don't know where to go from here, peto, but here is the only place I can be right now." She spins in place, taking in all the faces. So many faces. "Does anyone know about this? All of this?"

"Everyone had a part to play. Loki knows what the military has told him, but not all of it."

"So this is all government stuff?"

"No." I laugh darkly. "This is as far from the government as you can get."

"Mafia?" She gasps.

"No." A strange, warming sensation hits my chest. "Not mafia, princess. More vigilante, I guess."

"But the military knows about it? You said Loki..."

"They know and look the other way, as long as we keep doing their job and bringing these people home. Most of them, anyway."

"You're doing what the military can't."

There's nothing funny about this, but I can't contain a smirk. "I don't exactly follow the letter of the law, so yes. I get things done that others can't. Or won't."

"Are you a criminal?"

That's the crux of it, isn't it? Am I a criminal?

"I've done what needs to be done to those who deserve it." I pause when she frowns. I need her to understand me. "It's always for the innocent." I glance at the wall, then jerk my attention back to her.

"Why are these two in the center?"

"Because my father changed his course in life to save Loki, and in the process brought Pacen into our lives." Pinching the bridge of my nose, I hide my wince when the muscles pull at my sore ribs. "Nova, I...this is eighteen years' worth of shit I've been doing. I don't even know how to begin to explain it. And once I do, I'll lose you too."

As soon as I say it, I know it's the truth. My life is too dark and morbid for this beautiful princess. I'd only dim her light.

"You don't get to tell me how I'll react," she says trying to portray a sense of authority. "Wait, eighteen years? Ashton, are you telling me..."

I almost laugh when I see her mind working out the calculations in her head. Yeah, I was a kid when this all began. It's never hit harder than watching Sadie grow up. Shaking my head, I will myself to focus. It's never been this difficult before.

"I'm not telling you, sweetheart. I'm preparing myself. It's been a long time since I've wanted anything for myself enough to even consider opening this door."

Her shocked gasp sends a buzzing through my chest, and I have to actively force my hands to stay at my sides.

"What do you want, Ashton?" She speaks so low that it hides the trepidation in her tone, but I see it in the way her eyes go wide with emotion.

Standing, I ignore her question and cross the room with a neutral expression, even though every step is excruciating. Killian had only gotten in a handful of punches before my little hellion attacked him, but they were direct hits where he knew it would hurt the most.

"We will talk about you going all badass hellcat on Killian back there. Don't ever fucking do that again. I died a hundred times in less than five seconds. If he hadn't recognized you? Jesus, Nova. You could have been hurt."

"So I should have just let him beat the shit out of you? No, Ashton. No more deflecting. What do you want?" she demands.

I stop right in front of her. Lifting my arms, I cup her cheeks with both hands. The pain at my ribs is forgotten the second I make contact with her soft skin. "Isn't it obvious?" I whisper, then lean in so close my lips ghost over hers. "I want what I can't have. What isn't meant to be mine. What might ruin us both."

183

"What's that?" she murmurs, licking her lips, and I swear I can already taste them.

With her eyes on my mouth, I slowly lower my jaw to brush against her skin. "You. I want you, Nova. And all of your sunshine and starry nights. I want what might ruin us both. Your love."

"Ashton," she moans against me, and I'm lucky I remember how to breathe. The physical pain I need to feel alive is replaced by a feeling of hope that shreds me. The mental and emotional scars I've carried for longer than I can remember heal with the promise of her touch.

"If I put everything on the line, and I lose you anyway, at least then I'll die with something other than despair in my heart. I've never wanted to take that risk before, Nova. Do you understand what I'm saying?"

She shakes her head. I can feel her mouth opening and closing against my cheek, but she doesn't reply.

"I'm tired, baby. I'm tired of a fight I was never going to win. But I was prepared to see it through until my last breath. And then you walked in and made me see something other than the evil that fills my soul. I don't know how you do it. Or if you even mean to."

I'm losing my mind.

"I don't blame you if you walk away, Nova. There isn't a scenario in the universe where this is normal."

"You want my love? Even though I've spent years thinking happiness for me meant one-night stands. You're willing to risk…risk everything on the chance that I'll stay?"

Pulling back just an inch, I search her eyes. "I've been spiraling toward an end one way or another. Killian was right about that. I was either going to get out, or the darkness of what I do would have taken me under sooner rather than later. I've always known that. I thought it was my destiny. My duty."

"Ashton, I—"

I cut her off with a kiss. A kiss that numbs my pain better

than morphine. When she melts into me, my tongue darts into her mouth. Exploring. Tasting. Experiencing her in the most delicious of ways.

Fucking hell. I never knew a kiss could be like this. My limited sexual experiences mean nothing as instinct takes over and my hands fist in her hair. A primal need turning me into the beast I've always known I was.

Her body molds to mine, and I realize her hands have been roaming over my chest and biceps and I had no idea. But it makes me break the kiss anyway.

"I...fuck. This is hard. I need to tell you my story, Nova. Then give you time to decide where you want to be."

Her eyes are foggy with lust and, as fucked up as it is, pride hits me hard.

I did that to her.

Me.

Ashton.

The man. Not the ghost. Not the beast.

Me.

That is what she does for me. She makes me feel like a man. One who hasn't spent his life doing shady shit in the shadows of the worst parts of humanity. But one who has a chance. One who just might survive the guilt that threatens to crush him. A man with obligations he had no business taking on but did anyway.

A man who could be loved.

To my ultimate shock and disbelief, tears slide down my cheeks.

"Okay," she whispers and clears her throat. "Okay. Let's sit down." Nova laces our fingers together and tugs on my arm.

So much touch.

Touch that I'm beginning to crave when only a short time ago it felt like a branding.

Swallowing takes effort as I follow her to the sofa. When we reach it, she drops my hand to pull her hair back from her face. I watch fascinated as she wraps a band around it and twists. Her hands move like they've done it a million times, and when she drops her arms, her hair sits in a messy pile on her head.

I guess she has done it a million times. How weird that I notice something so mundane now. But I can't take my eyes off her hair as she tucks first one leg and then the other underneath her and pats the cushion, silently telling me to sit.

Have I really missed out on so much life that hair has become interesting?

Nova stares into my eyes with a small smile on her lips. "I came here because my brother knew you'd protect me, Ashton. Now I understand that protecting the people you love is all you know. But who protects you? Who keeps your heart safe while you're busy saving the world?"

Uncomfortable, I tug at the hair that's fallen onto my forehead and look out the window.

"We all need someone in our corner, peto. Even slightly scary vigilantes."

That has my attention. "You—You're scared of me?"

I drop onto the sofa with a thud, not caring about my aching body, but I'm careful to give her space.

She's scared of me?

Heavy breaths escape her nostrils like she's trying to calm herself down and failing spectacularly.

"No, Ashton. I've never once been scared of you. I'm scared for you. Scared that you won't be able to share the burden that's crushing you. Scared you won't be able to allow yourself to live and laugh and—and love."

CHAPTER 28

NOVA

*M*y hands shake so I tuck them under my legs. If I'm being honest, my entire body is trembling on the inside, and I work hard to keep it from Ashton.

A million different scenarios fill my head, making it hard to focus.

What has he done?

Why is he doing it?

Am I in danger?

Could I walk away even if I wanted to?

Do I want to?

No. The one thing I do know is that I belong here, even if it makes me the dumb woman in the horror movie who runs to the attic instead of out the door. With him, I belong. Even if only temporarily.

The certainty of that hits me with emotion so intense my heart flutters in my chest. If I walk away at the end of this as his friend, I know I'll always be tied to this man in a way I didn't know possible.

And that's the realization that steadies my fragile nerves.

Sometimes in life, you connect with another human, and

against all odds, you fit. For the first time in my life, I feel like I fit with this broken man.

"I don't even know where to begin, Nova," he admits, dragging me into the present with such defeat in his tone that my chest clenches painfully. "This is almost twenty years' worth of secrets."

Placing a hand on his, I scoot closer until my folded knees rest against his thigh. I scan his face for a grimace, a tensed muscle that says I'm too close, but it doesn't come, so I open my heart and tell him my truth.

"I'm not going anywhere. Take your time, peto. But in my experience, it always helps to start at the beginning. I'll be right here for as long as it takes. I'll be your safe space to fall as long as you'll allow."

He runs the fingers of his free hand through his hair multiple times, the movements rough and hurried. He's agitated but not at me. His truth is buried so deep he might split in two trying to excavate it.

"I was fifteen," he says with a burst of air that seems to deflate his entire body.

"Fifteen when what?"

"When my dad died, and I took over everything."

Surely he doesn't mean...

"I was in his office when I shouldn't have been," he admits. His voice is detached like he's talking about a movie, not a memory. "I was always doing shit I shouldn't be doing. Anyway, he had a fight with my brother, and I called him out on it. I—I didn't know what was happening at first. He became clumsy, stumbling around his office as I yelled at him to fix things with Halton. When he finally met my eyes, I knew. I knew I was going to lose him."

"Oh, God. Ashton. I'm so sorry."

He shakes his head to cut me off.

"He knew it too. I know that now. His very last struggle was if he should trust me with the information that changed my life. In the end, he didn't have a choice. He gave me a thumb drive I was supposed to get to his partner."

"But you didn't?" I guess.

"No, I did. But only after I hacked into it and changed the course of all our lives."

We're silent as I process this information, but any way I look at it, his comment about his dad doesn't sit well with me.

Picking at a cuticle on my left hand, I keep my eyes averted. My lips twist as I chew on the inside of my cheek, and my skin heats as Ashton's body leans into mine.

"What's troubling you?" he whispers.

Tit for tat.

I inhale so deeply that it's almost painful while I search for a way to address something that seems so obvious to me. When I glance up, he's staring at me with a look I can only describe as wonder. He watches me like I'm the extraordinary one here.

This broken man has no idea how special he is.

"Do you think that maybe he hesitated in giving you that information because he knew you'd be able to decode it? That you were smart enough to figure all this out and get caught up in a life he was trying to protect you from? I don't know anything about your father, but if he's anything like the rest of you, don't you think it's more likely he was trying to shelter you than he didn't trust you?"

His face screws up as he processes my question.

Ashton releases a heavy sigh. His chin hits his chest, and he sinks deeper into the sofa as exhaustion takes over. "It's possible," he finally concedes. He lifts both hands to tug on the ends of his hair, and I have the strongest desire to smooth his frazzled edges.

His haunted eyes lock with mine. I bet he's literally never shared this with anyone. He's been holding it inside, and it's slowly killing his soul.

He needs me. But more than that? I want to be his safe space like he's been for me this past month.

"What did you find on the thumb drive?"

"The worst humanity has to offer," he says with zero hesitation. "There were thirty-four children and young adults with coordinates for locations and very detailed profiles for each one. It took me a few hours because, at fifteen, you don't yet know that monsters aren't hiding under your bed. They're sitting in the mansions next door to yours, ready to sell off their firstborn for greed and power."

I gulp and squeeze his hand when I can't force my words to come.

"It wasn't until I got to the thirty-fourth dossier that things snapped into place."

"What was the thirty-fourth one?"

"Not what, who," he answers grimly. "It was Pacen. She had been my friend for years. Quiet. Painfully shy, but when she would come to my parents' house with her older sister, we just… hit it off. The information in her file led me to what my father had been doing since Loki was in grade school."

A sick feeling hits my stomach, and acid rises high in my throat. I'm not sure I want to know, but he needs this. Ashton needs me, and I force myself to remain silent.

He closes his eyes as if the memories themselves are too much to bear. I watch, barely breathing, as he collects himself. When he does, his expression is so sorrowful, so haunted, that I feel like I've been slapped.

"The real monsters in life, Nova? Are the ones who sell their souls to the devil while writing checks to charities and smiling for cameras."

"I don't know what you mean," I whisper. I search his eyes, hoping he can explain what he's talking about in a way I'll understand.

"There's a secret society called The Ravens. It's a group of rich and powerful men and women from all over the world. They use their influence and money to ensure they stay in power. And they keep it hidden from the rest of the world by ensuring loyalty from the very first day."

"H—How do they do that?" I stammer.

"A sacrifice," he spits. His jaw is so tight I hear his teeth grinding. "To enter the society, you're expected to give up a child."

My stomach heaves, and I gasp for breath.

"That's how my dad met Loki's mother. Loki's father had gotten his mother pregnant intentionally. He wined and dined her. Made her fall for him, all so he wouldn't have to sacrifice one of his legitimate children. Loki's father made the fatal mistake of underestimating a mother's love. When she found out what was happening, she fought back."

I open my mouth, but I can't speak. This is worse than a horror movie, but I can't look away.

"Loki's stepfather helped them get away," he continues. "As far as I can tell, Mr. Kane brought them to Waverley-Cay, where I grew up, around the same time The Ravens were circling my father." Ashton stands and paces in front of the coffee table.

I sit back, pulling my knees to my chest and wrapping my arms around them as tightly as they'll go. "Did your father join that group?"

He stops, and his expression softens as he stares at me. "No, princess. I may hate my father sometimes, but he was the best man I've ever known. He did the exact opposite. He made it his mission to ruin them. Shortly after Loki's family arrived in Waverley-Cay, Mr. Kane and my dad were contacted by SIA, a secret government organization that eventually recruited Loki."

"And you?"

His eyes slowly leave mine, and he stares out the window. Eventually, he nods. "And me. SIA tried to coerce them into going undercover, and at first, my dad was on board, at least according to his partner, Ryan. But when he realized the government wasn't really interested in saving those people, he took matters into his own hands. Loki's stepdad, my father, and his partner, Ryan Nicoles, started Envision. I own it now with Seth and Loki. Seth and I run the office here, Dillon Henry runs the New York office, and Loki runs a branch in North Carolina."

"But it's not just a security company?"

He turns a sad smile on me that steals my breath.

"We do regular security jobs for the rich and famous, but behind the curtain, it puts missions into place to rescue the sacrifices."

"What do The Ravens do with the kids?" I ask when I finally get the nerve.

"They send them away. Most go to a special boarding school where they're kept until they're old enough to marry, or they're sold to form allegiances with other families. No one is worried about their well-being other than how it pertains to The Ravens' agenda. Boys fare better than the girls most of the time, but they basically spend years being brainwashed into serving whatever The Ravens' end goal is. The ones who don't fall into line, they…" He swallows hard. "They go to auction." The venom in his voice causes tears to form at the corner of my eyes.

This is what he's given up his life for. No wonder he couldn't just walk away.

I drop my head into my hands and try to process this information, but thoughts are whirling through my mind faster than I can keep up. I'm drowning in information overload. "Why? How?" I hear myself mumble.

"Before my father died, a man named Macomb had been desperate to do business with him. He was the father of two girls. The older one dated Easton for a long time, and Pacen was my friend. Now I know those friendships were encouraged so my father could keep a closer eye on them. Anyway, Macomb was so desperate that after his oldest daughter died, he was ready to give up Pacen to join The Ravens. He was running out of money, and he was tied up with Loki's biological father, Antonio Black."

When I stare blankly, he explains. "Antonio Black was the head of a Boston area crime syndicate."

"Oh my God. It's all so…so complicated."

"There are a lot of bad people in this world, princess. And the worst of the worst are the Ravens."

"I— So, where is Pacen now?"

Do you love her? I desperately want to ask but zip my lips shut tight.

What would his answer be?

Am I strong enough to know?

Ashton sits down beside me. "I don't know. The night I was injured, I thought she had betrayed me. Her father's men found me, held me hostage, and tortured me right in front of her. I know now they were torturing her too, but where my torture was physical, hers was mental. A slip of a knife physically scarred me, but it sent a message to her that he could always get to her."

Ashton releases a sigh that sounds like it weighs a thousand tons. When I search his eyes, he's there, but his memory is far away.

"We only escaped alive that night because Loki's wife went all Lara Croft and caused enough of a distraction so backup could get to our location," he finally says. "SIA was disbanded right after that night, but Pacen decided to go out on her own. She's essentially doing the same thing I am, just on a smaller scale."

"Why do you call it an injury instead of an attack?"

"Because I'm not a victim." He says it like a curse. "If I had my head on straight that night, they wouldn't have gotten to me, and my entire family wouldn't have been in danger."

Watching his body go rigid, I know this is a battle I won't win, but I wonder if he'll ever be able to see himself through my eyes. He carries the weight of the world on his shoulders, and it's crushing him.

I shake my head and try to organize my thoughts. "It sounds like you and Pacen have shared trauma and experiences that would benefit others in this situation. Why wouldn't you work together?"

His sigh tells the story of a million secrets. "I honestly don't know. I've never gotten answers from her." He shifts uncomfortably and his gaze darts around the room. "Pacen and I, we were intimate a few times. The first time was shortly after my father died. The Ravens had kicked her out of boarding school, and I had just learned what they had planned for her. We thought it would keep her from the auction. It was her idea," he says quickly.

"We were fifteen, and I was just learning how to steal money from my brothers' trust funds—without getting caught—to keep the funding going for The Apollyon. That's who Killian and I are. Part of The Apollyon."

"Apollyon. The destroyer," I whisper.

"You know your Greek mythology," he says with a broken smile and tired eyes.

I shrug. One stupid class in college is coming in handy now.

"Do you love her? Pacen?" It's pulled from my lips without my permission.

The question catches him off guard, and he flinches away from me. "I have love for her," he says evasively. "I always will, but I've never loved her. But I have done her wrong, Nova. I did her so wrong." The guilt in his words nearly knocks me over.

I have my doubts about this, but it's not a hill I'm willing to die on, so I change the subject. "Why didn't you tell anyone about the Ravens? Or the impossible situation SIA put you in? It seems like Loki had a right to know this entire time. You could have had someone to talk to. Someone on your side."

"When I was fifteen, I thought I could do it all myself. I got cocky and made a stupid mistake. That's how SIA got to me. They promised I could keep Loki safe if I did things their way.

That meant keeping secrets. By the time I realized I had the power, one secret had snowballed into another. Then another. And another until I didn't know how to get out without hurting everyone I'd spent so many years trying to protect."

"Ashton?"

His face, drawn with lines of worry and regret, lifts to mine. "This was never a battle you could win on your own. You know that, right? No matter how hard you work or how close to death you bring yourself with each new secret, it was never a one-man job."

He nods but doesn't say anything. Doesn't blink. Doesn't even appear to breathe.

"A few years ago, Pacen told my brothers that the secrets of our father were slowly killing me from the inside out."

I nod because I agree, but I'm not the one who has to acknowledge it. "Do you think she's right?"

"My world has been closing in on me for years. I—I'm so tired, Nova." He stiffens next to me, and his fingernails scratch roughly at the scruff on his jaw. "I feel like I'm losing everything. I'm stuck somewhere between the living and the madness that takes better people than me into eternal darkness. The only time I've felt normal in the last twenty years is when…is when I'm with you."

His raspy, whispered admission knocks the wind out of me. It steals my breath and my words. All I have left are actions.

Without thinking too much about it, I stand and hold out my hand. He stares at it for three long beats. The scowl on his face tells me he doesn't understand.

"Trust me, peto."

"Oh, sweetheart. Don't you understand? I do trust you. I trust you more than I trust myself, and that's what worries me. What if I can't keep you safe from me?"

My beautiful peto. Always fighting. In the battle between trust and love, I'll always choose him.

Right then, I lay down my armor in favor of his war. The war for him—for us. For better or worse, I'm here for the long haul. I'll pick my battles to win his war that's raged on for far too long. The war of chaos. And love. Betrayal and loyalty. In the war of Ashton Westbrook versus the world, I'll be his loyal soldier. His sounding board. His friend.

"Ashton?"

He lifts his glistening eyes to mine.

"You can only hurt me if I allow it. Let me be the one to help you out of the dark?"

When he slips his fingers into mine, his expression softens. "You already have, princess. But I think I'm a sinking ship. If I go down, I can't take you with me."

"I'm an excellent swimmer, Ashton Westbrook. And I'm stubborn enough to keep you afloat until we're on even ground. That I promise you."

He stands, and we face each other without blinking, eyes locked on each other. The moment is intense and raw. I see the instant he lays down his sword, and it nearly guts me.

"Why would you do that for me?"

Slowly, I raise my hands and gently place them on his shoulders. I give him a second to adjust to the contact before speaking. "You said you wanted my love. Was that the truth?"

"More than anything. But I'm afraid of what it will do to you," he chokes out. His Adam's apple bobbing draws my attention, but I don't break our eye contact.

"Well, I want the same thing, but I'm not afraid, Ashton. I'm not afraid of you or the work it will take to get us there."

"You should be," he grumbles.

A smile tugs at the corners of my lips. "I've never been very good at shoulda, coulda, wouldas. I know there's a lot more you need to tell me, but not tonight. Tonight you need to sleep, and I need to process, so let's go to bed."

The air shifts between us, and the emotion of the moment is

replaced by lust, but I take a small step back. "Just to sleep, peto. For now, we need to replenish your body and soul, starting with a good night's sleep."

"I've only had a handful of those in twenty years."

Leaning in, I place my lips to his ear. "That's why I'm going to sleep next to you. Skin to skin, I'm going to chase away the darkness. I'm going to hold your hand while you dig your way out of the despair you're drowning in. I'm going to be your human life raft until you can swim again."

"Just promise me one thing?" he begs with more emotion than I've ever seen from him. The tears slide down his face and wet my cheek, but I don't pull away.

"Anything," I promise.

"Don't let me ruin you. Don't let me be the one to extinguish your light."

This man. He just can't help himself. Broken and battered, he'll go to his grave protecting those he cares about, but I'll be damned if I allow that to happen anytime soon.

"My light can't be extinguished, Ashton. It will always light the way home for us both. I promise."

His shoulders slump forward, as though he's finally shedding some of the burden he carries like shackles around his soul. It's all the sign I need to gently tug on his arm and lead him to his bedroom.

Once inside, I let his hand drop and take a step back. The room is shrouded in shadows, but the moon is high in the sky. It offers a sliver of light filtering in through the window, but it's enough. I can see his expression clearly as I lift my shirt over my head and drop it to the floor. My bra and leggings come off next.

His jaw clenches, but eventually, he sheds his clothes too. As much as I want to stand and stare at this beautiful man, I know it will make him uneasy, so I don't. Instead, I walk with purpose to the edge of his bed and pull down the covers.

"Which side do you sleep on?"

He opens his mouth, then closes it again. "I don't really have a side. I don't sleep in here much."

I press my lips into a thin line, but I nod and wave at the mattress. He slowly crosses the room, and I can't help but notice how his muscles strain with the movements.

When we're standing side by side, he lowers his head.

"Climb in, peto."

He does as I ask, and I slide in beside him. We lie there staring at the ceiling while our breathing slowly syncs, then I lift my arms above my head. "Come here, Ashton. Skin to skin."

"That's not a good idea," he growls.

"It is. Human touch is one of the most powerful healers we have at our disposal. There will be time for, ah, other things, but tonight is just about feeling safe. With each other. This is as much for me as it is for you."

He lifts up on his elbow to stare down at me. "What do you want me to do? Curl up into you? Are you going to spoon me?" The disbelief in his tone and the confusion on his face almost make me laugh. Almost.

"That's exactly what I'm going to do, Ashton. One way or another, I will hold you tonight just like you did for me those nights on your sofa."

"We weren't fucking naked then, Nova."

He drops his gaze, and it lands on my nipple. It puckers painfully under his scrutiny, and I barely contain a moan.

"Skin to skin." My words are wanton, and his eyes dart back to mine. Ashton's entire body is wound tight. But slowly, he slips in next to me and rests his head on my chest. His ragged breathing ghosts over my bare breast.

"Fuck," he mutters. The damp heat of his words floats over my nipple like he sucked it straight into his mouth, and I forget everything but him and me.

CHAPTER 29

ASHTON

*M*y cheek lands on her soft skin, the fleshy part just below her collarbone, and an involuntary exhale pulls the tension from my body at the contact.

Nova shivers beneath me, and my lips twitch into a smile, but my arms are still rigid at my side. It's not a comfortable position, so even as my soul relaxes, I don't know how to fit into her.

"Hug me, Ashton." Before she's even finished saying my name, Nova has pulled my arm across her middle and pats it into place.

More contact. My elbow rests on her hip with my forearm draped across her abdomen and like dominoes, the muscles in my arm race to relax.

My hips shoot forward, and I hook a leg over hers without thinking. The dominoes follow. Everywhere our skin touches my body relaxes.

I try to swallow past the lump lodging itself in my throat, but that fucker isn't going anywhere.

Nova doesn't say anything, but her fingers land in my hair. Gently, she massages my scalp, and a throaty groan escapes me.

More dominoes start at my head and work down through my neck.

Tears spring to my eyes, and I blink furiously.

I cannot be weak.

I will not cry.

I…

"Let it out, peto. Trust me," she murmurs as her lips press into the top of my head.

And just like that, the last domino falls.

My shoulders shake against her ribs as the tears slip free, and all my fears race through my mind.

I don't know how to do this with her.

I'm going to hurt her.

I can't be enough for her.

I can't live without her.

Nova.

∼

I don't remember falling asleep, and it's so rare to wake up moment by moment instead of gasping for breath that I savor the feeling.

My face still rests on Nova's breast. Our positions are exactly the same, but I've weaved my body through hers, and I'm holding on for dear life.

Except that's not exactly right. Opening my eyes, I take in our bodies without moving. I'm not ready to face the day yet, so I lie perfectly still.

I'm wrapped around Nova, but she's holding me. Just like she promised she would.

My stomach lurches as guilt consumes me.

Will I ever have happiness without that guilt?

Gently, I peel myself out of her embrace. A soft protest falls from her plump lips, and when I glance down, she rolls over in her sleep.

It's for the best. With her back to me, it's easier to leave. I carefully lift the sheet to cover her, then tiptoe out of my room, grabbing my clothes off the floor and dressing on my way down the stairs.

My only thought is getting out of my own house as quickly as possible.

By the time I reach the front door, sweat is trickling down my neck, and I can't get the door open fast enough.

Breathe, jackass. Breathe. The sweat coating my palm makes the door handle slide against my palm uselessly. I have to grip it with both of my shaking hands to get the knob to turn.

Once outside, I wait to hear the automatic locks click into place, then I race down the stairs two at a time. I don't realize I'm running until Halton's garage comes into view, but I don't stop. When I reach the edge of his property, I run faster until I'm standing in front of the bay doors, punching in the code.

When the lock disengages, I rip open the door, enter his studio, and slam the door shut behind me. I just need to be alone. To think. To get a grip on the chaos beating in my brain like a steel drum.

I frantically examine his space, taking in canvases of all shapes and sizes. There's artwork in various stages of completion, but I can't really focus on anything—it's all just swatches of color that flash before my eyes.

I walk back and forth, taking shallow breaths. Counting to ten and starting over. The air feels thick with promises I don't know how to keep anymore. I flare my nostrils with each harsh exhale. The effort of getting my emotions in check is staggering, but I clamp my mouth shut tight to keep the words I want to spew from becoming a reality.

Why did I tell Nova I wanted her love? How fucking selfish can I be? I can't have it. I want it, yes, but I can't have it.

I told her my secrets.

What if I can't walk away from The Apollyon?

What if it won't let me?

I stop in front of one of Halton's sketches. Since Rylan came back into his life, he's embraced his artistic abilities and uses more mediums now. His talent floors me.

Seeing the world through his unfiltered eyes is grounding. He sees things as they should be. Not tainted by evil and greed.

I've been coming here more often in the last year. I can usually find a piece of him here that helps settle the fears deep inside me.

When I'm drowning, this place has become my life vest.

My heart kicks against my ribs as I walk from canvas to canvas. I'm not finding any peace here today.

Because you left your true talisman in your bed.

Fuck. Tugging on the ends of my hair, I spin in place. My head falls back, and I stare at the ceiling, but something in the loft catches my eye.

When did he start working up there?

Curiosity pushes me up the old spiral staircase. My boots hit each metal step with a loud ding that echoes. When I reach the top, my heartbeat is throbbing in the vein at my neck. I'm lucky I don't fall back down the stairs because I move forward without seeing anything but the canvas before me.

It must be ten feet long and six feet high, and on it is…me.

All versions of me.

Hundreds of them in black and white. They all overlap like shadows chasing their owner. Each silhouette details only a piece of me. An eye. A scar. My hair. A tattoo. They all seem to be reaching for the man in the center. A faceless man with a scar on his right hand—it's too similar to my hand, and I know it's me.

But it's the woman he's facing that has my attention. I can only see her from behind, but I know it's Nova. She's cupping my cheeks with both of her small hands, and where she touches my skin is where the color seeps in. It gives the feeling of sunlight peeking over the tops of trees at sunrise, except it's my face she's lighting up.

Her light is seeping into me, bringing me to life.

"Are you okay?"

Halton's voice startles me, and I jump. Unable to speak, I shake my head.

"You weren't supposed to see this," he mutters. "Not yet, anyway."

Without turning to him, I point at the portrait before me. His footsteps come closer.

"I've been working on this for three years. Until recently, it was just different versions of you I couldn't finish." He isn't quite whispering, but his words are muted and unsteady.

"Why?" I have to push the word past the lump in my throat.

"Because whether you acknowledge it or not, your pain hurts us too. This is my way of working through it."

"Working through what?" My voice doesn't sound like my own, and I can't bring myself to face Halton. Not yet. I'm too afraid of what I'll find in his eyes.

"For years, I've been trying to capture you on canvas. I've done it with everyone else, but with you..." His voice cracks.

With sudden clarity, I realize how much my life choices have hurt my family. The one thing I've always tried to avoid, yet I've done it repeatedly.

"With you, I can only get the pieces right. I can't put you together because I don't know you anymore. I see you, Ashton. I see you hurting." He walks closer to the canvas. Pointing to one of the silhouettes, he outlines the position of the body. "I see how you hide away from us." He motions to another one that has a hand clutching his chest. "I see your pain."

In one iteration of me, the scar on my face seems to glow even in black and white. Another one has my head bowed, the face blank except for my eyes. I see all my fears reflected back in them, and I think I might be sick. He's crafted my pieces, but he's right. I'm not whole. I don't know if I can ever be again.

"But then..." He breaks off, and I follow his line of sight.

"Then Nova." I choke on her name, and he turns to face me.

Shame hits me like a lead weight to the face.

"She does something to you." It's not a question. He says it like you'd say the sky is blue. It's just a fact.

And it is. She brings me to life.

"What's going on Ash? Why are you here at five in the morning?"

CHAPTER 30

ASHTON

*W*hat am I doing here?

That's a great fucking question.

What was I doing in my father's office when I shouldn't have been? What was I doing when my enemies grabbed me out of the car like I weighed nothing?

What am I doing?

Time stands still, and my heart rate slows to a sluggish beat. My ribs feel as though they're caving in as dizziness descends like a wave hitting the shore in a hurricane.

I swear my body weighs a metric ton, and my knees tremble with the strain placed on them. I've been wading through quicksand my entire adult life.

Is this the moment it finally takes me under?

"Ash?" Halton asks hesitantly, shaking me from my thoughts.

"I—I'm lost and so fucking tired of life, Halt. I'm just so tired, and I don't know how to put the ghosts to bed." It's as close to the truth as I'll get. The words leave an acidic burn on my tongue.

My brother moves so fast I don't see him coming and slams his body into mine. He holds me like a small child who just fell off his bicycle for the first time, and I allow it. More than that, I welcome it. For the first time in years, I soak in his strength, and will it to rebuild another piece of my soul.

"You have been for a long time," he says with no judgment, but his voice is full of sadness. "But you're not quitting on us, you hear me?" He growls into my ear. "You have to fucking let us in now."

I push off Halton and take a step back.

"I don't know how," I shout. It feels like shards of glass are cutting each syllable from my throat.

"Then start with why you're here. Right now, what are you hiding from?"

"Nova. I..." Turning back to the canvas, my chest aches with the breath I can't release. The visual representation staring back at me is too close to the truth. Too honest. Broken. "She makes me feel alive."

"Thank God someone can," he mumbles. Emotion clogs his voice, but he forces his words to come. "What do you need from her, Ash?"

Though my eyes sting, I'm afraid to blink and break my connection with the canvas before me. What if I close my eyes and she's gone?

"Love," I whisper so low I barely hear myself.

"What are you afraid of?" Halton asks. "What are you afraid will happen if she loves you?"

"That I'll ruin her."

"Why?" he pushes, the words louder than before.

"I don't know how to love. Not like that. Not like she deserves. I'm not the man I could have been. I'm a man who has secrets..."

"Secrets that are not yours to keep. Secrets that are destroying you." I've never heard Halton so angry. It makes me rage so violently it's like the devil himself has taken over my body, and I spin on him.

He has no right to judge me.

"If I don't keep them, people die, or worse, they live a life of torment. How do you expect me to live with myself if that happens? I'm not holding family recipes here, Hattie." His childhood nickname slips from my lips as my body shakes viciously from my shoulders to my knees.

"You have to let us in."

My feet carry me closer to the canvas. I can't see it through my tears, but I feel the light at its center, and I know it's Nova. Through the darkness, she guides me home.

"What if I can't have a normal life with Nova? What if this is it for me?" I ask, pointing to the shadows.

Halton drags a chair across the room and pushes me into the one already there. I flop down without a fight. Resting my forearms on my thighs, I let my head drop into my hands. When Halton speaks again, he's in front of me, and I know if I lift my head, he'll be leaning forward, just as I am.

"What is it about Nova that has you clawing at your skin?"

His question has scenes playing in my mind like a film reel. I picture our time together. Her smile. Her sass. Her light.

Lifting my face to my brother's, another crack in my walls shakes my foundation. "She makes me feel like less of a monster."

"Jesus Christ, Ashton."

I don't have a chance to take it back. It's out in the world now, and Halton's chair falls backward as he leaps to his feet. Dragging me to stand, he wraps me in an embrace so tight it knocks the air from my lungs.

"What happened to you? When dad died, what happened?" Hattie's voice cracks with his own grief.

I hurt. Everywhere hurts. The secrets that infect my every pore burn with the need for release.

"I became the man that evil fears."

Halton's body goes rigid, and he takes a step back, but he doesn't release me. His firm grip on my shoulders tightens like he wants to shake me.

I hope he does.

But all I get is a slight nod of his head. "Tell me," he rasps.

And I do.

I tell him everything.

I speak until my voice gives out, and we sit in silence with the tears of loss and regret clinging to our faces.

My eyelids are heavy when the sun filters through the windows, telling me we've been sitting here for hours.

I clear my throat when the silence becomes unbearable.

What must he think of me now? But Halton holds up his hand to stop me from speaking.

Staring me straight in the eyes, he searches for answers. I don't know what he's looking for, but I know the broken man he finds isn't the brother he'd hoped for. Now I'm just a shell of a man.

"Will you fight till your last breath to love her back?"

I swallow bile as I nod. "I want to, Hattie. I want to love her. But what if I—"

"Are you ready to move on and finally live?"

My jaw hinges, then snaps shut. I shake my head, nod, shake again. I have no fucking clue what I'm ready to do, and he narrows his eyes as he watches me.

"I see the war in your eyes, brother. But it's our fight now, not just yours. Go home. For fuck's sake, sleep. I'm calling a family meeting, and there isn't a goddamn thing you can do to stop me."

A chill creeps down my spine as every what-if scenario runs through my mind.

"Ours, Ash."

I think he says something else, but he sounds like he's underwater. The instinct to flee has me moving toward the stairs. My mind is spiraling, trying to find a way out of this situation I've created.

I know I'm making no sense. I want what I want, and I'm smart enough to know I can't have it. It's making me crazy.

"Ashton!" Halton's angry voice cuts through my inner turmoil. "Don't fight us anymore, little brother. You won't win."

I don't have any words, so I don't even try. With heavy legs, I descend the stairs. One painful step at a time, but Halton's words stop me halfway down.

"Why didn't you say something sooner? If not to us, then why not to Loki or Seth?"

Glancing over my shoulder, I see the emotion in his expression, but he knows why. I can see that in his eyes too.

Preston was taking care of the family.

Easton could barely get through the day without killing someone.

Halton was struggling with his anxiety, and Colton had a lot of growing up to do.

Loki was fighting his own demons, and Seth had Sadie to think about.

"It was always meant to be my lot in life, Hattie. I couldn't take anyone else down with me," I finally answer. My foot hits the next metal step, breaking the tension hanging over us like the darkest cloud.

"You're not alone anymore, Ash. We won't ever let you down again," he promises. The vehemence in his tone gives me pause. I glance up just in time to see a small smile tug at the corner of his lips. "And we'll do what we should have done twenty years ago."

"You couldn't have—"

"We'll teach you how to get the girl," he finishes. "First, you're going to let everyone in, then we'll make a plan for the future so you can live a life free of guilt. After that, we're going to get that girl to fall in love with you. But honestly? I have a feeling she's already halfway there."

Of everything he just said, it's the loving Nova part that throat-punches me. "I don't know how to love her, Hattie."

"You do though." His voice is full of conviction I don't feel. "You may not know how to date, but you have more love to give than anyone I've ever known in my life. You wouldn't have given up the last twenty years of your life for strangers if you didn't know how to love. Trust your heart, Ash. It isn't as broken as you think it is."

"What if I screw it up?"

A crooked grin we all inherited from our father lights up his face, and my heart feels a little brighter just by looking at him.

"Oh, you'll screw up all right. We all do. And when you do, we'll teach you the fine art of groveling. Each Westbrook man has perfected it over the years. Now it's your turn."

"Now it's my turn," I mumble.

"In more ways than one. This is your time, Ash, and you're going to seize the fuck out of today."

Like it or not, I've put the final nail in the coffin of my time with The Apollyon.

Now the future will either embrace me or bury me next to my father.

Please, God, let it embrace me.

CHAPTER 31

NOVA

I've never really listened to the silence before. I know that sounds strange, but it's true. You'll always find a truth in the silence if you listen hard enough. Especially if you're used to city life, like me.

Tugging the thick wool blanket tighter around my shoulders, I listen. Wind rustles the leaves of the tree canopy above me, and somewhere the delicate jingle of a wind chime fights to be heard.

There's a calmness about the forest in the wee hours of the morning before the sun rises. But there's also a powerful sense of danger lurking around the next tree.

It reminds me of Ashton.

The calm before the storm or, perhaps, the storm itself.

I felt the moment he woke even though he tried not to disturb me. It wasn't hard since I never really fell asleep. I clung to him until his body relaxed, then held him tight through his dreamless night.

I'm not sure why I pretended to be asleep when he slipped away this morning. Maybe I needed some time alone too.

The life he's led? I can't possibly begin to comprehend his sacrifices. The all-consuming loneliness he's lived with.

The first rays of sunlight peek through the trees and assault my tired eyes while I fight a yawn. My head flops back against the old wooden rocking chair I've curled up in. I never noticed it on Ashton's front porch before, but sitting in it now, I picture him sitting here. Alone. Sadness makes my heart ache painfully.

"Oh, Nono. What the hell have we gotten ourselves into now?"

Waking up the phone in my hand, I check the time. Five fifty-five. My thumb scrolls my favorited contacts and hovers over the one person I know is up at this time. Penny.

I smile, picturing her running around the house, yelling at her three boys to get ready for school. Calling her now would be the epitome of selfishness. I'm sitting here wallowing in what-ifs while she's in Connecticut being supermom and dad and badass business lady.

Using my thumb, I exit out of the phone icon and text her instead.

Nova: FaceTime when you're on the train?

I swear the woman is glued to her phone because the dots bounce a second later.

Penny: You're lucky you texted me. I was about to round up the boys and come hunt you down on that mountain.

Penny: Yes to FaceTime.

Penny: You okay?

Penny: Give me five minutes, and I'll call you.

Penny: Gage lost the class bunny. Kaiser thinks he has it cornered. Landon, well, you know Landon.

I do. All three of her boys are amazing, but Landon, her middle son, and I have a special bond.

Nova: There's no rush. Get them to school.

Penny: No school today. I just have to find the damn bunny.

Nova: (laughing emoji)

I exhale the tension in my shoulders and watch the cloud of

air that forms before me. It's chilly here in the mornings. I can't imagine what it's like in the middle of winter.

Grabbing my phone, I take a selfie with the rising sun, then turn to head back inside. That's when I remember his automatic locks and hesitate.

What does it mean that I was able to get into his office?

Placing my hand on the scanner, the door unlocks immediately, and I go in search of coffee, resisting the urge to snoop. I scan the ceiling as I walk through his home, trying to detect the hidden cameras.

Loneliness hits me again as I prepare the coffee. His home is so empty. Devoid of anything personal, it feels cold. Even the one family portrait on his wall can't seem to bring the room to life. It doesn't suit him at all.

How long has he lived here?

He has a fancy coffee machine that has way too many options, and by the time I've selected one, my phone is ringing.

Penny flashes across the screen.

"That was fast," I say in greeting.

"No school today. Teacher workday. I'll never understand why they have these in the middle of the week, but here we are." Her always-frazzled tone makes me smile.

Penny Mulligan is the most amazing woman I've ever met. She's thirteen years older than me, which sometimes shows in her big sisterly concern, but she might be the most genuine friend I've ever had.

I wish I had listened when she gently tried to warn me about Kate.

Fucking Kate.

Penny bobbles the phone as she settles into a seat on the commuter rail, and I laugh. She always has four hundred things going on, but she never fails to make you feel like you're the most important one.

"Sorry." She sighs. "Well, it's about time. I've been worried about you, Nono. What the heck? Are you ever coming home?"

"I've missed you."

"Ah, the queen of evasivity. Is that a word? Evasiveness? Whatever. You're the queen of it, but I've missed you too. Seriously, what's going on? Lochlan has been holding your parents off, saying you needed some space—but, Nova! Get your ass back here and fight this bitch. It isn't like you to back down or to go into hiding."

I feel my nose scrunch up. "Is that what you think I'm doing?"

"Isn't it? Don't get me started on that scumbag, Sam. But Kate is a grade A bitch. They deserve everything coming to them. You know that, right?"

"Of course I do."

"Then why are you still in bum fuckle Vermont and not here with us?"

"It's…complicated."

"Because of Kate?" Penny takes a drink of her coffee, and I watch as it sloshes all down the front of her shirt. "Shit, shit, shit," she curses.

Pulling the phone closer, I take in her appearance. Lipstick. I narrow my eyes and try to remember what day it is. "Isn't today Thursday?"

"Yeah, why?"

I wait until she's finished wiping down her blouse, then scan her face again. She only spends time on her makeup on Wednesdays, when Dillon comes in for his weekly meeting with Lochlan. "Is Dillon coming in today?"

Her eyes go wide, and I laugh. "You look good, Penny."

"It's not what you think," she blusters, but can't hide the blush on her cheeks.

"I know things have changed since the last time you dated, but it's okay to ask a guy out. You don't have to wait for him to make a move."

"Nova," she hisses, glancing around the train. "First of all, I'm not from another century. I know women can ask men out. Secondly, Dillon is Lochlan's colleague."

"So are you."

"I'm his administrative assistant. That's hardly a colleague."

I roll my eyes. She's a pain in the ass sometimes. Her ex really did a number on her self-esteem, and it shows in situations like this.

"Anyway," she continues. "I have kids to think about. I have responsibilities. And Dillon is too young for me anyway."

"Excuses."

"Nova, we're not talking about me right now. We're talking about why you're still in Vermont, not at home with us. Lochlan keeps telling Kitty that you have a lot to work through, and he wants to give you the space to do that, but I doubt even he can keep her or Ollie from storming that mountain much longer. Don't you miss the city?"

I glance around Ashton's home, then down at the old T-shirt I'm wearing with a pair of his sweatpants. The pressure to look like a socialite, to have the latest styles, hasn't even crossed my mind since I walked through his door.

That's an oxymoron if I've ever heard one. A fashion designer who doesn't care about being fashionably relevant in her own life. I return my attention back to the phone just in time to hear Penny's gasp.

"You don't miss the city," she says with a hand over her mouth while slowly shaking her head in disbelief. "There's something else." Now it's her turn to pull the screen in close. "Or someone?" My throat is itchy as she stares at me, so I look out the window to break the building tension.

"I don't miss the city, and I'm not hiding." Resting my head against the window, I appreciate that Penny doesn't try to fill the silence while I collect my thoughts. "For the first time in a very long time, I feel free, Penny. Like, really free." Tears sting my eyes.

"Aw, sweetie. You're happy there."

"It's complicated," I say. My head rolls back and forth, relishing the cool glass against my heated skin.

"It's complicated, or he is?"

I pull away from the window. Watching my friend on the small screen, I cross the room with a quivering chin.

"Both?" I whine and then sink into the sofa. With my legs curled under me, I prop my phone up on a pillow next to me.

Penny's screen gives me motion sickness as she moves it all around her, giving me a great view of the train ceiling, then the passenger across from her, before finally resting back on her smiling face. "Sorry." She shrugs. "I had to find my headphones."

"AirPods," I correct as she slips one in her ear, then the other.

"Whatever, fancy pants." She smirks and adjusts her phone.

I return her smile, remembering her fight with my brother when he bought them for her for National Admin Day.

"Talk," she orders.

Penny and I have a friendship built on two things. Blunt honesty and profound loyalty. The two things we were both desperately lacking in our daily lives.

Guilt tries to bitch slap me for holding back with her for so long.

I take a deep breath, then another. "He's fucked up."

She raises an eyebrow and waits for me to continue.

"He's been really fucked up for a long time, but he does it to himself in a white knight kind of way."

"Yeah, I'm going to need more info than that."

Biting the corner of my lip, I hesitate. Ashton's secrets are not mine to tell, and the last thing I want to do is break the fledgling trust we've built.

"Think big secrets. Like CIA, FBI, NASA kind of secrets."

"Oh. Okay."

"So those secrets are doing really, really good things for innocent people."

"But?"

"But they're killing him."

I see Penny inhale and exhale three times before she speaks. "Are you in danger, Nova?"

"What? No. No. I don't think so."

"You don't think so?" she screeches, pulling the phone so close to her face I see straight up her nose.

"No. I know I'm not," I correct quickly.

"Nova, you know I love you, and I'm not going to give away anything, but I need to call you back so I can tell Lochlan I'm going to be late. Give me fifteen minutes to find a quiet place, and then we'll talk."

I nod. This isn't an argument I'll win. Not when she uses the mom voice on me like that.

"Fine, but—"

"I'll tell Lochlan I'm having some female issues. That will give me a good hour."

"The last time you did that, the executive restroom was filled with every box of tampons he could find at the nearest pharmacy."

Penny's laughter wraps me in a warm hug. "Your sister-in-law is training him well. Fifteen minutes. Hang tight."

She hangs up before I can argue.

Why couldn't I have always had friends like Penny? Loyal. Honest. Good, because above all else, that's what she is. Good. I'm lucky to have her.

CHAPTER 32

NOVA

"*That* was only ten minutes," I tease, avoiding Penny's gaze.

"Yeah, well, this is important." Penny huffs and rolls her eyes. People mill about around her.

"Where are you?"

"Fiddle the Bean." She holds up a coffee cup with a logo that makes me laugh. Two fingers pinching a coffee bean.

"Never in a million years did I think Loch would partner with a company like that."

"Love changes a person," she says with a knowing lilt to her voice.

"I don't know what I'm doing, Penny." I search my friend's face for any bits of wisdom she can impart. She flashes me a worried expression and I look away.

"What do you want to do?" she asks cautiously.

My eyes, which have been darting around the room, settle back on my phone. "What I want is crazy and irrational."

"I didn't ask for your judgment of it. I just asked what you wanted."

"Don't use your mom voice with me. It's weird."

"Nono. What do you want?"

"I want to stay. I want to see what happens next for Ashton. And me. For us. If there can even be an us. I don't think I can go back to the apartment. Even if Lochlan has every decorator in Manhattan redesign it. It doesn't feel like home anymore."

"It's not exactly prime apartment-hunting time in New York either. So what's stopping you? You're in between collections right now, so you can design anywhere. You normally travel for inspiration anyway. Why would this be any different?"

The salty taste of tears hits the back of my throat. "Ashton is different. He could really hurt me." Penny's eyes go wide in alarm, and I correct myself. "My heart, Penny. He could really hurt my heart."

"Oh, sweetie. That's part of life. Love will always come with a little pain at some point. It's how you work through it that matters. Will he be a partner? Will he work through the pain with you? Love is the hardest team you'll ever join, but when done right, it can form a bond so strong you can weather any storm."

Knowing the heartache her ex-husband has caused her, I have no idea how she can still be so optimistic. As if reading my mind, she offers a small smile.

"My parents weathered storm after storm. Kitty and Ollie? They've weathered the storm, though in a different way. Love is out there. Just because it didn't work once doesn't mean you stop believing."

"I don't think Ashton knows how to even be in a relationship."

"Have you asked him?"

"That's the most messed up part, Penny. I'm basing this all on unspoken conversations. He has so much to work through."

"But you feel something? Something with him that hasn't existed with anyone else? You don't let people get close to you, Nova. But I can already tell he's different."

"He is. I do. I just… I feel right with him. I don't know how to explain it."

"If he doesn't know how to be in a relationship, I'm guessing he hasn't had to let many people in or rely on many people either."

"No, he hasn't."

"Nono, can you be patient with him?"

My eyes fill with tears, and I bite the inside of my cheek to keep them from falling. "I'm not great with patience."

"I know." She laughs. "That's why I'm asking."

Sniffling, I dab at the corner of my eye. "I can. I think I can."

"There is a difference between being patient and being taken advantage of though. You must keep that distinction close to your heart. I know you. You go all in with people. I don't want you to lose yourself trying to find him."

"I won't."

She chews on her bottom lip but doesn't say anything for a long beat. "Promise me something?"

"What?"

"Promise me that you'll check in with yourself regularly. Love hurts sometimes, but it should never be one-sided. If you find yourself being the only one taking the pain and making sacrifices, promise me you'll step back. You can help and nudge and even shove, but you can't do the work for him. If he wants you, he has to put in the effort to make it work. Love is a partnership. Remember that."

"You don't think this is crazy? That I want to stay in a town where I know no one, for a man I've never even been on a date with?"

"Love is crazy and has made people do crazier things. Okay, so you're staying?"

"I want to. At least for a little while."

"Well, guess I'll have to plan a trip for me and the boys to check this guy out for myself." She leans in with a wicked gleam in her eye. "How's the sex?"

"You can't live vicariously through me with this one, Penny."

"What?" She gasps. "After everything you've told me about the other guys, you're holding out on me?"

"I might. When it happens."

Her eyes flicker back and forth like she's trying to see the tops of both eyebrows. "You haven't slept with him?"

Gnawing away at the cuticle on my thumb, I shake my head.

"Third base, then?"

When I don't say anything, her eyes go so wide I'm afraid they'll fall out of her head.

"Have you kissed him?" she hisses.

This time I nod. "I don't know if I kissed him, or he kissed me. It was more like clashing tsunamis."

Penny flops back into her chair with a dumbfounded expression on her face. I know how she feels. Normally these conversations go much differently.

"You said he has a lot of secrets. That's a lot of pressure." She says it almost to herself before turning her attention back to me. "Is he having trouble...you know?" She uses her index finger to point, then curls it like a deflating penis.

"Ah, no. That's not an issue. He's locked and loaded and so thick. Like, beastly thick."

"You've seen it but haven't touched it."

"I've seen it. And it's pressed against me a couple of times, but I haven't touched it, no."

"You've been naked together, and you haven't done anything but kiss?"

"Yeah."

She sips her coffee and watches me over the top of her cup. "You really like this guy."

"I really like him."

"What are you going to tell your family?"

Visions of Ollie and Kitty storming this mountain again make my chest flood with warmth. "The truth, I guess. They'll tease me because that's what they do, but all they've ever wanted for me was to be happy. They'll trust me to figure it out."

"Your parents will. Lochlan might kill the guy." She laughs, but I freeze because she's right.

"Maybe we don't tell Lochlan yet. Let me figure things out a little first."

"Or we could tell him that I really like you too, and I'll promise to do my best to learn to be the man you deserve."

My coffee goes flying at the low, growly voice that makes goosebumps sweep across my body. Turning my head, I find Ashton leaning against the wall just outside the foyer with his arms crossed and one leg bent, his bare foot resting on the wall. It's a relaxed position, but tension throbs wildly in the vein at his neck. His eyes are dark, and I swear he's seeing me naked right now.

Heat rises high on my cheeks as I wipe coffee off my lap with the edge of my T-shirt.

"Oh, lord. Is that him?" Penny squeals.

I'd forgotten she was on the phone, but I can't tear my eyes away from Ashton's. "Penny?" I squeak. "Ah, I'm going to need to call you back."

"I'd say so. Don't worry about—"

I hang up. She'll forgive me.

When the phone drops to the cushion beside me, Ashton pushes off the wall and stalks toward me. There is no other way to describe his movements. He is stalking me like prey, and I gulp at the intensity in his stare but frown when he's close enough for me to see the dark circles that ring his eyes.

"Peto, what's wrong?" I ask, wiping away the last drops of coffee that landed on my legs. Thank God the cup was almost empty.

He falls to his knees before me and pushes my legs apart to

get closer. I happily spread them and wrap them around his back. Holding him to me, I tentatively place my palms on his cheeks.

His eyes betray a million stories he doesn't want to tell, but he blinks them away, and then there's only us. Him and me and the story we'll write. Together.

CHAPTER 33

ASHTON

J hadn't meant to eavesdrop, but my insecurities got the better of me, and I needed to hear her unfiltered thoughts. What I heard in her fears and love shredded the last bit of control I had.

"What's wrong, peto?"

Everything and nothing. I've never felt more lost in my life.

Sitting on my knees before her, I allow myself a moment to get lost in her eyes. The eyes that glow like the hearts of stars. The eyes that lead me home.

"I need you, Super Nova. I need you and want you and am terrified that I'll ruin you. I haven't had a meaningful relationship in almost twenty years. Not one that wasn't shrouded in secrets and lies."

A tear slips down her cheek. I lift up and kiss it away before I can stop myself. "Don't cry, princess. Please don't cry."

"Penny told me to be patient with you."

"I think I like Penny," I whisper in her ear before placing a gentle kiss on her temple.

"Problem is, I'm not very patient, so you'll need to be patient with me too."

"I can do that." My heart drop-kicks my chest cavity as I press another kiss to the corner of her eye.

"For this to work, I need something from you too, Ashton."

I freeze with my lips pressed to her skin. "What do you need?"

"A promise that you'll put us first."

Fuck.

"You said this life is killing you. I see it, peto. I see what it's done to you. Do you want to keep living like this?"

Closing my eyes, I pull my lips away from her. When I open them, we're eye to eye. "No, Nova. I don't. But I haven't figured out how to walk away from it either."

"But you're going to? You want to?"

I run a hand through my hair. Back and forth until the friction causes my scalp to prickle. "Yeah, sweetheart. I need to. It's time to let Killian take over, but it's not as simple as handing someone a key."

"Ashton?"

Leaning forward, I rest my forehead against hers. "Yeah?"

Her exhale smells like coffee with a hint of mint from her toothpaste. "As long as you put us first when it matters, I can be patient while you make this transition. I just need to know that you're trying and that we're a priority too."

Blood rushes to every nerve ending in my body. This is happiness. Pure, uninhibited joy racing through my veins.

"When I mess up?"

"I'll tell you, don't worry about that." She smiles, and fireworks detonate in my heart.

"Does this mean you're my girlfriend?"

Nova's laughter fills my broken bits with hope. "Would you like me to be?"

"I should warn you. I've never had a girlfriend before."

"I'm a good teacher." Her words are breathy and full of innuendo that makes me rock-hard.

"I didn't mean to listen in on your phone call." Leaning in, I kiss the corner of her mouth and growl when a quiet moan slips out of her. "I like that you want to stay though."

"I'll need to find a short-term rental or talk to GG about a monthly arrangement."

My heart skips a beat, and my shoulders tense. "Why?"

She blinks, confused. "What do you mean, why?"

I scan the room. Why wouldn't she want to stay here? My gaze darts to the stairs, snags on the only photo hanging on the wall. That's when it hits me. This place is a fucking joke. No life happens here because I haven't been living. It's decorated like a model home, and it's never once bothered me. Until now.

"We can change whatever you want." Her confusion deepens in her furrowed brow, and panic claws at my chest. "We can bring your stuff from New York or go shopping. Whatever you want."

"Ashton." Nova gently places a hand on my shoulder, but I don't let her push me away. "What are you talking about?"

"If you don't like it here, we'll change it. You don't have to find an apartment."

Her mouth hangs open as she stares at me, unblinking.

I'm already fucking this up. "Shit." I stand with jerky movements. "I'm messing this up. I—"

"Peto."

My fists clench and unclench, but it doesn't release the tension. The fear. I stride to the window and stare out over the mountain below us.

Nova's hand lands in the center of my back, grounding me.

"Ashton, you're asking me to move in with you when we haven't even been on a date. And just a short time ago, you couldn't wait to hand me off to Rylan."

At the confirmation that I'm a fucking idiot, my shoulders slump.

"I thought I was doing the right thing sending you away," I mutter. "I don't know what I'm doing."

"You have to talk to me, peto. We haven't had a normal beginning, but I've never been normal. You just caught me off guard, that's all."

Spinning, I face her with hope trying to curl my lips into a smile. "So you'll move in."

"I just got a boyfriend five minutes ago. Let's see how the next couple of weeks go, and then we'll reassess. How's that?"

I don't suppress the growl rumbling in my chest. Nova winks.

In a move I didn't know I had, I spin us both so she's pushed up against the glass, and I hover over her.

"I've never been a boyfriend." There's no masking the lust in my voice. "Does it come with perks?"

Her sexy little body shimmies against mine, and my hips pin her to the window. Insecurity creeps in because I know I'll blow the second my cock touches her pussy. Maybe I should rub one out first? I glance at the bathroom, but her low, sultry voice draws my attention back.

"So." She rolls her hips.

"Many." Her teeth nip at my neck.

"Perks." Her hot little tongue trails fireworks down my throat.

"Nova," I warn before my mouth takes hers. Biology kicks in, instinct driving me. There's no thinking. No planning. Just me and her. Her tongue licks my bottom lip, and I growl as our mouths open, both tongues darting out to taste, tease, test.

I'm happy to let her take the lead. Precome seeps into my boxer briefs, and there isn't a damn thing I can do about it, so I embrace it.

By the time I realize her trembling fingers are pressed against my chest, my cock is so hard it's the only thing demanding my attention.

She proves she's been watching me as closely as I study her when she asks, "Is this…can I…?"

"For fuck's sake, touch me, princess." I ghost my lips over hers. Our breaths mingle and become one. I'm not sure where she stops or I begin. The softness of her skin contrasts with the roughness of my own, and it threatens to pull me from the moment.

"I want you, Ashton. Scars"—she kisses my collarbone—"wounds"—then she licks the spot she kissed—"baggage. I want it all."

Her cold fingers slip beneath my T-shirt, making me hiss, but I don't pull away as she lifts it over my head. Her lips turn down while she takes in my scars. The instinct to hide is overwhelming. But the emotion in her eyes keeps me standing ramrod straight with my hands flexing against her hips.

She leans forward, centimeter by agonizing centimeter. It takes my brain way too long to realize she's asking for permission. Permission to touch me. When I nod, she closes the distance. Her lips press to the most jagged scar, where the knife entered my skin just above my left nipple.

I nearly black out. But it's not from pain. It's lightning strikes and first breaths. It's being sucked from the depths of hell and landing at heaven's door.

Nova Blaine is an angel sent to save me.

"Breathe, Ashton."

I exhale at her command and brace myself on the window behind her.

My chest heaves as she kisses lower.

My shoulders shake with first kisses that tear me apart brick by brick.

Nova is on her knees before me, undoing my jeans, and my throat goes dry. Fucking fuck me. I've never been so desperately unhinged for another person. I've never felt the need for anyone as much as I need her. And I can't even form words to stop her, knowing I'm about to embarrass myself.

Her hands slide down my thighs as she pushes my pants and boxers down my legs, allowing my cock to stand like a beacon calling her home. My hips thrust greedily, and I'm useless to stop them.

"Princess," I howl through clenched teeth, but the words are lost as she wraps her lips around my tip.

I see stars, and sweat gathers on my forehead.

Super Nova.

Heaven.

I'm about to crack a tooth from grinding my jaw back and forth. She hums, and I pound my fist against the cool glass.

I cannot come in her mouth before she even...

Fuck. My tip hits the back of her throat. I drop my hands to her head and fist them in her hair when my tip hits the spongy wall of her throat.

"Stop," I say like a curse because the last fucking thing I want is for this goddess to stop sucking me down. "I—I can't stop myself if you keep this up."

Her teeth press into my sensitive flesh just enough to make my hips jerk, and my cock presses into her throat before she releases me. But the little minx leaves her lips on the side of my swollen flesh as she speaks.

"Don't you see, peto? That's what I want."

My cock twitches against her mouth, begging to be sucked whole again.

"What? What do you want?" I explode. All sense of chivalry is gone. I am the beast now. I am a monster unleashed.

"I want..." She licks the underside of my shaft with a stiff tongue, and I can't hold my head up. I stare at the ceiling, waiting for her to finish speaking.

My cock bobs, her lips following it.

"I want you to lose control. With me. For me. Because of me."

My vision goes red. Everywhere I look, I see her swollen red lips, but when I look down to take in her beautiful face, I know what she's saying.

She wants me to trust her enough to let go.

"I'm scared I'll hurt you. If I lose control, what happens then?"

Those damn eyes of hers shine so brightly they light the entire room. Or at least my soul. "Oh, peto. I'll stop you before that happens."

I open my mouth to ask her what the hell she thinks she's going to do to stop me when I outweigh her by at least eighty pounds and have a good foot on her in height, but she closes her lips around my dick and sucks me into the back of her throat.

Her tongue is like crushed velvet as it engulfs me.

I flex my fist in her hair. "You're sure?" I grunt.

She nods and swallows around me as my hips thrust forward. It's a battle within myself not to fuck her face. That's not what boyfriends do. Is it?

She moans, and I glance down to see her hand slipping beneath the waistband of her pants.

My pants.

"Are you wearing my sweatpants?"

She nods, her lips stretched even wider as she smiles around my cock. I've never seen anything so goddamn sexy in all my life. Her hand moves rapidly beneath the cotton, and when she moans around a mouthful of me, I pick up my speed.

I'm going to come. She needs a warning, so I try to pull back, but her free hand wraps around my ass and pulls me in closer.

"Nova," I rumble. My hips piston into her. Fuck. Can she breathe?

Then her finger presses against a sensitive spot just behind my balls. I come in a torrent of curses and groans that stammer from my lips like a victory cry to the Gods.

What the fuck did she just do?

My knees shake, and I tumble to the floor in front of her with wide eyes.

She licks her lips like she's savoring the taste of me, and my cock instantly twitches to life. Apparently, I have the stamina of a teenage boy and the recovery time too—at least, when it comes to her.

"I told you I'd stop you before you went too far." She grins.

I blink.

Then I pounce.

"You may have the tricks, darlin', but I have years worth of fuckery to make up for. Can you handle it?"

"There's only one way to find out," she murmurs. Reaching forward, she tries to grab my cock, but I swat her away.

"This time, sweetheart? This time, I lead."

CHAPTER 34

ASHTON

I crawl forward onto my hands and knees until my body presses against Nova's, then I slowly lower her to the floor.

Somewhere, in the back of my mind, I know I need to get us to a bed. The sofa. Anything but the hardwood floor I'm crowding her onto, but I'm moving on pure instinct and rational thought comes and goes in waves.

Right now, all I want to do is touch her. Feel her. Learn her. When she's flat against the floor, I lean to the side and hold my weight up on my left forearm. I press my right hand flat against her sternum. Her heart beats against my palm, and I hold it there, memorizing her rhythm.

She releases the slightest whimper, and my lip curls into a smirk. All the Westbrooks are cocky. It's a trait I thought had skipped right over me, but holding Nova like this, I know it didn't. My cocky alpha persona was just in hiding, waiting for her.

"Oh, baby. What I want to do to you."

Nova tries to lift her shoulders, but I hold her still without applying any pressure at all. Tilting my head to the side, I study her expression. I lower my lips just above hers. When I lick mine, I catch hers with the faintest flick of my tongue.

I don't give her any space. As I speak, my lips brush against hers. "When is the last time you gave up control, princess?"

Her eyes dance between mine, and her heart beats wildly beneath my palm. Tapping my fingers against her collarbone, I slowly inch higher until they land in the little divot at the base of her throat. I tap that hollow three times, and her nostrils flare, so I lift my hand higher until it holds her throat. She swallows against me and grins.

"You don't give up control, do you?"

She swallows hard against the heel of my hand. I don't apply any pressure. I simply hold it there, watching her reaction. Finally, she shakes her head with the smallest of movements.

"You've been in charge of every—" My brain catches on the next word. When I finally force my question, it sounds like an angry demand. "You've been in charge of every sexual encounter you've had?"

The thought of her with anyone else sets my body on fire. Jealousy burns a fiery path down my spine.

"Yes," she replies without hesitation. I'm not sure what I expected from her, but confidence in her answer wasn't it.

Shit. Okay. Time to rethink my next steps.

"Is—Is that how you want this to go? With us?"

Jesus. Can I do that? Give her complete control?

Her face softens with a smile I haven't seen before, and it's like someone injected me with adrenaline.

"No, peto." She shakes her head slowly but never breaks eye contact. "That's not what I want."

"Tell me," I plead. I don't even give a shit if it sounds like I'm begging. "Tell me what you want."

"A partner. Give and take. Yin and yang."

"Give and take," I mutter, but I can already feel my body relaxing. She's releasing the dominoes again, and my body melts into hers. That's when it clicks. "You just took."

A smile so sweet it should be illegal covers her face as she nods. "Now it's your turn." Nova lifts her arms above her head and lies prone. For me.

"If I take too much…"

"If you take too much, we'll talk. That's what you do in a relationship. Give and take and talk and fight and kiss and make up."

"It sounds like a vicious cycle," I tease. My fingers dance across the hem of her T-shirt before slipping underneath. Her breath catches when I skim up her stomach to cup her breast.

"It is. Can you handle it?" she moans.

Instead of answering, I pinch her nipple between my thumb and forefinger. Nova gasps, the sound spurring me into motion.

I lift her shirt over her head, loving that she isn't wearing a bra. I pinch and knead her right breast, then lower my mouth to her left one. A quick exhale of hot air has her nipple puckering enough to catch it between my teeth. When she moans and rocks her hips, I stiffen my tongue and flick at it relentlessly.

"Jesus."

Releasing her nipple, I grin against her damp skin. "Not Jesus, sweetheart. Just a broken man glued together again by the weight of promises."

"Ashton," she murmurs, and it's the most beautiful sound I've ever heard.

I know hard times are coming our way, but I need us to be one right now. To be whole. There's no doubt she's the better part of me. I need to connect us to finally know what it feels like to be me again.

I rise to my knees and pull down her pants, watching her face and her body for every reaction. Her eyes roll back in her head when my thumb skims over her mound, and I memorize the spot.

When she's naked before me, I work really fucking hard to control my breathing. The moment is so charged that I half expect to see sparks fly from her skin as I lower my mouth to her stomach and slowly, oh so fucking slowly, move south.

The first swipe of my tongue over her slit has her hips lifting from the floor. And a sexy mewl escapes from the back of her throat when she stabs her fingers through my hair.

I love it. So I do it again, but this time, I hold Nova's hip down with one hand and spread her pussy lips with the other. My tongue darts out, savoring her sweet taste. She bends her knees, pulling me closer, and I fucking love it.

I've watched more than my share of porn, but nothing compares to the real thing. Nothing compares to Nova.

She writhes beneath me as my fingers circle her opening. Slowly, I enter her with my index finger, but my gaze never leaves hers. I've been with two other women in my life, and fore-play was never on the table with either of them, so I will enjoy every goddamn minute of this.

I curl my finger inside her. I'm nothing if not a great student, and when she lifts her head with wide eyes and her mouth hanging open, I know I'm moving in the right direction.

"What do you need, princess?"

"More," she gasps. "More pressure. Faster."

Possibilities run through my mind. She must be talking about her clit, right? I keep up the slow exploration with my finger and press my thumb through her folds until I find the magical little nub. It's harder to find than I'd have thought, but when she screams my name, I know I've hit gold.

"Yes. Holy shit," she pants, and I increase my speed. Adding a second finger inside her, I push and pull, still seeking that myste-rious spot deep in her core.

Nova's entire body trembles, and pride hits me hard. "I want you to come on my mouth," I growl.

"I—I'm so close," she whines.

I drop my lips to her pussy and remove my hand. She protests until I open her enough to find her clit with my teeth. Sucking it into my mouth, I flick the tiny bundle of nerves, then fuck her with my fingers until she coats my face with her arousal.

It's sweeter than any fucking honey I've ever tasted.

She quivers below me. "More, Ash. I need you. Please. Please," she begs.

I move up her body without any grace. I'm a live wire ready to go off, but I take a minute to kiss her. Hard. Deep. And hope she feels what I can't say. How much I appreciate her. How much I need her. How much I want her.

She opens her legs wider, and I settle between them. The heat of our bodies coats my skin in perspiration as I rub the head of my cock up and down her drenched folds.

I'm a fool if I thought the blow job would be enough to take the edge off.

"Don't tease me, peto. Please."

I notch my tip at her entrance. The feel of skin on skin short circuits my brain. Then I freeze. Skin on skin.

"Shit," I curse. I search the space wildly like a condom will magically appear.

Nova's eyes dart from mine down to my cock and up again. "I'm on the pill," she breathes.

I enter her in one forceful thrust, and time ceases to hold meaning. The world, The Apollyon, my demons? It's as if they never existed when my body merges with hers.

If I were a religious man, I'd say I've reached nirvana.

Fuck it. I'm saying it anyway. This is a rebirth for me. I am a new man with her.

"Fuck, Nova. Fuck. Fuck, you feel good."

Her pussy spasms at my words, and I bite my tongue to keep from popping off prematurely. When I think I can control myself, I open my eyes and find her watching me. "I need to work on my stamina, sweetheart."

She graces me with a smile. "Move, peto. Fuck me, please. I'm so close. So, so close."

Her hands claw at my chest, and I place my forearms on either side of her head. Lowering my body to hers, I slowly ease my hips forward, then continue in a rocking motion. She wraps her legs around my waist, urging me to go faster, but I don't speed up.

Slow. Measured. Controlled.

I want this moment beneath the window, on a hardwood floor, to last forever.

"I don't deserve you," I murmur. "I need you, but I don't deserve you."

Nova silences me with a kiss. It's passion and heat. It's love and desire and all things good.

The kiss is all Nova.

My hips pick up speed, and I'm powerless to stop them. Each punishing thrust scoots us farther along the floor until Nova's head rests against the wall. Cupping her head with my hands, I buffer her scalp as I pound into her.

She moans and clenches around me. "I'm going to come," she announces, and I bury myself to the hilt just so I can watch her face as she falls apart.

Even with her face screwed up in ecstasy, she's still the most beautiful creature I've ever seen. I try to hold out, but as her pussy clenches and milks my dick, I come harder than I ever knew possible. I unload stream after stream of come inside her, and when I'm completely rung out, I cling to her.

Nova runs her hands through my hair as we wait for our tremors to subside. Eventually, I lift my head to look into her eyes. "You're amazing."

"Yeah, well, I've had some—"

I'm not sure what she's going to say, but I already know I won't like it, so I cut her off with a kiss.

Even after coming twice in a relatively short period of time, my cock stays rock-hard inside her. That little fucker was deprived for so long he now thinks it's party time.

Easing out of her, I slip an arm beneath her and start to lift her. But she outmaneuvers me and wraps her legs around my waist, locking them behind my back. Shaking my head with a smile, I hold her close as I rise.

"We need to get some sleep. I have a feeling the entire Westbrook clan is about to descend on us, and it's going to be a really long few days."

"Why? What happened?"

Pulling her a little closer, I leave our clothes on the floor and move toward the stairs. "I told Halton, Nova. I told him everything, and hell is about to rain down on me like never before."

Her small hands leave my shoulders to cup my cheeks, and I stop on the stairs. "It's going to be okay, Ash. I'm here with you. For all of it."

I take another step, and my cock bobs against her ass. Her eyes go wide, and my chest cracks wide open as laughter flies free from my soul.

The sound is so foreign that it takes me a minute to realize it's coming from me. But when I do, I laugh harder. For a second, I can almost imagine I'm just a normal guy, living a normal life. For a second, I forget my life has never been my own.

"I love when you laugh," Nova whispers in awe. She's probably never really heard me laugh, not like this. I don't even know if I have this freely in years.

"Me too, baby. Me too." More than anything, I want to laugh with this woman. Laugh, and love, and fucking hell, I want to live.

"Take me to bed, handsome. We'll figure the rest out later."

"Nova, I…"

"You really, really like me too?" She smirks, and I'm reminded of her phone call earlier.

"Yeah, princess. I really, really like you too." I place a kiss on her nose and carry her to bed, feeling the noose around my neck loosen a notch or two.

CHAPTER 35

NOVA

"So, when you say everyone, you mean..."

"I mean everyone. Well, my brothers and my mom." He winces, as if remembering just how many people that is. "Yeah, everyone. Preston, East, Halt, Colton, Dex, Trevor, Loki, and Seth. Dillon will probably show up at some point, but he's made it pretty clear he'd rather be in New York these days."

"The girls aren't coming?" I ask, then place the mug in the dishwasher. I've already washed down the counters three times.

I'm stress-cleaning, and he knows it. Ash places a hand on top of mine and takes the dish soap out of my hands. Moving around me, he fills the dispenser.

"I'm sure that's Halton's doing. I'm not great with groups, even if they are family, and knowing what I'm about to tell them..." He stares out the window above the sink.

"I'll be with you the entire time, peto. Unless...unless you don't want me here?"

He spins so fast I'm surprised he doesn't get dizzy and crowds me against the large island. "No, I need you here. I want you here."

It's the first time he's let me see the desperation in his eyes. He's terrified of what's coming.

Oh, peto.

We woke up at four p.m. to Halton shouting from the bottom of the stairs. He was agitated, but I could see the worry in the frown lines around his eyes. They've all been worried about Ashton for years, it seems. And now I know why.

"My secrets will hurt a lot of them," he whispers.

"Only because you kept them for so long." When he frowns, I'm quick to explain. "I understand why you did, Ash. I do, but it's time."

His front door opens, and I peer down the hallway to see who it is. Killian walks around the corner, and anger heats my blood. "What are you doing here?"

Ashton wraps an arm around my middle like he thinks I'll charge the animal. I hadn't thought about it, but if there was any chance of me getting a punch in, I just might. I don't like this guy at all. I'm not a fighter, but I bet a titty twister could take him down.

"Easy, princess. Killian isn't the enemy here."

"He hurt you," I spit out.

"Because I paid him to. It was always my doing."

"That's really what you think, isn't it?"

"Lass," Killian says, interrupting.

"What?" I hiss.

The giant of a man smiles at me like he expected nothing less. "Thank you for bringing him back." He nods toward Ashton, and my icy walls melt. Just a tiny bit.

"You're going to help him walk away?"

Ashton explained his exit strategy to me this morning. It was exhaustive and intense, and I know it will take months, maybe years, to extract himself completely. But as he showed me page after page of notes, I realized this was how he got through the daily heartache. Planning his eventual exit was the dream that gave him hope.

It claws at my heart like a wildcat protecting her babies.

"Aye, Lass. It won't be easy. He's emotionally attached to The Apollyon."

"Asshole. I'm right here," Ashton grumbles, but he doesn't argue Killian's point either.

Killian ignores him and stares me down. It feels like a challenge. One I refuse to back down from.

"His darkest days are ahead of him."

"Stop fucking talking about me like I'm an invalid," Ashton roars. Neither Killian nor I break eye contact though.

"Are ya strong enough to hold his hand while he searches for the light to guide him off of this path?"

Taking three long steps, I move into Killian's space. Close enough to be uncomfortable. Close enough that I have to crane my neck to glare into his emotionless eyes. But I don't back down. Not for him, not for anyone. Not ever again.

"I am the fucking light, fuckface."

His eyebrow twitches. It's the only sign he gives that I've shocked him. But it's enough. We stare daggers at each other until Ashton grabs my wrist and hauls me to his side.

"What the hell is with the pissing contest?" he mutters.

Killian breaks out a smile that shows off perfectly straight teeth. He's a handsome man in an ogreish kind of way.

"Ya want the truth, mate?"

"That's always been our rule." Ashton angles his body between Killian and me. It's a protective stance I'm not even sure he realizes he's taken. He's a protector through and through.

"Truth is, I wasn't sure you'd be able to walk away. I've always said there would have to be a damn good reason. Something stronger than yourself to make ya do it."

"And? What's your point?" Ashton rumbles. His hands flex at his sides, a sign I've learned to recognize. He's on edge.

Killian leans around Ash. He raises his eyebrows as he stares at me with a slight smirk lifting the corner of his lip. "My point is, mate, I think ya found yer reason. Now it's my job to make sure ya don't fuck it up."

Ash takes a menacing step forward, but the front door opens, and his home is immediately filled with the boisterous noise that can only come from a football team's worth of brothers.

"Fuck," Ashton curses. His hand brushes through his hair roughly, and his entire body goes rigid.

Leaning forward, I press my body into his. "It's okay. It's going to be okay," I whisper.

He turns and wraps me in an embrace, holding on for dear life. The scent of pine and clean laundry fills my nostrils, and I inhale deeply. I smile into his chest when I feel him do the same thing.

Ashton takes three large breaths of air before he lifts his head.

The room has gone silent around us though it's filled with Westbrooks. Each man stands in a similar position. Some with arms crossed over their chests. Some with their hands tugging at the back of their necks. All of them sporting various versions of the same smirk. And all of them are watching us.

"I knew it," Colton shouts, fist-pumping the air as he bounces on his toes. "You're going to marry her. I knew it. Loch will lose his shit, but who cares."

The room erupts around us as questions fly one after another.

"Is that true?"

"Oh my God."

"When is the wedding?"

"She's still here?"

I turn a panic-fueled expression on Ashton, who watches the chaos unfold with a rueful smile.

"Peto, what the hell?" I mutter. "What is wrong with your brothers?"

"Just let them get it out. Chaos is what they know. They'll quiet down in a second," he whispers.

"Time out," Preston shouts above his brothers. "Everyone shut up for two seconds."

The room holds an excited happiness that's infectious, but the smile trying to form on my lips fades when I realize how much they want this for their brother. How desperate they are for him to be happy. Tears prick my eyes, knowing we're about to burst their bubble with Ashton's secrets and possibly break their hearts.

"Oh, God," I murmur under my breath.

Ashton places a heavy hand on my shoulder and squeezes. He transfers his strength to me in that one small gesture. It's enough to snap me out of it. I'm here to be his pillar. His strength. Not the other way around.

I catch his attention and see the worry in his eyes. With a small nod, I turn to his brothers. "We aren't getting married." The words hurt coming out. I clear my throat and continue. "But I think everyone should sit." I hold out my hand and gesture toward the large dining room table I'm sure has never been used.

A regal-looking woman steps forward from the front door. She's older, in her mid-sixties I'd guess, but there is no mistaking her. She has the familiarity of a Westbrook and Ashton's kind eyes.

This must be Ashton's mother.

244

CHAPTER 36

NOVA

"*N*ova, it's so nice to meet you." Mrs. Westbrook steps forward, and I hold out a hand to greet her.

She shocks the hell out of me when she swats it away and pulls me into a hug.

My brother was right. They are a bunch of huggers.

I love it.

"Hi, Mrs. Westbrook. It's, ah, nice to meet you."

She smacks Ashton's arm. "Didn't you tell her we don't do formalities like that?"

I blink and watch Ashton lean down to kiss his mother's cheek. "I didn't have time, Mom. This wasn't a planned introduction."

Turning back to me, she smiles. I fight the urge to tug on my T-shirt as she scans me from head to toe. "I knew when my baby fell, it'd be for someone strong enough to part the tide and flexible enough to go with the flow." She steps forward and holds my face in her hands.

I'm glad I don't have boundary issues.

"You, my girl, are exactly who we've been waiting for."

The room is eerily silent. Is anyone else even breathing during this odd exchange? I know I'm not.

It's like no one dares to interrupt this woman. The power she wields in the silence is impressive.

"He's a good man, Nova. My Clinton made some mistakes that Ashton's been paying for, I think, but if you can be patient with him, he'll give you all the happiness in the world. He just has to find his way."

"Why does everyone talk about me like I'm not fucking here?" Ashton mumbles.

"Language, Ashton," Mrs. Westbrook says without looking at him or releasing my face. To me she says, "It's Sylvie or Mom. Your choice." She pats my cheek, hugs me once more, then releases me and walks to the table.

What the hell just happened?

Ashton sighs heavily beside me. "That's my mom. She can control the chaos or create it without ever raising her voice."

A laugh bubbles up in my chest. I can't help it. It escapes in an unladylike display that at the very least makes him smile. "I think I'm going to like her. But God help us if she ever meets Ollie."

He hooks his arm into mine and leans down to whisper so only I can hear. "When. When she meets Ollie, princess. You're stuck with me now."

I open my mouth to answer, but he gently guides me forward, and I remember our audience. When I find them all sitting and facing Killian with a sense of unease, I clamp my mouth shut.

Killian stands tall like a dark reminder of what's to come and doesn't seem at all put off by the glares of eight adult men.

Ashton walks us to the head of the table. Killian sits on a stool behind us, and that's when I realize there aren't enough chairs. Just as I'm about to pull away, Killian slides another stool in behind me with a nod to Ash.

My chest clenches when I see Ashton's shaking hands, but he eases himself down into the chair. Killian and I perch on the stools slightly behind him on either side. The bar stools have us raised to an uncomfortable height. We perch like gargoyles. Protecting. Offering strength to the man in front of us.

My eyes mist as the air in the room shifts. It's like everyone in attendance suddenly realizes there is a much more dire reason for this meeting.

The vein in Preston's neck bulges. Colton's leg bounces violently. Loki sits with steepled fingers, wearing a mask I know must have taken years to perfect.

The tension is palpable, and I wipe the sweat from my upper lip as nausea rolls through my stomach.

Easton opens his mouth like he wants to say something, but Halton holds up his hand to stop him. Eyes dart around the room as Ashton sits with his head bowed. I can see his eyelashes fluttering as the first tear drips onto his clasped hands, and I know in this instant that I'm never leaving this man's side again.

I can't explain it. I don't need to. He's mine and I'm his. From this day forward, we'll be a team.

Scooting my stool closer, I grab his right hand and pull it into my lap. Lifting my gaze to every Westbrook in the room, I silently dare them to speak, to rush him. They'll have to deal with me if they do.

Come on, baby. You can do this. Please, you can do this.

I chant the words in my head as I squeeze his hand so tightly my own knuckles turn white. Eventually, he tilts his head to the side, and with the saddest eyes I've ever seen, he gives me the smallest nod before returning his eyes to his lap and starting his tale.

"I was hiding in Dad's office," he says. The room is deathly silent. All eyes are on the youngest brother. "I was fucking around where I shouldn't have been."

I lift my gaze then and check on each man in turn.

Dexter's face is ashen, his eyes full of unshed tears.

Trevor sits stoically with a clenched jaw.

Preston stands and leans over his chair with his hands on the backrest. As Ashton tells one horrifying truth after another, he shakes his head slowly from side to side and stares at the floor.

"I stole from your trusts in order to fund the missions. First from Preston's, and then when he came of age, I moved down the line to Easton. Then to Halton's, and eventually Colton's. By the time I came of age for my own, I'd stolen and replaced nearly thirty-seven million. Now I fund The Apollyon solely from my own accounts."

Killian makes a strangled noise but doesn't interject.

"Some of the people we've saved have come back to us as adults. They make donations in time or money, but I foot the majority of it."

I can't tear my eyes away from the brothers' reactions. Each so different in their pain, yet so eerily similar as fear and regret flash in their eyes.

Ashton speaks with a slow vibrato that enunciates every syllable. Like he's taking great care with each word, and I get lost in the melodic notes of it instead of taking in the details of his story that would cause nightmares for years to come.

His hand squeezes mine, startling me into the present. His voice is shaky, his palm sweaty.

He needs me.

"When Macomb's men pulled me from the car, I knew I'd made my second mistake. I thought this one would cost all our lives. The physical torture was..." A sob chokes him, and I use my free hand to wrap his arm in a hug. It's as close as I can get to him without climbing into his lap. "I prayed they'd just kill me. I just wanted to die," he cries. "But then they brought in Pacen. I—"

No one moves a muscle as Ashton weeps. No one except Sylvie. But Preston places a hand on her shoulder to hold her in place. He must sense that Ashton needs to get through this without disruption. It makes me like him a little more.

Time ceases to exist as we sit in this bubble of torment, and when he composes himself enough to speak, everyone in the room inhales sharply as if they're bracing for the worst.

"I'd called her repeatedly on an unsecured line. Then I thought she'd betrayed me for turning her down. We were close, but when she said she wanted a relationship, I… It just didn't make sense. I thought she'd given my location to her father. God. I should have known better." Ashton's fist comes down on the table with a loud crash that startles a squeak from the back of my throat.

Killian draws my attention with a growl in the corner. I'd forgotten he was even here. He sits like an armed guard, but something in his expression seems off. Does he know Pacen?

I make a mental note to ask Ash later.

Movement to my right catches my eye, and I turn my attention to Sylvie. She seems so small sitting among all these men. And so much more fragile than when she walked in. She holds herself high, but openly cries as Ashton speaks.

I should have set out tissues like place settings.

Next to her, Halton holds her hand in his. He's the only one with a thick, neatly-cropped beard, and tears roll down his face only to get lost in the dense forest of hair.

Seth sits between Halton and Preston's empty chair. His expression is impassive, but his haunted eyes tell another story.

Across the table, Trevor and Dexter have very different reactions. I don't know either man, though I recognize them from the family portrait. Dexter is more open with his emotions and allows the tears to fall, while Trevor's expression is fierce, like a man ready to burn the world to the ground.

But it's Loki who scares me. He's wearing his rage openly and directing it solely at Ashton.

Colton sits beside Loki, witnessing the same thing. When he reaches over and places a hand on Loki's shoulder, I know I'm right. Loki shrugs him off with a *fuck you* glare. The hostility rolls off Loki like steam from wet pavement on a ninety-degree day.

He's simmering just below the surface. Waiting for his turn to explode.

"I didn't have Pacen's father arrested right away because I thought she needed to do it. For closure. He'd tried to sell her off. Christ, I just wanted to make things right with her. I made sure no one was ever in danger while he was free, but that was a choice I made, and it turned out to be the wrong one," Ashton says quietly. "One that could have cost GG her mountain."

Wait, what? I'm getting so lost in emotions I'm missing most of what he says. But maybe that's for the best.

Hearing this shit once was more than enough.

"Where is she now? Pacen? Where is she?" Loki demands.

"I don't know," Ashton admits.

I startle when Killian speaks for the first time. "Pacen Macomb is a victim in all of this too. She isn't your enemy."

"How the fuck do you know? Ashton almost died. My wife almost fucking died. Pacen was the only one who walked away that night unscathed. What the hell are you even doing here?" Loki demands. He stands quickly, and his chair tumbles to the floor behind him.

Killian stands too but makes no attempt to move. "If you think she walked away from anything unharmed, you have your head so far up your arse, even your burps smell like shit."

Loki rounds the table, but Colton steps in front of him.

"Killian is part of The Apollyon. The group I formed to extract children from The Ravens. He's the reason I'm still sitting here," Ashton says quietly. "And he is the man who will allow me to walk away from it all."

Silence falls over the room like the calm before the storm. But then I realize everyone is watching a battle of wills play out between Ashton and Loki.

A lifetime of stories explodes back and forth between them though they never utter a word.

Sadness and regret from Ashton. Rage and betrayal from Loki.

Dexter clears his throat. Then does it again before speaking. "This entire time, we thought Loki was playing the merry fucking fairy godfather—manipulating our lives behind the scenes." I have to lean forward to see Dexter around Ash. "But it wasn't him. You played us all, Ash. You never trusted anyone. It's always been just you."

"I spent years wrecked with guilt for dragging you into this, Ashton. Years!" Loki rumbles, and I fear that I'm watching thirty years of friendship vanish before my eyes. "But the truth is, you were already running the show. Weren't you? Are you the reason the FBI came looking for me? The reason they lured me into SIA? Tell me this, brother." He spits the word brother like it disgusts him.

"Did I ever have free will? Did I ever have a choice in where my life was going? Or did you sit behind your money and computer screens, directing my choices like a pawn in your game of chess? Because I have to tell you, Ashton, this was a pretty fucked up life you gave me. I thought I was your friend. I thought I was your goddamn brother," he roars, and I swear the entire room shakes.

"No." Ashton's words are a hoarse grumble. "SIA already wanted you. They already had plans. This was the only way I could stay with you. The only way I could protect you." The man I love deflates in his seat.

The man I love.

Well, isn't this a freaking inconvenient time for truths.

"And not once, in the last twenty years, was there a time you could have pulled me aside and said, 'hey buddy, guess what?' No time you could have said, 'hey, Loki. I fucked up, but I thought I was doing the right thing?'"

Ashton's weary gaze holds Loki's, and there are clear cracks in both their shields. "For so many years—so many years I couldn't.

I was following orders. I didn't know what would happen to you or The Apollyon if I brought you in. Then one secret spiraled into the next..."

"And now?" Seth asks with an eerie calmness. "After everything we've been through? Everything we've done together? You didn't think we might need redemption with The Apollyon as badly as you did? Did you ever once stop to consider how we could help you so you weren't killing yourself in the secrecy?"

Ashton tugs his hand free from mine and drops his head into his palms. "You have Sadie and the girls to think about now. Preston and his heart. Halton with his anxiety. Loki, you don't want to hear this, but you needed Sloane more than anyone I've ever known. She saved you. And you're a dad now. I couldn't bring you back into this. Any of you. You all have something to live for."

Loki moves with the precision of the Special Forces that trained him so well. He manages to maneuver me out of the way and pull Ashton out of his chair before anyone else can even lift an arm.

"Loki!" someone shouts from behind as he lifts Ashton from his chair. Before I can blink, Loki has him up against the wall with his forearm pressing into Ashton's throat, but he doesn't listen.

"You, Ashton. You have always had something to live for. So many things to live for, you fucking asshole. Don't you understand? You are this family. You are the Westbrooks. You're the heart and soul, the nucleus that keep us all living. Without you, we don't work." Loki pushes off him in a huff, and Ashton doubles over to catch his breath.

I stand, shaking, as Loki stalks toward the front door. Just before he's out of sight, he turns an anguished glare on Ashton. "I love you, Ashton. I'll always love you. But I don't know if I'll ever be able to trust you again."

The door slams, the crack of wood on metal echoing in the hallway.

"Pacen told us that the secrets of our father were slowly killing your soul," Colton says softly. He's unnaturally still, and that tells me more than any tantrum he could throw. "She was right, wasn't she?"

Ashton nods, and I go to him. Together, we slowly walk back to the table. I'm thankful when he sits and pulls me down with him. I straddle his chair awkwardly, but he holds me tight to his chest. He holds me like he needs me to anchor him in this world.

So I do.

CHAPTER 37

ASHTON

*M*y leg cramps, but I refuse to move. That would mean removing Nova from my lap, and that isn't possible right now. Right now, she is the only thing tethering me to my sanity.

It's been hours. Hours where my brothers rightfully grill me. Hours where their pain hurtles me into the darkest corners of my mind. But I deserve it. I deserve their ire.

I answer question after question until my voice gives out, and then Killian fills in the blanks. Eventually, my brothers leave. One by one, they filter out with promises and threats that they'll be back.

We're all running on emotionally borrowed time tonight.

Only Halton, Preston, and my mother have remained silent and in their seats. I'm not sure how she hasn't run out of tears yet, but with each new detail, a fresh wave of them sprang free. She cried silently though, and that knowledge burns deep in my chest.

How often has she cried so no one heard her? How often has it been because of me?

Halton is the next to stand, leaving me and Nova with Killian,

Preston, and Mom. He leaves without a word. He's had a few more hours to process this information, but I know he'll be back.

When Halton's footsteps fade in the distance, Preston clears his throat. "You're going to help him? Help him get out of this?"

Lifting my gaze, I see he's staring at Killian, but the rage I expect is replaced with something else. Something far more concerning. Brotherly indignation.

"I can't get out of it, Preston. I will always be involved. The money needs to come from somewhere."

Nova's foot taps at a rapid pace against the chair. Her legs swinging over the arm leave them suspended just enough that I can watch the jerky movements. I try to catch her eye, but she's staring at a point on the wall. She's also gnawing on her bottom lip, and it worries me.

What did I say that upset her now?

Is it always this hard to read girlfriends?

My heart hammers in my chest, and when she speaks, there's fear in her voice. "But you don't have to be the one to personally monitor the victims. You don't have to be so involved. Right?"

"Ashton?" It's the first time my mother has spoken in hours. When I turn to her, she appears to have aged, like each tear she's shed today has torn away a piece of her youth. The laugh lines that usually put people at ease frown at me with disapproval.

More guilt chokes me.

"I'm sorry, Mom. I'm so sorry." What else can I say to this woman who has done nothing but love me my entire life? I repaid her with secrets and lies. I don't blame her. I'm disappointed in myself too.

She stands and drags a chair closer so she can lean in. She presses her forehead to mine and draws Nova's in as well. The three of us sit like that for long minutes. Allowing the comfort and the pain to strip us bare.

"Do you remember when I told you that Daddy was like Bruce Wayne, but he was never Batman?" Mom asks. Her voice transports me back in time to the bedtime stories she would tell us as children. Calm. Strong. She kept the monsters away.

What does she think of her son now that she knows what I've become?

"Do you?" she asks again.

Of course I do. It hit hard, just as she'd intended. It was right after Colton had handed me a message from Pacen. Right after she'd told him I was keeping our father's secrets.

"Yeah, I remember."

Nova wiggles in my lap and tries to slip away, but I hold her tighter. My mother smiles and then moves back to give us some room.

"Your father was the money, Ash. He stepped in for Loki and would have done the same for Pacen, but I knew my husband. He couldn't have done what you're doing, and you don't have to be the dark avenger either, my sweet boy." Her voice cracks, and she shakes her head while straightening her spine. She's pulling herself together before my very eyes.

Where does her strength come from?

"We have more money than our grandchildren's grandchildren could ever spend. We can help these children, but you don't have to be the heart of it. Not anymore." She shoots a knowing look in Nova's direction, and my fragile emotions shatter. "It's slowly killing you. The ones you can't save?"

Nova stiffens in my lap, and I know I can't lie. "I failed them, Mom. The ones I can't save are either slaves in lives they didn't choose, or they just vanish. I'm not sure which fate is worse."

Her armor slips, but she doesn't try to replace it. Instead, she shows the power of honesty and love with her words. "You're focusing on the wrong things, Ashton. You take each loss as a personal affront. But how many have you saved?"

"Three thousand three hundred and seventy-two," Killian growls. "He's haunted by the two hundred and thirty-three we didn't save. Every year their classes get smaller. Because of

Ashton. Because of The Apollyon, but he remains consumed by the ones we've lost."

"I lost," I hiss through clenched teeth before I can stop myself.

"Why now?" Preston has always had a presence about him, a manufactured air when needed, but looking at him now, I only see my brother. Tired and beating himself up because he didn't see what I was hiding.

We've all kept secrets that have hurt each other. We've all been broken down by unattainable duties we were never meant to carry. Yet we all come back. For each other. Because of each other. We keep coming back together.

"I'm tired, Preston. Life, it hurts. Every day it hurts. So damn badly. I didn't think I could feel anything but despair ever again. I truly didn't. I honestly thought the darkness that nips at my heels would win."

"And?"

Nova's arms wrap tighter around my middle. Her face rests against my chest, but the wet spot from her tears doesn't burn like a fresh wound. The physical representation of her love that soaks my chest nurtures a new foundation that's quietly filling in all the cracks in my heart.

"And Nova showed up in my guest room," I admit.

"And Nova showed up in your guest room," he repeats with an easy smile.

I search his eyes for some pearl of wisdom. Some snarky remark he's about to hit me with, but all I see is hope.

"You know I've made a lot of mistakes." He speaks in that silky way he has, but his eyes never leave Nova's. "First with my own life, then with each of yours…"

"Pres, you were barely twenty-two when Dad died," I interject, and he smirks.

"And you were still a child, Ashton. This grace you so freely bestow to all of us? Where is it for yourself?"

"I'm smarter than all of you. I understand things differently."

Preston's bark of laughter makes me wince. Technically, I am a genius, but I've never said it out loud like a douchebag before.

"Academically, yes. You are. But there's something to be said for emotional growth, Ash. Lived experience. In some ways, you're still the scared fifteen-year-old. And it's those pieces where I should have stepped in to help guide you."

"We can go 'round and 'round, placing blame." My mother sighs. "The truth is, we all made mistakes. Starting with your father and me. He had the biggest heart, but it sometimes got in the way of what was best. When Colton was a newborn, your father brought home not one, but two puppies. One was blind in one eye and going blind in the other. The second puppy only had three legs. He loved an underdog. But he didn't always stop to think about the repercussions."

"Flopsy. We named the three-legged one Flopsy," Preston mutters, but he's smiling.

"We did. And my point is, you're all so much like your father in different ways. But, Ash? You're his heart and soul. Flopsy died of bone cancer two months after we got her, and your brothers were devastated. Your father took her in knowing he couldn't save her, and you take on this job knowing you can't save everyone."

She shifts in her chair and dabs at her eyes when she thinks no one's looking.

"You can't save the entire world, son, no matter how hard you try. You can only do your best to give those you do save a chance at happiness. But you can't pour from an empty well. You can't give from an empty cup. You can't help anyone if you give so much of yourself that there's nothing left."

I open my mouth to argue, but my mother isn't finished yet.

"I should have known," she says quietly. "When you were fifteen. Still a baby. I should have known what you were doing."

"Mom, no. I was a fifteen-year-old in college. A fifteen-year-old recruited by a secret organization. There were too many factors invested in keeping those secrets for you to have ever figured it out. Even if you weren't grieving the loss of your husband, SIA would have made sure you never found out. They played by their own rules. This was never on you."

"Tell me that again when you're a parent, son."

I blanch at the nonchalant comment, but no one seems to notice.

"Nova, dear? Can you and Killian walk me out? It's been a long night, and we all need to sleep on things."

Kissing the top of Nova's head, I help her stand but frown when I see the emotion swirling in her eyes. Something is troubling her.

You, asshole. *You* are troubling her.

That horrid voice inside my head that always points out my failures is loud tonight.

But it's not wrong either. This is not normal for anyone involved, let alone a new romantic partner.

Exasperated, I squeeze my forehead between my thumb and fingers to ease the tension there while Killian and Nova walk my mother outside.

"This is a lot for anyone," Preston comments easily. His lackadaisical tone makes me want to kick his chair out from under him.

"It's worse than a bad movie because this is real life," I grumble. "You can't just turn the channel. She doesn't deserve any of this."

"But you do?" He shakes his head and I look away. "She cares for you though." My brother stands and crosses the room. The clinking of metal on crystal tells me he's standing at my bar. When he returns, he slides a glass full of amber liquid in front of me.

We sip in silence as his words play in my head. I know Nova cares for me, but is it enough to put up with this shit?

As if reading my mind, Preston sets down his glass. "If she

didn't hop the first plane home when you told her this, I don't think she'll run now."

"She'd be smart to."

"Probably," he concedes. "Is that what you want?"

"Fuck no." I take another swig of whiskey and let the burn that fills my throat ground me. It takes a beat for my thoughts to regulate, but when they do, I turn to my eldest brother. "After everything I just told you, Nova is what you want to talk about?"

His goddamn smirk irritates me.

"I learned to focus on what's important in life, little brother."

"Lucky you," I grumble.

"Why do you think I'm asking about Nova?" He says it like we're discussing the weather.

"Because you're a nosy fucker?"

He laughs, and my shoulders drop some of their tension.

"That's part of it. But I've learned that sometimes you just have to move forward. Do I agree with what you did? Hell no. Do I understand why you did? Sadly, yes. But by talking to us, it tells me that you're committed to moving forward. To actually living. Is that the truth?"

"I want to." Suddenly I'm ten again, telling him I blew up his bike tire with a harebrained experiment.

"But you're scared." He places no judgment in those words, but I know he's seeking confirmation.

Eventually, I nod and down the rest of my whiskey in one fiery gulp.

"I think to move forward, you have to truly put The Apollyon behind you. If you don't, you're risking your relationship with Nova and possibly us."

I know that. I've always known that. It's why I've never told them what I do.

"If I don't, I won't survive, Preston. But I don't know how to do this. I don't know how to be normal. I don't know how to let go of the guilt. I don't even fucking know how to date, for Christ's sake."

Preston crosses one long leg over his knee and leans back in his chair. Clasping his hands behind his head, he flashes me the most devious grin I've ever seen. You can't look at that expression and not smile, so I do, and we sit there grinning at each other like two fucking fools.

"Dating is something we can help with. Dating in the most epic fashion is what your brothers excel at. Are you and your big brain ready to learn?"

"I didn't mean—"

"To call us idiots?" he teases. "I know. But we're also not going to let that big head of yours get any bigger." He drinks from his crystal tumbler and his smile slowly fades into seriousness. Dread fills my gut. "This won't be easy, Ash. I won't say you're broken, but you have work to do to get your head on straight. And I honestly don't think you can do that while being broken down every day with The Apollyon."

"I meant what I said. Killian is going to take over. I have to find the right balance though. I can't just up and leave. I know I can't keep doing what I'm doing, but it's been my whole life for twenty years."

"That's what I mean about moving forward, Ash. Is Nova your future?"

"I don't deserve her."

"That's not what I asked," he says harshly.

"I want her to be. I want her to be mine more than I've ever wanted anything for myself."

"She'll have to come first."

I glance at the empty hallway, but I don't know what I'm searching for. "Hattie said the same thing."

"I'm not surprised. He learned the hard way."

"Learned what?"

"That if you're not leading with love, you're following with regret."

If you're not leading with love, you're following with regret. Fuck. When did he become so smart?

"Can you put her first, Ashton?" The seriousness of his tone makes my heart thrash against my ribcage.

"I'm going to try. I swear I'm going to try, but…"

"But nothing. That's all I needed to know. We'll help with the rest."

"The rest of what?"

"The happily ever after. You do the work no one else can. Get your head straight, and we'll give you a crash course in landing the girl." His eyes dance like Colton's, telling me I'm in trouble.

"That sounds like a fucking terrible idea."

Preston's grin is blinding. "You have eight sisters-in-law, Ash. We've learned a thing or two. Welcome to the school of GTGs and HEAs."

"The what? And what's?" What the hell am I getting myself into?

"Getting the girls and happily ever afters. We'll throw in some classes on groveling for when you inevitably fuck up because you will. We all do. It's better to know when to say you're sorry than to chase her down after she's left."

Muted voices in the hallway have me sitting taller in my chair.

"I don't care who you are, Killian McPuncherface," Nova says. "But if you're hiding something, I will gut you myself." She stops short at the entrance to the dining room when she realizes Preston and I are staring. "Ah, well. Okay. It was nice to meet you, Killian. You can show yourself out."

Preston laughs, and I kick him under the table. I know why Nova hates Killian, but he truly isn't the enemy. I only relax when Killian himself laughs. His thick Irish brogue is hard to understand through fits of laughter.

"Aye, lass. I like ya." The laughter dies when he turns to me. I know what comes next. "It's time, Ashton. Make the call."

I nod. My gaze passing over three sets of eyes.

What will happen if I say it?

When I say it?

What if I can't truly walk away?

Nova.

Sweat trickles down my spine and acid rises in the back of my throat. It takes two tries before I can force the words to come. "Titan Falls." My back falls against my chair like I was shot. I know my eyes are wide. Too wide. Nova watches on in fear, but I can't speak.

Preston stands and gapes between Killian and me. "What the fuck is going on?"

My shoulders shake like an earthquake is swallowing me whole. Adrenaline. It must be adrenaline coursing through my body at the power those two little words wield.

I'm free.

"Peto?" Nova's voice cracks, and my eyes dart to hers, but my body is frozen. Paralyzed. I'm free.

Killian steps forward and slaps my face, then all hell breaks loose. Nova jumps on his back, and Preston tries to piledrive him. They tumble to the floor in a mess of limbs. But he did what he was supposed to, and I come back into my body.

"Stop. Nova, stop." It takes more strength than I thought I had to pry her off Killian. Preston released him the second he heard my voice. But my feisty little protector still claws at him. "Shh. I'm okay, princess. I'm okay."

She turns her anger on me. "What the fuck is going on?"

"I—I'm free. Titan Falls means..." I break down. Words fail me. My mouth opens and closes like a fish and once again, Killian steps in just as a sob breaks free from my soul.

"Titan Falls means he's out. It's his succession plan. For me to take over if something happened to him." He turns to me, and his expression is full of relief. "I'll let the team know immediately. You're a good man, Ashton. The best I've worked with, but I've never been so happy to see someone walk away. You've done great things, but you're so much better than this. You're meant to make the world a better place in much bigger ways."

"Jesus Christ," Preston blurts, still clutching his chest. "I may have a new heart, but I can't take this shit."

Killian chuckles and exits the room with barely a sound.

Preston stands before Nova and me with his hands on his hips like a father ready to scold unruly children, and I laugh. I laugh so hard my stomach cramps. He watches on until I've got it all out. Then his words sober me to the moment.

"Get some sleep. Now the real work begins."

He has no idea how right he is.

CHAPTER 38

NOVA

"You don't think I'm crazy?" I ask the only dad I've ever known.

Cradling his tea in both hands, he blows across the top of the mug and watches me.

It's hard to look at Ollie Blaine and not smile. Today he's dressed for fall with wide-leg faux denim pants and a neon green floral button-down. It's the first time I haven't seen him in parachute pants in almost three years, and I suppress a giggle. What fashion blogger told him this outfit was in style now?

"Nono," he coos fondly. "You know how quickly I fell in love with your mother. I'm not here to judge."

I tilt my head at him suspiciously. "What are you doing here then?"

It's been four days since Ashton ripped open old wounds to allow his family in. Then he slept for three days straight. When we woke this morning, his eyes had a brightness that's never been there before. With the weight of his world no longer holding him hostage, I think he's seeing life through new eyes.

I don't think he was expecting a visit from my family so soon, but I guess I should have expected that when I called home yesterday to have some things shipped here.

Sitting higher in my chair, I try to put my eyes on Ashton. Lochlan nearly dragged him from his own house without any shoes on before I stepped in.

"Don't worry so much, Nono. Kitty is out there keeping the peace, but you know Lochlan. You'll always be his baby sister. No matter how close he is to the Westbrooks, no one will ever be good enough for you."

I roll my eyes to hide my grin.

"We all love you and just want you to be happy."

Reaching across the table, I place my hand on top of my dad's. "I know, Papa. I am. I feel like I belong here."

"Then here is where you shall be. I have to ask though, or Kitty will kill me."

I scrunch my face up as I prepare for his question. It can't be good. "What?"

"You're not hiding out here because of what happened with the K word, are you?"

Ollie Blaine is insane. "The K word? You mean Kate?"

"Shh. We aren't saying that twat's name ever again."

"Papa."

"I mean it, Nono. You're not here because…"

"I'm here because I want to be, and because I think I'm in love with Ashton."

His smile lights up the entire room. "Very well. One more question, because I read your impact statement."

Oh, shit. I sent him an impact statement yesterday outlining all my interactions with Kate throughout our so-called friend-ship. He was supposed to give it to my lawyer. Of course he would have read it.

"Why did you put up with her for so long? You don't believe any of that. Do you? The shite she said was utter bullocks." I love that his British accent gets thicker when he's heated.

"No. Not really. Maybe for a while I did. But not now. She was just always there when I was alone. Now I know she planned it that way, but at the time, I truly thought she was my only real friend."

He scans my face but finally lets it go. "So, tell me about this boy."

"He's hardly a boy, Papa."

"Humor me," he teases. "He seems..." Papa stares out the window, and I follow his movements. Ashton stands with his back to us, arms crossed over his chest. "Troubled. He seems troubled."

Understatement of the century, but at some point in the last few days, I decided to keep most of Ashton's secrets from my family, at least for now. I don't want them to worry, and honestly, I still need some time to process it all.

My mind drifts to this morning when Ashton woke in a panic. He'd thought I'd left.

"God, princess. I felt like my heart was carved from my chest. I thought you were gone."

"I'm right here. I was just making some calls."

"I don't know how to do this, us, but I'm going to try. I promise I'm going to try."

"I know," I whisper, pulling his head into my chest. *"I know you will."*

"No secrets." His voice is hoarse like he's been screaming his entire life. *"Not with us. We can never keep secrets. It's nearly destroyed my family too many times. Not with us. Never between us. Promise me."*

"I promise, peto. I promise."

"Nono?" My father's words startle me, and I almost drop my tea into my lap.

"Sorry," I say sheepishly. "He is troubled, Papa. But there's something about him, our connection. It's...it's almost..."

"Magical," he supplies.

"Yeah, if magic had thorns and obstacles at every turn."

My father frowns with concern. "But it's worth it? Is he worth it?"

Carefully, I break eye contact with my father and focus on Ashton again. Lochlan stands before him, tugging on his vest with agitation very clearly written across his face, but Ash stays calm.

"Yeah, Papa. He's worth it. Don't ask me how I know because I can't explain it. I just feel it. It feels as simple as breathing and as hard as neuroscience. But I know it's right."

"That's what love is, baby girl. Something so tangible it hurts, but not something you can hold and show off. I just needed to make sure you were here for the right reasons."

We're both watching the men in the driveway, and Kitty is outside with them, swaying side to side while she monitors from the sidelines.

"Lochlan seems to be under the impression Ashton could hurt you. It's our job to make sure you have both eyes open. Just promise me that you'll never forget your worth, Nono. Any man who will hold your hand has to know it too. You deserve happiness that shines like the sun and love that guides you home. But you can't love with your whole heart if you don't love yourself first."

Tears prick the corners of my eyes. It isn't my self-worth I'm worried about though.

"Well, if this is going to be the place you call home, give me the tour. We'll have to talk to Preston about finding a house."

I pause halfway out of my chair. "A house?"

"You didn't think we would let you move to the boonies without us, did you?" He finishes his tea and tosses me a wink. My mouth goes dry. My dad is not a "boonies" type of guy. "Just for visits, Nono. Geez. I'm no country boy, and did you see Kitty's heels? She's probably sunk into the ground out there with those spikes. But if this is home for you, we'll need a place to visit without cramping your style. Something tells me your guy isn't too keen on filling up his house with our crazy."

"All he knows is crazy, Papa. Trust me."

I take his teacup and I'm rinsing it when I hear Sadie's voice in the hallway.

"Nova?" she calls.

My father's eyes sparkle. He's going to adore Sadie Sunshine.

"In the kitchen," I reply. She comes skidding to a halt in the doorway.

"Girls' night," she screeches, clapping her hands happily in front of her.

I dry my hands as I turn to her. "Girls' night? But it's Friday. Don't you have plans with your uncle?"

"I did." She laughs, causing her blond curls to bounce around her shoulders. "But Preston and Colt just told him he has class tonight, and he isn't getting out of it."

"Class? What kind of class?" I hurry to the window and gasp. Preston, Colton, Halton, and Dexter stand in a circle with Lochlan and Ash.

Sadie squeezes in next to me and presses her face to the glass. "Supposedly, my dad and Uncle Easton are going too."

"But what kind of class are they taking?" Worry worms into my chest. Ashton looks uncomfortable even from here.

"No." Sadie giggles, and my father joins us at the window. "Only Uncle Ash is taking the class. The others are teaching it."

I turn my head to look at her and frown. "Teaching him what?"

The little girl who harnessed the sun looks up at me and smiles. "They're teaching him how to date."

The front door bursts open, and Ashton barrels through, looking more haggard than I've ever seen him. His eyes are wide, and his hair stands on end like he's run his fingers through it a million times.

Pulling away from my dad and Sadie, I walk toward him slowly.

"Well, hello there, young lady. My name is Sir Ollie Blaine."

Sadie giggles and I suppress the urge to roll my eyes. My father has never been knighted, but he plays the part well.

"Nono was just going to give me a tour. Perhaps you could take over?"

"Sure. Come on. I'll show you the sunshine room first." Sadie is an intuitive little thing. She winks as she passes, dragging my father behind her. I don't speak until they reach the stairs.

"Are you okay?"

"I'm going to miss my first date night with Sadie in eight years," Ashton says.

I blink in confusion. I'm not sure which part he's upset about —missing his date with his niece or the dating lessons.

"Okay," I drawl. "She seems all right. She's actually excited about a girls' night."

He grunts and tugs me into him. I land against his chest with a thud. "Good. Good," he repeats. "She'll have fun."

"And you?" I tap his back to get him to ease up on his grip, but I swear the longer our bodies are connected the more I feel his body relax, so I don't pull away. I let him take comfort in our closeness.

"My brothers have a plan."

Now I'm glad my face is smooshed into his chest so he can't see me smile. He must feel it, though because he pulls his head back to peer down at me.

"Sadie told you."

"Dating school sounds—fun?"

Closing his eyes, he sighs loudly and mutters something under his breath that sounds a lot like *assholes*.

"They love you and they're trying to help," I remind him.

"I'm a thirty-three-year-old man who has never been on a date, but I'm pretty sure I could have figured it out."

Patting his chest, I smile up at him. "I'm sure you would have. But I think this is their way of making amends for their perceived missteps. Plus, I've heard there have been some pretty epic grand gestures in this family, so they've either got the Prince Charming thing down or they've messed up epically. Either way, they want to hand over their knowledge. Let them have their fun. Plus, is it really so bad? Spending quality time with your brothers without all the secrets keeping you apart from them?"

His shoulders droop. "No, it's not bad. Just different."

"It is different, peto. You're learning how to live for the love of living instead of the duty of protecting. It's going to feel uncomfortable for a while."

"You'll be here when I get back?"

I point to two large suitcases standing against the back wall. "That was my plan."

Ashton smiles, and it's such an innocent, happy expression I feel my heart flutter. "I'll put the boys to work." He hesitates, uncertainty in his eyes. I wait patiently for him to find his words. "You are moving in, right? With me? Like a couple? Or a roommate? Should we put them in the sunshine room? How does that work if we're sleeping together? Because I really want to keep sleeping with you." The words tumble from his mouth like he can't stop them.

He grips the back of his neck, and his cheeks flush bright red. "Shit. I suck at this."

I reach up and grab his hand. Pulling it to my lips, I kiss his knuckles and watch his eyes darken each time I press another against his skin.

"With you, peto. Always with you."

He exhales a harsh breath that breezes across my forehead. "Thank fuck." He lowers his head to mine and places a gentle kiss on my lips. "Always with you too," he whispers against my mouth.

When he pulls back, I hear Sadie giggle, which sets off a chain reaction. With his arm around my shoulder, he turns us to face Sadie and my dad standing with Kitty and a scowling Lochlan.

"Love looks good on you, Uncle Ash. It's about time."

Looking up at Ashton, I find his eyes already on me. The smile on his face finally reaches his eyes. "It does, doesn't it?" he whispers.

I nod and grin like a fool.

Love does look good. It looks good on us both.

CHAPTER 39

ASHTON

"*I* hope you're joking," I deadpan as Colton places another shot in front of me.

"Guys' night," he shrugs.

We've taken over the back room of the newly renovated bar in GG's lodge.

"Did she really have to name it The Pickled Peter?" I ask, noting the dancing pickles on everything from napkins to pint glasses.

"It could have been worse." Colton laughs.

"How the fuck could it have been worse?" I demand.

"She wanted to name it the Cocky Cooter," Halton informs me. He flops down into the seat next to me and places a box of cookies on the table. The box is huge. There must be close to a hundred cookies in it.

No one says a word though. Baking and painting are how Halton works shit out. Glancing across the table, I make eye contact with Easton. I'd bet money he's been in his workshop building something out of wood.

We each have our way of coping.

Their ways are just less destructive than mine.

"What happens next?" Preston asks on my left.

I don't bother pretending not to know what he's asking. Preston is the caretaker. The planner. He'll want an actionable, step-by-step process.

"We're moving The Apollyon into a vacant space downtown next to Envision's headquarters. Eventually, Killian will hire more people and move the organization wherever he wants to set up home base."

Everyone nods. A few take sips of their beers. It weighs heavily on me that Loki's not here.

"He feels betrayed," Seth says, guessing where my thoughts have drifted. "He's hurt too. We all are, but him especially. Granted, he did the same exact thing. He's probably a little butthurt that you outplayed him though. He's spent his entire life thinking he dragged you into the mud, when really, you set the hose in the dirt. He'll come around."

"And if he doesn't?"

"He will," Preston vows. "We're family. He will."

"My question is, will you be able to let Killian take the reins?" Seth asks. He knows me as well as anyone. "Nova is uprooting her life for you, and you know as well as I do that you can't live as you were and give her what she deserves. I'm not saying it's one or the other, but…"

"But it kind of is," Colton butts in. "Nova is a good girl, Ash. She's feisty and smart, but I get why Loch is concerned. Her heart can be bruised easier than your ego, so if you're making a commitment to her, she has to be your first priority."

"I know that," I say. Slamming my shot glass onto the table, I avert my eyes. "I know that, but I can't just walk away from The Apollyon tomorrow. It's a process. I couldn't live with myself if I didn't make sure they had everything they need."

"No one is asking you to abandon your responsibilities. We're just making sure that you're consciously making an effort to shift your priorities. It's something most of us learned the hard way," Preston says as diplomatically as a politician.

My ears burn with anger. None of them think I can do this. None of them have any faith in me.

Why would they? I've proved time and again that I'm an excellent liar. Secrets and lies.

"Ashton?" Dexter says my name like it isn't the first time he's tried to get my attention.

"Sorry, what?"

He smirks and rubs his hands together like he's preparing to tell me aliens are real. I lean back in my chair. I feel like the more space I can put between us, the better off I'll be.

"I said, Prince Charming is at your service. Are you ready to begin?"

"Begin? Begin what?"

"Your training." He cackles like GG, and I push my chair away from the table. If he's about to throw some tarot cards at me or sprinkle me with some fucking potion she made in her basement, I'm out of here.

When I don't say anything, all the assholes around me laugh.

"Relax, Ash. We're just talking about dating. You haven't done much of it, but since Nova brought you back to us, we want to make sure you don't do anything to fuck it up," Halton says and rolls his eyes. "Not all of us are into the theatrics, Dex."

"I'm thirty-three, not thirteen. I'm sure I can figure it out."

"Oh, yeah?" Colton asks with a raise of his brow. "Do you open the car door for her or not?"

"Yes, of course."

"What if she doesn't want you to open it?" Trevor asks. "How do you know?"

"How do you know what?"

"Some women want you to open the doors for them. Some think it's a slap in the face of feminism."

I slump back in my chair and reach for a beer.

"You're shitting me." I glance around at all my brothers. Well, almost all my brothers. I'll need to work on Loki.

"Nope, afraid not," Seth mutters. "Women are a fucking mystery, dude. And when you think you have them figured out?"

"They change their mind," Easton grumbles. "It's their prerogative too."

"What about the check? Do you pay, split it, or let her pay?" Halton asks.

Turning in my seat, I stare him down. Surely this is a trick question.

"You pay it," I say smugly.

All seven of them shake their heads sadly.

"Are you fucking with me?"

"Some women appreciate the white knight. Some get really pissed off if you expect anything but the unexpected."

Now I'm sure they're messing with me.

I glare at Dex. "What do you teach Tate?"

"Ah, now you're learning." Dexter laughs.

"Learning what? That you're all a bunch of assholes and I should have stayed home and let Sadie paint my nails?"

"Does she paint your nails?" Easton asks.

"If she wants to," I say with a shrug. "Who cares? It's just paint."

"No judgment. I guess I never really thought about what you do together."

"We do whatever the hell she wants because even if I'm a fuckwit to everyone else, I don't want her to see me that way." I shove out of my chair. No one moves as I pace the length of the table. "Until now, Sadie was the only one who didn't look at me like I was broken. She's a good kid with a kind heart, and I refuse to be the bastard who breaks that."

"Because you care," Preston states.

"Of course I fucking care. I'm not a monster."

As soon as the words are out of my mouth, they ring in my ears like I was hit in the head with a pair of cymbals.

All eyes are on me as I process my own words.

"No, Ash. You've never been a monster. Sadie loves you because you have the heart of a giant and the determination of a gladiator. She loves you because you've always asked her what she wanted. Because you listen to her. The same goes for dating," Seth says softly.

"Dating is simple if you let it be," Colton explains. "When you don't know something, you ask."

"You ask?" I reply numbly.

"Yup. If you can't tell something by her body language, you ask. When the check comes, you snatch it up and tell her that you don't want to make her uncomfortable, but you'd really like to buy her dinner. When you're walking on the street, if she gets to the door first and opens it, say thank you and take it from her. Usher her in under your arm. If you get there first, just do whatever feels natural."

"You guys are freaking him out. It isn't rocket science," Halton grunts.

"No, rocket science would be easier," I mumble.

"Listen," Halton continues, "it all comes down to communication. Something all of us, except maybe Colton, suck at. You have to talk to her. Talk about meals and dates and sex. Talk about her day and expectations and the future. Just talk. Even when it feels like you're talking in circles, keep talking until you're one hundred percent sure you're on the same page. And even then, ask for confirmation that you're both hearing the same thing because you can say the same words, and they could still have vastly different meanings."

My brothers all nod and hum their agreement.

"You say the same words and they mean different things? What the hell does that even mean? Blue is blue." I groan in frustration.

"Blue is blue unless it's baby blue," Halton says.

"Or cobalt blue."

"Or azure blue."

"Or navy blue." Colton smirks. "Lots of blue, Ash. And they're all a little different. See what we mean?"

"No!" I shout. "No, I have no fucking clue if I'm supposed to ask her out or get a color chart."

"What these boys are tryin' tell ya, warden, is ya have to communicate with her," GG's voice wobbles with age.

Halton reaches her first and attempts to guide her into the room. Her body is frailer than I remember, and it's a reminder that time doesn't stand still for anyone. She smacks Halton in the shin with her cane when he tries to hold her arm, instead taking her time to click-clack across the room unassisted.

When she eases down into a chair, I feel my brothers' collective sigh of relief. GG is a pain in the ass, but she's ours.

"This has been a long time comin', ain't it, warden?"

I gulp but nod. This crazy old lady has always told me my light was coming. After all her love matches, I should have known she wouldn't let me down.

"In love and life, you only need to know one thing." She grins, looking around the table.

"What's that, GG?" Halton is the only one with enough balls to ask.

"How to say yer sorry." She reaches across the table and grabs my whiskey that someone keeps refilling. Then she tosses it back without a wince.

She's a tough old bird, but she just might have the biggest heart of us all.

"So, have ya given him the sex talk yet?" she asks, ruining the moment.

Colton howls with laughter to my right, and even Seth breaks into a grin.

"Jesus, GG. I'm not a virgin."

Somehow, it's not even weird to be having this conversation with her.

"So ya know how to find the devil's doorbell then, do ya?"

Beer sprays across the table. Preston sits across from me, spluttering and wiping his mouth. "The devil's doorbell? Is that a thing?"

Suddenly I'm thankful Nova's brother decided not to stick around for this. Pinching the bridge of my nose, I pray it's almost over, but I should have known better.

"It was in my day. We're talkin' bout the clit, boy. Got it?"

"Yeah, GG. Got it. Thanks." I groan.

"But we didn't do all this butt stuff when I was young. Maybe it's called something else now, 'cause I sure as shit would think the devil's doorbell would be on the back end."

"Oh my God," Dex mutters.

I can't. This can't be real.

"Butt stuff, GG?" Colton goads with a grin that spells trouble. "What kind of butt stuff are you referring to?"

"Colt!" Dex scolds. "Do not encourage her."

"Oh, come on. You've all had a little." He twirls his finger in the air with a whistle. "Admit it."

Easton stands and drops a wad of cash on the table. "I'm not having this conversation with my wife's grandmother."

"Oh, he's definitely had the..." Preston makes the same motion with his finger, and Colton supplies the whistle.

Easton's face turns bright red.

"Oh my God. He has." Dex laughs.

Before I know what's happening, everyone has fingers in the air, and Colton alternates whistles with a full-on belly laugh.

Fuck, it feels good to laugh with these guys. Even if we're talking about butt stuff with an almost ninety-year-old woman.

In the midst of all the chaos, GG leans over and places a bony hand on mine. Her skin is nearly translucent. It's paper thin and cold. The laughter continues around us, but for a second, it's just her and me.

"You're going to be just fine, Ashton. Yer finally ready."

My throat feels as dry as the Sahara, and it's an effort to get the words out. "Ready for what, GG?"

"To love and be loved. You have the greatest capacity for it I've ever seen. You just needed someone to fill in yer cracks. You're a good boy, Ashton. A real good boy. You've done yer part to make this world a better place. Now it's finally yer turn to let love do the rest. Let it heal yer heart and yer soul. Forgive yourself, Ashton. Forgive yer past so you can live in the present and embrace yer future."

I don't remember her ever calling me Ashton before. It hits harder than any secret I've ever kept or truth I've told. That, more than anything, makes me believe she just might be right.

CHAPTER 40

"*D*o I look okay?" Taking a step back, I angle the phone so Penny can see all of me.

"You look hot, Nova. Where are you going?"

"Dinner and dancing. I'm not exactly sure where. Lexi took me out and showed me around town yesterday, but there's not much here. I don't even think there's a Target close by."

Penny laughs but sobers when she sees my face. "Wait, you're serious? How is there no Target? Even Chance Lake has a Target within driving distance."

I shrug because I'm confused too. "I don't know. I thought they were everywhere, but not here. The town sign said population 2,356. There were more people in my high school."

"Do you like it, though? Are you happy?"

"Everyone is really nice."

"That's not what I asked, Nono, and you know it."

"I am. It'll be better when Ashton is around more."

Penny bites her lip like she wants to say something.

"What?"

"Maybe the boys and I should come for a visit. You know, check this guy out."

That draws a laugh from me. "I would love it if you came to visit, and you'll love Ashton."

"Hmm."

"What's the hmm about."

"You have a habit of fixing everything, Nova."

I feel my defenses rising. "And?"

"And just make sure you don't spend so much time trying to fix this guy that you lose sight of yourself. That's all. I am happy for you. If you're happy, that's all that matters, but don't live your life waiting on someone else. It never turns out like you think it will."

I know she says this out of love and from her own lived experience, but it doesn't sit well with me. "I'm not," I promise. "I've been drafting new designs, and he's just moved his—his business out of the house into an actual office. It's just a lot. We'll settle into a routine. I'm sure of it."

"I'm sure you will," she placates, which pisses me off. I bite my tongue to keep from snapping at her. "I just worry about you. That's all."

That softens me. "I know, Penny. But I'm fine. Promise. I should probably go though. Our reservation is in half an hour.

"Call me tomorrow and let me know how it goes."

"I will. Bye, Pen."

"Bye, Nono."

Ending the call, I check the time. I feel unsettled, but I toss the phone into my clutch. With a final look in the mirror, I fix my lipstick, then head down the stairs to wait for Ash.

And wait.

And wait.

After an hour, I call Rylan.

"Hey. I thought you were on your date?" Someone cries in the background, and I realize it's probably bedtime for her toddler.

"Ah, we are. We do. I mean…"

"He's late? On your very first official date? You've got to be shitting me. Hattie!" she yells without moving the phone and nearly blows out my eardrum. "Where the hell is Ash? He's late on their first date."

There's grumbling, then the crying fades away and it's just Rylan.

"It's not a big deal. I know he's doing stuff with Killian today, I just…"

"You're worried," she finishes for me. "Seth lives the closest to the office. He'll run over and check on him."

"Oh, no. I don't want to bother him. I just—" Our front door crashes open and scares the shit out of me.

"He's home?"

"He's home," I say when my eyes land on Ashton's frazzled face.

"Call me later," Rylan grumbles. "I'm going to smack him when I see him."

"Bye." Disconnecting the call, I never take my eyes off Ash. He looks tired, and I just want to hold him. "Are you okay?"

"Fuck, princess. I'm so sorry. You look amazing." He runs his hand through his hair and then drops his head to his crumpled button-down. "Give me five minutes, and we can go. Okay?" Even his voice sounds tired.

I take a step toward him, bend down and remove one heel, take a step, then bounce on one leg while I take the other off and drop them both on the floor. "We don't have much in the fridge, but I can make a mean peanut butter and jelly." When I reach him, I lift up onto my toes and wrap my arms around his neck. "You look exhausted, peto. Give me a rain check instead."

"But our date," he pleads. "Dinner and dancing. I can't believe I lost track of time."

I can. I know how hard he's been working. I know he's been sneaking out of bed at night to get stuff done, and I know he's nearing burnout after only two weeks.

"Rain check," I say with my lips pressed to his cheek. "Tonight, we'll stay in, but you have to promise no more work tonight. No sneaking out of bed when you think I'm asleep. Tonight, it's just you and me."

His body goes stiff against me. "I don't want to miss time with you." He wraps his arms around my waist, and we sway to the song of our hearts.

"I know. That's why you're working all day, coming home to me until I fall asleep, then going back to work. But you can't do it all. You have to sleep. Tonight. Okay?"

His body melts into mine, and all my nervous energy from earlier evaporates. It's easy to worry about the what-ifs when we're apart, but our bodies know what we need. What our hearts long for. What our minds crave.

Each other.

We dance in the glow of the fading sun. Ashton sings above me, and my heart thunders heavily in my chest. "You—You sing? What song is that?"

His legs stop moving, but his hand on my lower back continues to rub rhythmic circles. His chin rests on my head and his body relaxes on a deep exhale.

"I used to sing," he rasps. "I forgot. I forgot I liked it. I forgot so much about life."

Lifting my head, I find his eyes on me, full of wonder and what I think is hope.

Oh, peto.

"It's The National."

I look at him, confused.

"Elpis, play The National, 'I Need My Girl,'" he commands, and a slow, melodic beat filters through the house. The man's voice is low, gravelly, and mesmerizing. But his words coming from Ashton's mouth as we slowly rock to the beat give me a sense of home I've never truly had.

"Don't give up on me," Ashton whispers. "I'll try harder, Nova. I will."

I nod against his chest. I know he will. He'll always try. He'll keep pushing until it kills him.

"Kiss me," I plead. I need to get out of my head. I need to feel him and know we're going to be okay. I need the calm that comes from the rawest of connections.

When his lips touch mine, my mind stops racing with what-ifs. It focuses on the here and now. On him. On me. On us.

He hooks his hands under my thighs and lifts me to him. I immediately wrap my legs around his waist, and he carries me upstairs. We don't break our kiss the entire time, and when we tumble to the bed as one, my heart races with worries of the future, but I ignore it.

Right now, I just need him.

"Tell me what you want," he growls.

"You. In me. Now."

His groan vibrates through his entire body as he lifts up onto his knees to release his cock. I'm so desperate for him, to feel like we're all right, that I lift my skirt and tug my panties to the side.

Ashton's eyes darken as I rub my hand over my pussy. I'm already soaked. I don't want foreplay. Not tonight.

"Now, peto. I need you," I whine.

He lowers his body and rests on his forearms above me. His eyes dance back and forth between mine as he enters me in one slow thrust. "Are you okay?" he whispers. Maybe he senses the turmoil stirring in my chest.

"Yeah. Yeah." It's all I can manage before his lips land gently on mine. He rolls his hips, and tears spring to my eyes. I have no idea why I'm so emotional, but it doesn't matter. Not right now.

"Faster," I beg, but he doesn't listen. He maintains that torturous pace until I think I'll lose my mind. Ashton fucks me lazily, thoroughly, deeply, and never once breaks eye contact.

When a tear slips free, he catches it with his thumb, but keeps riding the wave of bliss in his own time. He's taking my arousal to new heights. It's too intimate. So intimate.

"I want to be the man you deserve, Nova." He whispers his confession, and I feel the first tremors of an orgasm deep in my belly. "You make me want things I never thought I'd have. You're the best thing that's ever happened to me, and I'm so scared I'll lose you too."

Through all his words, his cock keeps up the almost painfully slow fucking. But once he's done talking, it's like the cord has snapped, and his hips hammer into mine.

It's delicious and devastating and so damn perfect that I come apart with a strangled cry and beg for more. He doesn't stop. If anything, he moves faster, harder. His strokes become longer and more erratic, and one spasm rolls into another.

"Fuck, yes. Nova. You are meant for me. For me," he roars, then stills so deep inside me it's like he's trying to imprint his body in mine. I feel every twitch as he releases in me, his come splattering against my walls in an erotic claiming that has my entire body trembling.

Ashton collapses on top of me. His weight settles the unease of earlier, and I gently run my fingers up and down his spine.

In moments like these, when he gives himself over to me so completely, I know we're going to be just fine.

"I thought," he mutters sleepily into my neck, "I thought I'd fucked up and you wouldn't be here."

My heart breaks at the reminder of all he's missed out on. All the things he never experienced.

"That's not how relationships work, Ash. We made promises, remember? Communication. Trust. That's what we said."

His eyes find mine in the darkened room. "Why? Why me? Wouldn't your life be much easier with someone less—less fucked up? Someone with less baggage to work through?"

I chuckle sadly. It makes my inner walls squeeze his dick, and his hips twitch involuntarily.

"It would probably be easier," I admit, and his face falls before I can finish. "But that's not how love works. You don't get to choose who you fall in love with. But even if you did, I'd choose you, Ashton Westbrook. I'd choose your giant heart and your battered soul. I'd choose your secrets and your truths. I choose you."

"Why?" he croaks. His insecurities seep through the cracks in his quickly crumbling walls.

"Isn't that obvious?"

He shakes his head, and his hands tremble on either side of my face. "No. Tell me?"

I smile and let him see all the way to my heart. "Because I love you. I love you, peto. I love all of you."

"Say it again," he growls.

"Three times wasn't enough?" I laugh.

His hips press me hard into the mattress, and his length grows harder. Thicker. Longer.

"No. Say it again."

"I love y—"

He cuts me off with a kiss that leads to another orgasm that leads to a dreamless and tranquil sleep.

CHAPTER 41

ASHTON

I wake slowly. Peacefully. It's a novelty that only happens with Nova at my side. I can smell her shampoo before I even open my eyes.

I want this every day. More than anything, I want mornings like this. I just wish I knew how to let go. How do I keep the guilt from consuming me?

Whenever I think I can hand The Apollyon over to Killian, I'm haunted by innocent faces that won't release me.

What if they never do?

"You're thinking awfully hard up there for six in the morning." Nova's voice is sexy with sleep. Her words blow gentle breaths across my chest.

Isn't it strange that I was having mental breakdowns only a month ago because she grazed my skin and now, she lies naked on top of me with no reaction?

How is that?

That question reminds me I have a session with Dr. Benson today, and my mood instantly sours.

"What is it?" Nova asks, turning to find my face. "What's making you grumpy before the sun can even shine?"

I fold my right arm under my head and prop it up so I can look down at her. I use my free hand to play with her hair. Even a snarled mess, it's still so silky soft.

"I have a therapy session today." I let her strands of hair slip through my fingers. A metaphor if I've ever seen one. If I'm not careful, everything is in danger of slipping away from me.

She sits up next to me, her hair sliding away from my fingers. The blankets pool at her waist, and I lick my lips with longing as her nipples pucker in the cool morning air.

"Do they help? Your sessions?"

I think about her question. Do they? Most of the time, I don't think so. But lately?

"Maybe," I finally say. "I don't know. I go because it's important to my mom and Sadie. I've always just gone to appease them."

She frowns like she's thinking hard. "So you're not putting in the work?"

"I— What do you mean?"

"Therapy is one of those things you only get out of it as much as you put in. If you're just going through the motions, you're not really getting anything out of it."

I don't like the way she's looking at me. It makes the hairs on my arms stand on end, so I adjust the pillows behind me and sit up straighter.

Nova places her hand on my arm. Her thumb swipes back and forth across my skin as she speaks. "Therapy is a useful tool, but like anything else, it takes work. Therapy isn't something you can do by osmosis, Ashton. We're all flawed in some way, but unless you can acknowledge your faults, your fears, and your ambitions, it isn't worth going. It has to be something you do for yourself, not for anyone else."

Her tone is clipped but gentle. It's confusing.

"You're mad." I don't mean to say it out loud, but it slips free.

She purses her lips and leans back against the headboard. "I'm not mad. I'm disappointed. I know you're trying. I do, but it seems counterintuitive to me that you have the best resources at your disposal to make things happen, and you're just going through the motions."

Am I?

Dr. Benson always asks the stupidest fucking questions. How can that possibly help me?

She sighs and moves to get out of bed, but I hook her around the waist and pull her into me. Big spoon, little spoon is my new favorite position.

My cock doesn't mind it, either.

"Ashton," she gripes. "I'm being serious."

Making sure my hips don't move without permission, I nestle her closer. "I know you are, baby." I keep my words low and breathy at her ear and love it when goosebumps appear all over her exposed flesh. "I'll talk to him today, okay? Really talk."

She presses her back into my chest, and I roll over so she can turn around. "You're still not getting it. Don't do it for me, Ash. It has to be for you."

I don't get the difference. I want to make her happy. So, if going at therapy differently does that, why does it matter?

I know better than to say that, though. Instead, I say sincerely, "I will."

It's not a lie. I will try. I'll try to figure out why it's so important. Try to figure out how to do this thing called love. I'll try to figure out how to live a normal life. If the good doc has some suggestions, great. If not, I'll do what I've always done. I'll make it happen.

Nova's stomach growls loudly, and that familiar pang of guilt slices my chest open.

I never took her to dinner last night.

Then I fucked her. Twice. And didn't feed her.

When she sees my expression, she rolls her eyes, then climbs out of bed. "Don't borrow guilt, peto. You have enough of that to last a lifetime. I'm a grown-ass woman. If I was that hungry last night, I wouldn't have let you maul me until I passed out. I made the choice not to eat. Not you."

"It's the second time I've failed to take care of you," I grumble. Tossing back the covers, I stomp from the bed. "A simple fucking date. That's what my priority should have been last night, and I failed."

She marches straight to me and shocks the shit out of me when she grabs my face between her hands and kisses every thought right out of my head.

"Do I have your attention now?" she asks, pulling away. Our lungs heave as we suck in air.

"Did you just kiss me stupid?" My mouth hangs open with a grin.

"It's my new signature move when my alpha man is being ridiculous. It works, right?"

"Fuck," I grumble, rubbing my swollen lips.

"Are you ready to listen now?"

"What? Yes. I'm listening."

She smirks and sits on the edge of the bed. Gently she pats the spot next to her. I stalk to the bed and can't help sulking as I sink onto the mattress.

"I love you," she states simply, and I realize I haven't said it back to her. Not because I don't want to, but because I'm terrified. "I love you," she repeats staring straight into my eyes. "But I'm not looking for a caretaker, a babysitter, or a father figure. I need a partner, Ashton. I need you. I need you as the man you are, the man you want to be, and the man you're working to be in the future."

"I like taking care of you."

It's the simplest truth I've ever told.

She smiles lazily. "I like it too, but not when you tear yourself apart because you failed at some duty you think you should have done. Take care of me because it's natural. Because it's what happens in the moment, but don't ever break yourself down because you think you failed at something I'm perfectly capable of handling myself. Okay?"

I nod, but truthfully, I'm fucking confused. Maybe I do need my brothers' help after all. Women are so goddamn confusing.

"Good," she says cheerfully. "Now, I am starving. So I'm going to make some breakfast while you get ready. Want some?"

"Yeah, thanks," I say on autopilot. My mind is still wondering how the hell to make this work.

She's at the door when it hits me. "Nova?"

She turns with the most brilliant smile that draws me to her like a zipline. When I'm close enough to touch her, I do. I hold her head tightly and bring her lips to mine. Just before we touch, I let the last domino fall.

"I love you. So fucking much it hurts. I love you, Nova Blaine."

I feel the tension I didn't know she was carrying leave her body when she sags into me. I hate that I didn't realize she was so wound up.

Life lesson learned. Grow the fuck up and make the therapy work.

"I love you too," she breathes against my skin. Her stomach growls again, and so do I. Placing a quick kiss on her lips, I turn her toward the door and watch her walk down the hall.

For this woman, I'll walk through hell. And today, I guess my hell just happens to be called Dr. Benson.

～

I storm through the door of Dr. Benson's old Victorian home. He's converted the back half of the house into a home office. It's the only place I'll see him. I fucking hate hospitals.

"Mr. Westbrook." The older woman sitting at the desk splutters. I realize in the two years I've been coming here, I never got her name. Strange. "You're early."

"Does he have a patient?" I ask, pointing to the door.

She glances at the clock ticking behind me. I know I'm his first appointment of the day.

"No. You always schedule the first appointment and the one after it."

Right. I never wanted to run into anyone else while I was here.

I scan the room, searching for a nameplate, or something that will tell me her name. Now that I know I've ignored her for so long, it claws at my conscience. There's nothing. Not even a picture frame.

"What's your name?" It comes out of my mouth like a grunted demand, but I can't help it.

My skin feels too tight for my body every time I walk in here. Today it's worse.

"Carol," she says.

I huff out a loud breath through my nostrils and nod my head at the same time. I feel marginally better.

"Thank you, Carol." At least that came out more civilized. "I'm going in now."

I don't wait for her to answer. I'm paying through the nose for these sessions. Even the one that follows mine, so it's time to get my money's worth.

Barging through the door, I find Dr. Benson sitting behind his desk. He's not at all surprised to see me in my current state.

For the first time since I've known him, he cracks a smile.

It's irritating.

"You're ready," he says mysteriously.

I hike the heavy backpack I'm carrying higher onto my shoulder.

"For what?"

"To be here."

When I stand in the doorway glaring at him, he sweeps his palm across the room, silently inviting me to sit.

"I've always been here when I said I would be," I mutter.

As I enter the room, my eyes dart back and forth between the sofa and the chair that sits directly across from Dr. Benson's.

On the sofa, I can stare at the ceiling. I've always chosen that spot so I don't have to make eye contact with the smartass. So he can't see too much.

I take a step toward the sofa, then two toward the chair. I hover in limbo between the two spaces while Dr. Benson watches.

It shouldn't be so goddamn hard to choose a seat.

What the hell is wrong with me?

My throat is itchy, and I cough to clear it. Finally, I turn to Dr. Benson. "Where should I sit?"

The fucker has been watching me this entire time without giving anything away in his expression. Once again, he opens his hands wide. "It's your choice, Ashton. It's always been your choice."

There are too many secrets in those words. Too many meanings, so I ignore them and fall, ungracefully, into the chair opposite his.

I have to put in the work. Opening the backpack that now sits in my lap, I dump its contents onto the coffee table.

Dr. Benson watches me but says nothing as he observes twenty years' worth of notebooks spill out onto his table.

"What's this?" he asks impassively.

"My journals. The real ones. Not the bullshit I brought in here every week."

He leans back in his chair and steeples his fingers. Silently, he observes me, and my neck grows hot. My right knee bounces wildly, giving life to my discomfort.

"You're a very intelligent man, Ashton. Much smarter than

me. For two years, I knew the only way to get to you was to wait you out."

My eyes snap to his. "What?" I bark.

I clench my fists so tightly that my knuckles crack.

"We've been playing chess, Ashton. Circling each other but never getting anywhere. You were simply going through the motions. You were never trying to heal. Now, you're ready."

"Ready for what?"

"To heal yourself."

My defenses build up their walls, even if he's right. I can't help it. My fight or flight is kicking in. I'm losing control.

"You can tell that by where I chose to sit?" I snarl.

"Yes," he says simply. "Look at you. Your body language says it all. You're ready to move forward even though it's causing you great discomfort. This is the greatest breakthrough you've had since I've known you."

Shaking my head, I resist the urge to shout. "Breakthroughs are not that simple or easy."

"Who says?" he argues.

"Science. Nature. Life," I yell. My thread of control unravels all around me.

"For once in your life, you're wrong, Ashton. Breakthroughs are simply acknowledging the need for change or making the decision to be the change. I think you're doing both. The work to get there won't be easy, no. But the breakthrough you've just had is half the battle."

He leans forward and picks up one of my journals. "Before we begin, I want to ask you something."

"What?" Fuck. My knee won't stop bouncing. Even placing my hand on it, I'm not strong enough to hold it down. It's distracting, and disconcerting, and so fucking annoying.

"Now that you're ready, what do you want to get out of our sessions?"

"Freedom." It comes without thought. But it's the truth, and Dr. Benson nods like he'd already guessed it.

"Very good, Ashton. One more thing. I'd like you to set two goals. One that you believe to be impossible and one you want to achieve through our sessions."

Resting my arms on my thighs, I drop my head into my hands. "Okay," I mutter.

"Tell me?" Dr. Benson asks. His pen scratches across the paper like the sharp edge of a knife.

"I want to see The Ravens fall." The pen stops moving. I've alluded to my past in prior sessions. Enough that he knows what I'm talking about, but I've never named them.

With all the courage I have, I lift my head to find him regarding me with new eyes. "And?" he encourages.

"I want to live and love fearlessly."

"Living and loving fearlessly doesn't mean you won't feel fear, Ashton. Love is one of the scariest things we can do as humans because it makes us vulnerable."

I swallow the lump in my throat. "I know. I just don't want the fear to keep me from experiencing them."

Dr. Benson holds my eyes for a beat too long before he nods and offers a sympathetic smile. "Those are very worthy goals, Ashton. Thank you for trusting me with them. We have our work cut out for us, but I have no doubt you'll get there. Welcome to the first day of the rest of your life."

"Thank you, Dr. Benson. W—What do we do?"

"I think we start by making a list of people you need to forgive or make amends with. Starting with yourself."

Starting with myself.

And just like that, the last wall around my heart tumbles to the ground, clearing the way for a new foundation. One moored in trust. And truth. And love.

CHAPTER 42

NOVA

*L*ightning flashes, illuminating the entire room, before thunder claps high in the sky. I can already tell Ashton isn't in bed with me, so I feel along the nightstand for my phone. When the screen lights up, I see it's three in the morning.

It's been a month since our first missed date, and Ashton has tried hard to be everything for everyone ever since. It exhausts me just thinking about it.

He is the best uncle for Sadie. Loving and attentive, but he's been late to two out of the last four date nights with her too. Two of them, he barely made it home before she was heading to bed, and I know it hurt her.

It gutted Ashton as well. I see the vicious cycle he has himself in. Working endlessly to be perfect at everything but perfecting nothing.

Sometimes, I'm not even sure he remembers I'm here.

My feet hit the cool wood floor as I slip from the warmth of our bed. It sends a chill through me. The robe that hangs on the chair is twice my size, but it's worn and soft, so I wrap it around me. It smells like Ashton. Tying it tightly at the waist, I lift it enough that it won't drag on the floor behind me.

I know where I'll find him. It's where I've found him every other night this week and last. In his office, toiling away over new intel or old clues. There's always one more case to follow up on. One last detail that doesn't sit right with him.

It's impossible to get angry at a man who compromises himself for the safety of innocents, but I'd be lying if I said my weary heart wasn't growing restless in the silence. Not knowing where I fall in his life leaves me needy and fragile in a way I've never been before.

My heart shatters, knowing things may never change.

He doesn't bother locking the Murphy door late at night anymore. Most of his sensitive documents and files are safely stored at a building owned by his security firm. The only one entering this late at night now—besides Ashton—is me.

I slip through the heavy door to find him standing with his hands on his hips, facing the wall of the lost. In the center is Pacen. Her photo stares back at me with listless eyes, but her presence looms like an ominous cloud.

"Ashton?" My voice is small and fearful. Not at all my normal self, but my insecurities rise anytime Ashton is troubled by something to do with his missing friend.

"Princess," he says in a whoosh. He uses a remote in his hand, and the photos all fade to black before he turns to me with a guarded expression. "Did I wake you?"

He knows he didn't.

"No, the thunder is pretty loud though. It woke me, and you weren't in bed."

"Yeah, I—I was just coming." He tugs on his ear, and sadness washes over me. We promised no lies. Not even little white ones, but I have no doubt that's what he just told me.

But I'm so desperate for a connection with him that I don't challenge it. Instead, I allow him to guide me back to our room and under the covers, where he wraps his body around mine just as he had a few hours before.

It takes longer than normal for his breathing to even out, and even longer for me to calm my racing heart and thoughts. But when I do, I know I need to help him find peace if we have any hope of a future.

I just wish finding peace didn't look so much like Pacen Macomb.

~

"Why are we doing this?" I ask, placing my bare feet in the icy cold sand.

"It's called grounding," Rylan explains.

Lexi bounces from foot to foot. "Is there a reason we're doing it at the break of dawn in a lake that feels like a glacier just broke off in it? Seriously, Chelle. Why is it so cold?"

Turning to our hostess, I see the wicked gleam in her eye, and I can tell she gives Lexi a run for her money. Chelle and her husband, Eric, own the campground across from the lake.

"Don't be a baby. The cold water is invigorating. Now, squish your toes in it and be quiet. Close your eyes. Feel the earth and the air. Just be in the moment," Chelle instructs.

Looking around, I almost laugh. The White Caps Campground sign is behind Lexi, and I really wish I had my camera. She screws up her face when the frigid water settles around her ankles.

"I can't," Lexi shrieks, jumping back from the water's edge. "If I wanted an ice bath, I'd go to physical therapy."

Chelle laughs and doubles over. "I'm just messing with you. It's too cold to be in the water. I just wanted to see if you'd follow directions this time."

Lexi turns a red face on the smaller woman. "Goat yoga was not my fault, Chelle. That little asshole was eating my hair."

Watching these women interact, even when they're annoyed with each other, does a funny thing to my chest. While Lexi and Chelle bicker, they're both suppressing loving smiles. I've never had a lifelong friendship like that.

I turn away before anyone can see the tears forming in my eyes.

Embarrassed, I shake out my towel and take a seat nearby. Close enough that I can hear them laughing but far enough away that I have a moment to rein in my overzealous emotions.

With a little distance between us, I grin. Lexi stands at least six feet tall, and Chelle might be five feet on a good day. They are truly an odd couple, but their friendship is as honest as I've ever seen.

"They're funny, huh?" Rylan asks. She clutches my shoulder and lowers herself to the ground next to me, holding her stomach.

"Are you okay?"

Her eyes dart to her stomach, and she blushes. "Yeah. It's funny how Mother Nature kicks in. We found out I'm pregnant again, but it's early so we're holding off on telling too many people for a few more weeks. Just in case, you know?"

I blink to ward off the now happy tears that are threatening. "That's amazing, Ry. I'm so happy for you."

"Thank you. Hattie and I just take it one day at a time. Having a wild two-year-old helps keep me occupied, but this pregnancy already seems easier than the last. I was sick every day with Gray."

"It's insane how much he looks like Halton."

"You should see their baby pictures." She smiles and bumps my shoulder. "The Westbrooks have strong genes, that's for sure."

"Strong personalities too," I mutter.

"And stronger opinions. These men have huge hearts, but they're pig-headed as hell."

I chuckle, but my thoughts are on Ashton.

"Wanna talk about it?"

Turning my head, I find her watching me closely. She has the look of a woman who has had to fight for her happiness and knows all too well how rocky the road can be.

"Ashton?"

She nods. "I'm assuming he's the reason you look so melancholy over here."

Whatever resolve I've had crumbles in the face of her sincerity. "I'm worried about him." Saying it out loud allows all my fears to take root in my heart. The ache grows to a steady throb.

"Nova, I say this as someone who has known Ashton his entire life. We're all worried. We've all tried to reach him. And we've all failed. He—" She looks out over the mirror-smooth lake, and I swear I can see all the thoughts swirling around in her head.

She tosses a rock into the water, and we stare at the ripples.

Sometimes it feels like Ashton is that rock and the rest of my life is tiny waves.

When the lake stills, it looks like a piece of glass. Shiny but breakable. Like me.

Rylan angles her body to face me. "He's different with you. So different. I can see slivers of our old Ash when he's with you, but he still sets himself apart from the rest of us. He's still shutting us out."

"I know."

"I tried to fix Hattie," she says, catching me off guard. Rylan smiles when she sees my expression. "I think everyone in this family has tried to fix someone or something before they came to the same conclusion."

"What's that?"

"You can't fix a person, even if they want you to. Working through your shit can feel like dying sometimes, but it's something he has to do on his own. I'm not saying you can't support Ashton. You can, and you should. I can see the difference it makes, but if you're twisting yourself up to do it for him, you'll lose yourself in the process."

"He's trying." My tone is defensive and harsher than I intend, but it doesn't seem to faze Rylan.

"Is he? Or is he trying to do it all without giving anything up? And I say this with all the love for him and you, but we have eyes, Nova. I'm worried about you. Hattie told me everything. I know the pressure Ash is under, but that doesn't mean you come second. Ever. If he's making the choice to move on, he will have to give something up. He doesn't fit in that world, and he's forgotten how to live in ours. I don't want him to wake up one day and realize that by trying to do it all, he lost you in the process. And I don't want you bending so far to fit into the space he gives that you lose yourself."

"She's right," Lexi hums, then flops her long limbs down next to me.

I blink through a teary haze to see Chelle walking back up the path to her campground with the colors of fall all around her. I guess our grounding session has become a therapy session.

"We love Ashton, and we'll always support you too, but he's spiraling, and if he isn't actively working toward the future, you're going to get hurt."

"Jesus, Lexi." Rylan rubs her temples with both hands. "Do you have to be so blunt?"

Lexi shrugs unapologetically. "It's the truth. We all want the same thing here, but I'd rather see the car coming than get blindsided."

"Neither of you think he can be happy?"

"That's not what we're saying." Rylan's voice is gentle as she places a hand on my forearm, holding me steady. "We're saying that with these stubborn Westbrook men, sometimes they can't see the forest through the trees until they're forced to."

"English, Ry." God, Lexi really is a younger, brasher version of GG.

"I'm just saying it's quite possible that Ash won't know what he has or wants until he doesn't have it anymore."

"You want me to give your brother-in-law an ultimatum?" My heart beats like a kid with bongo drums.

"No. Geez. Those never work," Lexi says, then tosses a large stone into the water. "What she's saying is, it's okay to put yourself first. Whatever and however you need to. When he crashes, it's okay to step back so you don't get burned. Self-preservation. You'll need all the strength you have when he has his come-to-Jesus moment, and you won't have any strength at all if you go down with him."

"You expect me to just watch him spiral?" What in the actual fuck? I thought this family cared about each other.

"No, Nova. We're just making sure you're prepared. If he isn't making changes on his own..." She lifts her face to the sky and inhales deeply. "We know you love him. And he loves you. So much I'm sure he's terrified, but the price for love shouldn't be never-ending pain. Just remember that, okay?"

I want to throttle these women. If ever there was a time for Ashton to need his family in his corner, it's now. Why would they choose me over him when he needs support like never before?

Don't they understand the pressure he's under? Don't they understand all he's given up?

A tiny voice in the back of my head tells me they're just watching out for me. That they see things more clearly than I do, but I don't listen.

"He'll come around," I finally say. "No one ever expected him to undo fifteen years' worth of heartache in a matter of days."

Rylan stares at me like I'm missing the point, but I know Ashton. I know what he's capable of.

"Are you still going home at the end of the month?" Lexi asks, giving me whiplash.

"Uh, yeah. I need to pick fabric samples for my next collection."

"Okay, well, GG turns eighty-nine in two weeks, so you can help us with the party."

I look at Rylan, then turn my head back to Lexi. Is that it? Are we just done talking about Ashton and me?

"Sometimes it's better to just go along with her," Rylan whispers.

Lexi stands, brushes the sand off her hands, then holds them out to help haul me and Rylan to our feet. "Come on, chicas. We have a party to plan." She puts a long arm around my shoulders and pulls me in close. "I've been in Ashton's shoes, Nova. I know how it feels to be suffocating in the choices you've made. But all you can do is toss him the life raft. You can't breathe for him without drowning first. We're all here for you both, but you can't give so much of yourself that there's nothing left."

She's the second person to say those exact words to me.

Fear steals my breath as understanding dawns. Maybe they're seeing what I can't. Am I so caught up in fixing Ash that I don't know my own needs anymore?

My brain catches on a memory. Ashton and I in bed this morning. Before the chaos intruded. Before reality kicked in.

And I have my answer. Love hurts. Ashton and I have a battle ahead, but I have no doubt we'll help each other through. Together.

CHAPTER 43

"*A*sh? Ash, yer late." Killian is an incessant nag these days. "Really late, mate. Ain't Nova waitin' on you?"

Fuck.

"It's fine. She's with my family. Rylan will keep her busy until I get there. I'm so close."

"That's what you said last week. And last month. There's always something, but yer missing the point."

It pains me to pull my eyes away from the screen, but I do and come face-to-face with Killian. "What is your point?" I growl.

"This is not supposed to be your life anymore. You have a woman who loves ya, and yer fecking it all to hell. How many times can you let her down before she realizes she's worth more than just being your dumping ground?"

"Watch it, Kill."

"Or what? What are you going to do, Ashton? You're so close to having the life you deserve. Why are you sabotaging it?"

"I'm not," I roar. "You don't know anything about Nova and me."

He doesn't. He doesn't know that I'm trying. That I'm quite

literally killing myself to be everything to everyone. He couldn't know what I've given up or what I'm trying to hold on to.

No one fucking understands.

He steps into my face. "I know she loves ya. I know she's bending herself in two to make this work. I see it every fecking day. How long until she bends so far she breaks, huh?"

I react without thought. My fist flies out from my side, but I've never been a fighter. Killian catches my arm easily and pushes me back.

"Why do you want this job so badly, Killian? Huh? Is it the power? What? Why do you want this? Why does it matter to you what the fuck I do?"

"The power?" He chuckles darkly. "Is that what you think this is? The Apollyon isn't a power, Ashton. It never has been."

"Then why are you pushing me so fucking hard to leave it?" I scream so hard the metallic taste of blood trickles down my throat.

"You dumb feck," he spits, and I charge him again. Only to have him slam me into a wall. "I'm pushing you to walk away because I'm yer mate. I see what happens to you every time The Ravens have a new class come through. Do you know how hard it is to watch someone you care about slowly die inside? That's why I'm pushing you, Ashton. You have a chance with Nova. A real chance at being happy, and yer sitting here pissing it away because you can't let go—or because you don't trust me with the weight of it. I don't know which, but I do know I can't sit here and watch this anymore."

"What makes you so much more capable of living this life?" I ask. Taking a step to the side, I put a few feet of space between us.

"Because I've never known what it's like to have a heart. I was born into this life. It's all I've ever known. I never had another option. You do. Take it. Take it now, before you lose the one person capable of keeping you in the light."

"I'm not going to lose her," I grumble.

Killian crosses his arms over his chest. He shakes his head in disappointment. "Like I said, the dumbest fucking genius I've ever met."

I huff and shake out my hands, which hang at my sides like lead weights. Energy zaps through my veins like an electric current.

"How was the concert last night?" he asks, and I can't contain my wince. "That's what I thought. I know ya love her, mate. But you're not doing right by her. Whatever it is you're punishing yourself for, you've got to get over it or let her go."

"He's right," a soft female voice says from the shadows in the corner. It's a voice I recognize, but I take a step back. Confusion and fear feel awfully similar, and I'm not sure which one I'm experiencing right now.

"Pacen?"

She steps forward, and my chest aches with a held breath.

I stumble back against the wall and blindly search for the light switch. Then I blink furiously, trying to acclimate to the bright overhead light.

"What are you doing here?" I ask, my head on a swivel, eyes darting back and forth between her and Killian.

"Killian said it was time."

"Time for what?" I growl. There was a time when I would have trusted Pacen with my life, but she's shut me out for eight years. I have no fucking clue what she's been up to. Or who she's partnered with.

"To help you."

Taking a step to the side, I put distance between us. I continue to move along the wall until I'm within reach of a desk drawer I know contains at least one gun.

"You don't need a weapon, mate."

"Don't I? I know she didn't get in on her own. Are you going to take her out if she's here to..." Turning to Pacen, I ask, "What are you here for?"

Her face relaxes, and it hits me how much healthier she looks than the last time I saw her. Her face has filled out, and her skin isn't a sallow color. And she's smiling.

"He isn't going to take out his own wife. At least, I don't think he would." She holds up her hands and spins in a slow circle. "I'm not here to hurt you, Ash. I would never have been able to hurt you. You're my friend."

"Friend?" I spit. "You've iced me out for eight goddamn years. I didn't know if you were alive or dead. I had no idea if you were okay, or if—if…" My throat closes, and I sink into a chair along the wall. "Why didn't you let me help you? Why…wait. Did you say wife?"

Pacen sits in a chair on the other side of the room like she's afraid of spooking me. Killian props a hip against the desk but doesn't say anything.

"I did," she says, casting a loving glance toward Killian. "You sent him after me."

"I sent him to find you. To make sure you were okay, not to fucking marry you," I hiss. I'm so enraged I can't bring myself to even look at Killian.

"And I am okay. Now. I never wanted to lose you as a friend, Ash. But after my father's men attacked you, I was lost. I was scared, and I was so damn angry at the world. I'll never understand why he was so desperate to become a Raven. Or why he did all the horrible things he did, but after that night, after he hurt you to prove loyalty to them, I knew he would never stop. I couldn't be near him, and I couldn't be with you. I was so confused. It just took me a long time to realize I wasn't in love with you. I simply craved the love you gave me. I'd never had that before."

"You should have talked to me, Pacen. You should have let me help you."

She tilts her head to the side and studies me. "Would you have though?"

Tension builds in my shoulders, making my muscles ache, and I stand abruptly. "Yes! I would have."

She shakes her head. "I don't think that's true. I think you would have done it for me, then presented it as a gift. This battle you've been fighting? It isn't only yours, and I think you forget that sometimes. I'm not so sure you would have ever let me be a partner or trusted me enough to share the weight of it all."

"What is that supposed to mean?"

"You've become an island with a moat and a twenty-foot-high stone wall. But this was always my fight too. I knew after your attack that you wouldn't trust me again. Not fully. I also knew that the little trust you did have in anyone would be shattered, so I had no choice but to go out on my own. We've spent eight years fighting the same war from different vantage points, but we've always been on the same team. You just have to take off your coach's hat long enough to see that you can trust your second string. We're ready to play."

Nostalgia hangs heavy on my heart. My friend always loved sports metaphors.

"I did trust you." Using my right hand, I squeeze the back of my neck, trying to ease the headache forming with each passing moment. I think I've just run through every emotion in the span of ten minutes. "I trusted you too, Kill. You know I've been searching for her, and she was with you all this time?"

"Nah, mate. You were looking for a lost little girl. The woman I met wasn't lost, and she had her own plan."

"I didn't think it would take eight years for someone to knock some sense into you though." Pacen smiles, and it unlocks a piece of guilt I've never been able to shed.

"I—I didn't know how to do things any differently," I confess.

"I know, Ash. We were kids thrown into adult situations bred straight from the devil himself. There was no playbook. No rules to follow. We did the best we could, but we're losing you, and you know it."

My shoulders slump forward. The weight of our world is reaching a breaking point.

"Don't be upset with Kill. He only did what I asked because we both care about you. I knew a day would come when you'd be torn between duty and love. You're too good of a man not to be someone's other half. But I also knew you wouldn't let anyone into The Apollyon until you had to let it go completely, so I stayed away until I knew you were ready to accept my help."

She stands and crosses the room slowly. Each step closer she comes, I feel the armor of half-truths I've used to keep myself safe start to slip. "She must be amazing and strong as hell if she's scaled your walls."

I swallow back the fear that comes with being vulnerable. Pacen sits next to me, but still gives me the space I need. "She makes me feel. She gives me hope. She—"

"Is going to run if you don't find balance," Killian interrupts.

"Fuck you." I jab my finger in his direction. "I'm so angry with you right now, Kill. Don't say a fucking word to me."

"But it's the truth, Ash." Even Pacen's cadence has changed. She's not an empty shell anymore. I realize she's found a way to move forward, to live through the static, and come out on the other side better than before.

I've never been a jealous man, but I feel the emotion now.

"You were born to invent and create and to make the world a better place, but not like this. Not by living in the underbelly of society," she says with the patience of a seasoned mother.

"And what? The two of you are better equipped to live this life?"

"Yeah," Killian states calmly. "We are."

Pacen holds up a hand, and he stops talking. I'm finally understanding their connection in the way their eyes communicate.

They're in love.

"Ash? My father would have gladly sold me to the highest

bidder. Killian's father is so entrenched with The Ravens that we can't even get eyes on him. We have a vested interest in this."

"So do I," I curse.

How dare they question my involvement? My intent?

"I know you do. But where ours is a personal affront, you've only ever been the protector. You and your father both. You saw an injustice, a slap in the face of humanity, and you burned the world to the ground to fix it. But it was never your fight. It's not your fight. It's time for you to choose your path. One with Nova. One where you're a player in your brothers' chaos, not just part of the scenery. It's time for you to live, Ashton. Live fully. With a purpose that's not based on survival. A life lived with love."

"I don't know how," I say through gritted teeth. "I keep trying, and I keep fucking it up. What if it's too late for me to do anything but what I'm doing right now?"

"It's not," Killian says quietly. "If Pacen and I can find love in the shadows, you can be loved in the light. It's where you belong. We've always known it."

I look at my friend. Really look at him, but his eyes remain on Pacen.

"How long have you been together?" What I really want to ask is *how long have you been betraying me?* but I know that's not fair.

"A little over a year," Pacen says quietly.

That's something. At least they haven't been plotting against me for the last eight years.

"We are not your enemy," Killian says. His eyes read mine too clearly.

I nod while trying to organize my thoughts.

"Why have you been holding onto this, Ash? Really, dig deep and ask yourself why?" Pacen asks softly.

Silence fills the room as I reflect on the life I've led. I know the answer, but the truth hurts, and she knows it.

"This is the only connection I have to right all my wrongs," I finally whisper. "With my dad. With you. My family. The children I couldn't save. How else do I fix those things?"

"Let Kill and me help you. We'll never be able to fix everything, Ashton. You know that. But we can do good in this world. Let us take some of the burden so you don't lose Nova."

My spine tingles like it's trying to tell me something. Like it might already be too late.

Lifting my wrist, I see it's after midnight. GG's party will have ended hours ago.

"Fuck."

"The most powerful tool in your arsenal are two little words," Killian advises.

"What's that?" I ask absentmindedly. My brain is already ten steps ahead.

"I'm sorry," Killian explains. "Say it and mean it."

I stand as fear clenches my heart. The computer screen lights up with an incoming message, and I know this will be a turning point for me. If I open that message, I'll be lost for hours. If I leave it, I hand over The Apollyon to Pacen and Killian.

I hesitate for half a second and see the worry written all over their expressions. Worry for me. Probably for Nova. Definitely for my future.

With sudden clarity, I know my next move. "Nightingale233."

"What?" Killian steps toward me when I march to the door.

"That's my password. The class is expected any day, so that message"—I point to one of the screens above the desk—"is probably urgent. I'll be back tomorrow to help decipher codes."

Pacen looks a little shell-shocked. "Just like that?"

"Are you going to let those kids down?" I ask, gesturing to the wall illuminated behind her.

"You know I'm not," she bites back.

"Then welcome to the team."

"Team?" Killian chokes.

"I don't know how this will work, but I've always known that if Pacen came back, I'd trust her. I'm trusting her." Turning to Killian, I see the man who's stood by me through every bad decision. The man who kept me alive when I wanted the darkness to take me. The man I consider a friend. "And I'm trusting you too. You've never let me down. I won't be good at relinquishing control, but I trust you enough to try. For Nova, I have to try. For real this time."

He claps me on the shoulder and pulls me into a one-armed hug. "You might have to grovel this time. You've got a lot of apologizing to do."

"I know." And I do. I have a lifetime of apologies to make, but it starts with the most important one.

Nova.

CHAPTER 44

ASHTON

The parking lot near the old barn is mostly deserted. It's proof that I've fucked up. Badly.

GG wanted an old-fashioned barn dance for her birthday, so my brothers and their wives spent the last week clearing out Easton's workshop.

I was too busy. I'm always too busy.

Or hiding.

Too busy or hiding has always been my normal M.O.

Even Nova put off a meeting with a supplier to help with decorations.

Fuck. I'm a selfish asshole.

I park in between two SUVs. One belongs to Halt, and the other to Easton. At least they're still here.

Maybe they can help me figure out a way to apologize. To Nova. To GG. Dammit. I probably owe everyone an apology.

My boots hit the ground with a loud crunch against the gravel. But I don't make it two steps before a heavy door on the side of the barn is thrown open and snaps back. The sound of wood on wood drowns out the rustling of dead leaves desperately clinging to their branches in the wind.

Familiar blond hair blows in the cool breeze, but it's the angry female it's attached to that has me stopping in my tracks.

The blood drains from my face, whooshing in my ears instead. Sadie Sunshine is stomping toward me with arms swinging wildly. She's too far away for me to hear what she's saying, but I catch bits and pieces as she gets closer.

I've seen Sadie mad before. But it's never once been directed at me. It's the dead of night, and I'm fairly certain there isn't anyone behind me, so this little ball of rage must be headed right for my jugular.

I've always been proud of this little girl. But seeing her now? I know she's going to do just fine in life.

"Never," she seethes when she stops mere inches in front of me. "Never have I ever been more disappointed in anyone."

That's when it hits me. Sadie isn't only mad. She's hurt. The one person I spent the last eight years bubble-wrapping so my thorns wouldn't scratch her just got caught by one of them.

"Sadie," I force out. My throat closes as guilt consumes me.

"No, Uncle Ash." She shakes her head and stares at the ground. My nephew Tate walks up behind her with his hands in his pants pockets, staring at his feet. He looks like he wants to be anywhere but here. But I know this kid too. He'll walk behind Sadie to the ends of the Earth just to make sure she doesn't float off on a cloud when she reaches for the stars.

It's how I should have been with Nova. Fuck. How can two teenagers teach me so much about love without saying a damn word?

"She refused to leave. Did you know that? The party ended four hours ago, and she has sat in that corner while everyone whispered around her. She's here for you, Ashton."

Sadie has never called me anything but Uncle Ash, and the use of my name now slices my heart in two.

"I—I know."

"Do you? Do you know that she sat in there, holding back

315

tears with near-strangers instead of celebrating at home with her own family?"

Wait. What? Shaking my head, I try to streamline my thoughts. "Why would she celebrate GG's birthday with her family? Do they know her?"

Sadie blinks with her mouth hanging open wide. She turns to Tate, and he grimaces.

"What am I missing here?"

"No cap, you're worse than mid," she says.

My eyebrows fall into my line of sight as I try to figure out what the hell she just said. Thankfully, Tate speaks both teen and old man. "No cap means not lying. Mid means, well, it means average."

Not lying, I'm worse than average.

I nod like I understand. But I don't. Not at all.

"I ship her, Ashton. And you have been my person. But you suck at relationships, and Nova deserves better."

"Sadie, ah, what am I missing? I know I missed the party. But why is Nova crying?"

Sadie throws her hand into the air and storms off. "I can't with him, Tate. I just can't."

Turning to my sixteen-year-old nephew, I realize for the first time he's grown into a man. He's the spitting image of Dexter with the heart of Lanie. "Help me out here?"

"Ashton. You've really kicked the pooch here."

Oh, God. More teen talk.

"Nova got her CFDA nomination for the American Emerging Designer of the Year today. If she's important to you, you should have at least known it was happening. Dad hates to shop, and even he knew she was up for a nomination."

Dexter Cross knew because he put the Prince in Charming. And he obviously puts in the time for those he cares about.

"But Ashton? If I'm being honest here, I don't think this is about the award. Nova doesn't seem to care that much about it.

But you not being there for her after everything she's given up for you? That speaks volumes."

Fuck. I really did kick the pooch here.

I pat Tate on the shoulder and move with urgency toward the barn. The closer I get, the faster I walk until I bolt through the door. My presence is like a record scratch and the entire group freezes in time.

I don't have to scan the room. My heart knows exactly where she is, and I find her immediately. Sitting in the corner, just as Sadie said. Her dress sparkles under twinkle lights that hang from the rafter. But she's small. Too small. Like she's spent the entire night trying to crawl in on herself instead of being the outgoing fireball I know her to be.

Did I do that to her?

As if sensing me, she lifts her head, and our eyes catch. Her expression ruins me. It's the way her chin trembles even as she clenches her teeth to control it. It's in the tiny smudges of mascara at the corner of one eye that show the first sign of tears.

No.

"The dumbest fucking genius." Killian's words hold true.

My heart refuses to beat as I cross the barn. There are so many sets of eyes on me, but I can't turn away from Nova. Not until my brothers step into my path.

"You really hurt her," Colton growls.

"I—I know. I owe a lot of apologies to a lot of people, but I have to start with her."

Colton nods, but Easton doesn't back down.

"She refused to leave because she believes in you. Or she did." He glances over his shoulder to where Nova sits, biting on the cuticle of her thumb. "It would have been so easy to make her happy, Ashton. She doesn't want anything from you but your time. If you can't give her that, don't tease her with your heart. She deserves better than that."

My stomach rolls with guilt that's hammering away at my

317

insides, and my entire body shivers. "I know she does." The words are a promise. To them. To her. To myself.

"We tried to help you, Ash. We tried to keep this from happening, but it doesn't seem like you're doing anything but what you want to do." Preston has disappointed dad down to a T.

Seth steps up to our semicircle. He wears his feelings in his stiff posture. "I'm not going to lay into you because I think my little girl already did that, but you will make this right with her tomorrow. Sadie has always been in your corner. Don't make me regret allowing that to happen."

I nod. Words evade me anyway. My brothers part and I feel their eyes on me as I walk toward Nova.

"Y—You came. I—I told them you would." She can't control the tremor of her chin, and I've never hated myself more than I do right at this very moment.

"Princess." The second I open my mouth, she falls into my open arms and buries her face in my chest. The whispers around us fade to a gentle hum before the room falls silent except for Nova's erratic breathing. "How do you have so much faith in me?"

Why did you stay? is what I really want to ask, but I'm too scared she won't be able to come up with an answer.

"Someone has to." She hiccups and holds me tighter.

"I'm so sorry, Nova. I know I'm a broken record, but I am so fucking sorry."

I wouldn't have thought it possible, but she seems to shrink even more in my arms.

"I'm tired." I can barely hear her words, so I bend my knees and lower my face to hers, but her eyes are squeezed tight. The smudged mascara streaks the corners of both eyes now. A dark line showing the damage I can cause.

"Let's go home." Kissing the top of her head, I don't release her, but guide her toward the door instead. I'm fully aware of my family's eyes on us. All disapproving. All staring. All rightfully pissed off. At me.

I ignore them. I'll make amends in time. But I have a sinking feeling my time with Nova is running thin.

We make it to the driveway, and Nova stumbles. For the first time, I notice she's all done up. The sparkly dress was just the wrapping. Her lips are painted a shade of red that complements her fair skin. The long locks of silky brown hair I love are twisted into an updo with a clip that shines even in the moonlight. But it's her eyes that arrest me.

Her amber eyes are framed in a smoky charcoal color that I bet looked sexy as fuck before I made her cry.

"I will never be the cause of your tears again, Nova. Not ever." I lift her off the ground and carry her to my truck. Her mouth opens like she wants to say something, but no words come.

I settle her into the seat and clasp the buckle for her. I'm backing out of the vehicle when she grabs my arm. "We promised truth, peto."

God, she sounds so wounded.

"I know."

"Then don't make promises you can't keep." Her words stun me into silence. I back away with a lump the size of Texas in my throat and shut her truck door.

The dumbest fucking genius.

Yeah, that's me all right.

I take a steadying breath before climbing into the truck and driving us home.

It's time to make some changes.

CHAPTER 45

NOVA

"*C*ome with me?"

I'm not sure why I ask. I already know what his answer will be. The same answer he gave me last night when we climbed into bed. The same answer as the night before when he missed the concert. The same answer he's given more times than not.

Work.

Is it selfish of me to be disappointed when I know how many lives depend on him? Probably. It doesn't stop my raging emotions from having a pity party though.

"Princess." He sounds so defeated. Exhausted. Overwhelmed. Sitting on the edge of his bed, barefoot and in jeans, his shoulders slumped forward, there's torment behind his eyes, despite his attempt to appear relaxed.

He runs a hand through his hair roughly.

"It's okay, Ashton. I know you have stuff to do."

"It won't always be like this. I promise. Pacen is here now. She and Killian will take the majority of the load."

I turn at the mention of her name. I don't have a great poker face, and there will be no masking the jealousy wrapping around my heart like a vice.

"So you said," I say with false cheer. "I'm glad she can give you peace." It's obvious that job was never mine. I hear him move, but I keep folding clothes and piling them into my suitcase. "Honestly, it's great. It sounds great, I mean. I'm happy she can share the burden you carry."

"Nova?" He's so close now his breath blows my hair. The heat of it makes me shiver.

"Hmm?" I can't talk. My jaw is clenched to keep my tears at bay. I don't know what's wrong with me, but Ashton Westbrook has me so twisted up that I have no self-control anymore.

"You're upset." The anguish in his voice nearly makes me cave, but I don't dare turn around.

"No. I'm happy for you," I force out, but it's shaky. Clearing my throat, I bend down to zip up my suitcase.

"Then why are you so sad?" God. This man.

"I'm just going to miss you. That's all." It isn't a lie. Not really. I will miss him. Terribly. But it isn't the only reason for my tears.

I don't know where I fit. New York feels like a distant memory. Burke Hollow feels like a vacation where I'm a visitor in his life, not a piece of it. Once again, I'm alone and without direction.

Running home seems like the safest solution.

"But…" His labored breathing behind me has goosebumps racing down my arms, and I bite my tongue to steady myself enough to face him. "But you're coming back. Right?"

My body tenses and my chin quivers.

"Right?" Ashton's voice cracks, and I hate that I've put fear in his eyes.

The best I can do is nod and look away. Staring into his eyes is like watching blood pour from an open wound. It makes you a little sick, and your heart pinches so painfully it's hard to breathe.

"Nova, I'm so sorry. So fucking sorry. Please believe me. I'm sorry I didn't know about your nomination. I'm sorry I wasn't home the night before so you could tell me. I…" His voice is higher than normal as he pleads. But the problem is, I do believe him. I do. His hands fist in his hair as he looks around the room like a wild animal.

Another dagger in my soul.

I step forward to place a hand over his heart, and a tear slips free when I feel it thrashing violently in his chest.

"I know you're sorry, Ashton. I will come back, but it doesn't feel like you have room for me in your life right now. Our timing might just be off. I have to go to New York to pick samples anyway. So it just seems like the most logical thing. Some space will help us reorient our thinking and our needs."

It happens in slow motion.

The small fleck of hope leaves his eyes.

His hands drop listlessly to his sides.

He blinks slowly. Once. Twice. Three times.

"Y—You're breaking up with me?" His eyes are vacant, and his arms dangle like broken tree branches. It's like the weight of his limbs is physically pulling him to the ground. He's so raw and exposed right now. It's the most heartbreaking thing I've ever witnessed.

"No. I'm…I think… Maybe a break? We need to figure out what we want."

"I know what I want," he growls. "Even I know *a break* never works. Be honest with me, Nova."

It's like he struck a match and lit me on fire. I stumble back.

Honesty? That's all I've ever given him.

"You want honesty, Ashton?" I say with fire in my veins and hurt in my soul. "I've been nothing but honest. I've told you what I need. What we need. I've bent and shifted. I've sacrificed and told myself it's okay to come in last with you. I'm the one making all the concessions here. I stayed here. With you. Without friends or family. I've twisted myself up so tight to fit into the moments you bless me with only to be cast aside without a second thought."

"That's not true," he roars. "I've said I'm sorry."

"Over and over again, yes. You have. But at some point, when your actions never change, the words just become broken promises."

He turns and drops heavily onto the edge of the bed. Keeping his eyes averted, he mumbles, "I don't know what you want from me."

"Oh, peto. It's simple. I've only ever wanted you, but right now, I'm not sure you have any pieces to give. You're so consumed by duty, and it's admirable. It truly is. But I deserve to have more than just spare parts and stolen moments. I've spent most of my life not knowing my worth. Not until you." A shiver runs through my body like I'm slowly being dipped in ice water.

"I see your potential and your progress, Ashton. And I know you care about me. More than you probably ever thought you could, but sometimes love just isn't enough."

"You are breaking up with me." He speaks so quietly I can barely make out the words.

"I don't want to, but I also don't want to give you an ultimatum. I want to be a partner in your life because you choose it. I'm just not convinced you have room for me right now. And I get it, please believe me there. I understand how important The Apollyon is. You're doing things for strangers that most people would never be able to accomplish. That's an amazing feat, Ashton. It shows just how big your heart is. But we all have a limit. I don't want to be the reason you break."

"You're not," he cries. "Don't you get it? You are my talisman. My center. My calm in the chaos."

"I want to be all those things," I say on a sob. "But you can only lean on me after you've learned to stand. Otherwise, we're both vying for a position where neither of us win."

The room spins, and a wave of nausea hits me like a speeding train. I sink to the floor next to my suitcase and swallow down the emotions that are crushing me. "We rushed into this because I was scared to go home, and because you were scared of not feeling anything again. But maybe if we just date for a while, you'll figure out if there is space for me in your life. And I'll figure out how to be there without losing myself."

"You're leaving."

My shoulders shrug like they know an answer I can't bring myself to say. "I have to."

"But you want to date?" This poor, emotionally stunted man. "I don't understand."

"We'll see how things go," I say evasively.

His spine straightens, and determination is written in the set line of his jaw. His brow furrows, and when he glances up, I know he's made a decision about something.

"We're not breaking up."

"Ah…"

"We're not. This is a problem. I find solutions to problems, and this will be no different." His knee bounces erratically, and I can't stop watching it. "But we're not breaking up. You are still mine, and I'm yours. We'll simply be apart for a little while." I can't tell if he's talking to me or to himself, but then his eyes dart to mine and hold me captive. "How long?"

I gulp, and it takes excruciating effort to form a word. "What?"

"How long do I have?"

Shaking my head, I glance down at my knees, trying to get a handle on this spiraling conversation. "This isn't a math equation, Ash. There's no formula to follow."

A rumble vibrates in his chest, and I swear I can feel it through the floor. "Then how long do I have until you come back?"

"Why can't we just see how things go?"

"Because if you walk out of here with no return date, I'm

going to lose my fucking mind. I can't get all my shit together with an open-ended date. I need a time. A date. And then I will fix my goddamn world."

"Ash. That's not what I'm asking you to do."

"It's what I have to do," he bellows. "My life is a fucking mess. The only thing that works in my entire world is you. You, Nova. I'll try harder. Delegate. Walk the fuck away at the end of my time if I can't fix it, but I know I won't survive without you by my side. I just need a time frame. A date. So when will you come home?"

This isn't what I want. What if he becomes free and realizes I'm not what centers him? What if I come back and no matter how hard he tries, he can't make room for me?

What-ifs are for the unimaginative. The lazy. What-ifs are what people say when they won't fight for their future. My stepmother's words smack me in the face. Kitty Bryer-Blaine doesn't back down out of fear. She has always fought for her future. Perhaps I can too.

"Um." My teeth sink into my bottom lip. I want to keep the worry out of my voice, but there's no masking my emotions today. They seem to be in overdrive and running this show. "A— A month?"

"Fine. We'll talk every night. Ten p.m." I can see his brain moving at warp speed behind his shadowed eyes. "You can read to me or ask me questions. We'll talk about whatever the fuck we need to, but it's a date I will not miss. Not once. I promise you that."

I want to believe him. God, do I want to believe him. My foolish heart nearly jumps out of my chest to cling to that promise, but there's a voice in the back of my head that tells me to be cautious. It's like a dark cloud on a sunny day. Ominous. Foreboding. Dangerous.

"Every night, Nova," Ashton says with urgency.

"Okay."

"Okay." His bare feet hit the hardwood floor with a plop that follows him as he pads across the room. Standing in front of me, he hooks me under my arms and lifts me to stand. He holds me like he's afraid to let me go, and despite my best judgment, I sink into him.

"I love you, Nova. So damn much."

My throat is thick with emotions I can't force down. "I know. I love you too. I'm not leaving because I don't love you. Please know that. I'm leaving because I do. So much it hurts."

"I don't understand any of this," he mutters into my scalp.

A sob breaks free. I try to muffle the sound, but it's useless.

"Hey," he demands. Leaning back, he uses two fingers to turn my face to his. "I don't understand, but I will figure it out. I swear to you I will."

Voices echo through the hall from the foyer, and Ashton's eyes go wide. He clutches me so tightly that I'll have bruises tomorrow, but I don't pull away. Not yet.

"Nova?" Rylan calls up the stairs.

"You called for a ride?" His words are choppy and gritty as he forces them out.

"I thought it would be easier. And I wasn't sure you'd be here this morning."

He grimaces and tugs on his collar. "I've really messed this up."

"We both made mistakes, but mistakes are not the end of the world. Well, not in my world. I know you've spent your life fighting for perfection. The Apollyon could have nothing less. But people by nature are flawed, peto. We're supposed to screw up. It's how we learn. And relationships are naturally messy."

"I don't have to fix mistakes very often. But I will fix this one," he vows.

A knock on the door has us tearing apart, but not letting go completely.

"Sorry," Rylan grimaces. "Are you ready? We're going to hit

traffic if we don't leave soon." Over her shoulder, Halton stands with his legs spread wide and arms crossed over his hulking chest. But it's his frown and sad eyes that have my heart ricocheting painfully in my chest again.

"Yeah, I'm ready," I whisper. Leaning down, I grab the handle of my large suitcase, but Ashton swats my hand away and picks it up with ease. Halton muscles his way past Rylan and picks up my two smaller bags.

Without a word, we exit the room single-file. Tension fires off the brothers like a pinball machine. Ashton grunts as he lifts my suitcase into the trunk, followed by Halton, who closes the lid with a loud thunk.

We stand in a circle. None of us are sure of the next move until Ashton steps forward and herds me against the car.

"One month," he growls through clenched teeth.

"Yeah," I reply then snap my mouth shut before I blurt out words and demands I have no right to say. Words like choose me. Keep me. Love me.

Instead, I turn before the tears spring free and duck into the car. Ashton closes the door behind me but stands watching as we pull away. He never moves as we roll out of sight, and I'm left wondering how long he'll stay there.

How long until he forgets I was ever there at all?

CHAPTER 46

ASHTON

Two Weeks Later

"*G*o home, Ash. You aren't going to find anything else when you're this tired. Honestly, The Ravens could move the class tonight, and we'd be ready."

"I know," I mutter. Removing my glasses, I rub my weary eyes. Twelve hours staring at a computer screen has everything looking a little blurry.

"Then what are you doing here?" Pacen asks. She keeps her face neutral, but she doesn't filter the disapproval in her tone.

"It's my last class. I just need to make sure I didn't miss anything. When they move in two days, I want to sit here, running communications, knowing there will be no surprises."

"I say this as one of your oldest friends, but it's a compulsion for you. And one you have to let go of, or you're going to lose Nova for good. Is that the real reason you're here right now? Are you avoiding going home?" Pacen asks.

Killian's chair makes a scraping sound as he pushes away from his desk to face us.

It takes a conscious effort not to roll my eyes at another group therapy session. "I told you, it's not home without her."

"Then what the feck ya doing here, Ghost? Get the hell out of town. Go get her." Killian's gruff voice belays his disgust.

"I can't get her until I know how the hell to live without the weight of this," I say, gesturing around the war room we've set up in a nondescript building adjacent to Envision.

"You're not going to learn that by spending twenty hours a day in this room, ya dumbass."

"Kill," Pacen says in warning.

I almost crack a smile when he deflates and backs off. A sliver of jealousy weaves its way into my heart at how easily they fit together.

"How did you do it?" I ask, staring at Pacen.

She chews on her lip as she studies me with the eyes of a professor. "You mean Killian and me?"

I nod, but my chest constricts, and I feel like I'm drowning.

"I made a choice, Ashton. A choice to live by my goals and dreams. My father set me on a course destined for self-destruction. But only if I allowed it. I went to therapy. A lot of damn therapy. And I chose to be the creator of my own happiness."

"Now, doll. It wasn't as easy as all that." Killian smirks. "You made the choice and then had to choose it every second of every minute of every day until it became reality. It was hard work to get to a place where you could breathe again."

Pacen's face softens as she looks at her giant of a husband.

"He's right," she says without taking her eyes off him. "When you wake up in the morning, the first thing you do is choose your happy. When your mind tells you to come here, you actively force yourself to listen to your heart. You choose to have a life, and you choose to love."

"But you have love and The Apollyon." Why do I keep fighting for this? I don't even want to fucking be here, but I keep trying to talk myself out of walking away. What is wrong with me?

"Because we were both born into this life, Ashton. It's all we've ever known, and we have each other. When we go home at night, we know what the other has gone through. We don't have to talk about it, so there's never a chance for a chasm to grow between us."

Her gaze lingers on Killian and for a moment, I can picture what their life is like. They bring each other peace.

Knowledge has always brought me peace.

"If Killian hadn't had the same lived experience as me," she says gently, "I'm not sure it would have worked. This isn't a life anyone chooses on their own. So you can't expect someone who has never seen pure evil on their doorstep to be able to accept it in their lives with open arms. Innocents shouldn't have to make that choice, and neither should the people we love."

I drop my head into my hands as she speaks. She's right. I don't want Nova anywhere near The Ravens. She's too good for this life. And I have no life without her.

"You're holding on because of your dad, but he wouldn't even want you here in the first place, and you know it. Your dad had the biggest capacity for love. It's all he ever wanted for any of us. To love with your whole heart and be loved in return. Let The Apollyon go, Ash. Choose life. Choose love."

"I've already said this will be the last class I see though. I know their names. Their faces, Pacen. I can't just abandon them."

"Okay," she says, sounding defeated. "I just hope all the time you're spending here instead of getting your shit together doesn't end up costing you the best thing that's ever happened to you."

I swallow, and it feels like razor blades are slicing me open.

"Go home, mate." Killian shakes his head and returns his chair to his computer just as Pacen sits down beside him.

I watch them, side by side, their heads angled toward each other as they work. It brings me peace, and a deep well of gratitude washes over me. They're going to be okay, and they're going to do amazing things for The Apollyon.

Rolling my shoulders, I'm thankful when some of the tension leaves my body. I might be able to do this after all. I snort at my thoughts, but neither of my friends turn to look at me, so I exit quietly and head for my truck.

My newfound calm doesn't last long. The drive is too short for that.

The tension builds again the closer I get to my house. My dark house sitting on a hill all by itself. I intentionally built it farther away from my brothers' homes to give me privacy. Now it feels like we're worlds apart.

I park in my normal spot and exit the truck with a sense of dread that nags at every cell in my body. The door closes with a deafening crack. I hadn't even realized I'd slammed it until right then. Turning toward the house, my breath stalls in my lungs.

I fall back against the truck, and let the cold metal hold me up. The large, unassuming log cabin has become something straight out of my nightmares. It's always felt safe. Always been the one place I knew I could hide. But staring at it now, it's empty and cold in a way I didn't know houses could be.

It's not a home anymore.

"Fuck," I curse, loud enough to startle wildlife.

But it's not a bear that walks from the shadows. It's Loki. I'd know his silhouette anywhere. I spent years following it in camera feeds and security footage.

Words escape me as he stalks closer.

"It's not a home, is it?" he asks.

"Not the way your houses are, no. But that's nothing new." I'm in unchartered territory with my oldest friend. My partner. My brother.

"No? I heard you call it home when Nova was here."

"That's because she made it a home."

"Did she?"

Crossing my arms, I turn to the man I know better than

myself. "What are you trying to say, Loki? What are you doing here?"

He ignores my question and walks to the back of my truck, releasing the tailgate with a clank and a thud. The truck dips behind me as he climbs on, so I follow him.

Loki sits patiently, swinging his legs and staring at my house. After counting to ten, I climb up next to him.

"I never really understood the saying 'your home is where your heart is' until I met Sloane."

Yeah, that hits like a bullet.

"Do you trust me, Ash?"

"Fuck, Loki. You know I do." My skin crawls like a million tiny bugs are executing an invasion.

"No. I really don't. Until a month ago, yeah, I would have bet my life that you trusted me as much as I've trusted you over the years. But that's not the case. If it were, you would have let me help you."

Those bugs crawling up my skin eat away at my heart. I'm struggling to breathe.

"I wanted to, Loki. So many times, I wanted to run to you, but my hands were tied by SIA for so long."

"And then you made the choice on your own," he says bitterly.

"You had Sloane," I plead. I need him to understand I did what I knew to be best.

"But it should have been a decision you and I made together. We were always a team, Ash. Always. Fuck SIA and the FBI. It was you and me first, and you know it."

I do.

"I was scared, Loki." I can't take the emotions overwhelming my body anymore. I claw at my chest, trying to ease the uncomfortable feelings there.

"Of what?"

"Of letting you in and fucking up again," I yell in frustration. "You and I both know if The Ravens got ahold of you, you'd end up in the ground instead of a cut-up monster, like me. They'd want to make a statement with you because you're Antonio Black's son."

"I'm sorry." Loki's voice sounds pained, and it catches me off guard.

"For what?"

"For not seeing. Not knowing. Jesus, Ashton. You've given up your entire life when it should have been me. You're in this mess because of me. Your father got involved because of me. You should be the one with a wife and kids. I…"

"You're exactly where you're supposed to be, Loki. My father would have stepped in if it were you, or later down the line when it was Pacen. He would have gotten involved regardless because that's who he was. The torch was always coming to me. I've made peace with that."

"But you haven't, Ash. You haven't. Look at you. This isn't living."

An alarm sounds on my phone, followed by another, and finally, a third.

"What's that?" Loki asks, jumping to his feet with military precision. He's ready to battle at my side, and it cuts me to my core.

He's right. This is how it should have always been.

"My reminders to call Nova. Every night at ten."

Loki glances down at his watch and smiles. "Call. Don't be late on my account."

"Loki?"

He turns to look me in the eye. "We'll talk later. Keeping a date with your woman is your most important job now." He gives me a two-finger salute and meanders away.

I want to stop him. To say something. But he's right. Lifting my phone, I let it scan my face and immediately FaceTime Nova.

It rings three times before it connects, but the face that comes into the screen isn't Nova's.

"Who the fuck are you?" I ask, jumping down from the tailgate.

Loki's footsteps stop and he spins to face me.

"M—Mr. Westbrook?" the woman stammers, and my entire body goes cold.

Something is wrong.

Something is terribly wrong.

"Who are you?" I manage to ask again.

"I'm Nova's friend. I'm Penny. She—She's been staying with me."

"What? Where is she, Penny?" Desperation has my voice rising.

I feel Loki at my side, and I nearly break when he places a comforting hand on my shoulder. After all my betrayals, he stands by my side.

How could I fuck up family and friendships so badly?

Penny hiccups, and that's when I notice her eyes are rimmed red like she's been crying.

"Oh, God." It's ripped from my lungs with my last bit of air.

Loki tightens his grip and leans in so his face is present in the phone screen. "Penny, can you tell us where Nova is now?"

Penny nods. Her expression says she's in shock, and my entire body trembles with a fear I've never known.

"She's at Port Chance Memorial Hospital."

"Why?" I demand.

Loki releases my shoulder and pulls out his phone. He's typing away feverishly with both thumbs, but I'm too busy watching Penny to figure out what he's doing.

"I took her phone because I knew it was important for her not to miss this call." Penny shakes on the screen, and I can't tell if it's from her hand or mine.

"Why is she in the hospital, Penny?" My patience is waning. I need some goddamn answers.

"Oh, right. Sorry."

Just get to the fucking point, Penny!

"She was taking my son Gage upstairs. I'm not exactly sure what happened next. Gage said her eyeballs looked funny, and then she collapsed. She hit her head and at least one arm on the fall back down."

"Is she okay?" I growl. If I don't keep my teeth clenched tight, I'm going to lose my shit on Nova's poor friend.

Penny shrugs, and the tears she's been holding back tumble free. "I don't know. No one will tell me anything because I'm not family. She's been in there for three hours now."

"Where is Lochlan?" I explode.

"I couldn't get ahold of him at first, but he's on his way now. There's construction heading out of the city and I—I just don't know when he'll get here. But I'm so scared. She was so, so pale. Mr. Westbrook, she was so pale." Her voice cracks, and sympathy for this woman nearly crushes me.

"Call me Ashton. I—" Turning in a slow circle, I feel my world crumbling.

"He's on his way," Loki says over my shoulder. "Call him with any updates."

"O—Okay. Port Chance Memorial, in Chance Lake, Connecticut. Okay?"

"We've got it, Penny. He'll be there soon."

Loki takes my phone and disconnects the call while I stand frozen in silence.

CHAPTER 47

ASHTON

"*C*olton is getting the plane ready," Loki says calmly. "You'll be there in about an hour, but you need to hold it together, okay? She doesn't need you freaking the fuck out."

My head spins with details. The Apollyon. Nova. Killian. Nova. The pressure in my head nearly brings me to my knees.

"Ash? Talk to me."

The engine of a four-wheeler invades my ears, and I turn in the direction it's coming from to see Easton flying around the corner. Even in the dark, I can tell he's wearing pajamas.

He screeches to a halt at our feet, kicking up rocks and dust along the way.

"Tell me," he demands. He's never been one to mince words.

Another motor sounds in the distance, and I know my brothers are rallying.

Loki must have been texting them.

"She's in the hospital, but we don't know anything else," Loki explains as Halton pulls up.

"Preston is in Boston, but he'll meet you there. Colton is already at the airfield, bribing the tower to get you in the air immediately," Halton says with worry written all over his face. "What else do you need?"

All eyes turn toward me, but I think I'm having an out-of-body experience. The pressure in my head is drowning out all their words while sweat drips down my forehead.

I have a duty to The Apollyon, but Nova is the only thing I can think about.

"Ash?" Loki stands in front of me and grabs my shoulders. He gives them a rough shake, and I snap my eyes to his. "Do you trust me?"

"Yes."

"Do you trust Seth?"

"Yes." I wouldn't have partnered with either of them if I didn't, but I can't make my words work.

Easton stands behind Loki with his arms crossed over his chest. "What's more important to you? The next Ravens class or Nova?"

"Nova," I spit angrily. Lifting my hands, I break Loki's hold on me.

"Good." Loki grins. "Right answer, brother. Then go. Seth and I are not rookies. We've been trained for this. We'll cover your spot so Killian and Pacen can run the mission. We may not have your genius brain, but between the two of us, we won't miss anything. They will not be in danger on our watch. I promise you."

"I know. I know," I repeat.

"Okay. Anything we need to know?"

"The Ravens classes are getting smaller. They're more desperate than they've ever been. It makes them more dangerous."

"We'll go to headquarters now and get caught up. You trust Killian?"

Shame smacks me in the face because I do. I trust Killian like I should have been trusting Loki.

"I do," I say. Regret is a nasty bitch.

"Then I will too. We've got this, Ash. Go get your girl."

I stare into the eyes of my friend. He has every reason to hate me. Every reason to walk away from me like I did him. But here he stands. At my side. On my team.

I tear my gaze away and find Halton watching me closely. He knows what's running through my head. He's the most intuitive person I've ever met.

"It's okay, Ash," Easton says. His breath leaves in an audible whoosh. "We're family. We can get pissed, throw shit, fight until our knuckles are bloody, but we're always going to have each other's backs. It's in the chaos that we find hope. Because of the chaos, we're strong enough to fight all the demons chasing us. We're stronger together. I was afraid you wouldn't make the right decision here."

"Is that why you're here in Mr. Rogers pajamas?" Halton teases.

"Fuck yes. I jumped out of bed. I didn't even put shoes on," he says lifting a foot to show us. "I'm proud of you, Ashton."

Emotion gathers and sits in my throat like a dry piece of toast.

Loki raises his fist in the air. "Welcome to the chaos," he says in solidarity.

Muscle memory kicks in, and we all raise our fists to his. "Welcome to the chaos," we repeat.

"Where's your go bag?" Loki asks.

"Ah, in the hallway closet." Before I finish the sentence, he's taking my front steps two at a time.

"Give me your keys," Halton says holding out his hand.

They're clutched in my palm so tightly that when I open my hand there are angry red marks where the metal has broken skin. It's a shock to see. I never felt a thing.

Easton tugs me in for a hug. "Take care of her." When he pulls away, I see the concern in his eyes. They're worried about Nova too.

Squaring my shoulders, I drop the keys into Halton's hand as Loki comes barreling down the steps with my go bag on his arm.

One thing working for a secret military organization taught us was to always be prepared to run at the drop of a hat. A go bag meant the difference between life and death sometimes. Thankfully, it's not something you ever stop doing once it's been so deeply ingrained in your survival.

Loki crashes into me like a meteor and almost knocks me over, but he wraps his giant arms around me and holds on for dear life. "We've got this. We've got you. It's time for you to take charge of your life. We'll take care of the rest."

"Thank you, Loki. I'm so sorry," I mumble into his shoulder, and he pushes back, giving us some space.

"No, don't do that. You can make up for your shitty choices with me after you get your girl. Right now, all you need to know is that we're good. You and me. Brothers, business partners, friends. From now on, we're equal in everything. Got it?"

"Yeah," I choke out. "Thank you."

He nods and walks to Halton's four-wheeler. "I'll grab Seth, then we'll go see Killian. Call me as soon as you have news."

"Let's go," Halton orders, opening the driver's side of my truck. "Colton's waiting."

I hurry to the passenger's side, beyond thankful I don't have to drive. I'm not sure I'd make it to the airfield in one piece.

"Call me with any news," Easton yells to us. "I mean it. Any news. My phone is on, and I'll be waiting for updates."

Gratitude for my family drowns out all other emotions. I'm a lucky asshole. I nod to Easton and wave before I shut my door.

Halton drives in silence, allowing the riot of voices in my head to reign. Guilt tries to claw its way into my conscience, but I push it back. Loki and Seth can handle this. Nova is my priority. If forced to choose between her and The Apollyon, there would be no hesitation on my part. Nova is all that matters to me.

It hits me with a clarity I didn't have before.

The Apollyon is my past. Nova is my future.

And just like that, my chest expands, and I feel like I can breathe for the first time in years. Relief rushes through me like a tidal wave. Tremors rack my body, making my teeth chatter.

Now I'm truly free.

"It's an incredible feeling, huh?" Halton asks without taking his eyes off the road.

"What feeling?"

"Forgiveness," he states plainly. "Letting go. Finally moving on. It feels a lot like I imagine birth to be. It's a new beginning. I'm proud of you, Ash. I'll be honest—I wasn't sure you'd make the right decision either."

Yeah, I haven't given anyone in my life any reason to believe I would. Especially Nova.

"So that lesson in groveling you guys promised?"

Halton slams his open palm on the steering wheel and howls with laughter.

Rolling my eyes, I turn away and stare out the window. "Smug isn't a good look on you, Hattie."

He laughs even harder. He's shaking the truck, and I turn my head, but I'm unable to hide my grin.

When he finally composes himself, we're turning onto the old dirt road that leads to the private airfield. "Just know that when you apologize, do it from your heart. Never hold back. A half-assed apology is worse than no apology at all. And, Ash?"

I turn to look at my brother.

"Be honest. Tell her why you need her. Why you love her. Then spend every day for the rest of your life proving your love like it's your last day on earth."

"A lifetime of groveling."

Halton smirks. "We're human. We'll make mistakes. It's how you learn from them that matters."

"I'll never make this kind of mistake again. I should have gone with her, Hattie. I should have been there when this happened."

"You're right," he says without remorse. "But you'll learn from this."

"Damn right. I'm never leaving her alone again. Ever."

His chuckle warms my chest. "Good luck with that. No one likes to be hovered over."

"She'll get used to it."

"Second rule. Learn to compromise. A lot. In fact, learn that she's right more times than not, and you'll live to have a long and happy life."

Halton puts the truck in park, and Colton materializes out of nowhere.

He's bouncing on his toes from foot to foot. This guy has more energy than Exxon. "Come on. Preston is already in the air." He rips my door open and nearly drags me out.

Halton stands in front of the truck with his hands in his pockets.

"Thank you, Hattie."

"You want me to come?" he asks, and I see he's torn.

Halton, like all of my brothers, has fought hard for his family. He's worried about me, but his heart begs him to stay home with Rylan and Grayson. His priorities are on straight. I really need to start taking notes.

"No, you have people here who need you. I'll update you as soon as I know anything."

His relief is palpable. "Okay. If anything changes, I'll be on the next flight out."

"I know. Thank you. Just hug Rylan and little Gray for me."

"Done."

Colton tugs me toward the plane by my sleeve, and suddenly it's real. I shrug him off and jog onto the tarmac. I need to get to my girl.

Dear God, please. Please let her be okay.

CHAPTER 48

ASHTON

"*A*re you sure this is the right place?" I ask Colton.

"Yeah, this is it. No wonder Lochlan only makes Penny commute a few times a week. This place is in the middle of fucking nowhere."

Colton puts the car in park, then continues while I stare straight ahead. "Google says Chance Lake is even smaller than Burke Hollow. You're lucky they even have a hospital here. According to Mr. Google, it was built as a community hospital for multiple towns a few years ago, but there are no hotels or bars. There wasn't even a gas station in town until they built the hospital and had to add one."

I give my brother the side-eye as we step out of the car. Surely, he's messing with me. There are gas stations everywhere.

We walk at a clipped pace toward the entrance. When we get close, Preston pushes off the wall and stalks toward us.

Preston has matured so much these last ten years. As the head of our family, he has more pressure on him than I could have ever imagined, yet he's always the first one to be there when something goes sideways.

"How is she?" I blurt in greeting.

"They wouldn't tell me anything," he growls. He's pissed. No one says no to Preston Westbrook. "I can't even find a goddamn person to bribe in this Podunk town. Where the hell are we anyway?"

"Chance Lake," a stranger supplies to our right while puffing on a cigarette. He's dragging an IV bag behind him, and his hospital gown is blowing in the breeze. I turn away quickly before he flashes his junk.

"Anyway," Preston continues, "here."

He holds out a small box, and my hands freeze at my sides.

"What's that?" I ask. Panic makes my voice crack like a fifteen-year-old's.

"Mom's ring."

"What?"

"She gave it to me years ago, before I even met Emory, but it wasn't right for Ems. Mom told me to hang on to it and that I would know when it was needed."

"I don't need it."

He tilts his head and studies me. "Don't you?"

"No. I mean, yeah. I am going to marry her, but—"

Preston cuts me off, and Colton stands beside us grinning like the fool he is.

"But nothing. If you want to choose your own ring, that's fine. But to get into her room, you might need this damn ring." He pops open the box, and the diamonds glitter under the overhead lights.

"I'd forgotten how pretty it is," Colton says with wonder in his eyes.

It really is. A large princess-cut diamond stands proudly above a thin antique band that has pavé diamonds encrusted in it.

Preston catches my eye and I know he's remembering our mother telling us how our father painstakingly chose each diamond when we were little. It was one of her favorite stories to tell after he passed away.

We learned a lot about diamonds the year after his death.

The band of smaller diamonds wraps around the large one like a hug. It's the center stone that holds my attention though. It stands out like a beacon. A bright flash in the night sky. A shooting star. Like Nova.

Stalking forward, I grab the box from my brother's hand. "It is a Nova ring."

"Not to be confused with a NuvaRing." Colton laughs like a teenage boy.

"A what?" I bark, then push through the hospital's front doors.

"Ignore him," Preston says as he walks beside me. Giving me a smirk, he nods toward the ring. "Was I right?"

My fist clenches around the box. "Yeah, Mr. Know-it-all. You're right."

His chuckle is annoying.

"Go ahead then. She's on the second floor."

"There's a second floor in this building?" Colton asks, looking up.

"Unfortunately," Preston grumbles. "Come on, Colty. Nova's friend could use a familiar face."

"I bet. Your ugly mug probably terrified her."

Preston rolls his eyes as we step onto the elevator. "We look just like each other, asshole."

"Yeah, except for the old man wrinkles. Have you thought about Botox?"

Preston's eyes go wide, and he runs his fingers along his forehead. He doesn't get a chance to retaliate because the elevator doors open, and we come face to face with the woman on the phone. Penny.

"Colton," she cries. Obviously relieved to see a familiar face.

"Penny." Colton steps forward and wraps the woman in a hug. She's older than Nova. Maybe early forties, but pretty, even with swollen eyes and dark circles under them.

"Thank you for being here with her," I say, then push past

them toward the nurse's desk that looks like it belongs to a librarian.

Colton's voice fades behind me as I zero in on the small woman watching us. "I told your friends, I cannot give any information unless you're a family member," she says. I must make her nervous because she looks anywhere but at me.

She pats the tight ballerina bun, then adjusts her cat's-eye glasses as I approach.

When I wave the ring box in front of her, she's forced to focus on me though. "I'm her fiancé. Her ring was being sized. I was on my way home with it when I got the call from her friend."

"Fiancé?" she asks with a furrowed brow. Papers fly all over her desk as she searches for something. "It doesn't say anything about a fiancé in her paperwork."

"Did you ask her?"

"Well, no. She's been—" She purses her lips then narrows her eyes. "When is her birthday?"

"October twentieth."

"Middle name?"

"Sky," I fume.

"Name?"

"Hers or mine?" I growl. Preston walks up and places a patient hand on my shoulder.

"Yours," she huffs.

"Ashton Westbrook. Now can I please see my future wife?"

"I'll need your license."

I'm about to flip her goddamn desk over, but Colton lifts my wallet from my back pocket, pulls out my ID, and hands it to her.

She takes her time scanning it into a computer that looks like it still runs Oregon Trail, and then we wait while it spits out a badge. One line at a time.

Slowly she hands it over, and I take it without a word. "Room 212. Down the hall on the right."

We move in that direction when she stops us. Again. "Only

345

you, Mr. Westbrook. Visiting hours were over at seven. The rest of your party will have to wait in the waiting room."

I feel Preston shake next to me. He isn't used to being told no, and it won't surprise me one bit if he explodes on this woman in the next thirty seconds.

"Go," Colton says to me while grabbing Preston by the arm. "We'll wait."

It takes everything in me not to sprint down the hall. But I quickly realize the rooms are not actually rooms. They're separated by metal rods with mismatched curtains hanging from them. What the actual fuck? It's like a military pop-up hospital straight out of the fifties.

The room numbers are pinned to the curtains, so I have to study each one as I pass. Then I hear her voice, and my heart finally beats again. At least until I register her words.

"Pregnant? But I'm on the pill. Are you sure?" Nova asks hesitantly. I freeze. Standing in the middle of the hallway, the floor sways beneath me.

"Pregnant?" I hear the unmistakable lilt of Lochlan's voice bellow in a muted sort of way that tells me he isn't in the room with her.

"L—Loch, I'll call you back." Her voice is as shaky as I feel. "Are you sure?" She asks again.

"I'm sure," a male voice says. "Even though it's early yet. The pill is only 99% effective. Have you been ill or under a lot of stress lately?"

I can't hear her reply, but he continues. "I'm estimating you to be about eight weeks along, but you do have options."

"Options?" Nova gasps.

I blink rapidly, trying to gather my wits to enter this conversation.

"Yes," the man responds. "I'm assuming this was unplanned. But you do have options if it's unwanted."

"It isn't unwanted," she squeaks. "It's just. It's just. Unexpected. The—The father…" Her voice cracks.

Thank God. She wants this baby. Our baby. Holy fuck. So do I! My feet move on their own even as my brain tries to process all this information. The one thing I know is I want Nova. And now I want this baby too.

I pull the curtain back. The scrape of metal on metal has them both turning toward me. Nova's face pales, and the doctor looks irritated, but my body relaxes for the first time in weeks when I finally see her.

"The father." I choke up as tears heat my eyes. "The father will never miss another second of this pregnancy."

Nova's hand flies up to cover a sob, and I charge forward. Some of my muscles are tense, but my shoulders droop when I'm close enough to touch her. Taking her hand in mine, I kiss her forehead. "I'm sorry I wasn't here, princess. I'm so sorry. I'll never make this mistake again. I swear to you."

She winces, and I pull back just enough to take her in. Fuck. She has bruises everywhere. And a cast on her left arm.

"Did I hurt you? Fuck. Is she okay?" I ask the doctor, my eyes glued to her injuries.

"Miss Blaine," he says dryly. "Is it okay to speak in front of him?"

She nods, and the doctor sighs. I'm not sure what the hell his problem is, but if he thinks I'm leaving he can fuck right off.

"Very well. Miss Blaine has a fracture in both the ulna and radius bones of her left arm. It's a common injury when arms are extended to brace against a fall. She has a deep bone bruise on her left hip, but no other broken bones. She also has a slight concussion that we're monitoring, but all in all, she was very lucky."

"And the baby?" I ask through tears. "Is the baby okay?"

The doctor finally shows some compassion. "The baby is very

well-protected, and from what we could see in the ultrasound, doing well."

"Thank God. Thank God," I repeat. Without thinking, I push the old-fashioned phone Nova's still cradling out of her lap and drop my head to her stomach. "Thank God." I take a deep breath like it's my first and exhale so many worries and fears my body trembles.

"I'll give you two some privacy. Visiting hours are over, but if you managed to get past Henrietta, I'll assume you're here for the night."

"I'm not leaving," I say definitively.

"The nurse will be back to check on you shortly. You have your call button if you need anything in the meantime."

Nova and I remain silent as he closes the curtain behind him. Tears slide down my nose and soak her hospital gown.

A baby.

I'm going to be a father.

A daddy.

"Peto? You can't be here," Nova whispers, and for the second time tonight I feel my world come tumbling down around me.

"I need to be here, Nova. There isn't anywhere else I need to be. I need to be here for you, baby."

"But—But the class? The mission…"

"Is being handled by a perfectly capable team."

Standing, I turn to face her. Careful not to sit on her, I lean against the edge of her bed.

"I don't want you missing it because you feel obligated just because I'm pregnant." Her lip trembles, and I know she's hurting. Because of me.

"Baby, don't you get it?"

She shakes her head, and a tear slips free.

"I'm not missing anything. I chose to be here, for you, always for you, before I knew about the baby. I walked away because you're the only one that matters. Well, now you and Bean."

"Bean?" she asks with wide eyes.

I nod toward the ultrasound on the table next to her. "She looks like a bean."

"She?"

With an embarrassed grin, I shrug one shoulder. "I hope she's a girl. I know what to do with them. Sadie taught me well, but if the baby's a boy, I'll learn."

"You want the baby? You want...us?"

My lips crash into hers. I'm not gentle. I'm not asking. I kiss her with every ounce of passion I have.

"I don't want you," I whisper when we come up for air. "I fucking need you more than the air that I breathe. I need you, Nova. There isn't any other path to happiness for me. My road always led to you."

She sobs, and I ache to hold her, but I don't know how to touch her without causing pain, so instead, I just cradle her face in my hands. "I love you, Nova."

"I asked him to protect her, not knock her up. Bloody fucket," Lochlan roars from down the hall. "How the hell did you beat me here?"

"I flew. Good to see ya, buddy." I can hear the smirk in Colton's voice. It's going to piss Lochlan off even more.

"Don't smile at me like that. Your brother got my sister pregnant."

Colton's laughter fills the hall, and I can hear the nurse scolding them both.

"Crap. He was on the phone. He's going to lose his damn mind," Nova grumbles. "And he's going to kill you."

"He can try, sweetheart. But we're going to be family. He can rant and even take a swing at me, but I'm not going anywhere."

Footsteps stomp closer, and the nurse is threatening to call security. I almost laugh. What kind of security can a place like this even have?

"Nova?" Lochlan bellows.

Her eyes go wide, so I step forward to open the curtain and come nose to nose with her big brother. I don't know what comes over me, but I have the irresistible urge to poke at him.

"Hi, uncle. I hope you'll have a better filter when you babysit. I'd rather 'bloody-fucket' not be my child's first word."

Lochlan winds up like he's going to punch me, but Colton pulls his arm back. "He kind of deserves it, but I can't let you hit my brother. He's just learning to live in the real world."

"Get off me, you bloody idiot." Lochlan's British accent is even more pronounced when he's angry. And right now, he's livid.

"Back down, Loch." His wife, Tilly, comes into view. "Well, Ashton. Fine mess you've created here," she says with a wink.

"No, Tilly. Not a mess. A family." Turning toward Nova, I think my body might actually explode from pure happiness. "I've created the family I never thought I could have, but now know I can never live without."

"Family?" Lochlan bellows. The guy pulls so hard on the bottom of his vest I half expect buttons to go flying. "Are you going to marry her?"

"Yes," I blurt, holding up the ring box just as Nova says, "No."
Shit.

Spinning in place, I search Nova's eyes. "Well, that's not how I meant to ask, but yes, I do plan to marry you."

"No," she repeats, and a cold chill invades my body. My palms are so sweaty I wipe them on my jeans, but nothing works. Sweat seems to be pouring out of every cell of my body.

"What do you mean, no? I'll ask you properly when your brother isn't barking orders."

"No, peto. The answer today is no. The answer tomorrow will be no, and the answer next week will be no."

CHAPTER 49

NOVA

*H*is body crumples like discarded tissue paper, but I hold firm to my word. I will not marry someone just because we made a baby together.

Colton steps forward and places a hand on Ashton's chest. He takes in a stuttering breath like Colton's touch shocked him to life.

"No?" Ashton's voice is so small. So utterly heartbreaking.

"I—I won't get married just because we're having a baby. When I get married, it'll be for love. Not some righteous belief of others who have no say in my life." I enunciate each word while glaring at my brother.

Ashton falls to his knees beside my bed and clutches my good hand to his chest. "You think I only want to marry you because you're pregnant?"

Gah! This man. How can he possibly have such a hold on my heart in such a short amount of time? "I think it's the motivating factor," I finally admit.

The nurse pushes into the room at that moment and Colton takes the opportunity to sweet talk her and usher everyone from the room. We're going to owe him big-time.

"No, Nova. No. Baby Bean isn't the only reason I want to marry you." The sincerity in his tone threatens to break me.

My heart bleeds for this man.

"I know, but it's the accelerant in our relationship." I pause to wipe my nose with the back of my hand. It doesn't do any good. My nose and eyes leak with emotions I can't hold in. Damn hormones. "I won't do it. Not to her. Not to me. And not to you. My mom learned that lesson the hard way. I won't follow in her footsteps."

"But I would have asked you even if it weren't for Bean."

"Ashton, I say this with all the love in my heart, but I know you only came here tonight because I was injured, and you didn't know how badly. If I had been able to call and tell you I just broke an arm, would you have rushed here the same way? Would you have walked away from your obligations for a broken arm?"

"Yes," he says adamantly. The stern set of his jaw tells me he believes what he says.

I'm not so sure.

"You are the only one who matters to me, Nova. It may have taken me a while to figure out my shit, but I would have been here before the month was over. No matter what, I was always coming to get you."

Tears slide down my face at an alarming rate. The doctor said I fainted from dehydration. This can't be helping things.

"Princess, I was always coming for you. I promise."

My heart aches to believe him. But I know where his loyalties have lain for over half his life. "What about the class? Or the next one?"

Letting go of my hand, he pulls himself to standing, then drags a chair closer to my bed. "Do you know what happened when I got into my truck and drove away from my house? From The Apollyon?"

I shake my head, but my tears flow faster.

"I broke free. I felt free. And after falling in love with you, it was the second-best feeling I've ever had in my life. Will I worry about each class? Yes. Will I regret not running the missions? No. No, I won't."

"How do you know?"

"Because I ran them with a sense of duty. Because with each new class we saved, another piece of me died. Because the only time I haven't hated myself so completely was with you. Because I know that you're my future. However we make it, I know it starts and ends with you."

"Ash—"

"You don't have to say anything. I'll show you. I'll prove it to you. I just—I just need to know that someday, someday you'll say yes when I ask you to marry me."

Staring into his eyes, it's impossible to deprive him of this. I see his truth, his sincerity. His honest-to-goodness hope in me, in us, and the only thing I can do is agree. "Someday," I whisper.

"But not today?"

Gah! His sad puppy-dog expression with a touch of hopefulness almost has me caving just to see him smile. But I know we have work to do. "Not today," I say with an awkward shrug.

"Someday," he says, more to himself than to me. "Okay. Someday. I can work with that."

Something in his tone tells me I'll be entertaining many more marriage proposals than I could have ever dreamed.

###

"Are you sure you'll be all right?" I ask, standing in the bedroom of Penny's youngest son, Gage. It's hard not to laugh at the sight before me. Ashton is curled up on his side on the bottom bunk. Gage is sprawled out, happy as a clam on top.

I know the second I close this door, Gage will tell Ashton every detail of whatever TV show currently holds his attention.

"I'll be fine. Go to bed, princess. It's late, and the doctor said you needed to rest."

"Ashton, you don't even fit in that bed. You should go into the city with Lochlan and stay at the hotel."

"Hey, my bed is normal-sized," Gage says, rolling over. He hangs his head over the edge to stare down at Ashton. "It's just not meant for giants like him." The boy's entire body shakes with laughter, and my heart melts a little when I see Ashton smile at him.

"Hey, kid. How many teeth are you missing?" Ashton asks after seeing his toothy grin.

"So many," Gage says with a lisp. "The tooth fairy came so much she ran out of money and had to leave me a special note," he says proudly.

Ashton's brow furrows at the little boy's response. He must be thinking the same thing I am. Penny is struggling more than I knew.

Her deadbeat ex-husband is no doubt behind on his child support. Again. I make a mental note to talk to her about it.

Penny's house is cute and well-loved, but I have noticed in my short time here things are breaking down. It's also much too small for both Ashton and me to be here for any amount of time.

"That happened to me once," Ashton says, and I realize he isn't angling his body to hide his scars. When did he stop doing that?

"It did?" Gage gasps. "Landon told me Mom just didn't have any money, but I know that's not true. Mom's too big to be the tooth fairy."

Ashton's face, usually full of hard lines and scowls, smiles gently at my friend's son. "Yeah, I had a lot of brothers, and four of us lost teeth on the same night. We all ended up with special IOUs from Tammy the Tooth Fairy."

Gage sucks in a breath so loudly he chokes. "She has a name?"

"Gage? Go to sleep and leave Mr. Westbrook alone," Penny calls from down the hall.

"We can whisper after the lights go out." Gage giggles with a conspiratorial thumbs-up.

Ashton holds up his hand, and the two high-five with wide grins.

When he looks back to me, he's more relaxed than I've ever seen him.

"Go to the city, Ash. Get a good night's sleep."

"Not happening, princess. I'm here for good. If you're here, so am I. If you want to stay in Chance Falls—"

"Chance Lake," Gage corrects.

"Chance Lake," Ashton says with the biggest smile. "Then I'm here too. If this is where we will be for a while, I'll find another place for us to stay though." He tries to stretch his legs and hits the wood frame of the bunk bed with a wince. "Maybe that will be the first thing I do."

Crossing the room, I sit on the edge of the bed. My body is starting to get stiff, but I hide the grimace as I lower myself down.

"Ashton, you can't just stay here."

"Why not?"

"Because you have a house. A family in Vermont. Work."

"I'm not sure if you're aware, but I am a billionaire by birth. If I want to pack up and move to Hong Kong, I can. Work is mobile, and my company, Envision, has an office in Manhattan. I can do pretty much whatever the hell I want, Nova. The question is, what do you want?"

"I don't want you making crazy decisions because you're afraid you'll lose me. Your family is important to you. That mountain town has been your home for years."

"Why was it okay for you to give up everything and everyone you loved to stay with me, but it's not okay for me to do the same?"

"That was different. I've never really had a home outside of the hotel. My parents are hotel nomads, for crying out loud, and I think we proved my friends were not really friends at all. Penny excluded anyway."

He raises his hand and gently runs his knuckles along my cheek. "I'm going to be where you are from now on, sweetheart. Get used to it."

Gage wiggles above us, and I know he won't be able to stay quiet much longer.

"We'll talk tomorrow, okay?"

"Okay. You good for tonight?" Ashton says gently. His eyes arrest me. They're unguarded. I've never seen him like this, and I feel a tiny sliver of hope weaving through my heart.

"Yeah, Landon is sleeping at a friend's house, so I've got his bed tonight."

Ashton sits up as much as the low-hanging bunk will allow and gently kisses my lips. "Sleep tight. Baby Bean needs her mommy well rested."

My mouth drops open and I can't close it.

"Mommy?" I mumble. It hadn't really sunk in before. I'm going to be a mom.

Oh, shit. I'm going to be a mom!

CHAPTER 50

ASHTON

I was up before the sun, knowing Killian and Pacen would already be leaving the ambush location. Loki was able to send the live feeds to my phone, and I've sat on Penny's porch, glued to the tiny screen for the last four hours while the house was asleep.

"They're clear," Loki says over the speaker.

"They work well together," I admit.

"Damn well. I've never seen a crew so tight. Not even my own. Killian's good," he admits.

"Pacen is better."

Loki is quiet for a minute, then agrees. "She is. This was her choice, Ash. And no one will ever have her back like Kill."

I grunt, but I know he's right.

"For what it's worth, I think you made the right choice. They're invested in The Apollyon, but they also have each other to get through the tough days. Take comfort in that."

"It's weird watching it all happen and not actually being a part of it," I mumble solemnly.

"That's a fairly common feeling when guys first come home from war. It's going to be an adjustment, but I'm so damn proud of you. You'll still be connected, but it won't consume your life anymore. And I was talking with Preston. We're creating a fund to help this run. It won't just fall on your shoulders anymore. We'll handle it all as a team."

"No. That opens up the entire family, Loki. I won't do that."

"It'll be done just as you are now, all anonymously, but we will do it. We're done letting you carry the burden alone." His tone is so stern that there's no use talking to him about this right now. "What are you going to do now?"

Leaning back in the rocking chair, I look around Penny's home. I won't admit it out loud yet, but I like it here. It has the small-town Vermont feel without all the baggage. Turning toward the rising sun, I exhale slowly. "I'm not sure. Honestly, I've never been so adrift yet anchored at the same time. I'm not sure what to do with myself."

"You'll find your way, Ash. You have had life-or-death situations hanging over your head since you were fifteen. It's normal to feel a little lost. In fact, I'd be worried if you weren't. Keep up your sessions with Dr. Benson. It's important. And as far as being anchored? That's what a good woman will do to you, man. I'm happy for you."

"Loki?"

"Nah, we're good. We have years to talk about your shitty choices. Right now, I just want to make sure you've got your head on straight. The only thing that should matter to you now is Nova."

"I'm going to be a father." I hear the words leave my mouth, but it sounds like another person talking.

"I know. You're going to be a great one too. Just like your dad."

The weight of his words sucker-punch me and the emotion of it overwhelms me.

"I think your dad led by example, and even though he made some choices that left us all scratching our heads sometimes, there was never a question that he loved us all. He believed in each one of us. He taught us how to love, and he taught us empathy. Even though his life was cut short, he left a lasting legacy in each one of us. Be proud of that, because I know wherever he is, he's looking down on us, shaking his fist and welcoming us all to his fucking chaos."

This pulls a laugh from me. "It's been a long time since I've thought of my dad and remembered the good."

Loki sighs through the phone. "I know. It's hard to see the fire through the smoke when you're in the middle of it with no lifeline. But you clawed your way out. You fulfilled everything your father wanted to do and then some. It's time to forgive, Ash. It's time to move on to the next phase of your life. Wherever that ends up being. Even if it means starting over somewhere else. Somewhere with less...baggage."

I hear what he isn't saying. It's hard not to agree with him. The next phase of my life is with Nova. Maybe that's why my Vermont house never felt like a home. Maybe home really is wherever Nova is.

"Yeah, I've been thinking about that all night," I say, tugging at the ends of my hair.

The sound of metal clanging together above me grabs my attention, and I glance up. When I don't see anything, I stand and walk down the porch steps but still can't find anything.

"You haven't taken a vacation in twenty years. Take time to figure out what you need. What Nova needs. Trust that we have your back whatever you decide."

Walking around the side of the house, I find the ladder. And at the top is Penny's oldest son, Kaiser.

What the hell is he doing on the roof?

"Yeah, thanks. Loki, I gotta go, okay? Send me a report when Killian and Pacen arrive?"

"Done. Love you, brother."

"Love you too. And Loki?"

"Yeah?"

"Thank you. For everything."

I swear he sniffles. "Always," he says gruffly, then hangs up quickly.

I pocket my phone and stare at the young man before me.

"Ah, hey, Kai. What's up?"

He stills on the roof but shifts his weight from one leg to another like he's about to get into trouble. My heart stops as I watch him. What the hell is he doing up there?

"Are you going to tell on me?"

I cross my arms over my chest and take in this kid. I like him already, but I understand the fear lurking in his eyes. "Depends on what you're doing, I guess."

His shoulders droop, but after a beat, he straightens his posture and stares straight down at me. "Mom had to go into the office early, and it takes her two hours on the train sometimes."

"Okay." I rock back on my heels, keeping the appearance of calm, but everything I've learned about this family has my skin itching with the sense that something isn't quite right.

"Well, the roof is leaking, and my dad..." He looks across the field, and I follow his gaze to a tiny home on the edge of the property. "Well, he isn't great at helping out."

"So is a roofer coming this morning?"

He shakes his head, and that's when I see the tools in his hands. This kid does not seriously think I'll let him fix the roof. Does he?

"We can't afford a roofer. I watched YouTube all week. I've got this." He sets his jaw stubbornly, daring me to stop him.

I fucking love this kid.

I quickly run through everything I know about roofing. It's limited at best, but I did help Easton with his workshop. I can at least help Kaiser and figure out what kind of damage is up there.

"How old are you?"

He lifts his jaw defiantly. "Thirteen."

Yup, I love him.

When I step onto the first rung of the ladder, he scoots back a few steps.

"Okay, stop right there," I order. "Don't move. Let me up there first."

"You're coming up?"

Against my better judgment, I guess I am. And I hate heights.

"Listen, kid. I understand why you don't want me to tell your mom, but if you think I'm leaving you up on this roof without me, you're nuts."

"You're going to watch me?"

Climbing onto the roof, I have the irresistible urge to hug him. Instead, I ruffle his hair on my way by. "No, kid, I'm going to help."

~

I sit on the hard edge of the roof with my makeshift safety harness pulled taut, trying to hide the fact that I'm terrified right now. Kaiser sits next to me, looking at the hole between us.

"It looked a lot easier on YouTube," he mumbles.

Scratching my head, I resist the urge to laugh. "It usually works that way, doesn't it?"

"Mom's going to kill me."

Yeah, she might kill me too. Luckily, Nova and the other boys are still sleeping. "Wait, don't you have school?"

"Not today. Teacher in-service or something."

Glancing back at the hole, I sigh. Who the hell do I call for this?

Easton.

That jackass is going to love this. Reaching into my pocket, I pull out my phone.

"My brother might be able to help," I tell Kaiser.

East picks up on the fourth ring. "What's wrong? Is Nova okay?"

"Yeah, sorry. She's sleeping."

He rubs his eyes, and I wait while he slips out of bed. When he turns on the light, I see he's in his kitchen and looking at me like he's confused. "Where are you?"

I scratch the edge of my hairline again. "Funny story that. Ah, I'm on a roof. With a thirteen-year-old."

Easton drops his glass of water and curses. "You're what?" he demands while sidestepping glass.

"There's a leak, and Kaiser wanted to fix it. He's Penny's son. You know, Nova's friend? He watched a bunch of videos. I thought I would help, but we kind of made it worse." I scan the camera over the hole. "How do we fix this?"

"Please tell me you don't have that kid up there tied in with a goddamn rope."

Looking around, I realize this might have been a really dumb idea. "He was already up here when I found him."

"Ashton. Get off the damn roof and get that kid's feet on the ground before we have a lawsuit on our hands."

"Oh, my mom would never sue you. She's too nice."

Maybe being too nice is why she doesn't have the money to fix this. I watch the kid's features and see his fear as plainly as my own.

"Do you know how to fix it?" I ask again.

"Yeah, you get off the damn roof and call a professional. Now, Ash."

"You don't think we can patch this up?"

"No. And honestly, I can't believe you let him get up there. Not to mention you hate fucking heights. Sorry, buddy. It's too early for my kid filter to kick in."

Kaiser smiles and looks away.

"All right. I'll think of something. Thanks, East."

"Get off the—"

I disconnect the call and slip the phone into my shirt pocket. "Here's the deal. I don't know how to fix this. You don't know how to fix it, though I admire your effort. How about if we get down, and I'll get someone over here to do the work before your mom gets home?"

"We can't afford it." He drops his eyes and won't look at me. The embarrassment rolls off him.

"That's okay. I've got it covered. I bet your mom doesn't like taking too much help, but what if we make a man's deal?"

He turns a skeptical gaze my way. "Men usually lie. I'd rather take a mom's deal."

Arrow, meet heart.

"You know what? Me too. A mom's deal then? I'll get the roof fixed, and you continue to fix what you can around here until it's paid off. But you stay off the roof from now on."

"Why would you do that? It's going to cost you money."

Smart kid.

"I'm doing it because I can. And because your mom has been a real good friend to Nova when she needed it most. That is worth more than money. And I'll let you in on a little secret. I have a lot of money. What good is being rich if you can't help your friends?"

"Okay." He sighs.

"Good. Down you go."

I hold his shirt as he turns and puts his feet on the ladder. He's halfway down when he looks up at me with questions just waiting to spill from his lips. "How much money is a lot of money?" His face turns a bright shade of red, and I laugh.

It feels so good to laugh.

"I have more money than my kids' kids' kids could spend."

His eyes go so wide that I'm afraid he'll faint. Then he nods. Just once. "I'm going to have that kind of money when I grow up. I'm going to take care of my mom and my brothers, and they'll never have to worry about anything."

My heart skips a beat while my eyes grow hot. "That's a very noble thing, Kaiser. You have a good heart. Just remember something, okay?"

"What's that?" he asks as he resumes his descent.

"Just make sure you remember to take care of yourself too. And don't help others so much that you forget how to ask for help when you need it. We all need it sometimes. It doesn't make you weak. It doesn't mean you've failed. It simply means you're human."

He chuckles and jumps past the last few rungs. "I know I'm human, Mr. Westbrook. I'm not an idiot. I'm a mammal too."

Laughter rumbles in my chest. Yeah, I really like this kid. I'm halfway down the ladder before I realize why. He reminds me of me.

With a million thoughts running through my head, I google emergency roofers, then follow Kaiser inside. Even with a leaky roof and cracked front step, this place feels like a home. This place feels like forever.

It's time to make forever a reality.

CHAPTER 51

NOVA

"What is this place?" My breaths are uneven and labored. This cannot be what I think it is.

"It's cute, right? And it's only fifteen minutes from Penny's house. It's kind of perfect." His smile is blinding. There has been a definite change in him over the last week. He's lighter. Happier. Calm.

I haven't even seen him attempt to hide his scars once. Not when we took Gage to the park. Not when we got Penny's oil changed. Not even when we stood in line for forty-five minutes at the post office to send Sadie a package when he missed his Friday date night.

But this? A house? In Chance Lake? Is he losing his mind? I'm starting to hyperventilate.

"Nova? Hey, take a deep breath. Sit down. What's wrong? Is it the baby?"

Shaking my head, I do as he asks. I sit on the stairs, then lower my head between my legs and focus on my breathing until my head stops spinning.

"Talk to me, princess."

"What are you doing, Ashton?" My voice cracks, and his face

falls. I hate to be the cause of it, but I need some ground rules here.

"I thought you'd want to be near Penny, but if you want to go back to New York, we can do that too. I have a realtor who can start setting up showings."

I hold up my palm to stop him.

"No, Ash. You don't understand. I mean, what are you doing?" I wave my finger around the room a little too wildly. "You have a house in Vermont. And North Carolina, if I'm not mistaken. People don't just go around buying houses because they're tired of sleeping in a bunk bed for a few days."

A sly smirk lifts the corner of his face, and I simultaneously want to smack and kiss him. "I'm not most people, Nova. And I can buy a house in every state if I want to, but I'm not wasteful like that. Yes, I am tired of sleeping in a toddler-sized bunk bed, but I'll keep doing it if that's where you want to be. Gage would love it if I moved in permanently."

A laugh bubbles up despite myself. "The boys do seem to love you."

He shrugs. "I like them. I'm worried about Penny, but I think if I fix anything else, she's going to kick me out."

"Buying her a new refrigerator as payment for room and board might have been a little much." I giggle. I love how hard he's trying with the people who matter in my life. I love that he's worried about them too. "Both Lochlan and I have tried to talk to her. Lochlan even gave her another raise, but she won't open up about what's going on with her ex, so I appreciate everything you've done for her."

"They're good people. I think she just needs a little help." He sits back and looks around the empty house. "You don't like it?"

"I love it, but this isn't home for you. What about your family?"

"Sweetheart, my family is spread out all over the country now.

We're only separated by a plane ride. And we happen to own three planes plus a helicopter."

I grew up with money. The Bryer-Blaines are in the upper echelon of society, but we have nothing on the Westbrooks. It's still a shock to have him state things so plainly.

"What about Sadie?"

I see the hurt flash across his face. She's his Achilles' heel.

His eyes dart around the room like he's searching for answers. Then he turns those devastatingly handsome blue eyes on me. "I've thought a lot about this, Nova. It's all I've done. I can't help it. My brain processes shit before I even realize I'm thinking about it. But yeah, I don't want to miss any more Fridays with Sadie."

He shifts and braces his forearms on his thighs. His head hangs low. "I know this sounds insane, but that girl saved me from my darkest days. I'm not sure where I would be without her. I only have a few years left before she leaves me and heads off to do great things in college." He turns a heartbreaking smile on me. "But I have a plan."

"Obviously," I say with a grin that ignites hope in my chest. I lean forward and rest my elbow on his shoulder. "Tell me."

"I'll fly back to Vermont on Fridays. You can come or stay if you have stuff going on. I can stay the night or do a day trip, depending on our schedules. This way I can check in with Envision and The Apollyon in person during the day and have my dates with Sadie at night. Then I'll come home. I'll go into the New York office sometimes, but I've never done well in that atmosphere, so I'll work from home most of the time. And Nova?"

I lift my eyes to his.

"Home for me is wherever you want to be. Chance Lake? New York? Or Bum Fuck Two, I'll follow you."

Tears that seem to be a part of my life these days roll down my face. "Are you happy?"

His entire face lights up. "As long as I have you, I'm happier than I ever thought I could be."

"And you're happy here?" I ask, waving my hand around the room.

"I don't want this to sound like I'm running away, because I'm not. But as much as I love my house in Vermont, it holds a lot of really dark memories. Even when I said I was moving on, that house always dragged me into the past. It wasn't until I got on that plane and left it all behind that I felt like I could breathe again." He exhales sharply and runs his fingers through his hair. "Does that make any sense?"

These damn tears. I wipe at them a little too aggressively, and he chuckles. Turning toward me, he clears them away with the pads of his thumbs.

"Yeah, it makes sense, peto. A fresh start looks different for everyone. I think that's why I adapted so easily when I first showed up at your place. Being out of my surroundings, which felt suffocating most of the time, allowed me to finally feel free. I get it. But are you sure this is where you want to start over?"

"Will you be okay with me flying to Vermont every Friday?"

"Will you be okay with me coming along for the ride?"

"Is that a threat?" He kisses the corner of my mouth. "Or a promise?"

Tit for tat with this guy. Smiling into his lips, I whisper, "It's both."

"Is this our fresh start, Nova? Is this our new beginning home?"

"It depends." I moan. He bites down on the sensitive skin of my neck, and my nipples harden.

"On?" His growl vibrates through my skin.

"How soon can we christen it?"

Ashton nips my neck again, and I gasp, but he pulls away so suddenly I almost fall forward. "Falling for me, huh?"

"Ugh. Are you starting with the dad jokes already? He isn't even born yet."

"I heard a strong heartbeat. She's going to be a pain in the ass just like her mother."

"You'd better hope not. He's going to be a know-it-all like his dad."

"She's going to drive you nuts answering every question you ask her with a question of her own."

"He's going to—gah! Ashton! Put me down." He's lifted me into a wedding hold.

"No can do, sweetheart. If I don't get us out of here, the realtor will come looking for us, and we'll never get the paperwork signed. Plus, I promised Gage we could build his new Lego tonight."

Placing my hands on either side of his face, I bring his lips to mine. "You're going to make a great dad."

He swallows as his fingers tighten around me. "I'm going to try," he promises. "Let's just pray that she has your confidence."

My head falls back, and laughter shakes my entire body. "I hope he looks like you."

"Oh, the Westbrook genes are strong. She'll look just like me. Let's hope she gets your eyes though. The world needs more stars."

"I love you, peto."

"I love you more."

Always one-upping, but when it comes to love, I'll take it.

∿

"Spill," Lexi orders. She fills my glass with sparkling grape juice then pours one for Rylan.

"I can't believe our babies will only be a couple months apart," Rylan squeals. "I'm so happy for you and Ash." She holds a napkin up to her face. If I thought my pregnancy hormones were tough, they have nothing on Rylan's.

Dear God, do they get worse the farther along you get? It's been a few weeks since I saw her last, but I make a mental note to pay closer attention to her symptoms.

Ari grins at Rylan, but hands her a pack of tissues under the table. "Tell me about the house."

"It's amazing," I gush. "I don't know what kind of voodoo magic Ashton pulled, but it will be ready for us to move in next week."

"That man would move mountains to give you whatever your heart desires." Lexi laughs.

We sit in silence for a minute, and I get the sense they all want to say something. "What? What is it?" I ask, looking at each of them in turn.

"We're sorry your nomination got pulled," Winnie says quietly.

I sigh heavily. "Yeah, it sucks, but it's not unexpected. With the trial going on, they don't want the publicity."

"Why give it to you in the first place then?" Lexi snarls.

"Honestly, I think they thought it would all die down by now. It's okay though. I think it might be opening the doors for me with some clients in L.A., so it's not all bad news."

Lexi assesses me with her drink paused at her lips. "You're sure you're okay with it?"

"Yeah." I nod. "I mean, it would have been an amazing accomplishment but it's not the end of the world."

The bell chimes as the door of the Marinated Mushroom opens, and we all turn to watch Ashton and Sadie walk in with Tate trailing behind them. My heart nearly implodes at the cuteness overload.

"I can't believe she got him to agree to this," Ari says, stifling a laugh.

"It's homecoming," Lexi says with an evil grin. "Who else would Sadie Sunshine have as her chauffeur?"

Sadie didn't hold back. Ashton is decked out in a three-piece suit with a cap to match. He narrows his eyes when he catches sight of me. I use my napkin to cover my grin, but it doesn't do any good. My entire body shakes with laughter.

He whispers something to Tate, who guides Sadie to a table like a gentleman, then Ashton makes a beeline to our table.

"Ladies," he growls. His eyes never leave mine as he stalks around the table until he's directly beside me. "Princess." A shiver runs down my spine. He bends in half to whisper in my ear. "Sloane sent me a new book. This one is just for you. As soon as I get these two home from the dance, we'll have our own date. Be naked."

My entire body heats from the tips of my ears all the way down to my toes. My hands fumble on the table, searching for the menu, but Lexi finally slips it to me, and I use it to fan myself.

"Someone is getting lucky tonight!" Rylan laughs like she's drunk. But I'm beginning to realize it's pregnancy hormones that make everything extra.

"You know it." Ashton grins and turns back to Sadie and Tate.

Ari whistles loudly, and he waves a hand over his shoulder in acknowledgment. "Did he just wink? Ashton Westbrook just smiled, winked, and sauntered away. What have you done and please keep doing it."

I take a sip of the juice and almost spit it out on the table.

"Oh, yeah. Sorry. I should have warned you. Sparkling grape juice tastes nothing like wine," Lexi says dryly.

"Welcome to the chaos, chica! Baby on board, but when we have our first post-baby girls' night, watch out. Now, tell us about the house. And be warned, the boys are planning a home invasion next month," Rylan says in one breath while fanning her face.

"A what?"

"Rotating weekends to visit. Get ready for the Westbrook

welcoming committee. They travel in packs, and it's not worth fighting," Winnie says.

"You're all coming to Connecticut?"

Ari grins. "A lot. Get those guest rooms ready. Welcome to the chaos isn't just a saying. It's a way of life."

Looking around the table, I see nothing but love. Yeah, this is the kind of chaos I can get behind. Lifting my glass in the air, I propose a toast. "Well, welcome to the chaos it is then."

Lexi whoops. Ari does a yeehaw of some sort, and Rylan? Rylan sits back and watches as friends become family.

CHAPTER 52

NOVA

"*A*sh? Where are you?"

We moved into the house a few months ago, and I instantly saw a change in Ashton. This house is nothing like his Vermont one. Thanksgiving in Vermont was tough for him. Our families wrapped us in love, but he never fully relaxed, so we thought we'd have a nice quiet Christmas, just the two of us, in our new home.

I should have known better.

The Westbrooks and Bryer-Blaines started arriving at six a.m. on Christmas morning and the parade of people didn't stop for a solid twelve hours. But since they all showed up unannounced, Ashton put them to work.

We had the entire house unpacked and semi-decorated within a few hours and we haven't looked back since.

"Bean's room," he calls.

Shaking my head at the holiday chaos we still haven't put away, I head up the steps and stop at the nursery, watching as he moves one picture frame, changes his mind, and replaces it with another one.

The first thing Ashton did after our families helped us unpack was fill every available surface with photos. It's almost overwhelming, especially in the family room, where hundreds of eyes smile back at you through glass barriers.

Every time I turn around, there's a new frame. A new smiling face. I've let him have his way, but we're bordering on hoarder territory now.

"What are you doing?"

He lifts his head with a smile and holds up two new picture frames. "I'm picking out a frame for today's ultrasound."

I enter the room and look at the bookcase on the back wall. New photos of Sadie and a few of his other nieces line the top shelf. "What about these?" I can't contain my smile. He went from living in a model home to modeling his home after the chaos he tried to avoid.

"That's from Sadie's eighth-grade graduation," he says, standing beside me.

Looking at the other photos in a line, I pick up a group one and find Ashton in the back, off to the side. "You were there." I point to him in the photo.

"I was," he says sadly. "I was there for most of these, but it's weird. I don't feel like I was part of any of them. It's like I was…"

"On the outside looking in?" I guess.

"Yeah. I know this is a lot. But every time I go through pictures, I'm reminded of how much I missed out on, even though I was physically there. I don't want to miss any more moments. And I want Bean to know her cousins. I removed myself for so long, but the rest of them have always been close." He moves about the room, and I'm thankful he no longer hides the emotion in his eyes.

"Even if they don't see each other every day, Dexter's kids count on Loki's kids, and Halton's son worships Preston's kids. I want that for our kids too."

"Oh, Ash." Turning, I wrap my arms around his middle, and he holds me tight.

"I think, in Vermont, I couldn't put up pictures because I didn't want to be reminded of what I was missing out on. Now, I'm so afraid I'll forget the memories, I'm putting them everywhere."

Everywhere is the truth. The walls are lined with family photos. The bookshelves and even the changing table endcap all have frames in varying sizes and shapes. Our family's stories are shown through pictures in this room.

"Does this make you happy? Seeing all the smiles? The happy moments?"

He nods against my head. "It does. When I can't sleep, I find myself in here, studying each frame and wondering what was going on in their heads when it was taken. Or how I could remove myself so completely that I missed all these special moments and the feelings they brought my family. They're like a reminder. A reminder to live in the moment, and not in the background."

"I get it," I say. And I do. This house is his memory wall. A reminder that love is all around him.

"Is it too much?" he asks warily. "It's too much, isn't it?"

I laugh into his side. "I think we'll eventually run out of space, but if it makes you feel good to be surrounded by so much love, then I'm happy. That's what you wanted, right? To feel the love every time you walk into this room?"

"Yeah," he says, running his finger along the wall that Ari and Halton painted. The nursery is a garden theme, at Ashton's request, and dancing, smiling beans sprout from the floor. It's a happy place for a happy baby.

"I got a call from Lochlan this morning."

His body tenses. Lochlan must have called him too. Kate took a plea deal, and while it will mean jail time, I know he'll think the sentence is about fifty years too short.

"How do you feel about it?" he asks cautiously.

I shrug. "She's going to be in jail for a very long time. It makes me happy and sad. She ruined her life, and for what?"

"The key word in that sentence is 'she.' She did this to herself, and so did Sam. Lochlan said he'll probably get the same deal next month."

"I know. It's just hard. I thought she was my friend for a lot of years. She had so much potential."

Ashton tugs me into his chest and kisses the top of my head. "You're a good person, Super Nova." A timer goes off on his phone and he jumps to get it. "Time to go. Today is the day. I can feel it. Today, baby Bean will tell us it's time to start picking girl names."

"I think he's going to give you the finger again." I love messing with him, but I can't hide my smile when his eyes narrow in on me.

Ashton laughs. We've had three ultrasounds, and the baby's refused to cooperate each time.

"But this time, we'll see her in 3D. Even if she flips us off, it'll be a great picture." He holds up a yellow frame. "I'm ready for her."

He places the frame on the table, then takes my hand. "Let's go see our girl."

"Our boy is going to start kicking if you keep calling him a girl."

Ashton bends at the waist and places his lips on my stomach. At five months, I'm just starting to show. "Baby Bean," he coos. "You're going to be a good little girl and show mommy I'm always right today, aren't you?"

"Ganging up on me already? How dare you!"

"Never, princess. You'll always be our queen."

Smiling up at him, I can't believe this is the same man who kicked me out of his house. "I have to pee again. I'll meet you downstairs?" I need a buffer because I know I'll say yes if he asks me to marry him right now. And I can't say yes. Not yet. It'll ruin the surprise Dexter has been working on.

He kisses my forehead, and I watch him walk away. Knowing he'll come looking for me if I take too long, I use the nursery bathroom, then go downstairs to meet him.

I find him in the family room, staring at the painting Halton brought with him on his last visit. The thing is huge, and cut into three equal pieces, but I can't tell if Ashton likes it, or if it makes him sad.

The first time I saw it, I cried so hard I peed my pants. All the different versions of him were too close to the truth. We could have lost him. But the connection that Halton captured where my hands touch Ashton's face always gives me hope.

This portrait could have had a very sad aesthetic, but the love that shines between us always makes me happy.

Ashton turns when he hears me approach. "I was a very dark man for a long time," he says, nodding toward the painting.

"You were hurting, peto. There's a difference."

"Every time I look at it, I should feel sad. Or angry. But for some reason, all I feel is hope."

My breath catches in my lungs. "Really?"

He stares at me with a funny look. "Yeah, why?"

"Because that's exactly what I say every single time I see it. It's a sign of hope."

He searches my eyes with a contemplative smile. "Where are we going to put it?"

"I think it should go above the fireplace, but I didn't say anything because I wasn't sure how you felt about it," I admit.

He nods and rubs his jaw with his thumb and forefinger. "Yeah, I think you're right. We can't outrun our past, but remembering it keeps us from making the same mistakes in the future." He's silent for a minute, and I know something's wrong when he turns to me.

"What is it?"

"What if Bean asks why I look so sad, or angry, or…" He points at the portrait. All the shadows of his life.

"Then we'll tell him that life is full of ups and downs, but love and family will always guide you through the dark times."

He purses his lips and nods like he's thinking. "We're going to be okay," he says. "This parenting thing, I mean. We make a good team."

Tears fill my eyes. "Yeah, peto. We do."

He ushers me out the door, and I wait on the porch while he locks it. It was a challenge for him not to outfit this place with the same level of security that he has in Vermont, but it was therapeutic for him too. Now we just have paranoid-dad-level security.

His life is changing. We're changing.

Change has never felt so good.

~

"Come on, Bean," Ashton pleads.

"I'm sorry, Mr. Westbrook. Your baby seems to be very camera-shy."

Ashton lowers his lips to my belly and blows a raspberry, then turns toward the small screen where we can see the baby sitting with its legs crossed. It appears to kick right where his lips had just been.

"She's a feisty little thing," he mutters.

"He was sleeping," I say. "Let him be."

"Fine." Ashton sighs. "Can we just see her face one more time?"

I wasn't sure how I would feel about the 3D ultrasound, but the second the technician moved the wand to show us the baby's face, tears streamed from my eyes.

She's beautiful.

Yeah, I think she's a girl too, but I like giving Ashton shit.

"She's perfect. So, so perfect." Ashton's eyes are glued to the monitor. The love and awe on his face are enough to have me agreeing to ten more kids, so I keep my mouth shut.

Pregnancy is not a walk in the park, and I know he'd love a football team of kids if that's what I wanted.

"She looks like you," he whispers, but we both know that's a lie. She has the Westbrook way about her. She may end up with my attitude, but she's all Westbrook.

CHAPTER 53

ASHTON

Four Months Later

"*G*irls' night!" Lexi yells at the next table over, and Winnie laughs.

They've taken up the biggest table at the Marinated Mushroom, and the happiness they exude filters into every corner of the restaurant.

Seeing Colton's wife, Winnie, so carefree eases a knot in the back of my neck. She may have helped him grow up, but he has given her life. I'm proud of him.

Tate sighs like a ninety-year-old man. "Should I call Uncle East to pick them up?"

Sadie gives him an indulgent smile. "Two of them are pregnant. They're perfectly capable of driving home, even if the other two get tipsy."

Tate looks over his shoulder, and I can see him mentally cataloging all the drinks on the table. Sadie, on the other hand, is a party in a bottle and ready to spill over with giddiness.

I've watched these two grow up. Sadie has said she was going to marry Tate since she was six years old, and observing them now, I have no doubt in my mind she'll get her way. It's a good match. The best, really. Tate has been an old man since he could talk, and Sadie is his opposite. They balance each other out.

Like me and Nova.

"Uncle Ash," Sadie says, waving her hand in front of my face.

"Sorry. What did you say?"

"Are you nervous?" she whispers. Leaning in conspiratorially, she grins, and it's infectious. Even Tate smiles in response. "Do you think she'll say yes this time?"

That's the question, isn't it? I've asked Nova to marry me no less than twelve times since that first time in the hospital months ago.

"Jesus. I hope so."

"My dad has a knack for this stuff," Tate says stiffly. "Mom even made him a Prince Charming T-shirt that lists all his matches. They're taking it a bit too far if you ask me, but he's confident this is the plan that will work."

I hated having to turn to Dexter for this. But Tate's right. The guy is a happily-ever-after-loving freak. If this doesn't work, I'll just have to wait for Nova to ask me.

Sadie rubs her hands together. Her grin is slightly scary. "So, the real question is, do I get to be an auntie?"

This kid has given me whiplash since she was six years old, and I still wasn't expecting this question.

"For Bean?" Her eyes go wide, and she nods like a bobblehead on the dash of a car. "You want Bean to call you auntie?" I can't even say it without getting choked up.

"Heck yeah, I do. Uncle Ash, you've been the biggest part of my childhood after Mom and Dad. I want to be that for Bean. You're who I turned to for everything. Even when I got my period and needed—"

Tate chokes on his root beer and holds up his hand. "Filter, Sadie. Filter. Good grief. I'm getting too old for this."

Sadie and I stare at him like he has ten heads.

"You're sixteen, Tate. Sixteen," I remind him.

"Yeah? You try growing up with Charlie and Deacon and see how fast you age. Those two are trying to put me in an early grave."

I stare at him and forget to blink. Deacon is his brother, and admittedly a handful. Charlie is Julia and Trevor's son, and yes, that kid is fucking nuts, but in all the best ways. It's funny to see how Tate has taken on the role of protector for all his younger cousins. Both by marriage and by choice. But he's always been that way.

He's a good kid. Dex and Lanie have done right by him.

Turning my attention toward Sadie, I find her pulling at her bottom lip with her thumb and index finger. It's something she only does when she's nervous. Does she really think I'd deny her this?

"Sadie Sunshine, I would love for you to be little Bean's auntie." A sudden wave of emotion hits me when the not-so-little girl I love so much jumps out of her chair and barrels into me for a hug.

"I'm so happy for you, Uncle Ash. I'm so, so happy."

I hug her, the girl who changed my life. I hug her and don't let go until I feel her body shudder. When I pull back, I find the tears she was trying to hide.

"Why the tears, sunshine?"

"I was so worried about you for so long. Every night when I went to bed—" She sucks in a deep breath, and I help her sit in the chair next to me. "Every night, I would pray to my mom in heaven and ask her to help you."

My chest feels like it's caving in, and I place a hand on my stomach to keep my dinner down.

"Sadie? Maybe do this at home?" Tate whispers, but I cut him off with a finger in the air.

"I called Tate every Saturday and cried because I was afraid you'd never remember how to love. I'm so happy Nova could fix you. I'm just…" A small sob escapes her, and a crushing sense of guilt tries to drown me.

"No. No, Sadie. Is that why you've insisted on these date nights?"

"I just didn't want you to be alone."

"Oh, sweetheart." I pull her chair to mine, aware of the onlookers and not giving a fuck. "Sadie, listen to me. You saved me in so many ways, sweetheart. In so many ways that a child should never be burdened with. But every time you would kiss my boo-boos better, you placed a stitch in my broken heart. You. Saved. Me. Just by being you. I'm so sorry I've been a burden, sweetheart. I—I never thought—"

"What?" she blurts. "No. That's not what I'm saying. I love our dates. It made me feel special, and it gave my parents time to themselves. No. Uncle Ash, our Fridays were never a burden. I just worried you'd never be happy. And now you are. You are happy, right?"

"Oh, sweetheart. I'm so happy. I'm sorry you've been worried about me."

She wipes her nose with the back of her hand, and Tate makes a strangled noise in his throat, then hands her a handkerchief. A freaking handkerchief.

Maybe Tate Cross is a ninety-year-old man trapped in a sixteen-year-old's body.

Sadie punches me in the shoulder. "We're family, Uncle Ash. Of course I worried about you."

Eight years' worth of memories play like a highlight reel in my head. Eight years of Sadie Sunshine bringing me to life. Eight years of her worrying about me.

Because that's what families do.

My gaze darts to a table just a few feet away to find five sets of worried eyes trained on us. Ari watches Sadie with the eyes of a mother ready to jump in if her baby needs her. Lexi eyes Tate, an old soul, like she'll cut a person that dares to bruise his gentle spirit. Rylan observes us all with the knowledge of time. She's seen us all change and grow. She's seen our ups and downs, and she loves us anyway. Winnie wipes a tear from the corner of her eye. And Nova. Nova's nervous eyes search mine. She sees my world like I've never been able to because she sees me. All of me.

"Yeah, Sadie. We're the best family."

She jumps from the table like Colton on Pop Rocks and hugs me in a chokehold. "Thanks for coming tonight, Uncle Ash. After Tate, you're my best friend. I know that's weird, but you are. I love you."

As odd as it is, she was my only friend for years. "Right back at ya, kid. Now, what do you say? Should we get this show on the road?"

She stands and waves at Nova. "Yup. I won't be able to sleep until I get a text saying I get to wear a suit."

My eyebrows raise in surprise. "Wear a suit?"

"Oh yeah, I'm totes going to be a groomslady."

"A groomslady? Is that a thing?"

Tate shakes his head. "Definitely not."

"Ah, definitely is. Tell him, Uncle Ash. I'm going to be a groomslady in your wedding, and you're going to be the man of honor in mine."

This time I don't hold back the laughter. Tate shifts uncomfortably in his chair, but I think even he knows what his future holds.

"Deal, sunshine. Groomslady and man of honor it is."

She places a big, slobbery kiss right over my scar, and I'm instantly transported back to the first time she did it at Loki's wedding. The first time I felt my heart beat again. And this time, with this kiss, my heart finally feels whole.

CHAPTER 54

ASHTON

*S*adie and Tate say their goodbyes, and my gaze follows them out the door. The conversations throughout the restaurant are spirited, but I ignore them all. My eyes are on the five women across from me.

With their heads together in the center of the table, you'd think they were conspiring against someone. When all five heads turn to me, I know it's me they're plotting against, and I smile.

I take my time finishing my coffee. It's not a hardship. I love watching Nova any chance I get, but seeing her with my family is a special kind of happiness. As I observe them, my mind drifts to my brothers and sisters-in-law back in Waverley-Cay.

They'd called me the merry fucking godfather or something equally insane. I almost snort thinking back on all the shady shit I've done over the years to guide their happily ever afters in the name of keeping them all safe. I'd never intended to play match-maker—it's just how life unfolded.

A year ago, an outsider never would have believed it, but it was all part of the double life I led. From one story to the next, I was the lone wolf who secretly manipulated whatever had to be done to ensure safety above all else. Love was a happy side effect for them all.

Lanie was a godsend. Getting her to Waverley-Cay was much easier than I had ever imagined. Julia, the smartass, was a happy accident, but her intellect sparked a new side of my brain and helped me see things in a new light. If she wasn't such a loose cannon, I would have loved to pick her brain.

Preston was a mistake. An oversight I never anticipated and should have. He hid his illness well, and Emory was the angel he needed. I'm just glad I found out in time to be there for their wedding.

Nova laughs, and my eyes naturally follow the column of her throat. She is truly my missing piece. Like Sloane tamed Loki, Nova is where my happiness lies. Each of the women in our lives has brought the piece we were missing, the part that was broken. They just fit.

By the time I've finished my coffee and paid my bill and theirs, Nova is making her way across the restaurant with a sheepish expression I can't place.

"Everything okay?" I ask casually but study every nuance in her posture.

She's nervous, I realize.

Why?

"Yeah, just tired. Everything okay with you and Sadie? Looked a little emotional over here for a while."

Nodding, I stand and reach for her hand. Lifting it to my lips, I kiss each of her knuckles, paying special attention to the one on her ring finger.

Will she let me put a ring there tonight?

Her breath hitches, and I smile while leading her out of the restaurant.

We step outside just as the first few flakes of snow fall from the sky.

Leave it to Vermont to have a springtime snowstorm, but walking hand in hand, I finally feel like all is right with my world.

"Peto? Is everything okay?"

I go to open the truck door and remember the conversation with my brothers. I'm done making mistakes, so I stop with my hand on the handle. "Do you like it when I open doors for you?"

"What?" She laughs. When she realizes I'm serious, her face falls. "Sorry, I didn't know that was a real question. Yes, I like it when you open doors for me."

"What about when we go out to eat—do you care if I pay the check?"

She shrugs, but I can tell she's confused. "Not if you don't. I mean, I have my own money. A lot of it, if that's what this is about."

"No. It's not about money," I say adamantly. "It's about making sure I don't do things that piss you off."

"And you think paying for dinner or opening my door would piss me off?"

I blow out a harsh breath. "I don't know. It's something my brothers said about dating. I just don't want to fuck this up."

"Dating? We live together. We bought a house together. We're having a baby together! That's a little more than dating."

"And why I don't want to screw this up."

She flashes me a lazy grin. "You're not going to screw anything up, peto. I'm yours and you're mine. Forever."

I move closer and press her against the door. I'm vaguely aware that I can't keep her out here much longer. The snow is coming down harder, and she isn't exactly dressed for a Mother Nature freak-out. But I take the moment to drink her in like a fine wine.

"Forever, huh?"

"Forever," she confirms.

I let my head fall back and feel the snow land on my face. It's such an innocent move, but as the wet flakes melt against my skin, I allow myself to feel it all. The happiness, the sadness, the extreme overwhelm. I take it all in and let it wash away with the drops of snow. When Nova shivers, I lift my head to hers.

"I love you. I had a whole plan for tonight. Sloane wrote a special story. I had a plan. But you've taught me something."

Nova burrows into my chest, and I hold her tight. "Oh, yeah? What's that?"

"To live in the moment. To live for my happiness."

Dropping to one knee, I look up at her. It's different this time, and we both know it.

"My brothers all made huge gestures to ask their wives to marry them. I had a plan for that too, but it's not us."

She bites her bottom lip and shakes her head. "No. It's not," she whispers.

"I've asked you to marry me in the hospital." She nods, her eyes gleaming in the moonlight. "In the shower. At the park. During a movie. While working out. Over dinner. I've asked you a bunch of different ways, and you've said no every time."

"The timing wasn't right," she murmurs.

I nod. "The timing wasn't right. And I wasn't right. I still had a few things left to figure out."

"Did you figure them out?" I notice she's shaking, and I don't think it has anything to do with the temperature.

"I did."

I'm still putting in the work with Dr. Benson on Fridays, and I finally understand what Nova meant by doing it for myself. It's a lot of work. Hard work that makes me want to poke my eyes out, but I want to be the healthiest version of myself for her and Baby Bean.

"What did you figure out, peto?" Her voice is barely audible.

"I'm not a monster. And I'm not a beast. I'm a man who faced unbelievable challenges and still managed to catch the eye of the most beautiful woman in the world. I'm a man who learned to forgive everyone in his life except himself. Until now."

"Ashton?"

"I forgave everyone else but couldn't forgive myself."

"And now?" Her words tumble from her mouth as her chin quivers.

"Now I know there's nothing to forgive. Every heartbreaking step I took led me to you. I wouldn't trade that for anything in the world. You are my future, Nova. You are my forever. Whether you marry me today or ten years from now, I'm happy. I'm content, and I'm not going anywhere."

I stare up at her with all the love in the universe shining in her eyes.

"But you're on your knee today." She quirks an eyebrow, and my heart thumps a wild tune in my chest.

"I am."

"Is there a question forthcoming?"

"Will I like the answer?"

"I guess it depends on the question." She smiles, and it's all white teeth and bright eyes. She's goading me.

"Hmm, I'm not sure then."

Nova looks at her nails like she's bored. "Yeah, it's probably not worth my—"

I pop open the ring box. Something I've never done until tonight. Every other time I've asked her to marry me, I've known it wasn't the right time, but I couldn't stop myself. Tonight just feels different.

Her eyes go wide, and I grasp her hip with my free hand just in case she goes and faints again.

"Princess, you are my happily ever after. You've pulled me from the dark. You've shown me how to love again. I can never repay any of that, but I can promise to love you every day for the rest of my life. Will you marry me?"

Nova's eyes shine like the hearts of stars as she nods her head. "Yes, Ashton. Yes. Today, tomorrow, and every day after that is a yes. I'll marry you."

An awkward groan sounds from behind the car, and I stand quickly, pulling her behind me.

Then my brothers file out one by one, followed by their wives and kids, before even GG hobbles out from the shadows.

"What in the actual hell?"

"I had two—two!—plans in place, Ashton. Two. You couldn't proceed and let one of them happen?" Dexter grumbles, walking past me and kicking at something on the ground.

"What is happening?" I grumble.

Nova giggles behind me. It turns into a full-on belly laugh that infects every member of my family. Turning in place, I find her brother scowling at me. But Tilly stands beside Nova's father, who is also laughing.

"Why is every member of both our families, minus Lochlan, laughing at me right now?" I mutter into Nova's ear.

But she can't stop laughing long enough to answer me. It's Sadie who bounces up beside me with Tate and Colton in tow. "Oh, Uncle Ash. We were going to pull you over and fake arrest you. Then Nova was going to ask you to marry her. We had it all planned out."

I stare at her in shock as Dexter paces beside us, muttering under his breath. "Two plans, Ash. Two freaking incredible plans, and you just had to go and mess them up because it snowed."

The back of my head is pelted with a snowball, and I turn in a fury to find Lochlan smirking at me with two snowballs in his hand.

"Hey, asshat. In case you forgot, your sister is pregnant. Stop throwing shit at us."

He hurls another snowball that hits me directly in the nose. "I'm not throwing them at her. Just you." Another one hits my chest. Then I hear his gruff *oompfh*. Clearing the snow from my face, I see he's been hit in the chest too.

"Stop throwing shit at my brother," Easton barks and tosses another one at Lochlan.

Before I can say a word, Nova darts into the car, and snow-balls erupt all around us.

Words are shouted. Laughter rings loud. And every single person gets a snowball in the face. Everyone except GG and my mother, who stand back, watching it all unfold with giant, happy smiles on their faces.

"Welcome to your chaos," GG mouths.

I watch her for a moment, and wonder what she must think of all us Westbrooks who have invaded her tiny mountain town. The way her eyes glisten with love, I hope we've made her life better.

I know she's made ours one hell of a ride.

I tip an imaginary hat in her direction, and she blows me a kiss. It's such an un-GG like thing to do, it gives me pause. She's always accepted me the way I am. She's always offered love, just as she has with everyone else in her life. But with me, she was different. She silently corralled me toward happiness while never once losing faith in the man I'd become.

She knew all along. She knew I'd find my way. And she always knew I would be okay.

I shake my head and jump into the truck next to Nova. I may have held the secrets of my family, but GG has held the heart of hope in her bony, bossy hands.

The headlights illuminate the chaos before us. Eight grown men, their wives, and too many kids to count scrape together the first bits of heavy snow and throw it at each other in an epic game of tag.

This is chaos. This is family. This is life.

Reaching across the center console, I take Nova's hand in mine. In all the craziness, I hadn't noticed that she'd slipped on the ring. Lifting it to my lips, I kiss the diamond and know without a doubt, that I've finally found peace.

EPILOGUE

Ashton

*H*olding Hope in one arm, I gently place the daffodils on my father's gravesite. It's the first time I've been here since his funeral, and it's harder than I thought it would be.

I almost didn't come, but an appointment with Dr. Benson made me see how important it was to find forgiveness before starting this next chapter in my life.

Fucking Dr. Benson.

I drop the diaper bag to the ground, fish out the blanket, and gently place Hope in the center of it. Hope Sky Westbrook is as perfect as I expected her to be. And today, I'm introducing her to my father for the first time.

I sit in the silence until Hope's cooing begs me to join her. Lying on my side, I face my little girl. She's perfection in the tiniest package.

"I can't believe I made something so perfect."

The wind picks up, and something red catches my eye. Turning my head, I find a cardinal sitting on my father's headstone, watching me.

I'm not usually one to believe in signs, but this might make me a believer. I talk to the damn bird like it's my father.

"T—This is Hope, Dad. She's a perfect little bundle of happiness I didn't think I'd ever have." Once the words start, they stumble out at an alarming rate, but I don't try to contain them. I let out all the hate and hurt and love I have for this man.

"There are so many questions I wish I could ask you. So many times I wondered if I was doing the right thing. I'll never know, and I've had to make peace with that. I have to take comfort in knowing I did what I thought was right. It just hurt for so long, Dad. I hated you for leaving me. I loved you for being the best man I've ever known. But at the end of the day, I realize you were just a man too, doing what you thought was best."

Hope puts a chubby fist in her mouth and smiles at me. My love for her outweighs any hate I've ever known.

And that's what it boils down to. Choosing to accept and give love.

"I wish you could have met Nova, Dad. You would have liked her. She would have given you a run for your money."

The cardinal turns its head from side to side like it's actually paying attention, so I keep going.

"I don't know what your plan was, Dad, but I hope you're proud of me. I hope that you're looking down on me and feeling good about where we have all ended up. All of your boys are married. We're all insanely happy. We've all kept the chaos going." I pump my fist in the air and another cardinal lands next to the first.

My fist freezes in midair.

"I love you, Dad. I'm sorry I thought I hated you for so many years. But I've learned it was easier to hate you for leaving than to hate myself for the choices I made."

A shadow falls over Hope, and I lift my head to find my mother smiling down at us. She gracefully slides to her knees next to the baby. "Daffodils, huh?"

"It seemed like the right time for forgiveness."

She reaches into her purse, pulls out a small box, and hands it to me. I take it with shaking hands.

Untying the delicate white ribbon, I remove the robin-blue cover. Inside sits a tie clip with a daffodil on it. Laughter wheezes through my nose.

"It seemed like the right time for me too," she says gently. "I wanted you to have that as a reminder for the days you question if you're doing the right thing or not. Because I know you, Ashton Westbrook. You're so much like your father, and even on his best days, a sliver of doubt would creep in at the least expected times."

Hope smiles up at my mom, and we both get lost in the innocence of her chubby little face.

"I'm sorry I didn't know enough to help you, Ashton." Her voice sounds frail but determined.

"There is absolutely nothing for you to apologize for, Mom. You had a small army of teenage boys that were relying on you. You did everything you were supposed to."

"Except see that my baby was troubled."

I open my mouth to interrupt her, but she gives me a look that only moms can, and I snap my lips closed.

"I'm not here to argue about this with you. We have all made mistakes, and we have all paid for them dearly. I only wish I had the foresight to teach you all to communicate better."

A rough chuckle eases some of the tension in my shoulders. "I think Colton is the only one who got that from you, but we're getting better, Mom. We are all going to be okay. I feel it."

She places a hand on top of mine. "I know you will. Daddy would be so proud of you, son. So incredibly proud."

My throat tries to close up on me, and I lick my unnaturally dry lips. "I hope so."

"I know so. Are you ready? It's almost time," she says.

Glancing down at my watch, a piece that belonged to my

father, I nod. Then I stand, help my mother up, and bend down to scoop up a giggling Hope.

Together, we head back to my childhood home, where I'll finally make the woman I love my wife.

Nova

"Oh, my business. You look gorgeous, honey. You look just like your mom did on our wedding day," my father blubbers. He's never been very good at keeping his emotions in check. It reminds me of the pictures from the day he adopted me. His face was bright red and swollen, and so very happy.

Kitty and Lochlan stand behind him. It would have been so easy for this family to turn their back on me after my mom died, but in their eyes, I've always just been theirs.

They're so similar to the Westbrooks in that way, and I vow to always keep my heart open just as they have.

Lochlan tugs on his vest, and I let an evil grin slip onto my face. He senses it and immediately covers his nipples. "Don't even think about giving me a titty twister today, Nova. I haven't done a damn thing. I even shook hands with the slimy bastard."

Even Lochlan can't say that with a straight face. Ashton has proved himself tenfold over the last year. He'd be hard-pressed to find a more dedicated husband or father than my peto.

"Okay, children. Lochlan, walk me out to my seat before my makeup runs. I can't believe both of my babies have babies and, after today, will be married." Kitty looks to the ceiling and fans her eyes. "I'm so proud of you both."

"Aw, Kitty. You're getting emotional," I tease.

"I am not," she snaps. Lowering her face, she winks. "I'm allowed. It's a big day, Nova. I only wish your mom were here to see how amazing you are."

It's my turn to get emotional. "Me too, Kitty."

"That's enough of that," Lochlan commands. The guy could pass for a drill sergeant sometimes. He steps forward and kisses my cheek. "I'm very happy for you, Nono. All I've ever wanted for you is to be happy. I'm glad you've found that, even if it is with a Westbrook."

I giggle beside him. "You're just upset that this will make you and Colton some weird version of brothers-in-law, and now you're really in for his pranks."

"If that bloody fucket guy sends me one more glitter bomb, I'll drown him in a pool full of that shit."

I zip my lips shut tight because I know what's hanging over his hotel room door. I'm not sure how Colton will ensure Lochlan enters first, but that guy always has a plan.

"I'll see you out there, Nono," he says with a fondness only a big brother can manage.

"Love you, Lochness."

"Love you too."

❧

We decided to have a small ceremony, but as I walk down the aisle, I realize how laughable that is.

Ashton's family alone is close to fifty people, if not more. There isn't a dry eye in the house. But my focus is on the man waiting for me. The man who watches me like I alone can make the sun rise.

Blinking back tears, I look to his right and smile. Sadie stands beautifully in a navy-blue pantsuit that we tailored to her perfectly. In her arms is my greatest accomplishment. Hope.

My father chokes up as we near the end, and he leans on me for support. "This is the happiest day of my life, Nono. I'm so proud of you, and I'm so proud to be your dad." We take two more steps, and Ashton steps down to take my arm from my dad.

Ollie crashes into Ashton with a bone-crushing hug. "Take care of my girl, okay? She acts tough, but she's got a squishy center."

Ashton's eyes never leave mine. "I know," he whispers. "She'll be my top priority. I promise."

Lochlan steps up from the front row, and I laugh. "Come on, Pops. You're holding up the ceremony." My father releases Ashton and steps back with a sob.

We managed to get him into a traditional suit, but true to form, he has a wild blue cummerbund that matches the sash on Hope's dress. I love that, in all these years, he's never conformed to anyone's idea of beauty. He's always stayed true to himself.

I pray that Hope gets that from her grandfather.

"You ready?" Ashton whispers. "I don't know how long I can stand up here."

I look around in confusion. It's been a long time since he's been self-conscious, but when my eyes find his again, I realize my mistake.

"You look so damn good, princess. The most beautiful woman I've ever seen." He no longer shutters his eyes from me. No, now I see all the way through to his dirtiest thoughts.

Thankfully, Penny steps forward to take my bouquet and bumps Ashton in the shoulder on the way by. "Tone it down, Romeo. Kids are watching."

He chuckles darkly, and we step up to where Preston waits. He got a special license to perform our ceremony, and I know the gesture means more to Ashton than he can ever express.

"Welcome, everyone," he says seriously. "Nova and Ashton opted for traditional vows, but in true Westbrook form, Ashton has gone off script. So I'll hand things over to him before we get down to the I-dos."

"What?" I gasp. Looking around at our friends and family, I see none of the Westbrooks seem overly surprised by this. "What did you do?" I hiss through a plastic smile.

Ashton smiles so handsomely I'm momentarily stunned into silence.

"Well, princess. I made you a promise once."

My eyes dart around. I'm not sure what I'm supposed to say. We had a plan. The plan was to recite vows that Preston spoon-fed us.

"What promise?"

"When you first arrived in Vermont. I promised you I could do anything I set my mind to. And now here, in front of everyone we love, I'm promising to love you until my last breath. I promise to answer your questions with a better one."

A giggle gurgles in my throat, and Penny leans forward to hand me a tissue.

"I promise to support you and cherish you. I promise to love our family and protect you with everything I have. I promise to love myself enough to accept your love in return. I promise to choose love today, tomorrow, and every day for the rest of our lives. I choose you, Nova Sky, to be the light in my darkness that leads me home. I choose to be the man you can rely on and trust in. I choose to trust the power of forgiveness and to say sorry when I mess up. I choose love."

Tears soak my face, but there's no use in trying to wipe them away. "How did you say all that without crying?"

He holds up his palm, showing me a tiny metal daffodil pressed into his hand. "Mind over matter," he says with a shrug.

"Well, Nova. Do you choose love?" Preston asks, throwing me off guard. I guess our traditional vows are out the window.

"I do. Every day, I'll choose love. I choose you, peto."

His lips crash into mine, and Preston tosses his papers into the air. "I should have known better than to plan," he grumbles. "By the power vested in me, I now pronounce you husband and wife."

Ashton doesn't break the kiss as he bends down to lift me into his arms, or as he carries me down the aisle, or down the path that will lead to our reception. He doesn't break the kiss until we're alone and gasping for breath.

"Thank you," he whispers above my lips.

"For what?"

"For releasing my secrets. For loving me enough to be patient while I found my way. Secrets and lies and heartbreak and mistakes. It all led to the one kiss that changed my life. The one truth I spent my entire life searching for."

"What's that?" I ask breathlessly.

"You, Nova. You are the one little truth that set me free."

"You saved me too, you know."

He nods and kisses me gently as voices grow closer.

"You're my wife."

"I'm yours, and you're mine."

"Forever," he growls.

"Forever and then some."

"Welcome to the chaos, Nono!" Colton sings merrily as he tugs me free from Ashton's grasp and wraps me in a hug.

"Thanks, Colty."

Laughter rings out as he spins me around.

"We're a crazy family, Nono, but we've never lacked for love. We were just missing the final piece to make us whole." He looks over at Ashton, who wears a grin so wide you can't help but return it. "We were missing you. Thank you for bringing him back to us. Thank you for loving him."

I stare at Colton and see his sincerity and old fears for his brother lingering behind bright blue eyes. "I truly believe everything happens for a reason, Colton. I do. I think everything that happened was just paving my road to him."

"Dance with me," rumbles a low voice I don't recognize.

Turning, I find Ashton's adopted brother Dillon, and he's staring intently at my very own Penny Mulligan.

Ashton wraps an arm around my waist and tugs me into him.

I'm sandwiched between Ashton and Colton as we watch Penny's face turn bright red.

"Perhaps the story doesn't end here after all," Ashton whispers, causing a shiver to race down my spine. "Maybe love stories will continue to find happy endings wherever we end up."

Lifting my eyes to his, I smile. "I hope so, peto." Turning back to Penny, I almost laugh at how uncomfortable she is. "I really hope so."

$\sim$

BONUS EPILOGUE

SUNSHINE LOVE STORIES

Tate

"It's good to have you home," my mother says, patting my cheek like I'm still a little boy.

I don't pull away from her like I would with others though. Lanie Cross may not be my biological mother, but she saved me when I was a young, scared little boy. I'm who I am because of her, and I always remember that.

"It's good to be home," I say. And even though I haven't lived in this house since the summer after I finished college, it'll always be home. She made sure of it. I give her a fond smile. Time has been good to her. She's a beautiful woman with a kind soul.

The front door crashes open, and I hold back a groan as Harper, Deacon, and Charlie fall through it, laughing like hyenas.

The bars in Waverley-Cay will never be the same now that they're old enough to drink. Well, most of them. Deacon isn't of age, but it doesn't seem to stop him. I narrow my eyes when he sees me.

Liam and Sarah walk in behind them, carrying all their shit. At least two of my siblings are responsible.

"I'm getting married tomorrow. It's after midnight." I growl, and my mother pats my arm.

"We know." Deacon smiles devilishly. "That's why we're celebrating."

The front door opens again, and my father stumbles through with Trevor and Preston.

"What in the fresh hell is happening? They're all going to be hungover in pictures."

"Dad!" Charlie laughs as Trevor trips over his feet and offers my mom a sheepish grin.

"Charlie," my uncle grumbles.

"Doesn't anyone care that I am getting married tomorrow? Why are you all trashed?"

There's a crash in the kitchen, and my temperature rises to dangerous levels. "My betrothed had something to do with this, didn't she?"

When no one will meet my eyes, I stalk toward the kitchen, knowing I'll never get any sleep until this shit show is cleared up.

But I enter the kitchen and stop in my tracks as Wes holds the back door open and the rest of my uncles file in.

"What the hell is going on?"

Wes is sixteen and should not be out at midnight.

"I went to pick them up," he shrugs. "Dad couldn't get them all in the van."

Colton—his dad and my uncle—walks through with Loki and Ashton, and I honest to fucking God think my head is about to explode.

"Tate." My mother's gentle voice forces me to look at her. "They're just excited for you. That's all. And it's been a while since everyone has been together."

"We have to be at the country club at eight a.m.," I whisper.

The noise in the kitchen gets louder when everyone descends on the island, searching for food to soak up the alcohol.

"I don't understand," I say to no one in particular. "Why

would you all get trashed the night before the biggest day of my life?"

A "woohoo" I know well yelps from the backyard, followed by one from my sister in the foyer. My future wife and my crazy sister *woohoo* through the house until Harper makes it outside and more laughter ensues, right before a giant splash.

Pinching the bridge of my nose, I count to ten.

"Sadie," I sigh.

"It's not our fault," my uncle Ashton says quietly. "The dads were having drinks after the rehearsal, and then—"

"And then Sadie happened," I finish for him. "It's the story of my life."

I try to be exasperated, but when it comes to Sadie, there's only ever been love.

Liam walks around the corner with towels, and I practice counting again. "She jumped in the pool, didn't she?"

"Man, your wife. She can't. I mean—"

Clapping my brother on the shoulder, I offer him a smile because I get it. "There's no containing her," I say fondly.

"That's the truth," Ashton says at my side. He's not quite slurring, but if I know Sadie, she did some damage on her aging uncles. "Never could bottle her sunshine."

Sadie Sunshine.

My almost-wife.

Liam hands me the towels with a grimace. "No offense, but Sadie was wearing a white dress at the rehearsal."

It takes a minute for my mind to catch up, but when it does, primal need takes over.

It's all family here. But that's not the point. If anyone is going to see my bride naked, it's going to be me.

Pausing at the door, I take in the chaos. My mother is at the stove, laughing and making everyone egg sandwiches. Dad sits at the table with all his brothers. Sadie's father, Seth, catches my eye and gives a proud nod.

He and I have had so many heart-to-hearts over the years, and he's always ended with the same thing. He just wants his baby to be happy.

And Sadie has only wanted one thing since she was six years old.

Me.

How the hell I got so blessed is beyond me. But I thank my lucky stars every day.

Once outside, I find a new kind of chaos.

Sadie is floating in the pool in her dress. Harper bobs in the deep end, but at least she has a swimsuit on. Ashton's three kids sit on the edge of the pool with their mother, Nova, watching nearby.

They were staying in the pool house. Of course the noise would wake them.

"Sorry, Nova."

She waves me off.

Rylan sits on the lounge chair, drying off an angry Grayson and his sister, Hazel.

"They heard the party and had to check it out," Rylan says with a smile.

Of all the aunties in this crazy family, Rylan is the one I'm closest with.

At her voice, Ashton's children, Hope, Reeva, and Leo, turn to find me standing there with towels and come running.

Sadie and I spend the most time with them. Hope is turning out to be Sadie 2.0, and she loves it.

I walk toward the pool, but Leo catapults himself into my arms. He's the youngest cousin, the baby, and he's the best little guy in the world. Holding him on my hip with one arm, I turn to my future wife and find her beaming her sunshiny smile my way.

"Took ya long enough." Her smile always eases that knot around my chest.

She's the only one who could ever cut me free.

"What are you doing, Sunny? We're getting married in less than twenty-four hours. We have to be at the country club in eight."

"Only because you didn't trust the pack to show up on time or on their own."

The pack. It makes me smile. Our parents started calling us the pack around the time Preston's kids were born. Now the cousins have grown to twenty-three and are all shockingly close, despite our age differences.

"Look around, sweetheart. Do you blame me?"

"Not at all. That's why I made sure everyone had fun tonight," she teases.

"I knew this was your doing."

"Oh, Tate. Relax. It's going to be the best day of our lives. I promise."

It will be. But not because it just happens. Because I've spent every day for the last six months carefully and meticulously planning every last detail.

"Sunny, please."

"Please, what?"

God, she's such a tease. I know she's holding herself under the water because her dress is see-through and there are kids present, but when she tilts her head and rises just enough that the water shows off the swell of her breasts, I nearly lose myself.

That's what she does to me. She helps me live with less constraint. It's terrifying and amazing. And so perfectly her.

"Get out of the pool," I grumble, and Leo twirls a lock of my hair around his tiny finger. He always does that when I hold him. He rests his head on my shoulder and observes everything but says very little.

We're a lot alike, Leo and me.

Nova walks to me with a smile and takes Leo from my arms. "You ready to end the night?" she asks.

"More like ready to start tomorrow."

Her eyes shine with unshed tears. Sadie has a special relationship with her, and because of that, I guess I do too.

"You're such a good boy, Tate. This has been a long time coming, hasn't it?"

I grunt, and Leo mimics me, causing a smile to form on my face.

"My entire life, Nova. I've been waiting for this day for as long as I can remember."

"Even when you were fighting it," she says with a knowing grin.

I roll my eyes and focus on my breathing. "I thought breaking up with her in college was the right thing to do. We'd only ever been together. I didn't want her to feel like she was missing out on anything."

Nova laughs, and Rylan joins us.

"Yeah, and you were miserable," Rylan says. "So miserable we had to remind you to shower."

"It wasn't about me," I grind out. "I told her we should see other people so we could be sure we were on the same page."

"Yeah, and how did that work out? Go on many dates, did ya?" Nova can be a real pain in the ass sometimes.

"Of course not. I was never going to go out with anyone else. It has always been Sadie for me."

"But you didn't trust her to make that same decision on her own?" Rylan asks cautiously.

"I— What? Why are you grilling me?"

They both laugh. At me. And my face burns hot.

"No, Tate. We're just giving you some advice."

"Then just say it already."

"Trust that she'll tell you what she wants and needs. Trust her enough and respect her enough to make the big decisions together."

My aunts share a look that speaks to shared heartache. I know they both had severe communication problems when they first got with my uncles. I love them for trying to make sure we don't fall victim to the same issues.

"Thanks, ladies." I hug them both, and when I turn, I find Sadie sitting on a lounge chair, wrapped in a towel.

Even in the dark, the sun seems to shine on this woman.

Tomorrow can't come soon enough.

Sadie

A knock at the door has us all turning in slow motion.

My dad pokes his head around the door with a hand over his eyes. "Okay to come in?"

Nova finishes pinning a piece of my train into place and speaks with pins sticking out of her teeth. "All set. Come on in. Tell Ash—"

"I'm here too," Uncle Ash calls through the door.

My father pushes it open and both men enter. Uncle Ash is pushing GG in a wheelchair. The two men look at me, then to each other, and they both break out in tears. Not just a few tears, but sobbing, slobbery, messy tears.

"Geez, guys! I just had my makeup done! Pull it together."

It does no good. They charge me like linebackers heading for a quarterback, but Nova steps in front of them.

"The lace on this dress is handsewn. If you get your blubbering all over it, I will make you both regret it."

That sobers them. Slightly. And I smile.

"Sadie," my dad starts and stops multiple times, while Uncle Ash just stares and openly cries.

"Seth, you've had an entire year to prepare," my mother chides.

"I know," he says with a shaky exhale. "But look at her."

"I have. She's beautiful."

I stare at my sister, Stella, with wide eyes. She's still young but intuitive enough to know that if they keep this up, I'm going to have a meltdown. And no one wants me to have a meltdown. Tate will burn this place to the ground if that happens.

"Okay, family time's over. Let's give Sadie a few minutes to collect herself."

I give my sister a grateful nod.

"She's had all day," my dad complains.

"That's Tate's doing. He's the one who insisted everyone show up nine hours early. You can come back in a few. Okay? Just go get some coffee or something."

My mother winks at us, then ushers my father out the door. Nova holds Ashton's hand, but he doesn't budge.

"Sadie." GG's voice has weakened with age, but her eyes still hold the stories she's yet to tell.

Glancing nervously at Ashton, I hurry to GG's side and lower myself in front of her chair. The move makes my princess dress poof out around me like a mushroom cloud. She holds out a bony hand that shakes as she reaches for my face. She's one hundred years old, and I wasn't sure she would make it for my wedding.

"I've been waiting for this day, girl. Hanging on so I could see my final match."

I nod but don't interrupt.

"Ya brought a little sunshine into our lives." She licks her lips and her chin trembles. "Tate changed our lives, but you set our course. Never doubt yourself, sweet girl. You've made it this far bringing light and love to everyone around you because that's your gift." Her eyes drift to the wall behind me, and her thought is gone.

"It's been happening more often these days," Ashton whispers.

Tears prick my eyes. I know our time with this crazy old lady is limited, but it means more to me than anyone will ever know that she's here.

"Stop cryin', ya ninny. You're going to mess up your face," GG scolds, and I choke on a laugh. She's even bossier at a hundred.

Nova leans down to kiss my cheek. "I'll take her out with the others."

I nod, and Uncle Ash holds out a hand to help me stand.

When the door closes behind Nova, I'm left in silence with one of my best friends.

"I can't say I thought you were serious about the whole Man of Honor thing, but I've never been prouder to stand by someone's side, Sadie Sunshine."

"Thanks, Uncle Ash. I can't believe this day is finally here."

"I can," he says adamantly. "Sadie, do you have any idea how much life and love you bring to people just by being you?" Taking my hand, he guides me toward the loveseat in the corner.

"You have been barreling through life at your own speed, with one destination in mind. You've always known exactly what you wanted, and you went for it. With college, then your career, and always, always with Tate. I know you've had your ups and downs, but that's bound to happen in a relationship built on a lifetime of love. You've brought us so much happiness, beautiful girl. It's time for your happily ever after to start."

"Jesus, Uncle Ash. When did you start writing Hallmark cards? Maybe you should be the one in PR, not me."

He recoils at the thought. "That's okay. One PR superstar in the family is plenty. Well, unless Deacon and Charlie don't get their shit together."

I laugh. "They're still young, Uncle Ash. How much trouble can they possibly get into?"

He raises his eyebrows, and I concede. "Fine. Okay. I'll keep a better eye on them."

"You ready?" he asks, and my stomach hollows out. It's not nerves making my hands shake. It's so much excitement I feel like I'll explode.

"I'm so ready."

"You sure you want to do this? Tate is going to be pissed off."

An evil grin slides across my lips. "I know, Uncle Ash. But I also know he's in there pacing and barking orders at anyone who tries to talk to him. Just give me twenty minutes to calm him down, and then we'll get this show on the road."

Uncle Ash looks a little green, and I burst out laughing. "Ugh, I'm just going to give him a shot and talk him down. Get your head out of the gutter."

His entire body deflates with a whoosh. "Thank God," he sighs. "Fine. I'll go. But if I get caught, I'm blaming you."

"Fair enough." I grin as he walks toward the door. "Lock this behind me and don't let anyone in until I get back. Seriously, Sunshine. The things I do for you."

I wink. "Right back at ya, Uncle."

He pauses and takes me in like he's memorizing the moment. "Yeah, I owe you the world, Sunshine."

And then he's gone. My favorite Uncle now has the perfect life, and I'm proud to say I had a hand in it.

Tate

"Is she okay?" My heart thrashes against my chest as we hurry around the back of the country club where we'll be married.

Ashton winces and an uncomfortable feeling settles in my chest.

"Ashton, is she fucking okay?" He knocks on the door three times, and it opens quickly.

He doesn't answer me, but he does give me a two-handed shove into the room. "Sorry, buddy. I promise, she made me do it." Then he slams the door and anger takes over.

"Don't be mad at him," Sadie says softly, and my entire body relaxes.

Slapping a hand over my eyes, I curse. "I should have fucking known. Expect the unexpected with Sadie Sunshine. That's what you told me when you were ten, right? When you were fourteen, you told me you'd always keep me on my toes. What in the fresh hell, Sunny? I cannot see you before we take our vows. It's bad luck."

Her hand lands on my shoulder, and I tense.

"Sadie," I groan.

"You're wound very tight, Tate. I bet you're in the groom's suite making everyone walk on eggshells."

"I am not."

I am. I know I am, but I can't help it. Today is a big day.

I track the sound of her dress swishing as she circles me, but I squeeze my eyes shut even tighter.

"Today is the happiest day of our lives," she whispers. But her words are too slow. Too controlled. I know she's up to something.

"It is the happiest day, Sadie. But if I see you before you walk down that aisle, I'm going to attribute every bad thing that happens for the rest of our lives to it."

"I know," she whispers against my chin. Then the softest silk wraps around my head.

"Sadie." It's all I can force out as she ties the slippery material over my eyes.

"You're not going to see me. But I am going to help you relax."

Her hands drop to the button on my pants, and my entire body goes hard as granite.

"For fuck's sake."

My hips thrust forward when she reaches into my pants and pulls out my cock.

"Take, Tate. But don't you dare mess up my hair."

It's the last thing I hear before her lips wrap around me. The sensations of it heightened by the fact that I can't see her.

Her tongue swirls around my tip, then licks down the underside of my shaft before she swallows me whole.

Grunting is the only sound I can manage as she picks up speed. This is not how I imagined things going today. But I should have known better. Sadie always knows me better than I know myself.

"Sadie," I say through clenched teeth, but she just wraps a hand around my base and squeezes tighter.

I can imagine her face as she bobs up and down on my cock. How her eyes sparkle when she knows I'm about to come. How her red-painted lips wrap around my length like the most delicious lollipop she's ever had.

"I'm going to come," I hiss.

She groans around my dick and my last shred of self-control snaps. I come with a string of words I can't make out, but I feel her smile against my swollen flesh.

While I catch my breath, she tucks me away and fixes my pants. She always thinks she has the upper hand, but not this time. When she presses against me to kiss my lips, I trace the length of her with my hands, then lower myself to the floor.

With the blindfold in place, I swat blindly with my hands until I finally make my way under layers of gauzy material.

"Tate," Sadie laughs. I slide my hands up her bare legs until I reach her panties, and she gasps.

A knock at the door has her standing up straighter, but I don't stop. She does this to me. She makes me lose control.

"Tate," she hisses as I pull her panties to the side. "Tate." She repeats with more urgency. When she realizes I have no intention of stopping, she picks up her skirt and drops it around me. "Tuck in your feet. Tuck them in." She sounds slightly hysterical when I lick up her center.

I chuckle against her mound but do my best to make myself as small as possible. Her dress must be fucking huge if she thinks she can conceal me under it.

I feel her move above me. "Am I good?" I growl.

"I—I think…"

"Sadie?" someone calls through the door, but I double down and suck her clit into my mouth.

"Oh, God," she whispers.

Using my teeth, I flick her pleasure point relentlessly and insert one finger, then two.

"Oh," she moans.

"I don't want to alarm you," the person says, "but Tate isn't with his groomsmen."

"He—"

I insert a third finger and steal her breath.

"He went for a walk," she yells in a rush.

The words become a jumbled mess in my ears as Sadie rides my face until I feel the first spasms of her release.

"Come for me, sweet sunshine."

And she does. She always does. I lick her until her legs shake and I'm afraid she'll fall over. When I'm sure she can stand, I release her legs.

"Can I come out now?" I whisper.

"That…I…" She lifts her dress and I crawl out from underneath.

Holding the blindfold to my face, I stand and reach for her. When she falls into my arms, I lean down until I find her face, then whisper in her ear. "All night, I'm going to know that you smell like come under this dress, and all night I'm going to be counting down the minutes until I can see that beautiful pussy."

She gasps, and I feel like all is right with the world. She's calmed my chaos, and I've tethered her to the ground.

We just work.

There's another knock at the door, and I freeze.

"Sadie, I have to get him back," Ashton hisses.

She leads me to the door, and I hear it open.

"For fuck's sake," Ashton curses. "You said you were just talking. Why is his hair all fucked up?"

I grin and he takes my arm to lead me into the hallway. "You don't want to know."

Ashton freezes next to me, and my grin grows wider.

"At least maybe now you'll stop scaring the shit out of everyone who works here," he rumbles.

"Maybe," I say, feeling more at ease in my own skin. Ashton removes my blindfold, and I see the smirk in his eyes.

"You've been barreling toward this day for so long you don't even know what to do with yourself, do you?" he asks. His eyes are full of understanding and a lifetime of love.

"I don't, but Sadie does."

He laughs beside me as we make our way to where the ceremony will be held. "She always has, hasn't she?"

"Since the first moment I met her, she claimed me, and I was happy to be hers."

He claps me on the shoulder. "Let's make it official then."

I head toward the front, as he turns back to get Sadie.

My future is only minutes away.

Sadie

I walk toward my future, and his emotions are written in every tear that he sheds.

"Breathe," I mouth and smile when he takes a shuddering breath.

"I couldn't have picked a better man for you, Sunny," my dad whispers at my side. "I never could have anticipated the chaos we'd create by joining this family, but I have no doubt, you were always meant to be together."

"Dad," I say through clenched teeth, "you're going to make me cry."

"Sorry, sweetheart."

We reach the altar, and Tate steps forward to hug my dad. My eyes scan over to Uncle Ashton. The three most important men in my life all stand in a circle around me. I am who I am because each of these men believed in me.

My eyes mist, and Preston clears his throat. He's become the unofficial officiant of family gatherings, so it only seemed fitting that he'd do our vows.

"I think I can honestly say this is a day we all saw coming," Preston begins, and everyone laughs. "We've all watched these two for years, knowing this is where we would end up. There were tears and heartache and growing pains—those teenage years were kind to no one."

More laughter.

"But the overarching theme of Sadie and Tate has always been love. A love so pure, so innocent, so magical, you'd think it was sent straight to us from angels." He glances at the sky, and I tear up, knowing it's a nod to my mom and his dad. "And maybe it was. I like to think we all had a helping hand in love. Though some of us had more help than others."

We all turn to look at Uncle Ashton, who has the grace to look chagrined.

"The thing about our family is that we find grace in the chaos. We find healing in our ability to love, and no one has a bigger capacity for love than Sadie Sunshine. So it's no surprise to anyone here that both Tate and Sadie tried to pull a Westbrook special."

My eyes shoot up to Tate accusingly. "You said we were going to do traditional vows because you didn't want to screw up."

He leans forward with a grin that makes my mind go to very dirty places. "And you said we were doing traditional vows so we could get them over with faster and get to the good stuff."

I gasp. He's out Sadie'd me and doesn't give me a chance to recover.

"Our first kiss was under the stars when you were sixteen," he projects loud enough for our guests to hear.

"Because you kept saying I wasn't ready," I huff.

"I still didn't think you were ready, and I was eighteen. It wasn't right."

If I wasn't holding a bouquet of flowers, I'm pretty sure I'd have my hands on my hips, ready to lay into him.

"It was right, Tate."

"You kissed me in GG's field." He smirks, and I realize this was his plan all along. Our vows would tell our love story. My heart tries to escape my chest with love for this man. He always knows what I want even before I do.

"I did. And you kissed me back."

"I did."

"When you went to college, you got a two-bedroom apartment. Just in case I wanted to visit."

"But I always knew it would be our first home together," he admits. His eyes glow with so much love.

"When you tried to break up with me—" My voice cracks, and he interrupts.

"I learned a valuable lesson in love that day. I learned that there are no rules. There is no timeline. Those two months were the worst of my entire life. I won't ever make that mistake again."

"You asked me to marry you on Sylvie's beach."

"Because it was where we first met, and it was the first time of thousands that you told me you'd marry me some day. It seemed like the only viable option."

I snort, and tears threaten to ruin my makeup. "I've always known what I wanted."

His grin grows so wide his eyes crinkle. "What's that, Sadie Sunshine?"

"You, Tate-o-nator."

We stare at each other, our friends and family forgotten until Preston clears his throat.

"I assume this is my cue?"

We both nod, but never break eye contact.

"Then, by the power vested in me, and by every family member who has waited for this day, I now pronounce you, husband and wife. You may—"

Tate doesn't wait for the words. He takes my face in his hands and devours my lips, my tongue. He tastes me like it's the first time, and only the hoots and howls keep me grounded on Earth. Because that's what he does to me. He keeps me grounded with love.

Today, tomorrow, and every day for the rest of our lives, we're bound by a life that was always bigger than either of us.

Chaos consumes us, and he finally breaks our kiss.

"I've waited a lifetime for you, Sadie Sunshine, and now, we have a new chapter to write."

"The next chapter is just beginning," Charlie yells at our side with a fist bump in the air, but we barely hear him over the pounding of our hearts.

Chaos, love, and a happily ever after were always my destiny. And Charlie's right. The next chapter is just beginning.

DEAR READER

Dear Luv,

I have attempted to write this letter no less than twenty times in the last two weeks. I don't know how to thank you all for believing in me. Or for trusting me with your time and your hearts.

Words just don't seem to be enough.

When I started writing, I never dreamed it would come to this. It happened because I was struggling to find my self-worth. I didn't know who I was if I wasn't a mom, or a wife, or a friend, or a daughter.

It was also the start of the Covid pandemic lockdown and we'd just moved twelve hours away from our friends and family.

I didn't know who I was, who I wanted to be, or even who I could be anymore. I felt lost, and broken, and like so many others, isolated.

Remote learning with my four kids also brought out the worst in me. I didn't like who I became under all the stress. I didn't like the dynamic it created for my family, so I started writing as an escape. When my children would do their morning work, I would sit beside them and let my mind wander.

And in walked Dexter Cross.

Before I knew what was happening, I had finished a book about love, and loss, and healing. I had written all my feelings into a story I was proud of. It was a sense of accomplishment I desperately needed.

Before Cross My Heart, I couldn't remember the last time I felt proud of myself, and that was a heart-wrenching realization. Sure, I was proud of raising great kids—it's hard freaking work. But this was different.

I knew it was different, but publishing my story was never my end goal. Thanks to a slightly pushy friend, I did.

And do you know what happened? You found it. And you found me. And suddenly, I had created an entire world I was so proud of.

Now, two years and ten books later, I thought I was ready to type the end for the very first time. It seems crazy that I've never typed the end before, right? But it never felt like the end to me. So maybe, just maybe, one character's HEA is another character's new beginning. I guess we'll have to wait and see.

The one thing I do know is that all of these new beginnings are because of you. The extreme overwhelm and gratitude I have for each of you who have followed me on this journey is not something I can put into words. I've tried.

But I'll try again.

Thank you for believing in me so much that I had no choice but to believe in myself too. Thank you for loving my characters and stories so much that even on the hard days, I knew I wanted to try again, to get better, to work harder.

Thank you for entrusting me with your hearts, and for mending mine along the way.

Thank you for reminding me that it's okay to be proud of yourself.

You, my readers, are the piece of my heart I didn't even know was missing.

Thank you for being you.
Kindness and Luv,
Avery

ACKNOWLEDGMENTS

I can't believe we've come to the end of the Westbrooks. There were times when I truly did not think it would happen. There were times when Mr. Maxwell thought for sure they were going to break me. But here we are. Ten books later, and I have a feeling the best is yet to come.

There is no way I could ever do this on my own. So here are my thanks to my village:

To my husband and my children: Thank you for my office. LOL. Well, not just my office. Thank you for believing in me enough to make our lives work around all the chaos my new career has brought. You are my greatest joy, my biggest accomplishment, and my entire heart. I couldn't do anything without you.

To Rhon, my fabulous PA: Thank you for putting up with my 2 a.m. meltdowns, my 2 p.m. imposter syndrome attacks, and everything in between. Thank you for all you do to keep team Avery working and thank you for being in my corner daily. I appreciate you.

To Joyce & Tammy: Thank you for telling me to simmer down, and for the votes of confidence when I struggle. Thank you for all you do in the romance community, and specifically, for being the friends I need every time I need them.

To Marie, Carissa, Liz, & Sarah: Thank you for all you do to keep The Luv Club afloat. It is still the kindest place on Facebook thanks to all of you. I appreciate your time and support more than you could ever know.

To my Beta Readers: I'm a needy author. I like to follow along and blow up your DMs. Thank you for allowing that and for helping me put out the best story I can.

To my Sensitivity Readers: Thank you for making sure my heart is always in line with my words.

To my Street & ARC teams: I couldn't do what I do without you. Thank you for always believing in me. Thank you for your time, your energy, and your feedback.

To The Luv Club: You have made my little corner of chaos one of the best parts of my day. Thank you for making it my safe space on social media. LUVS!

To Beth, my medical proofer, my longtime friend, and my cut-the-shit friend: Thank you for always being by my side. Family is what you make it, and I'm making you mine. Xoxo

To The Awesome Ass Authors: You know who you are. I hope you also know how much your support and daily check-ins mean to me. You make this job feel less lonely, you keep me sane, and you give me permission to open my wine at 3 p.m. For that, I'm eternally grateful.

To Tim: Thank you for believing in me. Thank you for working tirelessly on all the things I suck at so I can do what I do. And thank you for being one of the most genuinely caring individuals I've ever met.

To Dan: Thanks for putting up with me. Gold star day or not, you're one of my most favorite people.

To Chelle & Eric: Yes, they're real! And they really own White Caps Campground in Vermont. Thank you for being my lifelong friends. I am who I am because I got all my troublemaking ways out of my system with you when I was younger;)

To Jess, Emily & Team: Thank you for pushing me to be better. You make me think, learn, and rewrite without ever making me feel terrible for asking questions. I appreciate you. I appreciate the work you put in, and I will always appreciate you making me a better writer. Thank you for all that you do to make my words the best they can be.

To Jodi at Dark City Designs: Thank you for bringing my Westbrooks to life with nine amazing covers…and the four original covers too ;)

GET TO KNOW AVERY!

I'm a New-England girl born and raised, but now I live in North Carolina with my husband, our four kids, and two dogs.

I write sweet, sexy, small-town contemporary romance because I'm a romantic at heart. My stories are of friendship and trust, heartbreak, and redemption. I try to bring my characters to life and make you feel every emotion I pour onto the page.

I've always been a fan of the happily ever after and the stories that make them, and now I get to write a soul mate for us all. My heroines have sass, my heroes have steam, and together they create the stories you won't want to put down.

Want to hang out with me more? I'm in The Luv Club every day sharing my chaos, my crazy, my life. Pop in to say hi, meet the other luvables, and stay a while. It's the happiest, kindest group on the internet and I'd LUV to see you there!

twitter.com/AveryMa86771206

instagram.com/averymaxwellbooks

amazon.com/Avery-Maxwell/e/B0891X1667

ALSO BY AVERY MAXWELL

Standalone Romance:

Without A Hitch

The Westbrooks: Broken Hearts Series:

Book 1- Cross My Heart

Book 2- The Beat of My Heart

Book 3- Saving His Heart

Book 4- Romancing His Heart

The Westbrooks: Family Ties Series:

Book .5- One Little Heartbreak- A Westbrook Novella

Book 1- One Little Mistake

Book 2- One Little Lie

Book 3- One Little Kiss

Book 4- One Little Secret